just one day

ALSO BY GAYLE FORMAN

If I Stay

Sisters in Sanity

Where She Went

just one day

GAYLE FORMAN

DUTTON BOOKS
AN IMPRINT OF PENGUIN GROUP (USA) INC.

DUTTON BOOKS
An imprint of Penguin Group (USA) Inc.

Published by the Penguin Group
Penguin Group (USA) Inc., 375 Hudson Street, New York, New York 10014, USA
Penguin Group (Canada), 90 Eglinton Avenue East, Suite 700, Toronto, Ontario M4P 2Y3, Canada (a division of
Pearson Penguin Canada Inc.)
Penguin Books Ltd, 80 Strand, London WC2R 0RL, England
Penguin Ireland, 25 St Stephen's Green, Dublin 2, Ireland (a division of Penguin Books Ltd)
Penguin Group (Australia), 707 Collins Street, Melbourne, Victoria 3008, Australia
(a division of Pearson Australia Group Pty Ltd)
Penguin Books India Pvt Ltd, 11 Community Centre, Panchsheel Park, New Delhi–110 017, India
Penguin Group (NZ), 67 Apollo Drive, Rosedale, Auckland 0632, New Zealand
(a division of Pearson New Zealand Ltd)
Penguin Books (Sounth Africa), Rosebank Office Park, 181 Jan Smuts Avenue,
Parktown North 2193, South Africa
Penguin China, B7 Jiaming Center, 27 East Third Ring Road North,
Chaoyang District, Beijing 100020, China

Penguin Books Ltd, Registered Offices: 80 Strand, London WC2R 0RL, England

This book is a work of fiction. Names, characters, places, and incidents are either the product
of the author's imagination or are used fictitiously, and any resemblance to actual persons, living
or dead, business establishments, events, or locales is entirely coincidental.

Art on page 79 courtesy of Shutterstock.com

LIBRARY OF CONGRESS CATALOGING-IN-PUBLICATION DATA
Forman, Gayle.
Just one day / Gayle Forman.
p. cm.
Summary: "Sparks fly when American good girl Allyson encounters laid-back Dutch
actor Willem, so she follows him on a whirlwind trip to Paris, upending her life in just one day
and prompting a year of self-discovery and the search for true love."—Provided by publisher.
ISBN 978-0-525-42591-5 (hardcover : alk. paper)
[1. Voyages and travels—Fiction. 2. Self-actualization (Psychology)—Fiction. 3. Love—Fiction.
4. Actors and actresses—Fiction. 5. Europe—Fiction.] I. Title.

PZ7.F75876Jus 2013
[Fic]—dc23
2012030798

Published in the United States by Dutton Books,
an imprint of Penguin Group (USA) Inc.
345 Hudson Street, New York, New York 10014
www.penguin.com/teen
Designed by Danielle Delaney
Printed in USA   First Edition

1 3 5 7 9 10 8 6 4 2

For Tamar: sister,
travel companion, friend—
who, incidentally, went and
married her *Dutchman*

just one day

All the world's a stage,
And all the men and women merely players:
They have their exits and their entrances;
And one man in his time plays many parts....

From William Shakespeare's *As You Like It*

PART ONE
One Day

One

What if Shakespeare had it wrong?

To be, or not to be: that is the question. That's from Hamlet's—maybe Shakespeare's—most famous soliloquy. I had to memorize the whole speech for sophomore English, and I can still remember every word. I didn't give it much thought back then. I just wanted to get all the words right and collect my A. But what if Shakespeare—and Hamlet—were asking the wrong question? What if the real question is not whether *to* be, but *how* to be?

The thing is, I don't know if I would have asked myself that question—*how* to be—if it wasn't for *Hamlet*. Maybe I would have gone along being the Allyson Healey I had been. Doing just what I was supposed to do, which, in this case, was going to see *Hamlet*.

"God, it's so hot. I thought it wasn't supposed to get this hot in England." My friend Melanie loops her blond hair into a bun and fans her sweaty neck. "What time are they opening the doors, anyhow?"

I look over at Ms. Foley, who Melanie and pretty much the rest of our group has christened Our Fearless Leader behind her back. But she is talking to Todd, one of the history grad students co-leading the trip, probably telling him off for something or other. In the Teen Tours! Cultural Extravaganza brochure that my parents presented to me upon my high school graduation two months ago, the Todd-like graduate students were called "historical consultants" and were meant to bolster the "educational value" of the Teen Tours! But so far, Todd has been more valuable in bolstering the hangovers, taking everyone out drinking almost every night. I'm sure tonight everyone else will go extra wild. It is, after all, our last stop, Stratford-upon-Avon, a city full of Culture! Which seems to translate into a disproportionate number of pubs named after Shakespeare and frequented by people in blaring white sneakers.

Ms. Foley is wearing her own snow-white sneakers— along with a pair of neatly pressed blue jeans and a Teen Tours! polo shirt—as she reprimands Todd. Sometimes, at night, when everyone else is out on the town, she will tell me she ought to call the head office on him. But she never seems to follow through. I think partly because when she scolds, he flirts. Even with Ms. Foley. Especially with Ms. Foley.

"I think it starts at seven," I say to Melanie. I look at my watch, another graduation present, thick gold, the back engraved *Going Places*. It weighs heavy against my sweaty wrist. "It's six thirty now."

"Geez, the Brits do love to line up. Or queue. Or whatever. They should take a lesson from the Italians, who just mob. Or maybe the Italians should take a lesson from the Brits." Melanie tugs on her miniskirt—her bandage skirt, she calls it—and adjusts her cami-top. "God, Rome. It feels like a year ago."

Rome? Was it six days ago? Or sixteen? All of Europe has become a blur of airports, buses, old buildings, and prix-fixe menus serving chicken in various kinds of sauce. When my parents gave me this trip as a big high-school graduation present, I was a little reluctant to go. But Mom had reassured me that she'd done her research. Teen Tours! was very well regarded, noted for its high-quality educational component, as well as the care that was taken of its students. I would be well looked after. "You'll never be alone," my parents had promised me. And, of course, Melanie was coming too.

And they were right. I know everyone else gives Ms. Foley crap for the eagle eye she keeps on us, but I appreciate how she is always doing a head count, even appreciate how she disapproves of the nightly jaunts to local bars, though most of us are of legal drinking age in Europe—not that anyone over here seems to care about such things anyway.

I don't go to the bars. I usually just go back to the hotel rooms Melanie and I share and watch TV. You can almost always find American movies, the same kinds of movies which, back at home, Melanie and I often watched together on weekends, in one of our rooms, with lots of popcorn.

"I'm roasting out here," Melanie moans. "It's like middle of the afternoon still."

I look up. The sun is hot, and the clouds race across the sky. I like how fast they go, nothing in their way. You can tell from the sky that England's an island. "At least it's not pouring like it was when we got here."

"Do you have a pony holder?" Melanie asks. "No, of course you don't. I bet you're loving your hair now."

My hand drifts to the back of my neck, which still feels strange, oddly exposed. The Teen Tour! had begun in London, and on the second afternoon, we'd had a few free hours for shopping, which I guess qualifies as culture. During that time, Melanie had convinced me to get my hair bobbed. It was all part of her precollege reinvention scheme, which she'd explained to me on the flight over: "No one at college will know that we were AP automatons. I mean, we're too pretty to just be brainiacs, and at college, everyone will be smart. So we can be cool *and* smart. Those two things will no longer be mutually exclusive."

For Melanie, this reinvention apparently meant the new heavy-on-skimp wardrobe she'd blown half her spending money on at Topshop, and the truncating of her name from Melanie to Mel—something I can't quite remember to do, no matter how many times she kicks me under the table. For me, I guess it meant the haircut she talked me into.

I'd freaked out when I'd seen myself. I've had long black hair and no bangs for as long as I can remember, and the girl staring back at me in the salon mirror didn't look like anything like me. At that point, we'd only been gone two days, but my stomach went hollow with homesickness. I wanted to be back in my bedroom at home, with my familiar peach walls, my collection of vintage alarm clocks. I'd wondered how I was ever going to handle college if I couldn't handle this.

But I've gotten used to the hair, and the homesickness has

mostly gone away, and even if it hasn't, the tour is ending. Tomorrow, almost everyone else is taking the coach straight to the airport to fly home. Melanie and I are catching a train down to London to stay with her cousin for three days. Melanie is talking about going back to the salon where I got my bob to get a pink streak in her hair, and we're going to see *Let It Be* in the West End. On Sunday, we fly home, and soon after that, we start college—me near Boston, Melanie in New York.

"Set Shakespeare free!"

I look up. A group of about a dozen people are coming up and down the line, handing out multicolored neon flyers. I can tell straightaway that they're not American—no bright white tennis shoes or cargo shorts in sight. They are all impossibly tall, and thin, and different looking, somehow. It's like even their bone structure is foreign.

"Oh, I'll take one of those." Melanie reaches out for a flyer and uses it to fan her neck.

"What's it say?" I ask her, looking at the group. Here in touristy Stratford-upon-Avon, they stand out like fire-orange poppies in a field of green.

Melanie looks at the flyer and wrinkles her nose. "Guerrilla Will?"

A girl with the kind of magenta streaks Melanie has been coveting comes up to us. "It's Shakespeare for the masses."

I peer at the card. It reads *Guerrilla Will. Shakespeare Without Borders. Shakespeare Unleashed. Shakespeare For Free. Shakespeare For All.*

"Shakespeare for free?" Melanie reads.

"Yeah," the magenta-haired girl says in accented English.

"Not for capitalist gain. How Shakespeare would've wanted it."

"You don't think he'd want to actually sell tickets and make money from his plays?" I'm not trying to be a smart-ass, but I remember that movie *Shakespeare in Love* and how he was always owing money to somebody or other.

The girl rolls her eyes, and I start to feel foolish. I look down. A shadow falls over me, momentarily blocking out the glare of the sun. And then I hear laughter. I look up. I can't see the person in front of me because he's backlit by the still-bright evening sun. But I can hear him.

"I think she's right," he says. "Being a starving artist is not so romantic, maybe, when you're actually starving."

I blink a few times. My eyes adjust, and I see that the guy is tall, maybe a full foot taller than I am, and thin. His hair is a hundred shades of blond, and his eyes so brown as to almost be black. I have to tilt my head up to look at him, and he's tilting his head down to look at me.

"But Shakespeare is dead; he's not collecting royalties from the grave. And we, we are alive." He opens his arms, as if to embrace the universe. "What are you seeing?"

"*Hamlet,*" I say.

"Ah, *Hamlet.*" His accent is so slight as to be almost imperceptible. "I think a night like this, you don't waste on tragedy." He looks at me, like it's a question. Then he smiles. "Or indoors. We are doing *Twelfth Night*. Outside." He hands me a flyer.

"We'll *think* about it," Melanie says in her coy voice.

The guy raises one shoulder and cocks his head toward it so his ear is almost touching his very angular shoulder blade. "What you will," he says, though he's looking at me. Then he saunters off to join the rest of his troupe.

Melanie watches them go. "Wow, why are they not on the Teen Tours! Cultural Extravaganza? That's some culture I could get into!"

I watch them leave, feeling a strange tug. "I've seen *Hamlet* before, you know."

Melanie looks at me, her eyebrows, which she has overly plucked into a thin line, raised. "Me too. It was on TV, but still . . ."

"We could go . . . to this. I mean, it would be different. A cultural experience, which is why our parents sent us on this tour."

Melanie laughs. "Look at you, getting all bad! But what about Our Fearless Leader? It looks like she's gearing up for one of her head counts."

"Well, the heat was really bothering you . . . " I begin.

Melanie looks at me for a second, then something clicks. She licks her lips, grins, and then crosses her eyes. "Oh, yeah. I totally have heatstroke." She turns to Paula, who's from Maine and is studiously reading a Fodor's guide. "Paula, I'm feeling so dizzy."

"It's way hot," Paula says, nodding sympathetically. "You should hydrate."

"I think I might faint or something. I'm seeing black spots."

"Don't pile it on," I whisper.

"It's good to build a case," Melanie whispers, enjoying this now. "Oh, I think I'm going to pass out."

"Ms. Foley," I call.

Ms. Foley looks up from ticking names off her roll-call sheet. She comes over, her face so full of concern, I feel bad for lying. "I think Melanie, I mean Mel, is getting heatstroke."

"Are you poorly? It shouldn't be much longer now. And it's lovely and cool inside the theater." Ms. Foley speaks in a strange hybrid of Britishisms with a Midwestern accent that everyone makes fun of because they think it's pretentious. But I think it's just that she's from Michigan and spends a lot of time in Europe.

"I feel like I'm going to puke." Melanie pushes on. "I would hate to do that inside the Swan Theatre."

Ms. Foley's face wrinkles in displeasure, though I can't tell if it is from the idea of Melanie barfing inside the Swan or using the word *puke* in such close proximity to the Royal Shakespeare Company. "Oh, dear. I'd better escort you back to the hotel."

"I can take her," I say.

"Really? Oh, no. I couldn't. You should see *Hamlet.*"

"No, it's fine. I'll take her."

"No! It's my responsibility to take her. I simply couldn't burden you like that." I can see the argument she's having with herself play out over her pinched features.

"It's fine, Ms. Foley. I've seen *Hamlet* before, and the hotel is just over the square from here."

"Really? Oh, that would be lovely. Would you believe in all the years I've been doing this, I have never seen the Bard's *Hamlet* done by the RSC?"

Melanie gives a little moan for dramatic effect. I gently elbow her. I smile at Ms. Foley. "Well, then, you definitely shouldn't miss it."

She nods solemnly, as though we are discussing important business here, order of succession to the throne or something. Then she reaches for my hand. "It has been such a pleasure traveling with you, Allyson. I shall miss you. If only more young people today were like you. You are such a . . ." She pauses for a moment, searching for the right word. "Such a good girl."

"Thank you," I say automatically. But her compliment leaves me empty. I don't know if it's because that's the nicest thing she could think to say about me, or if it's because I'm not being such a good girl right now.

"Good girl, my ass." Melanie laughs once we are clear of the queue and she can give up her swooning act.

"Be quiet. I don't like pretending."

"Well, you're awfully good at it. You could have a promising acting career of your own, if you ask me."

"I don't ask you. Now, where is this place?" I look at the flyer. "Canal Basin? What is that?"

Melanie pulls out her phone, which, unlike my cell phone, works in Europe. She opens the map app. "It appears to be a basin by the canal."

A few minutes later, we arrive at a waterfront. It feels like a carnival, full of people hanging about. There are barges moored to the side of the water, different boats selling everything from ice cream to paintings. What there isn't is any kind of theater. Or stage. Or chairs. Or actors. I look at the flyer again.

"Maybe it's on the bridge?" Melanie asks.

We walk back over to the medieval arched bridge, but it's just more of the same: tourists like us, milling around in the hot night.

"They did say it was tonight?" Melanie asks.

I think of that one guy, his eyes so impossibly dark, specifically saying that *tonight* was too nice for tragedy. But when I look around, there's no play here, obviously. It was probably some kind of joke—fool the stupid tourist.

"Let's get an ice cream so the night's not a total write-off," I say.

We are queuing up for ice cream when we hear it, a hum of acoustic guitars and the echoey beat of bongo drums. My ears perk up, my sonar rises. I stand on a nearby bench to look around. It's not like a stage has magically appeared, but what has just materialized is a crowd, a pretty big one, under a stand of trees.

"I think it's starting," I say, grabbing Melanie's hand.

"But the ice cream," she complains.

"After," I say, yanking her toward the crowd.

"If music be the food of love, play on."

The guy playing Duke Orsino looks nothing like any Shakespearian actor I've ever seen, except maybe the movie version of *Romeo + Juliet* with Leonardo DiCaprio. He is tall, black, dreadlocked, and dressed like a glam rock-star in tight vinyl pants, pointy-toed shoes, and a sort of mesh tank top that shows off his ripped chest.

"Oh, we *so* made the right choice," Melanie whispers in my ear.

As Orsino gives his opening soliloquy to the sounds of the guitars and bongo drums, I feel a shiver go up my spine.

We watch the entire first act, chasing the actors around the waterfront. When they move, we move, which makes it feel like *we* are a part of the play. And maybe that's what makes it so different. Because I've seen Shakespeare before. School productions and a few plays at the Philadelphia Shakespeare Theatre. But it's always felt like listening to something in a foreign language I didn't know that well. I had to force myself to pay attention, and half the time, I wound up rereading the program over and over again, as if it would impart some deeper understanding.

This time, it clicks. It's like my ear attunes to the weird language and I'm sucked fully into the story, the same way I am when I watch a movie, so that I *feel* it. When Orsino pines for the cool Olivia, I feel that pang in my gut from all the times I've crushed on guys I was invisible to. And when Viola mourns her brother, I feel her loneliness. And when she falls for Orsino, who thinks she's a man, it's actually funny and also moving.

He doesn't show up until act two. He's playing Sebastian, Viola's twin brother, thought dead. Which makes a certain sense, because by the time he does arrive, I am beginning to think he never really existed, that I've merely conjured him.

As he races through the green, chased after by the ever-loyal Antonio, we chase after him. After a while, I work up my nerve. "Let's get closer," I say to Melanie. She grabs my hand, and we go to the front of the crowd right at the part where Olivia's clown comes for Sebastian and they argue before Sebastian sends him away. Right before he does, he seems to catch my eye for half a second.

As the hot day softens into twilight and I'm sucked deeper into the illusory world of Illyria, I feel like I've entered some weird otherworldly space, where anything can happen, where identities can be swapped like shoes. Where those thought dead are alive again. Where everyone gets their happily-everafters. I recognize it's kind of corny, but the air is soft and warm, and the trees are lush and full, and the crickets are singing, and it seems like, for once, maybe it can happen.

All too soon, the play is ending. Sebastian and Viola are reunited. Viola comes clean to Orsino that she's actually a girl, and of course he now wants to marry her. And Olivia realizes that Sebastian isn't the person she thought she married—but she doesn't care; she loves him anyway. The musicians are playing again as the clown gives the final soliloquy. And then the actors are out and bowing, each one doing something a little silly with his or her bow. One flips. One plays air guitar. When Sebastian bows, he scans the audience and stops dead on me. He smiles this funny little half smile, takes one of the prop coins out of his pocket, and flips it to me. It's pretty dark, and the coin is small, but I catch it, and people clap for me too, it now seems.

With the coin in my hand, I clap. I clap until my hands sting. I clap as if doing so can prolong the evening, can transform *Twelfth Night* into *Twenty-Fourth Night*. I clap so that I can hold on to this feeling. I clap because I know what will happen when I stop. It's the same thing that happens when I turn off a really good movie—one that I've lost myself to—which is that I'll be thrown back to my own reality and something hollow will settle in my chest. Sometimes, I'll watch a movie all over again just to recapture that feeling of being inside something real. Which, I know, doesn't make any sense.

But there's no restarting tonight. The crowd is dispersing; the actors drifting off. The only people left from the show are a couple of musicians passing around the donation hat. I reach into my wallet for a ten-pound note.

Melanie and I stand together in silence. "Whoa," she says.
"Yeah. Whoa," I say back.

"That was pretty cool. And I hate Shakespeare."

I nod.

"And was it me, or was that hot guy from the line earlier, the one who played Sebastian, was he totally checking us out?"

Us? But he threw *me* the coin. Or had I just been the one to catch it? Why wouldn't it have been Melanie with her blond hair and her camisole top that he'd been checking out? Mel 2.0, as she calls herself, so much more appealing than Allyson 1.0.

"I couldn't tell," I say.

"*And* he threw the coin at us! Nice catch, by the way. Maybe we should go find them. Go hang out with them or something."

"They're gone."

"Yeah, but those guys are still here." She gestures to the money collectors. "We could ask where they hang out."

I shake my head. "I doubt they want to hang out with stupid American teenagers."

"We're not stupid, and most of them didn't seem that much older than teenagers themselves."

"No. And besides, Ms. Foley might check in on us. We should get back to the room."

Melanie rolls her eyes. "Why do you always do this?"

"Do what?"

"Say no to everything. It's like you're averse to adventure."

"I don't always say no."

"Nine times out of ten. We're about to start college. Let's live a little."

"I live just plenty," I snap. "And besides, it never bothered you before."

Melanie and I have been best friends since her family moved two houses down from ours the summer before second grade. Since then, we've done everything together: we lost our teeth at the same time, we got our periods at the same time, even our boyfriends came in tandem. I started going out with Evan a few weeks after she started going out with Alex (who was Evan's best friend), though she and Alex broke up in January and Evan and I made it until April.

We've spent so much time together, we almost have a secret language of inside jokes and looks. We've fought plenty, of course. We're both only children, so sometimes we're like sisters. We once even broke a lamp in a tussle. But it's never been like this. I'm not even sure what *this* is, only that since we got on the tour, being with Melanie makes me feel like I'm losing a race I didn't even know I'd entered.

"I came out here tonight," I say, my voice brittle and defensive. "I lied to Ms. Foley so we could come."

"Right? And we've had so much fun! So why don't we keep it going?"

I shake my head.

She shuffles through her bag and pulls out her phone, scrolls through her texts. "*Hamlet* just let out too. Craig says that Todd's taken the gang to a pub called the Dirty Duck. I like the sound of that. Come out with us. It'll be a blast."

The thing is, I did go out with Melanie and everyone from the tour once, about a week into the trip. By this time, they'd already gone out a couple times. And even though Melanie had known these guys only a week—the same amount of time

I'd known them—she had all these inside jokes with them, jokes *I* didn't understand. I'd sat there around the crowded table, nursing a drink, feeling like the unlucky kid who had to start a new school midway into the year.

I look at my watch, which has slid all the way down my wrist. I slide it back up, so it covers the ugly red birthmark right on my pulse. "It's almost eleven, and we have to be up early tomorrow for our train. So if you don't mind, I'm going to take my adventure-averse self back to the room." With the huffiness in my voice, I sound just like my mom.

"Fine. I'll walk you back and then go to the pub."

"And what if Ms. Foley checks in on us?"

Melanie laughs. "Tell her I had heatstroke. And it's not hot anymore." She starts to walk up the slope back toward the bridge. "What? Are you waiting for something?"

I look back down toward the water, the barges, now emptying out from the evening rush. Trash collectors are out in force. The day is ending; it's not coming back.

"No, I'm not."

Two

---

*O*ur train to London is at eight fifteen—Melanie's idea, so we will have maximum shopping time. But when the alarm clock starts beeping at six, Melanie pulls the pillow over her head.

"Let's get a later train," she moans.

"No. It's already all arranged. You can sleep on the train. Anyway, you promised to be downstairs at six thirty to say good-bye to everyone." And I promised to say good-bye to Ms. Foley.

I drag Melanie out of bed and shove her under the hotel's weak excuse for a shower. I brew her some instant coffee and quickly talk to my mom, who stayed up until one in the morning Pennsylvania time to call. At six thirty, we trudge downstairs. Ms. Foley, in her jeans and Teen Tours! polo shirt as usual, shakes Melanie's hand. Then she embraces me in a bony hug, slips me her business card, and says I shouldn't hesitate to call if I need anything while in London. Her next tour starts on Sunday, and she'll be there too until it begins. Then she tells me she's arranged a seven-thirty taxi to take me and Melanie to the train station, asks once again if we're being met in London (yes, we are), tells me yet again that I'm a good girl, and warns me against pickpockets on the Tube.

I let Melanie go back to bed for another half hour, which means she skips her usual primp time, and at seven thirty I load us into the waiting taxi. When our train arrives, I drag our bags onto it and find a pair of empty seats. Melanie slumps into the one next to the window. "Wake me when we get to London."

I stare at her for a second, but she's already snuggled up against the window, shutting her eyes. I sigh and stow her shoulder bag under her feet and put my cardigan down on the seat next to hers to discourage any thieves or lecherous old men. Then I make my way to the café car. I missed the hotel's breakfast, and now my stomach is growling and my temples are starting to throb with the beginnings of a hunger headache.

Even though Europe is the land of trains, we haven't taken any on the tour, only airplanes for the long distances and buses to get us everywhere in between. As I walk through the cars, the automatic doors open with a satisfying whoosh, and the train rocks gently under my feet. Outside, the green countryside whizzes by.

In the café car, I examine the sad offerings and wind up ordering a cheese sandwich and tea and the salt and vinegar crisps I've become addicted to. I get a can of Coke for

Melanie. I put the meal in one of those cardboard carriers and am about to go back to my seat when one of the tables right next to the window opens up. I hesitate for a second. I should get back to Melanie. Then again, she's asleep; she doesn't care, so I sit at the table and stare out the window. The countryside seems so fundamentally English, all green and tidy and divvied up with hedges, the fluffy sheep like clouds mirroring the ever-present ones in the sky.

"That's a very confused breakfast."

That voice. After listening to it for four acts last night, I recognize it immediately.

I look up, and he's right there, grinning a sort of lazy half smile that makes him seem like he just this second woke up.

"How is it confused?" I ask. I should be surprised, but somehow, I'm not. I do have to bite my lip to keep from grinning.

But he doesn't answer. He goes to the counter and orders a coffee. Then he gestures with his head toward my table. I nod.

"In so many ways," he says, sitting down opposite me. "It is like a jet-lagged expatriate."

I look down at my sandwich, my tea, my chips. "This is a jet-lagged expatriate? How do you get *that* from *this*?"

He blows on his coffee. "Easy. For one, it's not even nine in the morning. So tea makes sense. But sandwich and crisps. Those are lunch foods. I won't even mention the Coke." He taps the can. "See, the timing is all mixed up. Your breakfast has jet lag."

I have to laugh at that. "The doughnuts looked disgusting." I gesture toward the counter.

"Definitely. That's why I bring my own breakfast." He

reaches into his bag and starts unwrapping something from a wrinkled piece of waxed paper.

"Wait, that looks suspiciously like a sandwich too," I say.

"It's not, really. It's bread and *hagelslag*."

"Hachuh what?"

"*Hach-el-slach*." He opens the sandwich for me to see. Inside is butter and some kind of chocolate sprinkles.

"You're calling *my* breakfast confused? You're eating dessert for breakfast."

"In Holland, this is breakfast. Very typical. That or *uitsmijter*, which is basically fried egg with ham."

"That won't be on the test, will it? Because I can't even begin to try to say that."

"*Out. Smy. Ter.* We can practice that later. But that brings me to my second point. Your breakfast is like an expatriate. And, go ahead, eat. I can talk while you eat."

"Thank you. I'm glad you can multitask," I say. Then I laugh. And it's all just the weirdest thing, because this is just happening, so naturally. I think I am actually flirting, over breakfast. About breakfast. "What do you even mean, an expatriate?"

"Someone who lives outside of their native country. You know, you have a sandwich. Very American. And the tea, very English. But then you have the crisps, or chips, or whatever you want to call them, and they can go either way, but you're having salt and vinegar, which is very English, but you're eating them for breakfast, and that seems American. And Coke for breakfast. Coke and chips, is that what you eat for breakfast in America?"

"How do you even know I'm from America?" I challenge.

"Aside from the fact that you were in a tour group of Americans and you speak with an American accent?" He takes a bite of his hagu-whatever sandwich and drinks more of his coffee.

I bite my lip to keep from grinning again. "Right. Aside from that."

"Those were the only clues, really. You actually don't look so American."

"Really?" I pop open my crisps, and a sharp tang of artificial vinegar wafts through the air. I offer him one. He declines it and takes another bite of his sandwich. "What looks American?"

He shrugs. "Blond," he says. "Big . . ." He mimes boobs. "Soft features." He waves his hands in front of his face. "Pretty. Like your friend."

"And I don't look that way?" I don't know why I bother to ask this. I know what I look like. Dark hair. Dark eyes. Sharp features. No curves, not much in the boob department. A little of the fizz goes out of my step. Was all this just buttering me up so he could hit on Melanie?

"No." He peers at me with those eyes of his. They'd looked so dark yesterday, but now that I'm up close, I can see that they have all kinds of colors in them—gray, brown, even gold dancing in the darkness. "You know who you look like? Louise Brooks."

I stare at him blankly.

"You don't know her? The silent film star?"

I shake my head. I never did get into silent films.

"She was a huge star in the nineteen twenties. American. Amazing actress."

"And not blond." I mean for it to come out as a joke, but it doesn't.

He takes another bite of his sandwich. A tiny chocolate sprinkle sticks to the corner of his mouth. "We have lots of blondes in Holland. I see blond when I look in a mirror. Louise Brooks was dark. She had these incredible sad eyes and very defined features and the same hair like you." He touches his own hair, as tousled as it was last night. "You look so much like her. I should just call you Louise."

Louise. I like that.

"No, not Louise. Lulu. That was her nickname."

Lulu. I like that even better.

He reaches out his hand. "Hi, Lulu, I'm Willem."

His hand is warm, and his grasp is firm. "Nice to meet you, Willem. Though I could call you Sebastian if we're taking on new identities."

When he laughs, little crinkles flower along his eyes. "No. I prefer Willem. Sebastian's kind of, what's the word . . . passive, when you think about it. He gets married to Olivia, who really wants to be with his sister. That happens a lot with Shakespeare. The women go after what they want; the men wind up suckered into things."

"I don't know. I was glad when everyone got their happy ending last night."

"Oh, it's a nice fairy tale, but that's what it is. A fairy tale. But I figure Shakespeare owes his comedy characters those happy endings because he is so cruel in his tragedies. I mean, *Hamlet.* Or *Romeo and Juliet.* It's almost sadistic." He shakes his head. "Sebastian's okay, he's just not really in charge of his own destiny so much. Shakespeare gives that privilege to Viola."

"So you're in charge of your own destiny?" I ask. And again, I hear myself and can hardly believe it. When I was little, I used to go to the local ice-skating rink. In my mind, I always felt like I could twirl and jump, but when I got out onto the ice, I could barely keep my blades straight. When I got older, that's how it was with people: In my mind, I am bold and forthright, but what comes out always seems to be so meek and polite. Even with Evan, my boyfriend for junior and most of senior year, I never quite managed to be that skating, twirling, leaping person I suspected I could be. But today, apparently, I can skate.

"Oh, not at all. I go where the wind blows me." He pauses to consider that. "Maybe there's a good reason I play Sebastian."

"So where is the wind blowing you?" I ask, hoping he's staying in London.

"From London, I catch another train back to Holland. Last night was the end of the season for me."

I deflate. "Oh."

"You haven't eaten your sandwich. Be warned, they put butter on the cheese sandwiches here. The fake kind, I think."

"I know." I pull off the sad wilted tomatoes and smear off some of the excess butter/margarine with my napkin.

"It would be better with mayonnaise," Willem tells me.

"Only if there was turkey on it."

"No, cheese and mayonnaise is very good."

"That sounds foul."

"Only if you've never had the proper sort of mayonnaise. I've heard the kind they have in America is not the proper sort."

I laugh so hard that tea comes spurting out my nose.

"What?" Willem asks. "What?"

"The *proper* sort of mayonnaise," I say in between gasps of laughter. "It makes me think that there's, like, a bad-girl mayonnaise who's slutty and steals, and a good-girl mayonnaise, who is proper and crosses her legs, and my problem is that I've never been introduced to the right one."

"That is exactly correct," he says. And then he starts laughing too.

We are both cracking up when Melanie trudges into the café car, carrying her stuff, plus my sweater. "I couldn't find you," she says sullenly.

"You said to wake you in London." I look out the window then. The pretty English countryside has given way to the ugly gray outskirts of the city.

Melanie looks over at Willem, and her eyes widen. "You're not shipwrecked after all," she says to him.

"No," he says, but he's looking at me. "Don't be mad at Lulu. It's my fault. I kept her here."

"Lulu?"

"Yes, short for Louise. It's my new alter ego, *Mel*." I look at her, my eyes imploring her not to give me away. I'm liking being Lulu. I'm not ready to give her up just yet.

Melanie rubs her eyes, like maybe she's still sleeping. Then she shrugs and slumps into the seat next to Willem. "Fine. Be whoever you want. I'd like to be someone with a new head."

"She's new to this hangover thing," I tell Willem.

"Shut up," Melanie snaps.

"What, you want me say that 'it's old hat for you'?"

"Aren't you Miss Sassy-pants this morning."

"Here." Willem reaches into his backpack for a small white container and shakes out a few white balls into Melanie's hand. "Put these under your tongue to dissolve. You'll feel better soon."

"What is this?" she asks suspiciously.

"It's herbal."

"Are you sure it's not some date-rape drug?"

"Right. Because he wants you to pass out in the middle of the train," I say.

Willem shows the label to Melanie. "My mother is a naturopathic doctor. She uses these for headaches. I don't think to rape me."

"Hey, my father is a doctor too," I say. Though the opposite of naturopathic. He's a pulmonologist, Western medicine all the way.

Melanie eyes the pills for a second before finally popping them under her tongue. By the time the train chugs into the station ten minutes later, her headache is better.

By some unspoken agreement, the three of us disembark together: Melanie and I with our overstuffed roller bags, Willem with his compact backpack. We push out onto the platform into the already-hot summer sun and then into the relative cool of Marylebone Station.

"Veronica texted that she's running late," Melanie says. "She says to meet her by the WHSmith. Whatever that is."

"It's a bookstore," Willem says, pointing across the interior of the station.

The inside of the station is pretty and redbricked, but I'm disappointed that it's not one of those grand stations with the clattering destination boards I was hoping for. Instead, there's just a TV departure monitor. I go over to look at it. The destinations are nowhere that exotic: places like High Wycombe and Banbury, which might be very nice for all I know. It's silly, really. I've just finished up a tour of big European cities—Rome, Florence, Prague, Vienna, Budapest, Berlin, Edinburgh, and now I'm in London again—and for most of it, I was counting the days until we went home. I don't know why now all of a sudden I should be struck with wanderlust.

"What's wrong?" Melanie asks me.

"Oh, I was just hoping for one of those big departure boards, like they had at some of the airports."

"Amsterdam's Centraal Station has one of those," Willem says. "I always like to stand in front of it and just imagine I can pick any place and go."

"Right? Exactly!"

"What's the matter?" Melanie asks, looking at the TV monitors. "Don't like the idea of Bicester North?"

"It's not quite as exciting as Paris," I say.

"Oh, come on. You're not still moping about that?" Melanie turns to Willem. "We were supposed to go to Paris after Rome, but the air traffic controllers went on strike and all the flights got canceled, and it was too far to go on the bus. She's still bummed out about it."

"They're always on strike for something in France," Willem says, nodding his head.

"They subbed Budapest in for Paris," I say. "And I liked Budapest, but I can't believe I'm this close to Paris and not going."

Willem looks at me intently. He twists the tie on his backpack around his finger. "So go," he says.

"Go where?"

"To Paris."

"I can't. It got canceled."

"So go now."

"The tour's over. And anyhow, they're probably still striking."

"You can go by train. It takes two hours from London to Paris." He looks at the big clock on the wall. "You could be in Paris by lunchtime. Much better sandwiches over there, by the way."

"But, but, I don't speak French. I don't have a guidebook. I don't even have any French money. They use euros there, right?" I'm giving all these reasons as if *these* are why I can't go, when in truth, Willem might as well be suggesting I hop a rocket to the moon. I know Europe is small and some people do things like this. But I don't.

He's still looking at me, his head tilted slightly to the side.

"It wouldn't work," I conclude. "I don't know Paris at all."

Willem glances at the clock on the wall. And then, after a beat, he turns to me. "*I* know Paris."

My heart starts doing the most ridiculous flippy things, but my ever-rational mind continues to click off all the reasons this won't work. "I don't know if I have enough money. How much are the tickets?" I reach into my bag to count my remaining cash. I have some pounds to get me through the weekend, a credit card for emergencies, and a hundred-dollar bill that Mom gave me for absolute emergencies if the credit card wouldn't work. But this is hardly an emergency. And using the card would alert my parents.

Willem reaches into his pocket, pulls out a fistful of foreign currencies. "Don't worry about that. It was a good summer."

I stare at the bills in his hand. Would he really do that? Take me to Paris? *Why* would he do that?

"We have tickets for *Let It Be* tomorrow night," Melanie says, assuming the Voice of Reason. "And we're leaving on Sunday. And your mom would freak out. Seriously, she'd kill you."

I look at Willem, but he just shrugs, like he cannot deny the truth to this.

And I'm about to back down, say thanks for the offer, but then it's like Lulu grabs the wheel, because I turn to Melanie and say, "She can't kill me if she doesn't find out."

Melanie's scoffs. "*Your* mom? She'd find out."

"Not if you covered for me."

Melanie doesn't say anything.

"Please. I've covered for you plenty on this trip."

Melanie sighs dramatically. "That was at a pub. Not in an entirely different country."

"You *just* criticized me for never doing things like this."

I have her there. She switches tacks. "How am I supposed to cover when she calls my phone looking for you? Which she'll do. You know she will."

Mom had been furious that my cell phone didn't work over here. We'd been told it would, and when it didn't, she called the company up in a tizzy, but apparently there was nothing to be done, something about it being the wrong band. It didn't really matter in the end. She had a copy of our itinerary and knew when to get me in the hotel rooms, and when she couldn't manage that, she called Melanie's cell.

"Maybe you could leave your phone off, so it goes to voice mail?" I suggest. I look at Willem, who still has the fistful of cash spilling out of his hand. "Are you *sure* about this? I thought you were going back to Holland."

"I thought so too. The winds are maybe blowing me in a different direction."

I turn to Melanie. It's on her now. She narrows her green eyes at Willem. "If you rape or murder my friend, I will kill you."

Willem tsk-tsks. "You Americans are so violent. I'm Dutch. The worst I will do is run her over with a bicycle."

"While stoned!" Melanie adds.

"Okay, maybe there's that," Willem admits. Then he looks at me, and I feel a ripple of something flutter through me. Am I really going to do this?

"So, Lulu? What do you say? You want to go to Paris? For just one day?"

It's totally crazy. I don't even know him. And I could get caught. And how much of Paris can you see in just one day? And this could all go disastrously wrong in so many ways. All of that is true. I know it is. But it doesn't change the fact that I want to go.

So this time, instead of saying no, I try something different.

I say yes.

Three

The Eurostar is a snub-nosed, mud-splattered, yellow train, and by the time we board it, I am sweaty and breathless. Since saying good-bye to Melanie and hastily exchanging plans and info and meeting places for tomorrow, Willem and I have been running. Out of Marylebone. Down the crowded London streets and into the Tube, where I got into some sort of duel with the gates, which refused to open for me three times, then finally did, before snapping shut on my suitcase, sending my Teen Tours! baggage tag flying underneath the automatic ticket machine. "I guess I'm really going rogue now," I joked to Willem.

At the cavernous St. Pancras station, Willem pointed out the destination boards doing that shuffling thing before hustling us to the Eurostar ticket lines, where he worked his charm on the ticket agent and managed to exchange his ticket home for a ticket to Paris and then used far too many of his pound notes to buy me mine. Then we rushed through the check-in process, showing our passports. For a second, I was worried that Willem would see my passport, which doesn't belong to Lulu so much as to Allyson—not just Allyson, but fifteen-year-old Allyson in the midst of some acne issues. But he didn't, and we went downstairs to the futuristic departure lounge just in time to go back upstairs to our train.

It's only once we sit down in our assigned seats on the train that I catch my breath and realize what I've done. I am going to Paris. With a stranger. With *this* stranger.

I pretend to fuss with my suitcase while I steal looks at him. His face reminds me of one of those outfits that only girls with a certain style can pull off: mismatched pieces that don't work on their own but somehow all come together. The angles are deep, almost sharp, but his lips are pillowy and red, and there are enough apples in his cheeks to make pie. He looks both old and young; both grizzled and delicate. He's not good-looking in the way that Brent Harper, who was voted Best Looking in the senior awards, is which is to say predictably so. But I can't stop looking at him.

Apparently I'm not the only one. A couple of girls with backpacks stroll down the aisle, their eyes dark and drowsy and seeming to say, *We eat sex for breakfast*. One of them smiles at Willem as she passes and says something in French. He replies, also in French, and helps her lift her bag into the overhead bin. The girls sit across the aisle, a row behind ours, and the shorter one says something, and they all laugh. I want to ask what was said, but all at once, I feel incredibly young and out of place, stuck at the children's table for Thanksgiving.

If only I'd studied French in high school. I'd wanted to, at the start of ninth grade, but my parents had urged me to take Mandarin. "It's going to be the Chinese century; you'll be so much better able to compete if you speak the language," Mom had said. *Compete for what?* I'd wondered. But I've studied Mandarin for the last four years and am due to continue next month when I start college.

I'm waiting for Willem to sit down, but instead he looks at me and then at the French girls, who, having deposited their things, are sashaying down the aisle.

"Trains make me hungry. And you never ate your sandwich," he says. "I'll go to the café for more provisions. What would you like, Lulu?"

Lulu would probably want something exotic. Chocolate-covered strawberries. Oysters. Allyson is more of a peanut-butter-sandwich girl. I don't know what I'm hungry for.

"Whatever is fine."

I watch him walk away. I pick up a magazine from the seat pocket and read a bunch of facts about the train: The Channel Tunnel is fifty kilometers long. It opened in 1994 and took six years to complete. The Eurostar's top speeds are three hundred kilometers per hour, which is one hundred and eighty-six miles per hour. If I were still on the tour, this would be exactly the kind of Trivial-Pursuit fodder Ms. Foley would read to us from one of her printouts. I put the magazine away.

The train starts to move, though it's so smooth that it's only when I see the platform is pulling away from us, as though it's moving, not the train, that I realize we've departed. I hear the horn blow. Out the window, the grand arches of St. Pancras glitter their farewell before we plunge into a tunnel. I look around the car. Everyone else seems happy and engaged: reading magazines or typing on laptops, texting, talking on their phones or to their seatmates. I peer over my seat back, but there is no sign of Willem. The French girls are still gone too.

I pick up the magazine again and read a restaurant review that I don't absorb at all. More minutes tick by. The train is going faster now, arrogantly bypassing London's ugly warehouses. The conductor announces the first stop, and an inspector comes through to take my ticket. "Anyone here?" he asks, gesturing to Willem's empty seat.

"Yes." Only his things aren't there. There's no evidence he ever was here.

I glance at my watch. It's ten forty-three. Almost fifteen minutes since we left London. A few minutes later, we pull into Ebbsfleet, a sleek, modern station. A crowd of people get on. An older man with a briefcase stops next to Willem's seat as if to sit there, but then he glances at his ticket again and keeps moving up the aisle. The train doors beep and then shut, and we are off again. The London cityscape gives way to green. In the distance, I see a castle. The train greedily gobbles up the landscape; I imagine it leaving a churned-up pile of earth in its wake. I grip the armrests, my nails digging in as if this were that first endlessly steep incline up one of those lunch-losing roller coasters that Melanie loves to drag me on. In spite of the blasting AC, a line of perspiration pearls along my brow.

Our train passes another oncoming train with a startling *whoomp*. I jump in my seat. After two seconds, the train is speeding past us. But I have the weirdest sensation that Willem is on it. Which is impossible. He would've had to fast-forward to another station to get that train.

But that's not to say he's on *this* train.

I look at my watch. It's been twenty minutes since he went to the café car. Our train had not yet left the platform. He might've gotten off with those girls even before we departed. Or at this last station. Maybe that's what they were saying. *Why don't you ditch that boring American girl and hang out with us?*

He is not on this train.

The certainty hits me with that same *whoomp* as the oncoming train. He changed his mind. About Paris. About me.

Taking me to Paris was an impulse buy, like all those useless gadgets grocery stores put at the checkout aisle so you're out the door before you realize what a piece of crap you just bought.

But then another thought hits me: What if this is all some sort of master plan? Find the most naïve American you can and lure her onto a train, then ditch her and send in the . . . I don't know . . . the thugs to nab her? Mom DVR'd a segment about something just like this on *20/20*. What if *that's* why he was looking at me last night, *that's* why he sought *me* out earlier today on the train from Stratford-upon-Avon? Could he have chosen easier prey? I've seen enough of those Animal Planet nature shows to know that the lions always go for the weakest gazelles.

And yet, as unrealistic as this possibility is, on a certain level, there's a nugget of cold comfort in it. The world makes sense again. *That* at least would explain why *I* am on *this* train.

Something lands on my head, soft and crackly, but in my panic, it makes me jump.

And there's another one. I pick up the projectile, a packet of Walker's salt-and-vinegar crisps.

I look up. Willem has the guilty grin of a bank robber, not to mention loot spilling out of his hands: a candy bar, three cups of assorted hot beverages, a bottle of orange juice under one armpit, a can of Coke under the other. "Sorry about the wait. The café is at the other end of the train, and they wouldn't open it until the train left St. Pancras, and there was already a queue. Then I wasn't sure if you liked coffee or tea, so I got you both. But then I remembered your Coke from earlier, so I went back for that. And then on the way back, I stumbled onto a very cranky Belgian and spilled coffee all over myself, so I had to detour to the loo, but I think I just made things worse." He plunks down two of the small cardboard cups and the can of soda on the tray table in front of me. He gestures to the front of his jeans, which now have a huge wet splodge down the front of them.

I am not the sort of person to laugh at fart jokes or gross-out humor. When Jonathan Spalicki let one rip in physiology last year and Mrs. Huberman had to let the hysterical class out early, she actually thanked me for being the only one to exhibit any self-control.

So it's not like me to lose it. Over a wet spot.

And yet, when I open my mouth to inform Willem that I actually don't like soda, that the Coke before was for Melanie's hangover, what comes out is a yelp. And once I hear my own laughter, it sets off fireworks. I'm laughing so hard, I am gasping for air. The panicked tears that were threatening to spill out of my eyes now have a safe excuse to stream down my face.

Willem rolls his eyes and gives his jeans a *yeah-yeah* look. He grabs some of the napkins from the tray. "I didn't think it was *so* bad." He dabs at his jeans. "Does coffee leave a stain?"

This sends me into further paroxysms of laughter. Willem offers a wry, patient smile. He is big enough to accept the joke at his expense.

"I'm. Sorry." I gasp. "Not. Laughing. At. Your. Pants."

Pants! In her tutorial of British English versus American English, Ms. Foley had informed us that the English call underwear pants and pants trousers, and we should be mindful of announcing anything to do with pants to avoid any embarrassing misunderstandings. She went pink as she explained it.

I am doubled over now. When I manage to sit upright, I see one of the French girls coming back down the aisle. As she edges behind Willem, she rests a hand on his arm; it lingers there for a second. Then she says something in French, before slipping into her seat.

Willem doesn't even look at her. Instead, he turns back to me. His dark eyes dangle question marks.

"I thought you got off the train." The admission just slips out on the champagne bubbles of my relief.

Oh, my God. Did I actually say that? The giggles shock right out of me. I'm afraid to look at him. Because if he didn't want to leave me on the train before, I've remedied that now.

I feel the give of the seat as Willem sits down, and when I gather up the courage to peer over at him, I'm surprised to find that he doesn't look shocked or disgusted. He just has that amused private smile on his face.

He begins to unpack the junk food and pulls a bent baguette out of his backpack. After he's laid everything out over the trays, he looks right at me. "And why would I get off the train?" he asks at last, his voice light and teasing.

I could make up a lie. Because he forgot something. Or because he realized he needed to get back to Holland after all, and there wasn't time to tell me. Something ridiculous but less incriminating. But I don't.

"Because you changed your mind." I await his disgust, his shock, his pity, but he still looks amused, maybe a little intrigued now too. And I feel this unexpected rush, like I just took a hit of some drug, my own personal truth serum. So I tell him the rest. "But then for a brief minute, I thought maybe this was all some sort of scam and you were going to sell me into sex slavery or something."

I look at him, wondering if I've pushed too far. But he is smiling as he strokes his chin. "How would I do that?" he asks.

"I don't know. You'd have to make me pass out or something. What's that stuff they use? Chloroform? They put it on a handkerchief and put up against your nose, and you fall asleep."

"I think that's just in movies. Probably easier for me to drug your drink like your friend suspected."

"But you got me three drinks, one of them unopened." I hold up the can of Coke. "I don't drink Coke, by the way."

"My plan is foiled then." He exaggerates a sigh. "Too bad. I could get good money for you on the black market."

"How much do you think I'm worth?" I ask, amazed at how quickly fear has become fodder.

He looks me up and looks me down, appraising me. "Well, it would depend on various factors."

"Like what?"

"Age. How old are you?"

"Eighteen."

He nods. "Measurements?"

"Five feet four. One hundred and fifteen pounds. I don't know metric."

"Any unusual body parts or scars or false limbs?"

"Does that matter?"

"Fetishists. They pay extra."

"No, no prosthetic limbs or anything." But then I remember my birthmark, which is ugly, almost like a scar, so I usually keep it hidden under my watch. But there's something oddly tempting about exposing it, exposing me. So I slide my watch down. "I do have this."

He takes it in, nodding his head. Then casually asks, "And are you a virgin?"

"Would that make me more or less valuable?"

"It all depends on the market."

"You seem to know a lot about this."

"I grew up in Amsterdam," he says, like this explains it.

"So what am I worth?"

"You didn't answer all the questions." '

I have the strangest sensation then, like I'm holding the belt to a bathrobe and I can tie it tighter—or let it drop. "No, I'm not. A virgin."

He nods, stares in a way that unsettles me.

"I'm sure Boris will be disappointed," I add.

"Who's Boris?"

"The thuggish Ukrainian who's going to do the dirty work. You were just the bait."

Now he laughs, tilting his long neck back. When he comes up for air, he says, "I usually work with Bulgarians."

"You tease all you want, but there was a thing on TV about it. And it's not like I *know* you."

He pauses, looks straight at me, then says: "Twenty. One point nine meters. Seventy-five kilos, last time I checked. This," he points to a zigzag scar on his foot. Then he looks me dead in the eye. "And no."

It takes me a minute to realize that he's answering the same four questions he asked me. When I do, I feel a flush start to creep up my neck.

"Also, we had breakfast together. Usually the people I have breakfast with, I know very well."

Now the flush tidal-waves into a full-on blush. I try to think of something quippy to say back. But it's hard to be witty when someone is looking at you like that.

"Did you really believe I would leave you on the train?" he asks.

The question is oddly jarring after all that hilarity about black-market sex slavery. I think about it. Did I *really* think he'd do that?

"I don't know," I answer. "Maybe I was just having a minor panic because doing something impulsive like this, it's not me."

"Are you sure about that?" he asks. "You're here, after all."

"I'm here," I repeat. And I am. Here. On my way to Paris. With him. I look at him. He's got that half smile, as if there's something about me that's endlessly amusing. And maybe it's that, or the rocking of the train, or the fact that I'll never see him again after the one day, or maybe once you open the trapdoor of honesty, there's no going back. Or maybe it's just because I want to. But I let the robe drop to the floor. "I thought you got off the train because I was having a hard time believing you'd be on the train in the first place. With me. Without some ulterior motive."

And *this* is the truth. Because I may be only eighteen, but it already seems pretty obvious that the world is divided into two groups: the doers and the watchers. The people things happen to and the rest of us, who just sort of plod on with things. The Lulus and the Allysons.

It never occurred to me that by *pretending* to be Lulu, I might slip into that other column, even for just a day.

I turn to Willem, to see what he'll say to this, but before he responds, the train plunges into darkness as we enter the Channel Tunnel. According to the factoids I read, in less than twenty minutes, we will be in Calais and then, an hour later, Paris. But right now, I have a feeling that this train is not just delivering me to Paris, but to someplace entirely new.

Four

Paris

Immediately, there are problems. The luggage storage place in the basement of the train station is shuttered; the workers who run the X-ray machines the bags have to pass through before they go into storage are on strike. As a result, all the automated lockers large enough for my bag are full. Willem says there's another station that's not so far from here we might try, but if the baggage handlers are on strike, we might have the same problem there too.

"I can just drag it behind me. Or toss it into the Seine." I'm joking, though there *is* something appealing about abandoning all vestiges of Allyson.

"I have a friend who works in a nightclub not so far from here. . . ." He reaches into his backpack and pulls out a battered leather notebook. I'm about to make a joke about it being his little black book, but then I see all the names and numbers and email addresses scrawled in there, and he adds,

"She does the books, so she's usually there in the afternoons," and I realize that it actually *is* a little black book.

After finding the number he's after, he pulls out an ancient cell phone, presses the power key a few times. "No battery. Does yours work?"

I shake my head. "It's useless in Europe. Except as a camera."

"We can walk. It's close to here."

We head back up the escalators. Before we get to the automatic doors, Willem turns to me and asks, "Are you ready for Paris?"

In all the stress of dealing with my luggage, I'd sort of forgotten that the point of all this was Paris. Suddenly, I'm a little nervous. "I hope so," I say weakly.

We walk out the front of the train station and step into the shimmering heat. I squint, as if preparing for blinding disappointment. Because the truth of it is, so far on this tour, I've been let down by pretty much everywhere we went. Maybe I watch too many movies. In Rome, I really wanted an Audrey Hepburn *Roman Holiday* experience, but the Trevi Fountain was crowded, there was a McDonald's at the base of the Spanish Steps, and the ruins smelled like cat pee because of all the strays. The same thing happened in Prague, where I'd been yearning for some of the bohemianism of *The Unbearable Lightness of Being*. But no, there were no fabulous artists, no guys who looked remotely like a young Daniel Day-Lewis. I saw one mysterious-looking guy reading Sartre in a café, but then his cell phone rang and he started talking in a loud Texas twang.

And London. Melanie and I got ourselves completely lost

on the Tube just so we could visit Notting Hill, but all we found was a fancy, expensive area full of upscale shops. No quaint bookstores, no groups of lovable friends I'd want to have dinner parties with. It seemed like there was a direct link between number of movies I'd seen about a city and the degree of my disappointment. And I've seen a lot of movies about Paris.

The Paris that greets me outside Gare du Nord is not the Paris of the movies. There's no Eiffel Tower or fancy couture stores here. It's just a regular street, with a bunch of hotels and exchange bureaus, clogged with taxis and buses.

I look around. There are rows and rows of old grayish-brown buildings. They are uniform, seeming to ripple into one another, their windows and French doors thrown open, flowers spilling out. Right across from the station are two cafés, catty-corner. Neither one is fancy, but both are packed—people clustered at round glass tables, under the awnings and umbrellas. It's both so normal and so completely foreign.

Willem and I start walking. We cross the street and pass one of cafés. There's a woman sitting alone at one of the tables, drinking pink wine and smoking a cigarette, a small bulldog panting by her legs. As we walk by, the dog jumps up and starts sniffing under my skirt, tangling me and him in his leash.

The woman must be around my mom's age, but is wearing a short skirt and high-heeled espadrilles that lace up her shapely legs. She scolds the dog and untangles the leash. I bend over to scratch behind its ears, and the woman says something in French that makes Willem laugh.

"What did she say?" I ask as we walk away.

"She said her dog is like a truffle hog when it comes to beautiful girls."

"Really?" I feel flush with pleasure. Which is a little silly, because it was a dog, and also I'm not entirely sure what a truffle hog is.

Willem and I walk down a block full of sex shops and travel agencies and turn a corner onto some unpronounceable boulevard, and for the first time, I understand that *boulevard* is actually a French word, that all the big streets called boulevards at home are actually just busy roads. Because *here* is a boulevard: a river of life, grand, broad, and flowing, a plaza running down the middle and graceful trees arcing out toward one another overhead.

At a redlight, a cute guy in a skinny suit riding a moped in the bike lane stops to check me out, looking me up and down until the moped behind him beeps its horn for him to move on.

Okay, this is, like, twice in five minutes. Granted, the first one was a dog, but it feels significant. For the past three weeks, it's been Melanie getting the catcalls—a result of her blond hair and LOOK AT ME wardrobe, I cattily assumed. Once or twice, I huffed about the objectification of women, but Melanie rolled her eyes and said I was missing the point.

As this lightness buoys me, I wonder if maybe she was right. Maybe it's not about looking hot for guys, but about feeling like a place acknowledged you, winked at you, accepted you. It's strange because, of all the people in all the cities, I'd have thought that to Parisians I'd be invisible, but apparently I'm not. Apparently, in Paris, not only can I skate, but I practically qualify for the Olympics!

"It's official," I declare. "I love Paris!"

"That was fast."

"When you know, you know. It's just become my favorite city in the whole world."

"It tends to have that effect."

"I should add that there wasn't much competition, seeing as I didn't actually enjoy most of the places on the tour."

And again, it just slips out. Apparently when you only have one day, you can say anything and live to tell. *The trip has been a bust.* How good it feels to finally admit this to someone. Because I couldn't tell my parents, who had paid for what they believed was the Trip of a Lifetime. And I couldn't tell Melanie, who really was on the Trip of a Lifetime. And not Ms. Foley, whose job it was to ensure I had the Trip of a Lifetime. But it's true. I've spent the last three weeks trying to have fun—and failing.

"I think maybe traveling is a talent, like whistling or dancing," I continue. "And some people have it—you seem to. I mean, how long have you been traveling?"

"Two years," he says.

"Two years with breaks?"

He shakes his head. "Two years since I've been back to Holland."

"Really? And you were supposed to go back today? After two years?"

He throws his arms up into the air. "What's one more day after two years?"

I suppose to him, not a lot. But to me, maybe something else. "That just proves my point. You have the talent for traveling. I'm not sure that I do. I keep hearing everyone go on about how travel broadens your horizons. I'm not even sure what that means, but it hasn't broadened anything for me, because I'm no good at it."

He's mostly silent as we walk over a long bridge spanning dozens of railroad tracks, graffiti everywhere. Then he says, "Traveling's not something you're good at. It's something you do. Like breathing."

"I don't think so. I breathe just fine."

"Are you sure? Have you ever thought about it?"

"Probably more than most people. My father's a pulmonologist. A lung doctor."

"What I mean is, have you ever thought about *how* it is that you do it? Day and night? While you sleep. While you eat. While you talk."

"Not so much."

"Think about it now."

"How do you think about breathing?" But then all of sudden I do. I get tangled up in thoughts about breathing, the mechanics of it, how is it that my body knows to do it even when I'm sleeping, or crying, or hiccupping. What would happen if my body somehow forgot? And sure enough, my breath grows a little labored, as if I'm walking uphill, even though I'm walking down the slope of the bridge.

"Okay, that was weird."

"See?" Willem asks. "You thought too hard. Same with travel. You can't work too much at it, or it feels like work. You have to surrender yourself to the chaos. To the accidents."

"I'm supposed to walk in front of a bus and then I'll have a good time?"

Willem chuckles. "Not those accidents. The little things

that happen. Sometimes they're insignificant; other times, they change everything."

"This all sounds very Jedi. Can you be more specific?"

"A guy picks up a girl hitchhiking in a faraway country. A year later, she runs out of money and winds up on his doorstep. Six months after that, they get married. Accidents."

"Did you marry a hitchhiker or something?"

His smile unfurls like a sail. "I'm giving examples."

"Tell me a *real* one."

"How do you know that's not real?" he teases. "Okay, this happened to me. Last year when I was in Berlin, I missed my train to Bucharest and caught a ride to Slovakia instead. The people I rode with were in a theater troupe, and one of the guys had just broken his ankle and they needed a replacement. On the six-hour ride to Bratislava, I learned his part. I stayed with the troupe until his ankle got better, and then a while after that, I met some people from Guerrilla Will, and they were in desperate need of someone who could do Shakespeare in French."

"And *you* could?"

He nods.

"Are you some kind of language savant?"

"I'm just Dutch. So I joined Guerrilla Will." He snaps his fingers. "Now I'm an actor."

This surprises me. "You seemed like you'd been doing it a lot longer."

"No. It's just accidental, just temporary. Until the next accident sends me somewhere new. That's how life works."

Something quickens in my chest. "Do you really think that's how it works? That life can change *justlikethat*?"

"I think everything is happening all the time, but if you don't put yourself in the path of it, you miss it. When you travel, you put yourself out there. It's not always great. Sometimes it's terrible. But other times . . ." He lifts his shoulders and gestures out to Paris, then sneaks me a sidelong glance. "It's not so bad."

"So long as you don't get hit by a bus," I say.

He laughs. Then gives me the point. "So long as you don't get hit by a bus," he says back.

Five

We arrive at the club where Willem's friend works; it seems completely dead, but when Willem pounds on the door, a tall man with blue-black skin opens up. Willem speaks to him in French, and after a minute, we're allowed into a huge dank room with a small stage, a narrow bar, and a bunch of tables with chairs stacked on them. Willem and the Giant confer a bit more in French and then Willem turns to me.

"Céline doesn't like surprises. Maybe it's better if I go down first."

"Sure." In the hushed dim, my voice seems to clang, and I realize I'm nervous again.

Willem heads to a staircase at the back of the club. The Giant resumes his work polishing bottles behind the bar. Obviously, he didn't get the message that Paris loves me. I take a seat on the barstool. They twirl all the way around, like the barstools at Whipple's, the ice-cream place I used to go to with my grandparents. The Giant is ignoring me, so I just sort of spin myself this way and that. And then I guess I do it a little fast, because I go spinning and the barstool comes clear off its base.

"Oh, shit! Ow!"

The Giant comes out to where I am sprawled on the floor. His face is a picture of blasé. He picks up the stool and screws it back in, then goes back behind the bar. I stay on the floor for a second, wondering which is more humiliating, remaining down here or getting back on the stool.

"You are American?"

What gives it away? Because I'm clumsy? Aren't French people ever clumsy? I'm actually pretty graceful. I took ballet for eight years. I should tell him to fix the stool before someone sues. No, if I say that, I'll definitely sound American.

"How can you tell?" I don't know why I bother to ask. Since the moment our plane touched down in London, it's like there's been a neon sign above my head, blinking: TOUR-IST, AMERICAN, OUTSIDER. I should be used to it. Except since arriving in Paris, it felt like it had maybe dimmed. Clearly not.

"Your friend tells me," he says. "My brother lives in Roché Estair."

"Oh?" Am I supposed to know where this is? "Is that near Paris?"

He laughs, a big loud belly laugh. "No. It is in New York. Near the big lake."

Roché Estair? "Oh! Rochester."

"Yes. Roché Estair," he repeats. "It is very cold up there. Very much snow. My brother's name is Aliou Mjodi. Maybe you know him?"

I shake my head. "I live in Pennsylvania, next to New York."

"Is there much snow in Penisvania?"

I suppress a laugh. "There's a fair amount in Penn-syl-vania," I say, emphasizing the pronunciation. "But not as much as Rochester."

He shivers. "Too cold. Especially for us. We have Senegalese blood in our veins, though we both are born in Paris. But now my brother he goes to study computers in Roché Estair, at university." The Giant looks very proud. "He does not like the snow. And he says, in summer, the mosquitoes are as big as those in Senegal."

I laugh.

The Giant's face breaks open into a jack-o'-lantern's smile. "How long in Paris?"

I look at my watch. "I've been here one hour, and I'll be here for one day."

"One day? Why are you here?" He gestures to the bar.

I point to my bag. "We need a place to store this."

"Take it downstairs. You must not waste your one day here. When the sun shines, you let it shine on you. Snow is always waiting."

"Willem told me to wait, that Céline—"

"*Pff*," he interrupts, waving his hand. He comes out from behind the bar and easily hoists my bag over his shoulder. "Come, I take it downstairs for you."

At the bottom of the stairs is a dark hallway crowded with speakers, amplifiers, cables, and lights. Upstairs, there's rapping on the door, and the Giant bounds back up, telling me to leave the bag in the office.

There are a couple of doors, so I go to the first one and knock on it. It opens to a small room with a metal desk, an old computer, a pile of papers. Willem's backpack is there, but he's not. I go back in the hall and hear the sound of a woman's rapid-fire French, and then Willem's voice, languid in response.

"Willem?" I call out. "Hello?"

He says something back, but I don't understand.

"What?"

He says something else, but I can't hear him so I crack open the door to find a small supply closet full of boxes and in it, Willem standing right up close to a girl—Céline—who even in the half darkness, I can see is beautiful in a way I can never even pretend to be. She is talking to Willem in a throaty voice while tugging his shirt over his head. He, of course, is laughing.

I slam the door shut and retreat back toward the stairs, tipping over my suitcase in my haste.

I hear something rattle. "Lulu, open the door. It's stuck."

I turn around. My suitcase is lodged underneath the handle. I scurry back to kick it out of the way and turn back toward the stairs as the door flies open.

"What are you doing?" Willem asks.

"Leaving." It's not like Willem and I are anything to each other, but still, he left me upstairs to come downstairs for a quickie?

"Come back."

I've heard about the French. I've seen plenty of French films. A lot of them are sexy; some of them are kinky. I want to be Lulu, but not *that* much.

"Lulu!" Willem's voice is firm. "Céline refuses to hold your bags unless I change my clothes," he explains. "She says I look like a dirty old man coming out of a sex shop." He points to his crotch.

It takes me a minute to understand what she means, and when I do, I flush.

Céline says something to Willem in French, and he laughs. And fine, maybe it's not what I thought it was. But it's still pretty clear that I've intruded upon *something*.

Willem turns back to me. "I said I will change my jeans, but all my other shirts are just as dirty, so she is finding me one."

Céline continues yapping away at Willem in French, and it's like I don't even exist.

Finally, she finds what she's looking for, a heather-gray T-shirt with a giant red sos emblazoned on it. Willem takes it and yanks off his own T-shirt. Céline says something else and reaches out to undo his belt buckle. He holds his hands up in surrender and then undoes the buttons himself. The jeans fall to the floor and Willem just stands there, all miles and miles of him, in nothing but a pair of fitted boxer shorts.

"*Excusez-moi,*" he says as he brushes past me so close his bare torso slides up against my arm. It's dark in here, but I'm fairly certain Céline can tell I'm blushing and has marked this as a point against me. A few seconds later, Willem returns with his backpack. He digs in it for a rumpled-but-stain-free pair of jeans. I try not to stare as he slips them on and threads his worn brown leather belt through the loops. Then he puts on the T-shirt. Céline glances at me looking at him, and I look away as though she's caught me at something. Which she has.

Watching him get dressed feels more illicit than seeing him strip.

"*D'accord?*" he asks Céline. She appraises him, her hands on her hips.

"*Mieux*," she says back, sounding like a cat. *Mew.*

"Lulu?" Willem asks.

"Nice."

Finally, Céline acknowledges me. She says something, gesticulating wildly, then stops.

When I fail to answer, one of Céline's eyebrows shoots up into a perfect arch, while the other one stays in neutral. I've seen women from Florence to Prague do this same thing. It must be some skill they teach in European schools.

"She is asking you if you have ever heard of *Sous ou Sur*," Willem says, pointing to the SOS on the shirt. "They are a famous punk-rap band with strong lyrics about justice."

I shake my head, feeling like a double loser for not having heard of the cool French anarchist whatever justice band. "I'm sorry, I don't speak French."

Céline looks disdainful. Another stupid American who can't be bothered to learn any other languages.

"I speak a little Mandarin," I offer hopefully, but this fails to impress.

Céline deigns to switch to English: "But your name. Lulu, it is French, *non?*"

There's a small pause. Like at a concert in between songs. A perfect time to say, ever so casually, "Actually, my name is Allyson."

But then Willem answers for me. "It's short for Louise." And he winks at me.

Céline points at my suitcase with a manicured purple fingernail. "That is the bag?"

"Yes. This is it."

"It is so big."

"It's not *that* big." I think about some of the bags other girls brought on the tour, the hair dryers and adapters and three changes of clothes per day. I look at her in her black mesh tunic that stops at her thighs, a tiny black skirt that Melanie would pay too much for, and suspect this knowledge would fail to impress her.

"It can live in the storage room, not in my office."

"That's fine. Just so long as I can get it tomorrow."

"The cleaner will be here at ten o'clock. And here, we have so many extra, you can have one too," she says, handing me the same T-shirt she gave Willem, only mine is at least a size larger than his.

I'm about to open my suitcase and stuff it in, but then I visualize the contents: the sensible A-line skirts and T-shirts that Mom picked out for me. My travel journal, the entries I hoped would be breathless accounts of adventure but wound up reading like a series of telegrams: *Today we went to the Prague Castle. Stop. Then we saw* The Magic Flute *at the State Opera House. Stop. Had chicken cutlets for dinner. Stop.* The postcards from Famous European Cities, blank because after I'd mailed the obligatory few to my parents and grandmother, I'd had no one left to send them to. And then there's the Ziploc bag with one lone piece of paper inside. Before the trip, my mom made me a master inventory of all the things to bring and then she made copies, one for every stop, so each time I packed, I could check off each item, to ensure I didn't leave anything behind. There is one sheet left for my supposed last stop in London.

I stuff the T-shirt into my shoulder bag. "I'll just hang on to this. To sleep in tonight."

Céline's eyebrow shoots up again. She probably never sleeps in a T-shirt. She probably sleeps in the silky nude, even on the coldest of winter nights. I get a flash of her sleeping naked next to Willem.

"Thanks. For the shirt. For storing my bag," I say.

"Merci," Céline says back, and I wonder why it is that she's thanking me, but then I realize she wants me to say thank you in French, so I do, only it comes out sounding like *mercy*.

We go upstairs. Céline is nattering away to Willem. I'm beginning to understand how his French got so fluent. As if this didn't make it clear enough that she was a dog and Willem her hydrant, when we get upstairs, she links arms with him and walks him slowly to the front of the bar. I feel like waving my arms and saying "Hello! Remember me?"

When they do that cheek-cheek-kiss-kiss thing, I feel so much of the excitement from earlier dwindle. Next to Céline, with her mile-high stilettos, her black hair, the underneath dyed blond, her perfectly symmetrical face, which is both marred and enhanced by so many piercings, I feel short as a midget and plain as a mop. And once again, I wonder, Why did he bring me here? Then I think of Shane Michaels.

All through tenth grade, I'd had a huge crush on Shane, a senior. We'd hang out, and he'd flirt with me and invite me lots of places and pay for me even, and he'd confide all kinds of personal things, including, yes, about the girls he was dating. But those relationships never lasted more than a few weeks, and I'd told myself that all the while, he and I were growing closer and that he'd eventually fall for me. When months went by and nothing happened between us, Melanie said it was never going to happen. "You have Sidekick Syndrome," she said. At the time, I thought she was jealous, but of course, she was right. It hits me that, Evan notwithstanding, it might be a lifetime affliction.

I can feel myself shriveling, feel the welcome Paris bestowed on me earlier fading away, if it even really happened. How stupid to think a dog sniffing my crotch and a quick look from some random guy meant anything. Paris adores girls like Céline. Genuine Lulus, not counterfeits.

But then, just as we're at the door, the Giant comes out from behind the bar and takes my hand and, with a jaunty "*à bientôt*," kisses both my cheeks.

A warm feeling tickles my chest. This is the first time on the trip a local has been unabashedly nice to me—because he wanted to, not because I was paying him to. And it doesn't escape my notice that Willem is no longer looking at Céline but is watching me, a curious expression lighting up his face. I'm not sure if it's these things or something else, but it makes that kiss, which I get was just platonic—a friendly, cheek-handshake thing—feel momentous. A kiss from all of Paris.

Six

"Lulu, we have something very important to discuss."

Willem looks at me solemnly, and I feel my stomach bottom out in anxiety over another unpleasant surprise.

"What now?" I ask, trying not to sound nervous.

He crosses his arms in front of his chest and then he strokes his chin. Is he going to send me back? No! I've already had that freak-out once today.

"What?" I ask again, my voice rising in spite of my best efforts.

"We lost an hour coming to France, so it's after two o'clock. Lunchtime. And this is Paris. And we just have the day. So we must consider this very seriously."

"Oh." I exhale relief. Is he *trying* to mess with me now? "I don't care. Anything except chocolate and bread, please. Those might be your staples, but they don't seem particularly French," I snap, not entirely sure why I'm so peeved except that even though we've now walked several blocks away from Céline's club, it's like she's following us somehow.

Willem feigns offense. "Bread and chocolate are not my staple foods." He grins. "Not the only ones. And they are *very* French. Chocolate croissants? We can have those for breakfast tomorrow."

Breakfast. Tomorrow. *After tonight*. Céline beings to feel a little farther away now.

"Unless, that is, you prefer crisps for breakfast," he continues. "Or pancakes. That's American. Maybe crisps with your pancakes?"

"I don't eat *chips* for breakfast. I do occasionally eat pancakes for dinner. I'm a rebel that way."

"Crêpes," he says, snapping his fingers. "We will have crêpes. Very French. And you can be rebellious."

We walk along, menu-browsing the cafés until we find one on a quiet triangle corner that serves crêpes. The menu is hand-scrawled, in French, but I don't ask Willem to translate. After that whole thing with Céline, my lack of fluency is starting to feel like a handicap. So I stumble through the menu, settling on *citron*, which I'm pretty sure means lemon, or orange, or citrus of some kind. I decide on a *citron crêpe* and a *citron pressé* drink, hoping it's some kind of lemonade.

"What are you getting?" I ask.

He scratches his chin. There is a tiny patch of golden stubble there. "I was thinking of getting a chocolate crêpe, but that is so close to chocolate and bread that I'm afraid you'll lose respect for me." He flashes me that lazy half smile.

"I wouldn't sweat it. I already lost respect for you when I found you undressing for Céline in her office," I joke.

And there's that look: surprise, amusement. "That wasn't her office," he says slowly, drawing out his words. "And I would say she was more undressing me."

"Oh, never mind, then. By all means, order the chocolate."

He gives me a long look. "No. To repent, I will order mine with Nutella."

"That's hardly repenting. Nutella is practically chocolate."

"It's made from nuts."

"And chocolate! It's disgusting."

"You just say that because you're American."

"That has nothing to do with it! You seem to have a bottomless appetite for chocolate and bread, but I don't assume it's because you're Dutch."

"Why would it be?"

"Dutch Cocoa? You guys have the lock on it."

Willem laughs. "I think you have us confused with the Belgians. And I get my sweet tooth from my mother, who's not even Dutch. She says she craved chocolate all through her pregnancy with me and that's why I like it so much."

"Figures. Blame the woman."

"Who's blaming?"

The waitress comes over with our drinks.

"So, Céline," I begin, knowing I should let this go but am somehow unable to. "She's, like, the bookkeeper? At the club."

"Yes."

I know it's catty, but I'm gratified that it's such a dull job. Until Willem elaborates. "Not the bookkeeper. She *books* all the bands, so she knows all these musicians." And if that's not bad enough, he adds, "She does some of the artwork for the posters too."

"Oh." I deflate. "She must be very talented. Do you know her from the acting thing?"

"No."

"Well, how did you meet?"

He plays with the wrapper from my straw.

"I get it," I say, wondering why I'm bothering to ask what is so painfully clear. "You guys were an item."

"No, that's not it."

"Oh." Surprise. And relief.

And then Willem says, ever so casually, "We just fell in love once."

I take a gulp of my *citron pressé*—and choke on it. It turns out it's not lemonade so much as lemon juice and water. Willem hands me a cube of sugar and a napkin.

"*Once?*" I say when I recover.

"It was a while ago."

"And now?"

"We are good friends. As you saw."

I'm not sure that's exactly what I saw.

"So you're not in love with her anymore?" I run my fingers along the rim of my glass.

Willem looks at me. "I never said I was in love with her."

"You *just* said you fell in love with her once."

"And I did."

I stare at him, confused.

"There is a world of difference, Lulu, between *falling* in love and *being* in love."

I feel my face go hot, and I'm not entirely sure why. "Isn't it just sequential—A follows B?"

"You have to fall in love to be in love, but falling in love isn't the same as being in love." Willem peers at me from under his lashes. "Have you ever fallen in love?"

Evan and I broke up the day after he mailed in his college tuition deposit. It wasn't unexpected. Not really. We had already agreed we would break up when we went to college if we didn't wind up in the same geographical area. And he was going to school in St. Louis. I was going to school in Boston. The thing I hadn't expected was the timing. Evan decided it made more sense to "rip the bandage off" and break up not in June, when we graduated, or in August, when we'd leave for school, but in April.

But the thing is, aside from being sort of humiliated by the rumor that I'd been dumped and disappointed about missing prom, I wasn't actually sad about losing *Evan*. I was surprisingly neutral about breaking up with my first boyfriend. It was like he'd never even been there. I didn't miss him, and Melanie quickly filled up whatever gaps he'd left in the schedule.

"No," I reply. "I've never been in love."

Just then the waitress arrives with our crêpes. Mine is golden brown, wafting with the sweet tartness of lemon and sugar. I concentrate on that, cutting off a slice and popping it in my mouth. It melts on the tip of my tongue like a warm, sweet snowdrop.

"That's not what I asked," Willem says. "I asked if you've ever *fallen* in love."

The playfulness is his voice is like an itch I just can't scratch. I look at him, wondering if he always parses semantics like this.

Willem puts down his fork and knife. "*This* is falling in

love." With his finger, he swipes a bit of the Nutella from inside his crêpe and puts a dollop on the inside of my wrist. It is hot and oozy and starts to melt against my sticky skin, but before it has a chance to slither away, Willem licks his thumb and wipes the smear of Nutella off and pops it into his mouth. It all happens fast, like a lizard zapping a fly. "*This* is being in love." And here he takes my other wrist, the one with my watch on it, and moves the watchband around until he sees what he's looking for. Once again, he licks his thumb. Only this time, he rubs it against my birthmark, hard, as if trying to scrub it off.

"Being in love is a birthmark?" I joke as I retract my arm. But my voice has a tremble in it, and the place where his wet thumbprint is drying against my skin burns somehow.

"It's something that never comes off, no matter how much you might want it to."

"You're comparing love to a . . . stain?"

He leans so far back in his seat that the front legs of his chair scrape off the floor. He looks very satisfied, with the crêpe or with himself, I'm not sure. "Exactly."

I think of the coffee stain on his jeans. I think of Lady Macbeth and her "Out, damned spot," stain, another speech I had to memorize for English. "*Stain* seems like an ugly word to describe love," I tell him.

Willem just shrugs. "Maybe just in English. In Dutch, it's *vlek*. In French, it's *tache*." He shakes his head, laughs. "No, still ugly."

"How many languages have you been stained in?"

He licks his thumb again and reaches across the table for my wrist, where he missed the tiniest smudge of Nutella. This time he wipes it—me—clean. "None. It always comes off."

He scoops the rest of the crêpe into his mouth, taking the dull edge of his knife to scrape the Nutella off the plate. Then he runs his finger around the rim, smearing the last of it away.

"Right," I say. "And why get stained when getting dirty is so much more fun?" I taste lemons in my mouth again, and I wonder where all the sweetness went.

Willem doesn't say anything. Just sips his coffee.

Three women wander into the café. They are all impossibly tall, almost as tall as Willem, and thin, with legs that seem to end at their boobs. They are like some strange race of human-giraffes. Models. I've never seen one in the wild before, but it is obvious what they are. One of them is wearing a tiny pair of shorts and platform sandals; she checks Willem out, and he gives her his little half smile, but then it's like he catches himself and looks back at me.

"You know what it sounds like to me?" I ask. "It sounds like you just like to screw around. Which is fine. But at least own that about yourself. Don't make up some bogus distinctions about falling in love versus being in love."

I hear my voice. I sound like Little Miss Muffet, all goody-two-shoes and sanctimonious. So not like Lulu. And I don't know why I'm upset. What is it to me if he believes in falling in love versus being in love, or if he believes that love is something the tooth fairy shoves under your pillow?

When I look up, Willem's eyes are half lidded and smiling, like I'm his court jester here to amuse him. It makes me feel covetous, a toddler about to tantrum for being refused something outrageous—a pony—she knows she can't have.

"You probably don't even believe in love." My voice is petulant.

"I do." His voice is quiet.

"Really? Define love. What would 'being stained'"—I make air quotes and roll my eyes—"look like?"

He doesn't even pause to think about it. "Like Yael and Bram."

"Who's that? Some Dutch Brangelina? That doesn't count, because who knows what it's really like for them?" I watch the herd of models disappear inside the café, where they will no doubt feast on coffee and air. I imagine them one day fat and ordinary. Because nothing that beautiful lasts forever.

"Who's Brangelina?" Willem asks absently. He reaches into his pocket for a coin and balances it between two knuckles, then flips it from knuckle to knuckle.

I watch the coin, watch his hands. They are big, but his fingers are delicate. "Never mind."

"Yael and Bram are my parents," he says quietly.

"Your *parents*?"

He completes a revolution with the coin and then tosses it into the air. "Stained. I like how you put it. Yael and Bram: Stained for twenty-five years."

He says it with both affection and sadness, and something in my stomach twists.

"Are your parents like that?" he asks quietly.

"They're still married after nearly twenty-five years, but stained?" I can't help but laugh. "I don't know if they ever were. They were set up on a blind date in college. And they've always seemed less like lovebirds than like amiable business partners, for whom I'm the sole product."

"Sole. So you are alone?"

Alone? I think he must mean *only*. And I'm never alone,

not with Mom and her color-coded calendar on the fridge, making sure every spare moment of my time is accounted for, making sure every aspect of my life is happily well managed. Except when I pause for a second and think about how I feel, at home, at the dinner table with Mom and Dad talking at me, not to me, at school with a bunch of people who never really became my friends, I understand that even if he didn't mean to, he got it right.

"Yes," I say.

"Me too."

"Our parents quit while they were ahead," I say, repeating the line Mom and Dad always use when people ask if I'm an only child. *We quit while we were ahead.*

"I never understand some English sayings," Willem replies. "If you're ahead, why would you quit?"

"I think it's a gambling term."

But Willem is shaking his head. "I think it's human nature to keep going when you're ahead, no matter what. You quit while you're behind." Then he looks at me again, and as if realizing that he has maybe insulted me, he hastily adds, "I'm sure with you it was different."

When I was little, my parents had tried to have more children. First they went the natural route, then they went the fertility route, Mom going through a bunch of horrible procedures that never worked. Then they looked into adoption and were in the process of filling out all the paperwork when Mom got pregnant. She was so happy. I was in first grade at the time, and she'd worked since I was a baby, but when the baby came, she was going to go on an extended leave from her job at a pharmaceutical company, then maybe only go back half time. But then in her fifth month, she lost the baby. That's when she and Dad decided to quit while they were ahead. That's what they told me. Except even back then, I think I'd recognized it as a lie. They'd wanted more, but they'd had to settle with just me, and I had to be good enough so that we could all pretend that we weren't actually settling.

"Maybe you're right," I tell Willem now. "Maybe nobody quits while they're really ahead. My parents always say that, but the truth is, they only stopped with me because they couldn't have any more. Not because I was enough."

"I'm sure *you* were enough."

"Were *you*?" I ask.

"Maybe more than enough," he says cryptically. It almost sounds like he's bragging, except it doesn't look like he's bragging.

He starts doing the thing with the coin again. As we sit silently, I watch the coin, feeling something like suspense build in my stomach, wondering if he'll let it fall. But he doesn't. He just keeps spinning it. When he finishes, he flips it in the air and tosses it to me, just like he did last night.

"Can I ask you something?" I say after a minute.

"Yes."

"Was it part of the show?"

He cocks his head.

"I mean, do you throw a coin to a girl at every performance, or was I special?"

Last night after I got back to the hotel, I spent a long time examining the coin he'd tossed me. It was a Czech koruna, worth about a nickel. But still, I'd put it in a separate corner of my wallet, away from all the other foreign coins. I pull it out now. It glints in the bright afternoon sun.

Willem looks at it too. I'm not sure if his answer is true or just maddeningly ambiguous, or maybe both. Because that's exactly what he says: "Maybe both."

Seven

When we leave the restaurant, Willem asks me the time. I twist the watch around my wrist. It feels heavier than ever, the skin underneath itchy and pale from being stuck under the piece of chunky metal for the past three weeks. I haven't taken it off once.

It was a present, from my parents, though it was Mom who'd given it to me on graduation night, after the party at the Italian restaurant with Melanie's family, where they told us about the tour.

"What's this?" I'd asked. We were sitting at the kitchen table, decompressing from the day. "You already gave me a graduation present."

She'd smiled. "I got you another."

I'd opened the box, seen the watch, fingered the heavy gold links. Read the engraving.

"It's too much." And it was. In every way.

just one day

"Time stops for no one," Mom had said, smiling a little sadly. "You deserve a good watch to keep up." Then she'd snapped the watch on my wrist, shown me how she had an extra safety clasp installed, pointed out that it was waterproof too. "It'll never fall off. So you can take it to Europe with you."

"Oh, no. It's way too valuable."

"It's fine. It's insured. Besides, I threw away your Swatch."

"You did?" I'd worn my zebra-striped Swatch all through high school.

"You're a grown-up now. You need a grown-up watch."

I look at my watch now. It's almost four. Back on the tour, I'd be breathing a sigh of relief, because the busy part of the day would be winding down. Usually we had a rest around five, and most nights, by eight o'clock, I could be back in my hotel room watching some movie.

"We should probably start seeing some of the sights," Willem says. "Do you know what you want to do?"

I shrug. "We could start with the Seine. Isn't that it?" I point to a concrete embankment, underneath which is a river of sorts.

Willem laughs. "No, that's a canal."

We walk down the cobblestoned pathway, and Willem pulls out a thick Rough Guide to Europe. He opens to a small map of Paris, points out, more or less, where we are, an area called Villette.

"The Seine is here," he says, tracing a line down the map.

"Oh." I look out at the boat, which is stuck now between two big metal gates; the area is filling up with water. Willem explains that this is a lock, basically an elevator that lifts and drops the boats down differing depths of the canals.

"How do you know so much about everything?"

He laughs. "I'm Dutch."

"So that means you're a genius?"

"Only about canals. They say 'God made the world, but the Dutch made Holland.'" And then he goes on to tell me about how so much of the country was reclaimed from the sea, about riding your bike along the low embankments that keep the water out of Holland. How it's an act of faith to ride your bike around, with the dikes above you, knowing somehow, even though you're below sea level, you're not under water. When he talks about it, he seems so young that I can almost see him as a towheaded little kid, eyes wide, staring out at the endless waterways and wondering where they all led to.

"Maybe we can go on one of those boats?" I ask, pointing to the barge we just watched go through the lock.

Willem's eyes light up, and for a second, I see that boy again. "I don't know." He looks inside the guidebook. "It doesn't really cover this neighborhood."

"Can we ask?"

Willem asks someone in French and is given a very complicated answer full of hand gestures. He turns to me, clearly excited. "You're right. He says that they have boat rides leaving from the basin."

We go along the cobblestoned walkway until it lets out in a large lake, where people are paddling in canoes. Off to one side, next to a cement pier, a couple of boats are moored. But when we get over there, we find out that they're private boats. The tourist boats have left for the day.

"We can take a boat along the Seine," Willem says. "It's much more popular, and the boats run all day." His eyes are downcast. I can see he's disappointed, as if he let me down.

"Oh, no big deal. I don't care."

But he's staring wistfully out at the water, and I see that *he* cares. And I know I don't know him, but I swear the boy is homesick. For boats and canals and watery things. And for a second, I think of what it must be like—away from home for two years, and here he postponed his return for another day. He did that. For me.

There's a row of boats and barges tied up, bobbing in the breeze that's kicked up. I look at Willem; a melancholy expression is deepening the lines on his face. I look back at the boats.

"Actually, I do care," I say. I reach into my bag for my wallet, for the hundred-dollar bill folded inside. I hold it up in the air and call out, "I'm looking for a ride down the canals. And I can pay."

Willem's head jerks toward me. "Lulu, what are you doing?"

But I'm walking away from him. "Anyone willing to give us a lift down the canals?" I call. "I got good old-fashioned American greenbacks."

A pock-faced guy with sharp features and a scrubby goatee pops onto the side of a blue-canopied barge. "How many greenbacks?" he asks in a very thick French accent.

"All of them!"

He takes the C-note and stares at it up close. Then he smells it.

It must smell legit, because he says, "If my passengers

agree, I will take you down the canal to Arsenal, close to Bastille. It is where we dock for the night." He gestures to the back of the boat where a quartet of gray-haired people are sitting around a small table, playing bridge or something. He calls out to one of them.

"Aye, Captain Jack," the man answers. He must be sixty. His hair is white, and his face is burnished red from the sun.

"We have some hitchhikers who want to come aboard with us."

"Can they play poker?" one of the women asks.

I used to play seven-card stud for nickels with my grandfather before he died. He said I was an excellent bluffer.

"Do not bother. She gave all her money to me," Captain Jack says.

"How much is he charging you?" one of the men asks.

"I offered him a hundred dollars," I say.

"To go where?"

"Down the canals."

"This is why we call him Captain Jack," one of the men says. "Because he's a pirate."

"No. It is because my name is Jacques, and I am your captain."

"A hundred dollars, Jacques?" a woman with a long gray braid and startlingly blue eyes asks. "That seems a little much, even for you."

"She offered this much." Jacques shrugs. "Also, now I will have more money to lose to you in poker."

"Ahh, good point," she says.

"Are you leaving now?" I ask.

"Soon."

"When is soon?" It's after four. The day is speeding by.

"You cannot rush these things." He flicks his hand in the air. "Time is like the water. Fluid."

Time doesn't seem fluid to me. It seems real and animate and hard as a rock.

"What he means," says the guy with the ponytail, "is that the trip to Arsenal takes a while and we were just about to open a bottle of claret. Come on, Captain Jack, let's shove off. For a hundred bucks, you can have your wine later."

"We'll continue with this fine French gin," the braided lady says.

He shrugs and then pockets my bill. I turn to Willem and grin. Then I nod at Captain Jack. He reaches out for my hand to escort me onboard.

The four passengers introduce themselves. They are Danish, retirees, and every year, they tell us, they rent a barge and cruise a European country for four weeks. Agnethe has the braid and Karin has short spiked hair. Bert has a shock of white hair and Gustav has the bald spot and the rat's tail of a ponytail and is sporting the ever-stylish socks-with-sandals look. Willem introduces himself, and almost automatically, I introduce *myself* as Lulu. It's almost as if I've become her. Maybe I have. Never in a million years would Allyson have done what I just did.

Captain Jack and Willem untie the line, and I'm about to say that maybe I should get some of my money back if Willem is going to play first mate but then I see that Willem is bounding about, having a blast. He clearly knows his way around a boat.

The barge chugs out of the broad basin, giving a wide view of a white-columned old building and a silver-domed modern-looking one. The Danes return to their poker game.

"Don't lose all your money," Captain Jack calls to them. "Or you won't have any left to lose to me."

I slip away to the bow of the boat and watch the scenery slip by. It's cooler down here in the canals, under the narrow arched footbridges. And it smells different too. Older, mustier, like generations of history are stored in the wet walls. If these walls could talk, I wonder what secrets they'd tell.

When we get to the first lock, Willem clambers to the side of the barge to show me how the mechanism works. The ancient-looking metal gates, rusted the same brackish color as the water, close behind us, the water drains out from beneath us, the gates reopen to a lower section.

This part of the canal is so narrow that the barge takes up almost the entire width. Steep embankments lead up to the streets, and above those, poplar and elm trees (per Captain Jack) form an arbor, a gentle respite from the hot afternoon sun.

A gust of wind shakes the trees, sending a scrim of leaves shimmying onto the deck. "Rain is coming," Captain Jack says, sniffing the air like a rabbit. I look up and then over at Willem and roll my eyes. The sky is cloudless, and there hasn't been rain in this part of Europe for ten days.

Up above, Paris carries on, doing her thing. Mothers sip coffee, keeping eyes on their kids as they scooter along the sidewalks. Vendors at outdoor stalls hawk fruits and vegetables. Lovers wrap their arms around each other, never mind the heat. A clarinet player stands atop the bridge, serenading it all.

I've hardly taken any pictures on this trip. Melanie teased me about it, to which I always said I preferred to experience something rather than obsessively record it. Though, really, the truth of it was, unlike Melanie (who wanted to remember the shoe salesman and the mime and the cute waiter and all the other people on the tour), none of that really mattered to me. At the start of the trip, I took shots of the sights. The Colosseum. Belvedere Palace. Mozart Square. But I stopped. They never came out very well, and you could get postcards of these things.

But there are no postcards of this. Of life.

I snap a picture of a bald man walking four bushy-haired dogs. Of a little girl in the most absurdly frilly skirt, plucking petals off a flower. Of a couple, unabashedly making out on the fake beach along the waterside. Of the Danes, ignoring all of this, but having the time of their lives playing cards.

"Oh, let me take one of the two of you," Agnethe says, rising, a little wobbly, from the game. "Aren't you golden?" She turns to the table. "Bert, was I ever that golden?"

"You still are, my love."

"How long have you been married?" I ask.

"Thirteen years," she says, and I'm wondering if they're stained, but then she adds, "Of course, we've been divorced for ten."

She sees the look of confusion on my face. "Our divorce is more successful than most marriages."

I turn to Willem. "What kind of stain is that?" I whisper, and he laughs just as Agnethe takes the picture.

A church bell rings in the distance. Agnethe hands back the phone, and I take a picture of her and Bert. "You will send me that one? All of the ones?"

"Of course. As soon as I have reception." I turn to Willem.

"I'll text them to you too, if you give me your number."

"My phone is so old, it doesn't work with pictures."

"When I get home, then, I'll put the pictures on my computer and email them to you," I say, though I'll have to figure out a place to hide the pictures from Mom; it wouldn't be beyond her to look through my phone—or computer. Though, I realize now, only for another month. And then I'll be free. Just like today I'm free.

He looks at one of the pictures for a long time. Then he looks at me. "I'll keep you up here." He taps his temple. "Where you can't get lost."

I bite my lip to hide my smile and pretend to put the phone away, but when Captain Jack calls to Willem to take the wheel while he visits the head, I pull it back out and scroll through the photos, stopping at the one of the two of us that Agnethe took. I'm in profile, my mouth open. He's laughing. Always laughing. I run my thumb over his face, halfway expecting it to emanate some sort of heat.

I put the phone away and watch Paris drift by, feeling relaxed, almost drunk with a sleepy joy. After a while, Willem returns to me. We sit quietly, listening to the lapping of the water, the babble of the Danes. Willem pulls a coin out and does that thing, flipping it from knuckle to knuckle. I watch, hypnotized by his hand, by the gentle rocking of the water. It's peaceful until the Danes start bickering, loudly. Willem translates: Apparently they're hotly debating whether some famous French actress has ever made a pornographic film.

"You speak *Danish* too?" I ask.

"No, it's just close to Dutch."

"How many languages do you speak?"

"Fluently?"

"Oh, God. I'm sorry I asked."

"Four fluently. I get by in German and Spanish too."

I shake my head, amazed.

"Yes, but you said you speak *Chinese*."

"I wouldn't say I speak it so much as murder it. I'm kind of tone deaf, and Mandarin is all about tone."

"Let me hear."

I look at him. "*Ni zhen shuai.*"

"Say something else."

"*Wo xiang wen ni.*"

"Now I hear it." He covers his head. "Stop. I'm bleeding from my ears."

"Shut up or you will be." I pretend to shove him.

"What did you say?" he asks.

I give him a look. No way I'm telling.

"You just made it up."

I shrug. "You'll never know."

"What does it mean?"

I grin. "You'll have to look it up."

"Can you write it too?" He pulls out his little black book and opens to a blank page near the back. He rifles back into his bag. "Do you have a pen?"

I have one of those fancy roller balls I swiped from my dad, this one emblazoned BREATHE EASY WITH PULMO-CLEAR. I write the character for sun, moon, stars. Willem nods admiringly.

"And look, I love this one. It's double happiness."

"See how the characters are symmetrical?"

"Double happiness," Willem repeats, tracing the lines with his index finger.

"It's a popular phrase. You'll see it on restaurants and things. I think it has to do with luck. In China, it's apparently big at weddings. Probably because of the story of its origin."

"Which is?"

"A young man was traveling to take a very important exam to become a minister. On the way, he gets sick in a mountain village. So this mountain doctor takes care of him, and while he's recovering, he meets the doctor's daughter, and they fall in love. Right before he leaves, the girl tells him a line of verse. The boy heads off to the capital to take his exam and does well, and the emperor's all impressed. So, I guess to test him further, he says a line of verse. Of course, the boy immediately recognizes this mysterious line as the other half of the couplet the girl told him, so he repeats what the girl said. The emperor's doubly impressed, and the boy gets the job. Then he goes back and marries the girl. So, double happiness, I guess. He gets the job and the girl. You know, the Chinese are very big on luck."

Willem shakes his head. "I think the double happiness is the two halves finding each other. Like the couplet."

I'd never thought of it, but of course that's what it is.

"Do you remember how it goes?" Willem asks.

I nod. "Green trees against the sky in the spring rain while the sky set off the spring trees in the obscuration. Red flowers dot the land in the breeze's chase while the land colored up in red after the kiss."

— — —

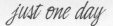

The final section of the canal is underground. The walls are arched, and so low that I can reach up and touch the slick, wet bricks. It's eerie, hushed but echoey down here. Even the boisterous Danes have shushed. Willem and I sit with our legs dangling over the edge of the boat, kicking the side of the tunnel wall when we can.

He nudges my ankle with his toe. "Thank you."

"For what?"

"For arranging this." He gestures to the boat.

"My pleasure. Thank you for arranging *this*." I point above us, to where Paris is no doubt going about its business.

"Any time." He looks around. "It's nice, this. The canal." He looks at me. "You."

"I'll bet you say that to all the canals." But I flush in the musty, rich darkness.

We stay like that for the rest of the ride, swinging our legs against the side of the boat, listening as the odd bit of laughter or music from Paris seeps underground. It feels like the city is telling secrets down here, privy only to those who think to listen.

Eight

---

*A*rsenal Marina is like a parking lot for boats, tightly packed into cement piers on both sides of the water. Willem helps Captain Jack guide the barge into its narrow mooring, hopping out to tie the lines in complicated knots. We bid farewell to the Danes, who are now truly soused, and I take down Agnethe's cell phone number, promising to text her the pictures as soon as I can.

As we get off, Captain Jack shakes our hands. "I feel a little bad to take your money," he says.

"No. Don't feel bad." I think of the look on Willem's face, of being in the tunnel. That alone was worth a hundred bucks.

"And we'll take it off you soon enough," Gustav calls.

Jacques shrugs. He kisses my hand before he helps me off the boat, and he practically hugs Willem.

As we walk away, Willem taps my shoulder. "Did you see what the boat is named?"

I didn't. It's right on the back, etched in blue lettering, next to the vertical red, white, and blue stripes of the French flag. *Viola. Deauville.*

"Viola? After Shakespeare's Viola?"

"No. Jacques meant for it be called *Voilà*, but his cousin painted it wrong, and he liked the name, so he registered her as *Viola*."

"Okaaay—that's still a little weird," I say.

As always, Willem smiles.

"Accidents?" Immediately, a strange little tremor goes up my spine.

Willem nods, almost solemnly. "Accidents," he confirms.

"But what does it mean? Does it mean we were meant to take *that* boat? Does it mean something better or worse would've happened to us if we *hadn't* taken that boat? Did taking that boat *alter* the course of our lives? Is life really that random?"

Willem just shrugs.

"Or does it mean that Jacques's cousin can't spell?" I say.

Willem laughs again. The sound is clear and strong as a bell, and it fills me with joy, and it's like, for the first time in my life, I understand that *this* is the point of laughter, to spread happiness.

"Sometimes you can't know until you know," he says.

"That's very helpful."

He laughs and looks at me for a long moment. "You know, I think you might be good at traveling after all."

"Seriously? I'm not. Today is a total anomaly. I was miserable on the tour. Trust me, I didn't flag down a single boat. Not even a taxi. Not even a bicycle."

"What about before the tour?"

"I haven't traveled much, and the kind I've done . . . not a lot of room for accidents."

Willem raises a questioning eyebrow.

"I've been places. Florida. Skiing. And to Mexico, but even that sounds more exotic than it is. Every year, we go to this time-share resort south of Cancún. It's meant to look like a giant Mayan temple, but I swear the only clue that you're not in America is the piped-in mariachi Christmas carols along the fake river waterslide thing. We stay in the same unit. We go to the same beach. We eat at the same restaurants. We barely even leave the gates, and when we do, it's to visit the ruins, but we go to the same ones every single year. It's like the calendar flips but nothing else changes."

"Same, same, but different," Willem says.

"More like same, same, but same."

"Next time when you go to Cancún, you can sneak out into the real Mexico," he suggests. "Tempt fate. See what happens."

"Maybe," I allow, just imagining my mom's response if I suggested a little freelance traveling.

"Maybe I'll go to Mexico one day," Willem says. "I'll bump into you, and we'll escape into the wilds."

"You think that would happen? We'd just randomly bump into each other?"

Willem lifts his hands up in the air. "There would have to be another accident. A big one."

"Oh, so you're saying that *I'm* an accident?"

His smile stretches like caramel. "Absolutely."

I rub my toe against the curb. I think of my Ziploc bags. I think of the color-coded schedule of all my activities that we've kept tacked to the fridge since I was, like, eight. I think of my neat files with all my college application materials. Everything ordered. Everything planned. I look at Willem, so the opposite of that, of me, today, also the opposite of that.

"I think that might possibly be one of the most flattering things anyone has ever said to me." I pause. "I'm not sure what that says about me, though."

"It says that you haven't been flattered enough."

I bow and give a sweeping be-my-guest gesture.

He stops and looks at me, and it's like his eyes are scanners. I have that same sensation I did on the train earlier, that he's appraising me, only this time not for looks and black-market value, but for something else.

"I won't say that you're pretty, because that dog already did. And I won't say you're funny, because you have had me laughing since I met you."

Evan used to tell me that he and I were "so compatible," as if being like him was the highest form of praise. *Pretty and funny*—Willem could stop right there, and it would be enough.

But he doesn't stop there. "I think you're the sort of person who finds money on the ground and waves it in the air and asks if anyone has lost it. I think you cry in movies that aren't even sad because you have a soft heart, though you don't let it show. I think you do things that scare you, and that makes you braver than those adrenaline junkies who bungee-jump off bridges."

He stops then. I open my mouth to say something, but nothing comes out and there's a lump in my throat and for one small second, I'm scared I'm going to cry.

Because I'd hoped for baubles, trinkets, fizzy things: *You have a nice smile. You have pretty legs. You're sexy.*

But what he said . . . I did once turn in forty dollars I found at the food court to mall security. I have cried in every single Jason Bourne movie. As for the last thing he said, I don't know if it's true. But I hope more than anything that it is.

"We should get going," I say, clearing my throat. "If we want to get to the Louvre. How far is it from here?"

"Maybe a few kilometers. But it's fast by bike."

"You want me to wave one down?" I joke.

"No, we'll just get a Vélib'." Willem looks around and walks toward a stand of gray bicycles. "Have you ever heard of the White Bicycle?" he asks.

I shake my head, and Willem starts explaining how for a brief time in Amsterdam in the 1960s, there used to be white bicycles, and they were free and everywhere. When you wanted a bike, you grabbed one, and when you were done, you left it. But it didn't work because there weren't enough bikes, and people stole them. "In Paris, you can borrow a bike for free for a half hour, but you have to lock it back up, or you get charged."

"Oh, I think I just read they started something like this back home. So, it's free?"

"All you need is a credit card for the deposit."

I don't have a credit card—well, not one that doesn't link back to my parents' account, but Willem has his bank card, though he says he isn't sure if there's enough. When he runs it through the little keypad, one of the bikes unlocks, but when he tries it again for a second bike, the card is declined. I'm not entirely disappointed. Cycling around Paris, sans helmet, seems vaguely suicidal.

But Willem's not replacing the bike. He's wheeling it over to where I'm standing and raising the seat. He looks at me. Then pats the saddle.

"Wait, you want *me* to ride the bike?"

He nods.

"And you'll what? Run alongside me?"

"No. I'll ride you." His eyebrows shoot up, and I feel myself blush. "On the bike," he clarifies.

I climb onto the wide seat. Willem steps in front of me. "Where exactly are you going to go?" I ask

"Don't worry about that. You just get comfortable," he says, as if it's possible in the current situation, with his back inches from my face, so close I can feel the heat radiating off of him, so close I can smell the new-clothes aroma of his T-shirt mingling with the light musk of his sweat. He puts one foot on one of the pedals. Then he turns around, an impish grin on his face. "Warn me if you see police. This isn't quite legal."

"Wait, what's not legal?"

But he's already pushed off. I shut my eyes. This is insane. We're going to die. And then my parents really will kill me.

A block later, we're still alive. I squint an eye open. Willem is leaning all the way forward over handlebars, effortlessly standing on the pedals, while I lean back, my legs dangling alongside the rear wheel. I open my other eye, release my clammy grip on the hem of his T-shirt. The marina is well behind us, and we are on a regular street, in a bike lane, cruising along with all the other gray bicycles.

We turn onto a choked street full of construction, half the avenue blocked by scaffolding and blockades, and I'm looking at all the graffiti; the SOS, just like on the T-shirt for that band *Sous ou Sur* is scrawled there. I'm about to point it out to Willem, but then I turn in the other direction and there's the Seine. And there's Paris. Postcard Paris! Paris from *French Kiss* and from *Midnight in Paris* and from *Charade* and every other Paris film I've ever seen. I gape at the Seine, which is rippling in the breeze and glimmering in the early-evening sun. Down the expanse of it, I can see a series of arched bridges, draped like expensive bracelets over an elegant wrist. Willem points out Notre Dame Cathedral, just towering there, in the middle of an island in the middle of a river, like it's nothing. Like it's any other day, and it's not the freaking Notre Dame! We pass by another building, a wedding-cake confection that looks like it might house royalty. But, no, it's just City Hall.

It's funny how on the tour, we often saw sights like this as we whizzed by on a bus. Ms. Foley would stand at the front of the coach, microphone in hand, and tell us facts about this cathedral or that opera house. Sometimes, we'd stop and go in, but with one or two days per city, most of the time, we drove on by.

I'm driving by them now too. But somehow, it feels different. Like, being here, outside, on the back of this bike, with the wind in my hair and the sounds singing in my ears and the centuries-old cobblestones rattling beneath my butt, I'm not missing anything. On the contrary, I'm inhaling it, consuming it, becoming it.

I'm not sure how to account for the change, for all the changes today. Is it Paris? Is it Lulu? Or is it Willem? Is it his nearness that makes the city so intoxicating or the city that makes his nearness so irresistible?

A loud whistle cuts through my reverie, and the bike comes to an abrupt halt.

"Ride's over," Willem says. I hop off, and Willem starts wheeling the bicycle down the street.

A policeman with a thin mustache and a constipated expression comes chasing after us. He starts yelling at Willem, gesticulating, wagging a finger at me. His face is turning a bright red, and when he pulls out his little book and starts pointing to me and Willem, I get nervous. I thought Willem had been joking about the illegal thing.

Then Willem says something to the cop that stops the tirade cold.

The cop starts nattering on, and I don't understand a word, except I'm pretty sure he says "Shakespeare!" while holding a finger up in an *aha* motion. Willem nods, and the cop's tone softens. He still wagging his finger at us, but the little book goes back into his satchel. With a tip of his funny little hat, he walks away.

"Did you just quote Shakespeare to a cop?" I ask.

Willem nods.

I'm not sure what's crazier: That Willem did that. Or that the cops here know Shakespeare.

"What did you say?"

"*La beauté est une enchanteresse, et la bonne foi qui s'expose à ses charmes se dissout en sang,*" he says. "It's from *Much Ado About Nothing.*"

"What does it mean?"

Willem gives me that look of his, licks his lips, smiles. "You'll have to look it up."

We walk along the river and onto a main road full of restaurants, art galleries, and high-end boutiques. Willem parks the bike in a stand, and we take off on foot under a long portico and then make a few more turns into what, at first, seems like it should be a presidential residence or a royal palace, Versailles or something, the buildings are so huge and grand. Then I spot the glass pyramid in the middle of the courtyard, so I know we have arrived at the Louvre.

It's mobbed. Thousands of people are flooding out of the buildings, like they're evacuating it, clutching poster tubes and large black-and-white shopping bags. Some are energized, chatty, but many more look shell-shocked, weary, glazed after a day spent ingesting epic portions of Culture! I know that look. The Teen Tours! brochure bragged that it offered "young people the full-on European immersion experience! We'll expose your teen to a maximum number of cultures in a short period of time, broadening their view of history, language, art, heritage, cuisine." It was supposed to be enlightening, but it mostly felt exhausting.

So when we discover that the Louvre just closed, I'm actually relieved.

"I'm sorry," Willem says.

"Oh, I'm not." I'm not sure if this qualifies as an accident or not, but I'm happy either way.

We do an about-face and cross over a bridge and turn up the other bank of the river. Alongside the embankment there are all kinds of vendors selling books and old magazines, pristine issues of *Paris Match* with Jackie Kennedy on the cover and old pulp paperbacks with lurid covers, titled in both English and French. There's one vendor with a bunch of bric-a-brac, old vases, costume jewelry, and in a box on the side, a collection of dusty vintage alarm clocks. I paw through and find a vintage SMI in Bakelite. "Twenty euro," the kerchiefed saleslady says to me. I try to keep a poker face. Twenty euro is about thirty bucks. The clock is easily worth two hundred dollars.

"Do you want it?" Willem asks.

My mom would go nuts if I brought this home, and she'd never have to know where it was from. The woman winds the clock, to show me that it works, but hearing it tick, I'm reminded of what Jacques said, about time being fluid. I look out at the Seine, which is now glowing pink, reflecting the color of the clouds that are rolling in. I put the clock back in the box.

We head up off the embankment, into the twisty, narrow warren of streets that Willem tells me is the Latin Quarter, where students live. It's different over here. Not so many grand avenues and boulevards but alley-like lanes, barely wide enough for even the tiny, space-age two-person Smart Cars that are zooming around everywhere. Tiny churches, hidden corners, alleys. It's a whole different Paris. And just as dazzling.

"Shall we take a drink?" Willem asks.

I nod.

We cross onto a crowded avenue, full of cinemas, out-door cafés, all of them packed, and also a handful of small hotels, not too expensive judging by the prices advertised on the sandwich boards. Most of the signs say *complet*, which I'm pretty sure means full, but some don't, and some of the rooms we might be able to afford if I were to exchange the last of my cash, about forty pounds.

I haven't been able to broach tonight with Willem. Where we're staying. He hasn't seemed too worried about it, which has me worried our fallback is Céline. We pass an exchange bureau. I tell Willem I want to change some money.

"*I* have some money left," he says. "And you just paid for the boat."

"But I don't have a single euro on me. What if I wanted to, I don't know, buy a postcard?" I stop to spin a postcard caddy. "Also, there's drinks and dinner, and we'll need somewhere for, for . . ." I trail off before getting the courage to finish. "Tonight." I feel my neck go warm.

The word seems to hang out there as I wait for Willem's response, some clue of what he's thinking. But he's looking over at one of the cafés, where a group of girls at a table seem to be waving at him. Finally, he turns back to me. "Sorry?" he asks.

The girls are still waving. One of them is beckoning him over. "Do you know them?"

He looks over at the café, then back at me, then back at the restaurant. "Can you wait here for a minute?"

My stomach sinks. "Yeah, no problem."

He leaves me at a souvenir shop, where I spin the postcard caddy and spy. When he gets to the group of girls, they do the cheek-cheek-kiss-kiss thing—three times, though, instead of twice like he did with Céline. He sits down next to the girl who was gesturing to him. It's clear they know each other;

she keeps putting her hand on his knee. He throws darting glances in my direction, and I wait for him to wave me over, but he doesn't, and after an endless five minutes, the touchy girl writes something down on a bit of paper and gives it to him. He jams the slip deep into his pocket. Then he stands up, and they do another cheek-cheek-kiss-kiss thing, and he strides back to me, where I am feigning a deep interest in a Toulouse-Lautrec postcard.

"Let's go," he says as he grabs my elbow.

"Friends of yours?" I ask, jogging to keep up with his long stride.

"No."

"But you know them?"

"I knew them once."

"And you just randomly bumped into them?"

He spins toward me, and for the first time today, he's annoyed. "It's Paris, Lulu, the most touristy city in the world. It happens."

Accidents, I think. But I feel jealous, possessive, not just over the girl—whose number, I suspect, he now has in his hip pocket if he hasn't already transcribed it into his little black book—but over accidents. Because today it has felt like accidents belonged solely to us.

Willem softens. "They're just people I knew from Holland."

Something in Willem's whole demeanor has changed, like a lamp whose bulb is dimming before it burns out. And it's then that I notice the final and defeated way he says *Holland*, and it makes me realize that all day along, not once has he said he was going *home*. And then another thought hits me. Today, he was meant to be going home—or to Holland, where he's from—for the first time in two years.

In three days, I will go home, and there will be a crowd at the airport. Back at my house, there will be a welcome-home banner, a celebratory dinner I'll probably be too jet-lagged to eat. After only three weeks on a tour in which I was led around like a show pony, I'll be given a hero's welcome.

He's been gone *two years*. Why isn't Willem getting a hero's welcome? Is anyone even waiting for him?

"When we were at Céline's," I ask him now, "did you call anyone?"

He turns to me, his dark eyes furrowed and confused. "No. Why?"

Because how does anyone know you're delayed? Because how do they know to postpone your hero's welcome until tomorrow?

"Isn't anyone expecting you?" I ask.

Something happens to his face, for just the slightest of moments, a slip of his jaunty mask, which I hadn't realized was a mask until I see how tired, how uncertain—how much like me—he looks underneath it.

"You know what I think?" Willem asks.

"What?"

"We should get lost."

"I've got news for you, but I've been lost all day."

"This is different. This is getting on purpose lost. It's something I do when I first come to a new city. I'll go into the metro or on a tramline and randomly pick a stop and go."

I can see what he's doing. He's changing the scenery, changing the subject. And I get that, in some way, he needs to do this. So I let him. "Like traveler's pin the tail on the donkey?" I ask.

Willem gives me a quizzical look. His English is so good that I forget not everything computes.

"Is this about accidents?" I ask.

He looks at me, and for half a second, the mask slips again. But then just like that, it's back in place. It doesn't matter. It slipped, and I saw. And I understand. Willem is alone, like I am alone. And now this ache that I can't quite distinguish as his or mine has opened up inside of me.

"It's always about the accidents," he says.

Nine

I pick a doozy.

Using the pin-the-tail-on-the-donkey strategy, I close my eyes and spin in front of the Metro map and land my finger on the benign-sounding Château Rouge.

When we come out of the Metro, we are in yet another Paris altogether, and there's not a chateau, rouge or otherwise, in sight.

The streets are narrow, like in the Latin Quarter, but grittier. Tinny, drum-heavy music blares out from the shop windows, and there's such an onslaught of smells, my nose doesn't know what to breathe first: curry coming out of the patisseries, the ferric tang of blood from the giant animal carcasses being trundled through the street, the sweet and exotic smell of incense smoke, exhaust from the cars and motos, the ubiquitous smell of coffee—though there aren't so many of the big cafés here, the kind that take up an entire corner, but more smaller, ad-hoc ones, bistro tables shoved onto the sidewalk. And they're all packed with men smoking and drinking coffee. The women, some wearing full black veils with only their eyes showing through the slits, others in colorful dresses, sleeping babies tied to their backs, bustle in and out of the stores. We are the only tourists in this area, and people are looking at us, not menacingly, but just curiously, like we're lost. Which we are. This is precisely why, on my own, I would never in a million years do this.

But Willem is loving it here. So I try to take a cue from him and relax, and just gape at this part of Paris meets Middle East meets Africa.

We go past a mosque, then a hulking church, all spires and buttresses, that seems like it landed in this neighborhood the same way we did. We twist and turn until we wind up in some sort of park: a quadrangle of grass and paths and handball courts sandwiched in between the apartment buildings. It's packed with girls in head scarves playing some version of hopscotch and boys on the handball courts and people walking dogs and playing chess and sitting out for a smoke at the end of a summer afternoon.

"Do you have any idea where we are?" I ask Willem.

"I am as lost as you are."

"Oh, we are *so* screwed." But I laugh. It feels kind of nice to be lost, together.

We flop down under a stand of trees in a quiet corner of the park under a mural of children playing in the clouds. I slide off my sandals. I have tan lines made from dirt and sweat. "I think my feet are broken."

Willem kicks off his flip-flops. I see the zigzag scar running up his left foot. "Mine too."

We lie on our backs as the sun throws shadows down between the clouds that are really starting to roll in on the cooling breeze, bringing with them the electric smell of rain. Maybe Jacques was right, after all.

"What time is it?" Willem asks.

I shut my eyes and stick my arm out for him to see. "Don't tell me. I don't want to know."

He takes my arm, checks the time. But then he doesn't let go. He examines my wrist, rotating it forward and back, as if it were some rare object, the first wrist he has ever seen.

"That's a very nice watch," he says finally.

"Thank you," I say dutifully.

"You don't like it?"

"No. It's not that. I mean, it was a really generous gift from my parents, who'd already given me the tour, and it's a very expensive watch." I stop myself. It's Willem, and something compels me to tell him the truth. "But, no, I don't really like it."

"Why not?"

"I don't know. It's heavy. It makes my wrist sweaty. And it ticks loudly, like it's always trying to remind me that time is passing. Like I can't ever forget about time."

"So why do you wear it?"

It's such a simple question. Why do I wear a watch that I hate? Even here, thousands of miles from home, with no one to see me wearing it, why do I still wear it? Because my parents bought it for me with the best of intentions. Because I can't let them down.

I feel the gentle pressure of Willem's fingers on my wrist again. The clasp opens, and the watch falls away, leaving a white ghost imprint. I can feel the refreshing breeze tickle against my birthmark.

Willem examines the watch, the *Going Places* engraving. "Where are you going, exactly?"

"Oh, you know. To Europe. To college. To medical school."

"Medical school?" There's surprise in his voice.

I nod. That's been the plan ever since eighth grade, when I gave the Heimlich maneuver to some guy who was choking on his lamb shank at the next table. Dad had been out front, answering a call from the service when I'd seen the guy next to us go purple. So I just got up and calmly put my arms around the guy's diaphragm and pushed until a piece of meat arced out. Mom was beyond impressed. She'd started talking about my becoming a doctor like Dad. After a while, I started talking about it too.

"So you'll take care of me?"

His voice has the usual teasing tone, so I get that he's joking, but this wave comes over me. Because who takes care of him now? I look at him, and he makes everything seem effortless, but I remember that feeling before—a certainty—that he is alone.

"Who takes care of you now?"

At first I'm not sure I said it aloud and, if I did, that he heard me, because he doesn't answer for a long time. But then finally, he says, "I take care of me."

"But what about when you can't? When you get sick?"

"I don't get sick."

"Everybody gets sick. What happens when you're on the road and you get the flu or something?"

"I get sick. I get better," he replies, waving the question away.

I prop myself up on my elbow. This weird chasm of feeling has opened in my chest, making my breath come shallow and my words dance like scattered leaves. "I keep thinking about the double happiness story. That boy was traveling alone and got sick, but someone took care of him. Is that what happens to you when you get sick? Or are you alone in some gross hotel room?" I try to picture Willem in a mountain village, but all I get is an image of him in a dingy room. I think of how I get when I'm sick, that deep sadness, that aloneness that strikes—and I have Mom to take care of me. What about him? Does anyone bring him soup? Does anyone tell him about the green trees against the sky in the spring rain?

Willem doesn't answer. In the distance, I can hear the pop of the handball slamming against the wall, the coquettish sound of women's laughter. I think of Céline. The girls on the train. The models at the café. The slip of paper in his pocket. There's probably no shortage of girls wanting to play nurse with him. I get a weird feeling in my stomach. I've made a wrong turn, like when I am skiing and I accidentally swerve onto a black-diamond run full of moguls.

"Sorry," I say. "It's probably just the doctor in me coming out. Or the Jewish mother."

Willem gives me a peculiar look. Another wrong turn. I keep forgetting that in Europe, there are hardly any Jewish people, so jokes like that don't make sense.

"I'm Jewish, and apparently that means when I get older, I'm doomed to fuss about everyone's health," I hastily explain. "That's what 'Jewish mother' means."

Willem lies on his back and holds my watch up to his face.

"It's strange you mention the double happiness story. Sometimes I do get sick and wind up puking into squat toilets, and it's not so nice."

I wince at the thought of it.

"But there was this one time, I was traveling from Morocco to Algeria by bus, and I got dysentery, a pretty bad case. So bad I had no choice but to get off the bus in the middle of nowhere. It was some town at the edge of the Sahara, not even mentioned in any book. I was dehydrated, hallucinating, I think, stumbling around for a place to stay when I saw a hotel and restaurant called Saba. Saba was what I used to call my grandfather. It seemed like a sign, like he was saying 'go here.' The restaurant was empty. I went straight to the toilets to throw up again. When I came out, there was a man with a short gray beard wearing a long djellaba. I asked for some tea and ginger, which is what my mother always uses for upset stomachs. He shook his head and told me I was in the desert now and had to use desert remedies. He disappeared into the kitchen and returned with a grilled lemon, cut in half. He sprinkled it with salt and told me to squeeze the juice into my mouth. I thought I would lose it again, but in twenty minutes, my stomach was okay. He gave me some terrible tea that tasted like tree bark and sent me upstairs, where I slept maybe eighteen hours. Every day, I came downstairs, and he would ask how I was feeling and then prepare me a meal specifically based on my symptoms. After that we would talk, just as I had done with Saba as a child. I stayed there for a week, in this town on the edge of the map that I am not even sure exists. So it is a lot like your story from before."

"Except he didn't have a daughter," I say. "Or you'd be married by now."

We are on our sides, facing each other, so close I can feel the warmth radiating off him, so close it's like we are breathing the same air.

"You be the daughter. Tell me that couplet again," he says.

"Green trees against the sky in the spring rain while the sky set off the spring trees in the obscuration. Red flowers dot the land in the breeze's chase while the land colored up in red after the kiss."

The last word, *kiss*, hangs in the air.

"Next time I get sick, you can tell that to me. You can be my girl in the mountains."

"Okay," I say. "I'll be your mountain girl and take care of you."

He smiles, like it's another joke, another volley in our flirtation, and I smile back, even though I'm not joking.

"And in return, I will relieve you of the burden of time." He slips my watch onto his lanky wrist, where it doesn't seem quite so much like a prison shackle. "For now, time doesn't exist. It is, what did Jacques say . . . fluid?"

"Fluid," I repeat, like an incantation. Because if time can be fluid, then maybe something that is just one day can go on indefinitely.

Ten

I fall asleep. And then I wake up, and everything feels different. The park is quiet now. The sound of laughter and echoes of handballs have disappeared into the long dusky twilight. Fat, gray rainclouds have overtaken the darkening sky.

But something else has shifted, something less quantifiable yet somehow elemental. I feel it as soon as I wake; the atoms and molecules have rearranged themselves, rendering the whole world irrevocably changed.

And that's when I notice Willem's hand.

Willem has also fallen asleep; his long body is curved in the space around mine like a question mark. We aren't touching at all except for his one hand, which is tucked into the crease of my hip, casually, like a dropped scarf, like it blew there on the soft breeze of sleep. And yet now that it's there, it feels like it belongs there. Like it's always belonged there.

I hold myself perfectly still, listening to the wind rustle

through the trees, to the soft in-out of Willem's rhythmic breathing. I concentrate on his hand, which feels like it's delivering a direct line of electricity from his fingertips into some core part of me I didn't even know existed until just now.

Willem stirs in his sleep, and I wonder if he's feeling this too. How can he not? The electricity is so real, so palpable, that if someone waved a meter around, it would spin off the dial.

He shifts again, and his fingertips dig in right there into that tender flesh in the hollow of my hip, sending a shock and a zing so deliciously intense that I buck, kicking his leg behind me.

I swear, somehow I can feel his eyelashes flutter open, followed by the heat of his breath against the back of my neck. *"Goeiemorgen,"* he says, his voice still pliant with sleep.

I roll over to face him, thankful that his hand remains slung over my hip. His ruddy cheeks bear little indentations from the grass, like tribal initiation scars. I want to touch them, to feel the grooves of his otherwise smooth skin. I want to touch every part of him. It's like his body is a giant sun, emitting its own gravitational pull.

"I think that means good morning, though technically it's still evening." My words come out sounding gaspy. I've forgotten how to talk and breathe at the same time.

"You forget, time doesn't exist anymore. You gave it to me."

"I gave it you," I repeat. There's such delicious surrender in the words, and I feel myself slipping away to him. Some small part of me warns against this. This is just one day. I am just one girl. But the part that can resist, that *would* resist, I woke up finally liberated of her.

Willem blinks at me, his eyes dark, lazy, and sexy. I can feel us kissing already. I can feel his lips all over me. I can feel the jut of his sharp hipbones against me. The park is almost deserted. There are a couple of younger girls in jeans and head scarves talking to some guys. But they are off in a corner of their own. And I don't care about propriety.

My thoughts must be like a movie projected on a screen. He watches it all. I can tell by his knowing smile. We inch closer to each other. Beneath the chirp of cicadas, I can practically hear the energy between us humming, like the power lines that buzz overhead in the countryside.

But then I hear something else. At first, I don't know how to place it, so discordant is it from the sounds in this bubble of electricity we are generating. But then I hear it a second time, cold and jagged and bracingly clear, and I know exactly what it is. Because fear needs no translation. A scream is the same in any language.

Willem jumps up. I jump up. "Stay here!" he commands. And before I know what has happened, he is striding away on those long legs of his, leaving me whiplashed between lust and terror.

There's another scream. A girl's scream. Everything seems to slow down then, like a slow-motion sequence in a movie. I see the girls, the ones with the head scarves, there are two of them, only now one isn't wearing her scarf anymore. It is on the ground, revealing a fall of black hair that is wild and staticky, as if her hair is frightened too. She is huddled with the other girl, as if trying to disappear from the boys. Who I now see aren't boys at all, but are men, the kind who sport shaved heads, and combat fatigues, and big black boots. The essential wrongness of *these* men with *these* girls in this now-quiet park hits me all at once. I pick up Willem's backpack, which he's just abandoned there, and creep closer.

I hear the soft cries of one of the girls and the men's guttural laughter. Then they speak again. I never knew French could sound so ugly.

Just as I'm wondering where he went, Willem steps between the men and the girls and starts saying something. He's speaking softly, but I can hear him all the way over here, which must be a kind of actor's trick. But he's also speaking in French, so I have no idea what he's saying. Whatever it is, it's gotten the skinheads' attention. They answer him back, in loud staccato voices that echo off the empty handball courts. Willem replies in a voice as calm and quiet as a breeze, and I strain to understand just a word of it, but I can't.

They go back and forth and as they do, the girls use the cover as it was intended and slip away. The skinheads don't even notice. Or don't care. It's Willem they are interested in now. At first, I think that Willem's powers of charm must know no bounds. That he has even made friends with skinheads. But then my ear attunes to the tone of what he is saying as opposed to the words. And I recognize the tone because it's one I've been privy to all day. He's teasing them. He is mocking them in that way that I'm not even sure they fully recognize. Because there are three of them and one of him, and if they knew what he was doing, they wouldn't still be standing there talking.

I can smell the sickly sweet odor of booze and the acrid tang of adrenaline, and all at once, I can *feel* what they are going to do to Willem. I can feel it as if they are going to do it to me. And this should paralyze me with fear. It doesn't. Instead it fills me with something hot and tender and vicious.

Who takes care of you?

Without even thinking about it, I'm reaching into Willem's bag and grabbing the thickest thing I can find—the Rough Guide—and I'm striding toward them. No one sees me coming, not even Willem, so I have the element of surprise on my side. Also, apparently, some serious fight-or-flight strength. Because when I hurl that book at that guy closest to Willem, the one holding a beer bottle, it hits him with such force that he drops the bottle. And when he raises his hand to his brow, there's a welt of blood blooming like a red flower.

I know I should be scared, but I'm not. I'm oddly calm, happy to be back in Willem's presence after those interminable seconds apart. Willem, however, is staring at me wide-eyed and slack-jawed. The skinheads are looking right past me, surveying the park, as if they can't quite believe that I could be the source of the attack.

It's their moment of confusion that saves us. Because in that moment, Willem's hand finds mine. And we run.

Out of the park, past the church, and back into that crazy mishmash neighborhood, past the tea shops and cafés and the animal carcasses. We leap over the overflowing gutters, past the congregation of motorcycles and bicycles, dodging delivery vans disgorging racks of clothing heavily bejeweled with glitter and sparkles.

The neighborhood's residents stop to watch us, parting to let us through like we are a spectator sport, an Olympic event—the Crazy-White-People Chase.

I should be scared. I am being chased by angry skinheads;

the only person who's ever run after me before is my dad when we've gone out jogging. I can hear the clomp of their boots beat in time with the heartbeat in my head. But I'm not scared. I feel my legs magically lengthen, allowing me to match Willem's long stride. I feel the ground undulating under our feet, as if it too is on our side. I feel like we are barely touching the earth, like we might just take off into the sky and run right over the Paris rooftops, where no one can ever touch us.

I hear them shouting behind us. I hear the sound of glass breaking. I hear something whizz past my ear and then something wet on my neck, as if my sweat glands have all opened up and released at once. And then I hear more laughter and the boot steps abruptly stop.

But Willem keeps going. He pulls me through the tiny jigsaw streets until they open up onto a large boulevard. We dash across as the light changes, running by a police car. It's crowded now. I'm pretty sure we aren't being chased. We are safe. But still, Willem carries on running, yanking me this way and that down a series of smaller, quieter streets until, like a bookcase revealing a secret door, a gap in the streetscape emerges. It's the keypadded opening to one of those grand apartment houses. An old man with a wheeled cart leaves the inner courtyard just as Willem skids us into the entryway. Our momentum crashes from sixty to zero as we slam together against a stone wall just as the door clicks shut behind us.

We stand there, our bodies pressed together, barely an inch of space separating us. I can feel the fast, steady thud of his heart, the sharp in-out of his breath. I can see the rivulet of perspiration trickling down his neck. I feel my blood, thrumming, like a river about to spill over its banks. It's as if my body can no longer contain me. I have become too big for it somehow.

"Willem," I begin. There is so much I need to say to him.

He puts a finger up to my neck, and I fall silent, his touch at once calming and electrifying. But then he removes his finger and it's red with blood. I reach up to touch my neck. My blood.

"*Godverdomme!*" he swears under his breath. With one hand, he reaches into his backpack for a bandanna, and with the other, he licks the blood on his finger clean.

He holds the bandanna against the side of my neck. I'm definitely bleeding, but not badly. I'm not even sure what happened.

"They threw a broken bottle at you." Willem's voice is pure fury.

But it doesn't hurt. I'm not hurt. Not really. It's just a little nick.

He's standing so close to me now, gently pressing the bandanna against my neck. And then the cut on my neck is not the point of exit for blood, but the point of entry for this weird line of electricity that is surging between us.

I want him, all of him. I want to taste his mouth, his mouth that just tasted my blood. I lean into him.

But he pushes me away, pulls himself back. His hand drops from my neck. The bandanna, now clotted with blood, hangs there limply.

I look up then, into his eyes. All the color has drained out of them, so they just seem black. But more disconcerting is what I see in them, something instantly recognizable: fear.

And more than anything, I want to do something, to take that away. Because I should be scared. But today, I'm not.

"It's okay," I begin. "*I'm* okay."

"What were you *thinking?*" he interrupts, his voice icy as a stranger's. And maybe it's that or maybe it's just relief, but now I feel like I might cry.

"They were going to hurt you," I say. My voice breaks. I look at him, to see if he understands, but his expression has only hardened, fear having been joined by its twin brother, anger. "And I promised."

"Promised what?"

An instant replay runs through my head: No punches had been exchanged. I hadn't even been able to understand what they'd been saying. But they *were* going to hurt him. I could feel it in my bones.

"That I'd take care of you." My voice goes quiet as the certainty drains out of me.

"Take care of me? How does *this* take care of me?" He opens his hand, which is stained with my blood.

He takes a step away from me, and with the twilight blinking between us now, it hits me how utterly *wrong* I have gotten this. I haven't just skied onto the diamond run; I've flown off the face of the cliff. It was a *joke*, this request to take care of him. When have I ever taken care of anybody? And he certainly never said he needed taking care of.

We stand there, the silence curdling around us. The last of the sunlight slips away, and then, almost as if waiting for cover of darkness to sneak in, the rain starts to fall. Willem looks at the sky and then looks at his watch—my watch—still snug around his wrist.

I think of those forty pounds I have left. I imagine a quiet, clean hotel room. I think of us in it, not as I imagined it an hour before in that Paris park, but just quiet, listening to the rain. *Please*, I silently implore. *Let's just go somewhere and make this better.*

But then Willem is reaching into his bag for the Eurostar schedule. And then he's unclasping my watch. And then I realize, he's giving time back to me. Which really means he's taking it away.

Eleven

There are two more trains back to London tonight. Willem tells me it's after nine, so there's probably not enough time for me to exchange my ticket and get on the next one, but I can definitely catch the last train. Because I gain an hour back going to England, I should get to London just before the Tube stops running. Willem tells me all this in a friendly helpful way, like I'm a stranger on the street who stopped him for directions. And I nod along, like I'm the kind of person who actually takes the Tube alone, day or night.

He is oddly formal as he opens the door to the apartment courtyard for me, like he's letting the dog out for its nightly pee. It's late, the night edge of the long summer twilight, and the Paris I walk out into seems wholly changed from the one I left a half hour ago, though once again, I know that it's not the rain or all the lights that have come on. Something has shifted. Or maybe shifted back. Or maybe it never shifted in the first place and I was just fooling myself.

Still, seeing this new Paris, it brings tears to my eyes that turn all the lights into a big red scar. I wipe my face with my dampening cardigan, my returned watch still grasped in my hand. Somehow I cannot bear to put it back on. It feels like it would hurt me, far more than the cut on my neck. I attempt to walk ahead of Willem, to put space between us.

"Lulu," he calls after me.

I don't answer. That's not me. It never was.

He jogs to catch up. "I think Gare du Nord is that way." He takes me by the elbow, and I steel myself against the zing, but, like tensing against a doctor's shot, that only makes it worse.

"Just tell me how to get there."

"I think you follow this street for a few blocks and then turn left. But first we have to go to Céline's club."

Right. Céline. He's acting so normal now, not normal like Willem, but normal compared to how he was twenty minutes ago, the fear gone out of his eyes, replaced with some kind of relief. The relief of unloading me. I wonder if this was always the plan. Drop me off and circle back for Céline for the evening shift. Or maybe it's the other girl, the one whose number is sitting snugly in his hip pocket. With so many options, why would he choose me?

You're a good kid. That's what my crush, Shane Michaels, had told me when I'd come as close as I ever would to admitting my feelings for him. *You're a good kid.* That's me. Shane used to hold my hand and say flirty, sweet things. I'd always thought it meant something. And then he went off with some other girl and did things that actually *did* mean something.

We follow a large boulevard back toward the station, but after a few blocks, we turn back off into the smaller streets. I look for the club, but this isn't an industrial neighborhood. It's residential, full of apartment houses, their flowering window boxes soaking up the rain, their fat cats happily dozing inside closed windows. There's a restaurant on the corner, its fogged-up windows glowing. Even from across the street, I can make out the sound of laughter and silverware clanking against plates. People, dry and warm, enjoying a Thursday-night dinner in Paris.

The rain is coming down harder now. My sweater is soaking through to my T-shirt. I pull the sleeves down over my fists. My teeth start to chatter; I clench my jaw to keep it from showing, but that just detours the shivering to the rest of my body. I pull the bandanna off my neck. The bleeding has stopped, but my neck is now grimy with blood and sweat.

Willem looks at me with dismay, or maybe it's disgust. "We need to clean you up."

"I have clean clothes in my suitcase."

Willem peers at my neck and winces. Then he takes my elbow and crosses the street and opens the door to the restaurant. Inside, candlelight flickers, illuminating the wine bottles lined up against a zinc bar and the menus scribbled on little chalkboards. I stop at the threshold. We don't belong in here.

"We can clean your cut here. See if they have an emergency kit."

"I'll do it on the train." Mom packed me a first-aid kit, naturally.

We just stand there, facing off. A waiter appears. I expect him to ream us out for letting in the chilly air, or for looking like dirty, bloodied riffraff. But he ushers me inside like he's the host to a party, and I'm the guest of honor. He sees my neck, and his eyes go wide. Willem says something in French, and he nods at once, gesturing to a corner table.

The restaurant is warm, the air tangy with onions and sweet with vanilla, and I am too defeated to resist. I slump down into a chair, covering my cut with one hand. My other hand relaxes and releases my watch onto the white cloth, where it ticks malevolently.

The waiter returns with a small, white first-aid box and a blackboard menu. Willem opens the kit and pulls out a medicated wipe, but I snatch it from him.

"I can do it myself!" I say.

I dab the wound with ointment and cover it with an oversize bandage. The waiter returns to check my work. He nods approvingly. Then he says something to me in French. "He's asking if you want to hang your sweater in the kitchen so it can dry," Willem says.

I have to fight the urge to bury my face into his long, crisp, white apron and weep with gratitude for his kindness. Instead, I hand over my soaked sweater. Underneath, my damp T-shirt clings to me; there are bloodstains on the collar. I have the T-shirt Céline gave me, the same obscure, too-cool-for-school band T-shirt Willem is wearing, but I'd rather parade around in my bra than put that on. Willem says something else in French, and moments later, a large carafe of red wine is delivered to our table.

"I thought I had a train to catch."

"You have time to eat a little something." Willem pours a glass of wine and hands it to me.

I am technically of age to drink all over Europe, but I haven't, not even when, at some of the prepaid lunches, wine was offered as a matter of course and some of the kids sneaked glasses when Ms. Foley wasn't looking. Tonight, I don't hesitate. The wine glints shades of blood in the candlelight, and drinking it is like receiving a transfusion. The warmth goes from my throat to my stomach before setting to work on the chill that has settled in my bones. I drain half a glass in one go.

"Easy there," Willem cautions.

I gulp the rest of it and thrust out my glass like a middle finger. Willem appraises me for a second, then fills the glass to the rim.

The waiter returns and makes a formal show of handing us a chalkboard menu and a basket of bread with a small silver ramekin.

"*Et pour vous, le pâté.*"

"Thank you," I say. "I mean, *merci.*"

He smiles. "*De rien.*"

Willem breaks off a piece of bread and spreads it with the brown paste and offers it to me. I just glare at him.

"Better than Nutella," he teases in an almost singsong voice.

Maybe it is the wine or the prospect of getting rid of me, but Willem, the Willem I've been with all day, is back. And somehow, *this* makes me furious. "I'm not hungry," I say, even though I am, in fact, famished. I haven't eaten anything since that crêpe. "And it looks like dog food," I add for good measure.

"Just try." He holds the bread and pâté up to my mouth. I snatch it from his hands, take a tiny sample. The flavor is both delicate and intense, like meat butter. But I refuse to give him the satisfaction of seeing me enjoy it. I nibble a bite and make a face. Then I put the bread back down again.

The waiter returns, sees our emptying wine carafe, gestures to it. Willem nods. He returns with a full one. "The sole is . . . it is *finis*," he says in English, wiping the entry off the chalkboard. He looks at me. "You are cold and have lost blood," he says, as if I hemorrhaged or something. "I recommend something with *force*." He makes a fist. "The beef bourguignon is excellent. We also have a fish pot au feu, very good."

"Just keep it coming," I say, gesturing to the wine.

The waiter frowns slightly and looks to me, then Willem, like I am somehow their joint responsibility. "May I suggest to start, a salad with some asparagus and smoked salmon."

My traitorous stomach gurgles. Willem nods, then orders for both of us, the two things that the waiter recommended. He doesn't even bother to ask me what I want. Which is fine, because right now all I want is wine. I reach out for another glass, but Willem puts his hand on top of the opening of the carafe. "You have to eat something first," he says. "It's from duck, not pig."

"So?" I shove a whole piece of baguette and pâté into my mouth, defiantly and noisily chomping on it, hiding any satisfaction I'm actually taking from it. Then I hold out my glass.

Willem looks at me for a long moment. But he does oblige with a refill and then that lazy half smile. In one day, I've come to love that smile. And now I want to murder it.

We sit in silence until the waiter returns to deliver the salad with a flourish befitting the beautiful dish: a still life of pink salmon, green asparagus, yellow mustard sauce, and toast points scattered around the side of the plate like blossoms. My mouth waters, and it's like my body is waving the white flag, telling me to just give in, to quit while I'm ahead, to accept the nice day I had, which really, is far more than I had any right to hope for. But there's another part of me that is still hungry, hungry not just for food, but for everything that's been laid out in front of me today. On behalf of that hungry girl, I refuse the salad.

"You're still upset," he says. "It's not so bad as I thought. It won't even scar."

Yes, it will. Even if it heals up next week, it'll scar, although maybe not in the way he means. "You think I'm upset about *this*?" I touch the bandage on my neck.

He won't look at me. He knows damn well I'm not upset about that. "Let's just eat something, okay?"

"You're sending me back. Do what you have to do, but don't ask me to be happy about it."

Over the dancing candlelight, I see his expressions pass by like fast clouds: surprise, amusement, frustration, and tenderness—or maybe it's pity. "You were going to leave tomorrow, so what's the difference?" He brushes some bread crumbs off the tablecloth.

The difference, Willem? The difference is the night.

"Whatever," is my stellar reply.

"Whatever?" Willem asks. He runs his finger along the rim of his glass; it makes a low sound, like a foghorn. "Did you think about what would happen?"

It's all I've been thinking about, and all I've been trying not to think about: What would happen tonight.

But again, I've misunderstood him. "Did you think about what would happen if they caught us?" he continues.

I could feel what they wanted to do to him. I could taste their violence in my own mouth. "That's why I threw the book at them; they wanted to hurt you," I say. "What did you say to them to get them so angry?"

"They were already angry," he says, evading my question. "I just gave them a different reason." But by his answer and the look on his face, I can tell that I'm not wrong. That they were going to hurt him. What I felt about that, at least, was real.

"Can you imagine if they'd caught us? You?" Willem voice is so quiet I have to lean in to hear him. "Look what they did." He reaches over as if to touch my neck, but then pulls back.

In the adrenaline of the chase and the weird euphoria that followed, I hadn't thought about them catching *me*. Maybe because it hadn't seemed possible. We had wings on our feet; they had leaden boots. But now, here, with Willem sitting across from me, wearing this strange, somber expression, with his bloody bandanna crumpled into a ball on the side of the table, I can hear those boots getting closer, can hear them stomping, can hear bones cracking.

"But they didn't catch us." I swallow the tremble in my voice with another gulp of wine.

He finishes his wine and stares at the empty glass for a moment. "This is not what I brought you here for."

"What *did* you bring me here for?" Because he never

answered that. Never said why he asked me to come to Paris with him for the day.

He rubs his eyes with the heel of his hands. When he removes his hands, he looks different somehow. Stripped bare of all the masks. "Not for things to get out of control."

"Well, a little late for that." I'm trying to be flip, to summon whatever dregs of Lulu I have left. But when I say it, the truth of it wallops me in the stomach. We, or at least, I, have long since passed the point of no return.

I look back at him. His eyes lock on mine. The current clicks back on.

"I suppose it is," Willem says.

Twelve

---

*M*aybe Jacques was right, and time really is fluid. Because as we eat, my watch sits there on the table and seems to bend and distort like a Salvador Dalí painting. And then at one point, somewhere between the beef bourguignon and crème brûlée, Willem reaches for it and looks at me for a long moment before slipping it back on his wrist. I feel this profound sense of relief. Not just that I'm not being sent back to London tonight, but that he is taking charge of time again. My surrender is now complete.

It is late when we spill out onto the streets, and Paris has turned into a sepia-toned photograph. It's too late to get a hotel or youth hostel, and there's no money left, anyhow. I gave the rest of my cash, my forty pounds, to Willem to help pay for dinner. The waiter protested when we paid, not because we gave him a grab-bag of euros and pounds, but because we gave him the equivalent of a twenty-five-dollar tip. "Too much," he protested." Wholly insufficient, I thought.

But now here I am: No money. No place to stay. It should be my worst nightmare. But I don't care. It's funny the things you think you're scared of until they're upon you, and then you're not.

And so we walk. The streets are quiet. It seems to be just us and street sweepers in their bright-green jumpsuits, their twig-like neon-green brooms looking like they were plucked from a magical forest. There's the flash of headlights as cars and taxis pass by, splashing through the puddles left by the earlier downpour, which has now softened to a misty drizzle.

We walk along the quiet canals and then along the park with the lake where we hitched a ride earlier in the day. We walk under the elevated railroad tracks.

Eventually, we wind up in a small Chinatown. It's closed up for the night, but the signs are all lit up.

"Look," I say to Willem, pointing to one. "It's double happiness."

Willem stops and looks at the sign. His face is beautiful, even reflected in the bright neon glow.

"Double happiness." He smiles. Then he takes my hand.

My heart somersaults. "Where are we going?"

"You never got to see any art."

"It's one in the morning."

"It's Paris!"

We wend deeper into Chinatown, cutting up and down the streets until Willem finds what he's looking for: a series of tall, dilapidated buildings with barred windows. They all look the same except for the building on the far right; it is covered in red scaffolding from which hangs a series of very modern, very distorted portraits. The front door is completely covered in colorful graffiti and flyers.

"What is this place?"

"An art squat."

"What's that?"

Willem tells me about squats, abandoned buildings that artists or musicians or punks or activists take over. "Usually, they'll put you up for the night. I haven't slept here, but I've been inside once, and they were pretty nice."

But when Willem tries the heavy steel front door, it's locked and chained from the outside. He steps back to look at the windows, but the whole place, like the surrounding neighborhood, is tucked in for the night.

Willem looks at me apologetically. "I thought someone would be here tonight." He sighs. "We can stay with Céline." But even he looks less than thrilled at that prospect.

I shake my head. I would rather walk all night in the pouring rain. And, anyway, the rain has stopped. A thin sliver of moon is dodging in and out of the clouds. It looks so fundamentally Parisian hanging over the slanting roof-tops that it's hard to believe this is the same moon that will shine in my bedroom window back home tonight. Willem follows my gaze up to the sky. Then his eyes lock on something.

He walks back toward the building, and I follow him. Along one corner, a piece of scaffolding runs up to a ledge that leads to an open window. A curtain billows in the breeze.

Willem looks at the window. Then at me. "Can you climb?"

Yesterday I would've said no. Too high. Too dangerous. But today I say, "I can try."

I sling my bag over my shoulder and step onto the ladder Willem has made with the loop of his hands. He heaves me halfway up, and I get a foothold in a groove in the plaster and use the scaffolding to get myself to the ledge. I sort of belly-slide across it and grab at the spiral railings by the window, heaving myself through headfirst.

"I'm okay!" I call. "I'm fine."

I poke my head out the window. Willem is standing just below. He has that private little half smile again. And then as effortlessly as a squirrel, he shimmies up, steps upright onto the ledge, crosses it with his arms out like a tightrope walker, bends his knees, and slips into the window.

It takes a minute for my eyes to adjust to the darkness, but once they do, I see white everywhere: white walls, white shelves, white desk, white clay sculptures.

"Someone left us a key," Willem says.

We are both quiet. I like to think it's a moment of thanksgiving for the providence of accidents.

Willem pulls out a small flashlight. "Shall we explore?"

I nod. We set off, examining a sculpture that looks like it's made of marshmallows, a series of black-and-white photos of naked fat girls, a series of oil paintings of naked skinny girls. He shines the flashlight around a giant sculpture, very futuristic, metal and tubes, all twisted and turning, like an artist's rendition of a space station.

We pad down the creaking stairs to a room with black walls and enormous photographs of people floating in deep blue water. I stand there and can almost feel the soft water, the way the waves caress when I sometimes go swimming in Mexico at night to escape the crowds.

"What do you think?" Willem asks.

"Better than the Louvre."

We go back upstairs. Willem clicks off the flashlight.

"You know? One day one of these might be in the Louvre," he says. He touches an elliptical white sculpture that seems to glow in the darkness. "You think Shakespeare ever guessed Guerrilla Will would be doing his plays four hundred years later?" He laughs a little, but there's something in his voice that sounds almost reverent. "You never know what will last."

He said that earlier, about accidents, about never knowing which one is just a kink in the road and which one is a fork, about never knowing your life is changing until it's already happened.

"I think sometimes you *do* know," I say, my voice filling with emotion.

Willem turns to me, fingers the strap on my shoulder bag. For a second, I can't move. I can't breathe. He lifts my bag and drops it to the floor. An eddy of dust flies up and tickles my nose. I sneeze.

"*Gezondheid,*" Willem says.

"*Hagelslag,*" I say back.

"You remember that?"

"I remember everything from today." There's a lump in my throat as I understand just how true this is.

"What will you remember?" He drops his backpack next to my messenger bag. They slump into each other like old war buddies.

I lean back against the worktable. The day flashes before me: From Willem's playful voice over my breakfast on the first train to the exhilaration of making my strange admission to him on the next train to the Giant's amiable kiss in the club to the cooling stickiness of Willem's saliva on my wrist at the café to the sound of secrets underneath Paris to the release I experienced when my watch came off to the electricity I felt when Willem's hand found me to the shattering fear of that girl's scream to Willem's brave and immediate reaction to it to our flight through Paris, which felt just like that, like *flight*, to his eyes: the way they watch me, tease me, test me, and, yet, somehow understand me.

That's what I see before *my* eyes when I think of this day.

It has to do with Paris, but more than that, it has to do with the person who brought me here. And with the person he allowed me to become here. I'm too overcome to explain it all, so instead I say the one word that encapsulates it: *"You."*

"And what about this?" He touches the bandage on my neck. I feel a jolt that has nothing to do with the wound.

"I don't care about that," I whisper.

"I care," he whispers back.

What Willem doesn't know—what he can't know, because he didn't know me before today—is that none of that matters. "I wasn't in danger today," I tell him in a choked voice. "I *escaped* danger today." And I did. Not just getting away from the skinheads, but I feel like the whole day has been an electrical shock, paddles straight to my heart, bringing me out of a lifelong torpor I hadn't even known I was in. "I escaped," I repeat.

"You escaped." He comes closer so he towers over me.

My back is pressed into the worktable, and my heart starts to pound because there's no escaping this. I don't want to escape this.

As if disconnected from the rest of my body, my hand raises in the air and goes to touch his cheek. But before it arrives, Willem's hand whips around and grabs my wrist. For one confused second, I think I've misread the situation again, am about to be refused.

Willem holds my wrist for a long moment, looking at that birthmark. Then he lifts it to his mouth. And though his lips are soft and his kiss is gentle, it feels like a knife jamming into the electrical socket. It feels like the moment when I go live.

Willem kisses my wrist, then moves upward, along the inside of my arm to the tickly crook of my elbow, to my armpit, to places that never seemed deserving of kisses. My breath grows ragged as his lips graze my shoulder blade now, stopping to drink at the pool of my clavicle before turning their attention to the cords of my neck, to the area around the bandage, then gently to the top of the bandage. Parts of my body I never even realized existed come alive as the circuits click on.

When he finally kisses my mouth, everything goes oddly quiet, like the moment of silence between lightning and thunder. One Mississippi. Two Mississippi. Three Mississippi. Four Mississippi. Five Mississippi.

Bang.

We kiss again. This next kiss is the kind that breaks open the sky. It steals my breath and gives it back. It shows me that every other kiss I've had in my life has been wrong.

I tangle my hands into that hair of his and pull him toward me. Willem cups the back of my neck, runs his fingers along the little outcroppings of my vertebrae. *Ping. Ping. Ping,* go the electric shocks.

His hands encircle my waist as he boosts me onto the table, so we are face-to-face, kissing hard now. My cardigan comes off. Then my T-shirt. Then his. His chest is smooth and cut, and I bury my head in it, kissing down the indentation at his centerline. I'm unbuckling his belt, tugging down his jeans with hunger I don't recognize.

My legs loop around his waist. His hands are all over me, migrating down to the crease of my hip where they'd rested during our nap. I make a sound that doesn't seem like it could come from me.

A condom materializes. My underwear is shimmied down over my sandaled feet and my skirt is bunched into a petticoat around my waist. Willem's boxers fall away. Then he lifts me off the table. And then I realize that I was wrong before. Only now is my surrender complete.

After, we fall to the floor, Willem on his back, me resting next to him. His fingers graze my birthmark, which feels like it is flashing heat, and mine tickle his wrist, the hairs so soft against the heavy links of my watch.

"So *this* is how you'd take care of me?" he jokes, pointing to a red mark on his neck where I think I bit him.

Like with everything, he's turned my promise into something funny, something to tease me with. But I don't feel like laughing, not now, not about this, not after that.

"No," I say. "That's not how." Part of me wants to disavow the whole thing. But I won't. Because he asked me if I'd take care of him, and even if it was a joke, I made a promise that I would, and that wasn't a joke. When I said I'd be his mountain girl, I knew I wasn't going to see him again. That wasn't the point. I wanted him to know that when felt alone out there in the world . . . I was there too.

But that was yesterday. With a clench of my chest that makes me truly understand why it's called *heartbreak*, I wonder if it's not him being alone that I'm worried about.

Willem fingers the fine film of white clay dust that covers my body. "You're like a ghost," he says. "Soon you disappear." His voice is light, but when I try to catch his eye, he won't meet my gaze.

"I know." There's a lump in my throat. If we keep talking about this, it'll become a sob.

Willem wipes off a bit of the dust and my darker, tour-tanned skin reemerges. But other things, I now realize, won't come off so readily. I take Willem's chin in my hands and turn him to face me. In the wispy glow of the streetlamp, his planes and angles are both shadowed and illuminated. And then he looks at me, really looks at me, and the expression on his face is sad and wistful and tender and yearning, and it tells me everything I need to know.

My hand shakes as I raise it to my mouth. I lick my thumb and rub it against my wrist, against my birthmark. Then I rub again. I look up, look him right in his eyes, which are as dark as this night I don't want to end.

Willem's face falters for a moment, then he grows solemn, the way he did after we were chased. Then he reaches over and rubs my birthmark. *It's not coming off,* is what he is telling me.

"But you leave tomorrow," he says.

I can hear the drumbeat of my heart echo in my temples. "I don't have to."

For a second, he looks confused.

"I can stay for another day," I explain.

Another day. That's all I'm asking. Just one *more* day. I can't think beyond that. Beyond that things get complicated. Flights get delayed. Parents go ballistic. But one more day. One more day I can swing with minimal hassle, without upsetting anyone but Melanie. Who will understand. Eventually.

Part of me knows one more day won't do anything except postpone the heartbreak. But another part of me believes differently. We are born in one day. We die in one day. We can change in one day. And we can fall in love in one day. Anything can happen in just one day.

"What do you think?" I ask Willem. "One more day?"

He doesn't answer. Instead, he flips me under him. I sink into the cement floor, submitting to the weight of him. Until something sharp jabs into my rib cage.

"Ow!"

Willem reaches under me and pulls out a small metal chisel.

"We should find somewhere else to stay," I say. "*Not* with Céline."

"*Shh.*" Willem quiets me with his lips.

Later, after we have taken our time, exploring every hidden crease of each other's bodies, after we have kissed and licked and whispered and laughed until our limbs are heavy and the sky outside has started to purple with predawn light, Willem pulls a tarp over us.

"*Goeienacht*, Lulu," he says, his eyes fluttering with exhaustion.

I trace the creases of his face with my fingers. "*Goeienacht*,

Willem," I reply. I lean into his ear, push the messy bramble of his hair aside and whisper, "Allyson. My name is Allyson." But by then, he is already asleep. I rest my head in the crook between his arm and shoulder, tracing the letters of my true name onto his forearm, where I imagine their outlines will remain until morning.

Thirteen

———

After a ten-day heat wave, I'm used to waking up sweaty, but I wake up to a cool breeze gusting through an open window. I reach for a blanket, but instead of getting something warm and feathery, I get something hard and crinkly. A tarp. And in that hazy space between wake and sleep, it all comes back to me. Where I am. Who I'm with. The happiness warms me from the inside.

I reach for Willem, but he's not there. I open my eyes, squinting against the gray light, bouncing off the bright white of the studio walls.

Instinctively, I check my watch, but my wrist is bare. I pad over to the window, pulling my skirt around my naked chest. The streets are still quiet, the stores and cafés still shut. It's still early.

I want to call to him, but there's a church-like hush, and to disrupt it feels wrong. He must be downstairs, maybe in the bathroom. I could sort of use it myself. I pull on my clothes and tiptoe down the stairs. But Willem isn't in the bathroom, either. I quickly pee and throw water on my face and try to drink away the beginnings of my hangover.

He must be exploring the studios by daylight. Or maybe he went back up the staircase. *Calm down,* I tell myself. He's probably back upstairs right now.

"Willem?" I call.

There's no answer.

I run back upstairs to the studio we slept in. It's messy. On the floor is my bag, its contents spilling out. But his bag, his stuff, is all gone.

My hearts starts to pound. I run over to my bag and open it up, checking for my wallet and passport, my minimal cash. Immediately I feel stupid. He paid for me to come over here. He isn't going to rip me off. I remind myself of the tizzy I got myself into yesterday on the train.

I run up and down the stairs, calling his name now. But it just echoes back to me—Willem, *Willem!*—like the walls are laughing at me.

Panic is coming. I try to push it away with logic. He went out to get us something to eat. To find us somewhere to sleep.

I go stand next to the window and wait.

Paris begins to wake. Store grates go up, sidewalks are swept. Car horns start honking, bicycles chime, the sound of footfalls on the rainy pavement multiply.

If stores are open, it must be nine o'clock? Ten? Soon the artists will arrive, and what will they do when they find me squatting in their squat like Goldilocks?

I decide to wait outside. I put on my shoes and sling my

bag over my shoulder and head to the open window. But in the cold light of day, without wine emboldening me or Willem helping me, the distance between the second floor and the ground seems like an awfully long way to fall.

You got up, you can get back down, I chastise myself. But when I hoist myself onto the ledge and reach for the scaffolding, my hand slips and I feel dizzy. I imagine my parents getting the news of me falling to my death from a Paris building. I collapse back into the studio, hyperventilating into the cave of my hands.

Where is he? Where the hell is he? My mind pinballs through rationales for his delay. He went to get more money. He went to fetch my suitcase. What if he fell going out the window? I jump up, full of twisted optimism that I will find him sprawled underneath the drain pipe, hurt but okay, and then I can make good on my promise to take care of him. But there's nothing under the window except a puddle of dirty water.

I sink back down onto the studio floor, breathless with fear, which is now on an entirely different Richter scale than my little scare on the train.

More time goes by. I hug my knees, shivering in the damp morning. I creep downstairs. I try the front door, but it's locked, from the outside. I have the sense that I'm going to be trapped here forever, that I'll grow old and wither and die locked in this squat.

How late can artists sleep? What time is it? But I don't need a clock to tell me Willem has been gone too long. With each passing minute, the explanations I keep concocting ring increasingly hollow.

Finally, I hear the clank of the chain and keys jangle in the locks, but when the door swings open, it's a woman with two long braids carrying a bunch of rolled up canvases. She looks at me and starts talking to me in French, but I just spring past her.

Out on the street, I look around for Willem, but he's not here. It seems like he would never be here, on this ugly stretch of cheap Chinese restaurants and auto garages and apartment blocks, all gray in the gray rain. Why did I ever think this place was beautiful?

I run into the street. The cars honk at me, their horns strange and foreign sounding, as if even they speak another language. I spin around, having absolutely no idea where I am, no idea where to go, but desperately wanting to be home. Home in my bed. Safe.

The tears make it hard to see, but somehow I stumble across the street, down the sidewalk, ricocheting from block to block. This time no one is chasing me. But this time I am scared.

I run for several blocks, up a bunch of stairs and onto a square of sorts, with a rack of those gray-white bicycles, a real estate agency, a pharmacy, and a café, in front of which is a phone booth. Melanie! I can call Melanie. I take some deep breaths, swallow my sobs, and follow the instructions to get the international operator. But the call goes straight to voice mail. Of course it does. She left the phone off to avoid calls from my mother.

An operator comes on the line to tell me I can't leave a message because the call is collect. I start to cry. The operator asks me if she should call the police for me. I hiccup out a no, and she asks if perhaps there is someone else I might call. And that's when I remember Ms. Foley's business card.

She picks up with a brisk "Pat Foley." The operator has to ask her if she'll accept the collect call three times because I start crying harder the minute she answers, so she can't hear the request.

"Allyson. Allyson. What's the matter? Are you hurt?" she asks over the line.

I'm too scared, too numb to be hurt. That will come later.

"No," I say in the tiniest of voices. "I need help."

Ms. Foley manages to pull the basics out of me. That I went to Paris with a boy I met on the train. That I'm stuck here, lost, with no money, no clue where I am.

"Please," I beg her. "I just want to go home."

"Let's work on getting you back to England, shall we?" she says calmly. "Do you have a ticket?"

Willem bought me a round trip, I think. I rifle through my bag and pull out my passport. The ticket is still folded neatly inside. "I think so," I tell Ms. Foley in a quivery voice.

"When is the return booked for?"

I look at it. The numbers and dates all swim together. "I can't tell."

"Top left corner. It'll be in military time. The twenty-four-hour clock."

And there I see it. "Thirteen-thirty."

"Thirteen-thirty," Ms. Foley says in that comfortingly efficient voice of hers. "Excellent. That's one-thirty. It's just past noon now in Paris, so you have time to catch that train. Can you get yourself to the train station? Or to a Metro?"

I have no idea how. And no money. "No."

"How about a taxi? Take a taxi to the Gare du Nord?"

I shake my head. I don't have any euros to pay for a taxi. I tell Ms. Foley that. I can hear the disapproval in her silence. As if nothing I've told her before has lowered me in her esteem, but coming to Paris without sufficient funds? She sighs. "I can order you a taxi from here and have it prepaid to bring you to the train station."

"You can do that?"

"Just tell me where you are."

"I don't know where I am," I bellow. I paid absolutely no attention to where Willem took me yesterday. I surrendered.

"Allyson!" Her voice is a slap across the face, and it has just the intended effect. It stops my caterwauling. "Calm down. Now put the phone down for a moment and go write down the nearest intersection."

I reach into my bag for my pen, but it's not there. I put the phone down and memorize the street names. "I'm at Avenue Simon Bolivar and Rue de l'Equerre." I'm butchering the pronunciation. "In front of a pharmacy."

Ms. Foley repeats back the information, then tells me not to move, that a car will be there within a half hour and that I'm to call her back if one doesn't arrive. That if she doesn't hear from me, she will assume that I will be on the one-thirty train to St. Pancras, and she will meet me in London right at edge of the platform at two forty-five. I'm not to leave the train station without her.

Fifteen minutes later, a black Mercedes cruises up to the corner. The driver holds a sign, and when I see my name—*Allyson Healey*—I feel both relieved and bereft. Lulu, wherever she came from, is truly gone now.

I slide into the backseat, and we take off for what turns out to be all of a ten-minute drive to the train station. Ms. Foley has arranged for the driver to take me inside, to show me right where to board. I'm in a daze as we make our way through the station, and it's only when I am slumped into my seat and I see people wheeling bags through the aisles that I realize that I've left my suitcase at the club. All my clothes and all the souvenirs from the trip are in there. And I don't even care. I have lost something far more valuable in Paris.

I keep it together until the train goes into the Tunnel. And then maybe it's the safety of the darkness or the memory of yesterday's underwater journey that sets everything loose, but once we leave Calais and the windows darken, I again start to quietly sob, my tears salty and endless as the sea I'm traveling through.

At St. Pancras, Ms. Foley escorts me to a café, stations me at a corner table, and buys me tea that grows cold in its cup. I tell her everything now: The underground Shakespeare play in Stratford-upon-Avon. Meeting Willem on the train. The trip to Paris. The perfect day. His mysterious disappearance this morning that I still do not understand. My panicked flight.

I expect her to be stern—disapproving, for deceiving her, for being such a not-good girl—but instead she is sympathetic.

"Oh, Allyson," she says.

"I just don't know what could've happened to him. I waited and waited for a few hours at least, and I got so scared. I panicked. I don't know, maybe I should've waited longer."

"You could've waited until next Christmas, and I scarcely

imagine it would have done a spot of good," Ms. Foley says.

I look at her. I can feel my eyes beseeching.

"He was an actor, Allyson. An *actor*. They are the worst of the lot."

"You think the whole thing was an act? Was fake?" I shake my head. "Yesterday wasn't fake." My voice is emphatic, though I'm no longer sure who I'm trying to convince.

"I daresay it was real in the moment," she says, measuring her words. "But men are different from women. Their emotions are capricious. And actors turn it on and turn it right back off."

"It wasn't an act," I repeat, but my argument is losing steam.

"Did you sleep with him?"

For a second, I can still feel him on me. I push the thought away, look at Ms. Foley, nod.

"Then he got what he came for." Her words are matter-of-fact, but not unkind. "I imagine he never planned on it being more than a one-day fling. That was exactly what he proposed, after all."

It was. Until it wasn't. Last night, we declared our feelings for each other. I am about to tell Ms. Foley this. But then I stop cold: Did we declare anything? Or did I just lick some spit on myself?

I think about Willem. Really think about him. What do I actually know about him? Only a handful of facts—how old he is, how tall he is, what he weighs, his nationality, except I don't even know that because he said his mother wasn't Dutch. He's a traveler. A drifter, really. Accidents are the defining force in his life.

I don't know his birthday. Or his favorite color, or favorite book, or favorite type of music. Or if he had a pet growing up. I don't know if he ever broke a bone. Or how he got the scar on his foot or why he hasn't been home in so long. I don't even know his last name! And that's still more than he has on me. He doesn't even know my first name!

In this ugly little café, without the romantic gleam of Paris turning everything rose-colored pretty, I begin to see things as they truly are: Willem invited me to Paris for one day. He never promised me anything more. Last night, he'd even tried to send me home. He knew Lulu wasn't my real name, and he made absolutely no attempt to ever find out who I really was. When I'd mentioned texting or emailing him the picture of the two of us, he'd cleverly refused to give out his contact details.

And it wasn't like he'd lied. He said he'd fallen in love many times, but had never been in love. He'd offered it up about himself. I think of the girls on the train, Céline, the models, the girl at the café. And that was just in a single day together. How many of us were out there? And rather than accept my lot and enjoy my one day and move on, I'd dug in my heels. I'd told him I was in love with him. That I wanted to take care of him. I'd begged for another day, assumed he wanted it too. But he never answered me. He never actually said yes.

Oh, my God! It all makes sense now. How could I have been so naïve? *Fall in love? In a day?* Everything from yesterday, it was all fake. All an illusion. As reality crystallizes into place, the shame and humiliation make me so sick, I feel dizzy. I cradle my head in my hands.

Ms. Foley reaches out to pat my head. "There, there, dear. Let it out. Predictable, yes, but still brutal. He could have at least seen you off at the train station, waved you away and then never called again. A bit more civilized." She squeezes my hand. "This too shall pass." She pauses, leans in closer. "What happened to your neck, dear?"

My hand flies up to my neck. The bandage has come off, and the scabby cut is starting to itch. "Nothing," I say. "It was an . . . " I'm about to say accident, but I stop myself. "A tree."

"And where's your lovely watch?" she asks.

I look down at my wrist. I see my birthmark, ugly, naked, blaring. I yank down my sweater sleeve to cover it. "He has it."

She clucks her tongue. "They'll do that, sometimes. Take things as a sort of trophy. Like serial killers." She takes a final slurp of her tea. "Now, shall we take you to Melanie?"

I hand Ms. Foley the scrap of paper with Veronica's address, and she pulls out a *London A–Z* book to chart our way. I fall asleep on the Tube, my tears wrung out, the blankness of exhaustion the only comfort I have now. Ms. Foley shakes me awake at Veronica's stop and leads me to the red-bricked Victorian house where her flat is.

Melanie comes bounding to the door, already dressed up for tonight's trip to the theater. Her face is lit up with anticipation, waiting to hear a really good story. But then she sees Ms. Foley, and her expression skids. Without knowing anything, she knows everything: She bid Lulu farewell at the train station yesterday, and it's Allyson being returned to her like damaged goods. She gives the slightest of nods, as if none of this surprises her. Then she kicks off her heels and opens her arms to me, and when I step into them, the humiliation and heartbreak bring me to my knees. Melanie sinks to the ground alongside me, her arms hugging me tight. Behind me, I hear Ms. Foley's retreating footsteps. I let her leave without saying a word. I don't thank her. And I already know that I never will, and that is wrong considering the great kindness she's done me. But if I am to survive, I can never, ever visit this day again.

PART TWO
One Year

Fourteen

Allyson. Allyson. Are you *there*?"

I pull the pillow over my head and scrunch my eyes shut, faking sleep.

The key turns in the lock as my roommate Kali pushes open the door. "I wish you wouldn't *lock* the *door* when you are *here*. And I *know* you're not *asleep*. You're just playing *dead*. Like *Buster*."

Buster is Kali's dog. A Lhasa apso. She has pictures of him among the dozens tacked up on the wall. She told me all about Buster last July when we had our initial howdy-roommate phone call. Back then, I thought Buster sounded cute, and I found it quirky that Kali was named for her home state, and the way she talked—as if she were punching her words somehow—seemed sweet.

"Okaay, Allyson. *Fine*. Don't answer, but look, can you *call* your parents back? Your *mother* called *my* cell looking for *you*."

From under the pillows, I open my eyes. I'd wondered how long I could leave my phone uncharged before something would happen. Already there's been a mysterious UPS delivery. I was half expecting a carrier pigeon to arrive. But calling my roommates?

I hide under the pillow as Kali changes into going-out clothes, applying makeup and spritzing herself with that vanilla-scented perfume that gets into everything. After she leaves, I take the pillow off my head and swing my legs over the side of the bed. I push aside my chemistry textbook, the highlighter sitting in the crease, uncapped, ever hopeful it'll get used before it dries up from neglect. I locate my dead phone in my sock drawer and kick through the dirty laundry piled in my closet for the charger. When it charges back to life, the voice mail box tells me I have twenty-two new messages. I scroll through the missed calls. Eighteen are from my parents. Two from my grandmother. One from Melanie, and one from the registrar.

"Hi, Allyson, it's your mother. Just calling to check in to see how everything is going. Give me a call."

"Hi, Allyson. It's Mom. I got the new Boden catalog, and there are some cute skirts. And some warm corduroy jeans. I'll just order some and bring them up for Parents' Weekend. Call me back!"

Then there's one from my dad. "Your mother wants to know where we should make reservations for Parents' Weekend: Italian or French or maybe Japanese. I told her you'd be grateful for anything. I can't imagine dorm food has improved that much in twenty-five years."

Then we're back to Mom: "Allyson, is your phone broken?

Please tell me you did not lose that too. Can you please touch base? I'm trying to schedule Parents' Weekend. I thought I might to come to classes with you. . . ."

"Hi, Ally, it's Grandma. I'm on Facebook now. I'm not sure how it works, so make me your friend. Or you could call me. But I want to do it how you kids do it."

"Allyson, it's Dad. Call your mother. Also, we are trying to get reservations at Prezzo. . . ."

"Allyson, are you ill? Because I can really think of no other explanation for the radio silence. . . ."

The messages go downhill from there, Mom acting like three months, not three days, have gone by since our last phone call. I wind up deleting the last batch without even listening, stopping only for Melanie's rambling account about school and hot New York City guys and the superiority of the pizza there.

I look at the time on my phone. It's six o'clock. If I call home, maybe Mom will be out and I'll get the machine. I'm not quite sure what she does with her days now. When I was seven, she wound up leaving her job, even though she didn't take that maternity leave after all. The plan had been to go back to work once I went to college, but it hasn't quite got off the ground yet.

She picks up on the second ring. "Allyson, where have you been?" Mom's voice is officious, a little impatient.

"I ran off to join a cult." There's a brief pause, as if she's actually considering the possibility of this. "I'm at college, Mom. I'm busy. Trying to adjust to the workload."

"If you think this is bad, wait until medical school. Wait until your residency! I hardly saw your father."

"Then you should be used to it."

Mom pauses. This snarkiness of mine is new. Dad says ever since I came back from Europe, I have come down with a case of delayed teenageritis. I never acted like this before, but now I apparently have a bad attitude and a bad haircut and an irresponsibility streak, as evidenced by the fact that I lost not just my suitcase and all its contents, but my graduation watch too, even though, according to the story Melanie and I told them, the suitcase and the watch inside it were stolen off the train. Which theoretically should make me blameless. But it doesn't. Perhaps because I'm not.

Mom changes the subject. "Did you get the package? It's one thing if you ignore me, but your grandmother would appreciate a note."

I kick through the rumpled sour clothes for the UPS box. Wrapped in bubble wrap is an antique Betty Boop alarm clock and a box of black-and-white cookies from Shriner's, a bakery in our town. The sticky note on the cookies says *These are from Grandma.*

"I thought the clock would go perfect in your collection."

"Uh-huh." I look at the still-packed boxes in my closet, where my alarm clock collection, and all my nonessential stuff from home, still remains.

"And I ordered you a bunch of new clothes. Shall I send them or just bring them up?"

"Just bring them, I guess."

"Speaking of Parents' Weekend, we're firming up plans. Saturday night we are trying to get dinner reservations at Prezzo. Sunday is the brunch, and after that, before we fly home, your father has an alumni thing, so I thought I'd splurge on spa treatments for us. Oh, and Saturday morning, before the luncheon, I'm having coffee with Kali's mother, Lynn. We've been emailing."

"Why are you emailing my roommate's mother?"

"Why not?" Mom's voice is snippy, as if there is no reason for me to be asking about this, as if there is no reason for her not to be present in every single part of my life.

"Well, can you not call Kali's cell? It's a little weird."

"It's a little weird to have your daughter go incommunicado for a week."

"Three days, Mom."

"So you were counting too." She pauses, scoring herself the point. "And if you would let me install a house phone, we wouldn't have this issue."

"No one has landlines anymore. We all have cells. Our own numbers. Please don't call me on hers."

"Then return my calls, Allyson."

"I will. I just lost my charger," I lie.

Her aggrieved sigh on the other end of the line makes me realize I've picked the wrong lie. "Must we tie your belongings to you with a rope these days?" she asks.

"I just loaned it to my roommate, and it got put away with her stuff."

"You mean Kali?"

Kali and I have barely shared a bar of soap. "Right."

"I'm looking forward to meeting her and her family. They seem lovely. They invited us to La Jolla."

I almost ask my mother if she really wants to get chummy with people who named their daughter Kali for California.

Mom has a thing about names; she hates nicknames. When I was growing up, she was kind of fascist about it, always trying to prevent anyone from shortening my name to Ally or Al. Grandma ignored her, but everyone else, even teachers at school, toed the line. I never got why, if it bothered her so much, she didn't just name me something that couldn't be truncated, even if Allyson is a family name. But I don't say anything about Kali because if I get bitchy, I'll blow my cover as Happy College Student. And my mother especially, whose parents couldn't afford to send her to the college of her choice and who had to work her way through college and later support Dad while he was in medical school, is very intent that I be a Happy College Student.

"I should go," I tell her. "I'm going out with my roommates tonight."

"Oh, how fun! Where are you going?"

"To a party."

"A keg party?"

"Maybe the movies."

"I just saw a great one with Kate Winslet. You should see that one."

"Okay, I will."

"Call me tomorrow. And leave your phone on."

"Professors tend to frown on calls in classes." The snark comes out again.

"Tomorrow's Saturday. And I know your schedule, Allyson. All your classes are in the mornings."

She *would* know my schedule. She basically created it. All those morning classes because she said they'd be less attended and I'd get more attention and then I'd have the whole rest of the day for studying. Or, as it turns out, for sleeping.

After we hang up, I shove the alarm clock into a box in my closet and take the cookies and bring them into the lounge where the rest of my roommates have started in on a six-pack. They're all dressed up and ready to go out.

When school started, the rest of them were so excited. They really were Happy College Students. Jenn made organic brownies, and Kendra drew up a little sign on our door with all our names and a moniker, the Fab Four, atop it. Kali, for her part, gave us coupons to a tanning salon to ward off the inevitable seasonal affective disorder.

Now, a month in, the three of them are a solid unit. And I'm like a goiter. I want to tell Kendra that it's okay if she takes down the little sign or replaces it with one that says something like Terrific Trio* and Allyson.

I shuffle into the lounge. "Here," I say, handing over the cookies to Kali, even though I know she watches her carbs and even though black-and-whites are my favorites. "I'm really sorry about my mom."

Kendra and Jenn cluck sympathetically, but Kali narrows her eyes. "I don't want to be a *bitch* or anything, but it's bad enough having to fend off my *own* parents, okaay?"

"She's having Empty Nest or something." That's what Dad keeps telling me. "She won't do it again," I add with more confidence than I possess.

"My mom turned my bedroom into a craft room two days after I left," Jenn says. "At least you're missed."

"Uh-huh."

"What kind of cookies are they?" Kendra asks.

"Black-and-whites."

"Just like us," Kendra jokes. She's black, or African American; I'm never sure which is right, and she uses both.

"The racial harmony of cookies," I say.

Jenn and Kendra laugh. "You should come out with us tonight," Jenn says.

"We're going to a party over at Henderson and then there's this bar over on Central that apparently has a very liberal carding policy," Kendra says, twisting her just-straightened black hair up into a bun, then thinking twice about it and pulling it down. "Lots of fine male specimen."

"And female specimen, if that's your thing," Jenn adds.

"It's not my thing. I mean, none of it is my thing."

Kali gives me a bitchy smirk. "Think you enrolled in the *wrong* school. I believe there's a *convent* in Boston."

Something twists in my stomach. "They don't take Jews."

"Back off, you two," Kendra says, ever the diplomat. She turns to me. "Why not come out for a few hours?"

"Chemistry. Physics." The room goes silent. They're all liberal arts or business majors, so invoking Science shuts them up.

"Well, I'd better get back to my room. I have a date with the Third Law of Thermodynamics."

"Sounds hot," Jenn says.

I smile to show I actually get the joke, then shuffle back to my room, where I diligently pick up *Foundations of Chemistry*, but by the time the Terrific Trio are heading out the door, my eyes have sandbags in them. I fall asleep under a mountain of unread science. And thus begins another weekend in the life of the Happy College Student.

Fifteen

OCTOBER
College

I put off thinking about Parents' Weekend as long as I can and then the Thursday before they're due to arrive, I look around my dorm and see it not as I see it—walls, a bed, a desk, a dresser—but as my parents will see it. This is not the dorm of a Happy College Student. There's dirty laundry spilling out of every drawer, and my papers are everywhere. My mother despises clutter. I ditch my classes and spend the day cleaning. I haul all the dirty laundry down to the washing machines and sit with it as it turns and gyrates. I wipe down the dusty surfaces. In the closet, I hide away all my current schoolwork—the Mandarin worksheets, piling up like unread newspapers, the Scantron chemistry and physics exams with their ominously low scores scrawled in red; the lab reports with comments like "Need to be more thorough" and "Check your calculations!" and the dreaded "See me." In their place, I set out a bunch of decoy notes and graphs from early in the term, before I started obviously bombing. I unwrap the duvet cover we bought at Bed, Bath & Beyond last summer and put it over the plain quilt I've been sleeping under. I grab some of the photos from the boxes and scatter them around the room. I even drop by the U bookstore and buy one of the stupid banners with the school name on it and tack it above my bed. *Voilà*. School Spirit.

But somehow I forget the clocks. And this gives me away.

When Mom comes into the dorm, after cooing over our tiny dump of a lounge, she oohs over Kali's pictures of Buster and then looks at my relatively bare walls and gasps. By her look of horror, you'd think I'd decorated with crime-scene photos. "Where's your collection?"

I point to the boxes in the closet, unopened.

"Why are they there?"

"They're too noisy," I quickly lie. "I don't want to bother Kali with them." Never mind the fact that Kali blasts her radio at seven in the morning.

"You could put them out and not wind them," she says. "Those clocks are you."

Are they? I don't remember when I started collecting them. Mom liked to go to flea markets on weekends and then one day, I was a clock collector. I got really into it for a while, but I don't remember the moment I saw an old alarm clock and thought, *I want to collect these.*

"Your half looks terribly barren next to Kali's," Mom says.

"You should've seen my dorm," Dad says, lost in his haze of nostalgia. "My roommate put tinfoil on the windows. It looked like a spaceship. He called it the 'Future Dorm.'"

"I was going for Minimalist Dorm."

"It has a certain penitentiary charm," Dad says.

"It's like a before/after on one of those home décor shows." Mom points to Kali's half of the room, over which every inch of wall space is covered either with posters, art prints, or photos. "You're the before," she says. As if I didn't already get that.

We head off to one of the special workshops, something insanely dull on the changing face of technology in the classroom. Mom actually takes notes. Dad points out every little thing that he remembers and every little thing that is new. This is what he did when we toured the school last year; both he and Mom were so excited about the prospect of me going here. Creating a legacy. Somehow, back then, I was excited too.

After the workshop, Dad meets up with other legacy parents, and Mom has coffee with Kali's mom, Lynn. They seem to get along famously. Either Kali hasn't told her mom what a dud I am, or if she has, her mom has the good grace to shut up about it.

Before the President's Luncheon, all four members of the Fab Four and their respective families meet back at the suite and the parents all introduce themselves and cluck over the tininess of our rooms and admire what we've done with our tiny lounge and take pictures of THE FAB FOUR WELCOMES THE FAB EIGHT sign that the rest of the group made. Then we all walk out onto the quad together and tour the campus, going the long way around to point out some of the older, statelier buildings, reddening ivy creeping up old bricks. And everyone looks nice together in flannel skirts and tall black boots and cashmere sweaters and shearling jackets as we swish through the autumnal leaves. We really do look like the Happy College Students in the catalogs.

The luncheon is fine and boring, rubber chicken and rubber speeches in a big, cold echoey hall. It's only after the luncheon that the myth of the Fab Four starts to unravel. Ever so subtly, Kendra's and Jenn's and Kali's families all peel off together. I'm sure they're talking about Christmas and Thanksgiving holidays and spring breaks and potlucks and things like that. My mom gives them a look but doesn't say anything.

She and Dad go back to the hotel to get ready for dinner. Mom tells me the place is fancy and suggests I wear my black and red wrap dress. And that I wash my hair, which is looking greasy.

When they come back to pick me up, there's an awkward moment as my family meets up with the rest of the Fab Four and their Fab Families, who are all going together to a big group dinner at some famous seafood place in downtown Boston. There's a sort of standoff as my parents face the other parents. The rest of my roommates, their faces pinking, take a huge interest in the industrial gray carpeting. Finally, Jenn's dad steps in and offers a belated invitation for us to join the rest of them for dinner. "I'm sure we can squeeze three more in."

"Oh, that won't be necessary," Mom says in her haughtiest voice. "We have reservations at Prezzo in Back Bay."

"Wow! How'd you manage that?" Lynn asks. "We tried and couldn't get in until next month." Prezzo, according to Mom, is the hottest restaurant in town.

Mom smiles mysteriously. She won't tell, though Dad told me one of his golf buddies had a friend on the faculty at a hospital in Boston and he pulled some strings to get us in. Mom had been so pleased about it, but I can see now the victory is sullied.

"Enjoy your chowdah," she says. Only Dad and I catch how condescending she's being.

Dinner is painful. Even sitting at this chichi place with all the best Bostonians, I can tell Mom and, by extension, Dad feel like rejects. And they're not. It's my rejection they're feeling.

They ask me about my classes, and I dutifully tell them about chemistry, physics, biology, and Mandarin, neglecting to tell them how hard it is stay awake in class, no matter how early I go to bed, or how badly I'm doing in subjects I aced in high school. Talking about, or not talking about, all this makes me so tired I want to put my head down into my thirteen-dollar salad.

When the entrees come, Mom orders a glass of Chardonnay, Dad a Shiraz. I try not to look at the way the candlelight dances against the colors of the wine. Even that hurts. I look down at my plate of ravioli. It smells good, but I have no desire to eat it.

"Are you coming down with something?" Mom asks.

And for just the tiniest of seconds, I wonder what would happen if I told them the truth. That school is nothing like I imagined it would be. That I'm not the girl in the catalog at all. I'm not a Happy College Student. I don't know who I am. Or maybe I do know who I am and I just don't want to be her anymore.

But this is not an option. Mom would just be aggrieved, disappointed, as if my unhappiness were some personal insult to her parenting. And then she'd guilt me out about how I'm so lucky. This is college! The college experience she didn't get to have. Which was one of the reasons she spent all of high school like an army general, plotting my extracurriculars, getting me tutors for weak subjects, signing me up for SAT prep.

"I'm just tired," I say. This, at least, isn't a lie.

"You're probably spending too much time in the library," Dad interjects. "Are you getting enough sunlight? That can really affect your circadian rhythms."

I shake my head. This too is true.

"Have you been running? There are some nice tracks around here. And it's not too far to the river."

I think the last time I went running was with Dad, a couple days before I left for the tour.

"We'll go out tomorrow morning, before the brunch. Burn off dinner. Get some air in those lungs."

Just the thought of it makes me exhausted, but this isn't an invitation so much as an expectation, and the plans are being made even before I've agreed to them.

———

The following morning, the rest of the girls are sitting in the lounge drinking coffee, happily chattering about their dinner, which included some incident with a cute waiter and a lobster mallet that's already being mythologized into a tale called "The Hammer and the Hottie." They double-take when they see me in tracksuit bottoms and a fleece sweatshirt, looking around for my running shoes. Our dorm has a state-of-the-art gym that Kendra and Kali are addicted to and Jenn gets dragged along to, but I have yet to set foot in.

I just expect my dad, but Mom is there too, all perky in her black wool pants, a cashmere cape. "I thought we were meeting at brunch," I say.

"Oh, I just wanted to spend some time in your dorm. It'll help me to picture where you are when I'm not with you." She turns to Kali. "If that's okay with you." Her voice is so polite, Kali might never catch the bitchiness in it.

"*I* think it's *sweet*," Kali says.

"Are you ready, Allyson?" Dad asks me.

"Almost. I can't find my running shoes."

Mom gives me a look, like I obviously lose everything all the time now.

"Where's the last place you left them?" Dad asks. "Just picture it. That's how you find missing things." This is his typical advice, but it usually works. And sure enough, when I picture my shoes, still packed in the suitcase under my bed, that's where they are.

When we get downstairs, Dad does some halfhearted stretches. "Let's see if I remember how to do this," he jokes. He's not much of a runner, but he's always telling his patients to exercise, so he tries to practice what he preaches.

We take off on a path toward the river. It is a true autumn day, clear and brisk with a sharp bite of winter in the air. I don't love running, not at first, but usually after ten minutes or so, that thing kicks in and I sort of zone out and forget what I'm doing. Today, though, every time I even begin to lose myself, it's like my mind defaults to that other run, the best run, the run of my life, the run *for* my life. And then my legs turn into waterlogged tree trunks, and all the beautiful fall colors fade to gray.

After about a mile, I have to stop. I claim a cramp. I want to go back, but Dad wants to check out the downtown and see what's changed, so we do. We stop at a café for cappuccinos, and Dad asks me about my classes and waxes nostalgic for his days in organic chemistry. Then he tells me how busy he's been and that Mom is having a really hard time and I should go easy on her.

"Isn't she supposed to be going back to work?" I ask.

Dad looks at his watch. "Time to go," he says.

Dad leaves me at the dorm to change before brunch. As soon as I step inside, I know something's wrong. I hear ticking. And then I look around, and for a second, I'm confused because the dorm no longer looks like my dorm but like my bedroom at home. Mom has dug up all the posters from my closet and put them up in the exact same configuration as at home. She's moved my photos around, so they too are a mirror image of my old room. She's made the bed with a mountain of throw pillows, the throw pillows I specifically said I didn't want to bring because I hate throw pillows. You have to take them off and reorganize them every day. On top of the bed are clothes that Mom is folding into neat piles and laying out for me, just like she did when I was in fourth grade.

And along my windowsills and bookcases are all my clocks. All of them wound up and ticking.

Mom looks up from snipping the tags off a pair of pants I haven't even tried on. "You seemed so glum last night. I thought it might perk you up if it looked more like home in here. This is so much cheerier," she declares.

I begin to protest. But I'm not sure *what* to protest.

"And I spoke to Kali, and she finds the sound of the clocks soothing. Like a white-noise machine."

They don't sound soothing to me at all. They sound like a hundred time bombs waiting to explode.

Sixteen

The last time I saw Melanie, she had a fading pink streak in her blond hair and was wearing her micro-skimp Topshop uniform with some teetering platform sandals she'd picked up at the end-of-season sale at Macy's. So when she charges at me on a crowded street corner in New York's Chinatown as soon as I'm disgorged from the bus, I hardly recognize her. Now the pink streak is gone; her hair is dyed dark brown with a reddish tint. She has severe bangs cut short across her forehead, and the rest of her hair is secured back into a bun with a pair of enamel chopsticks. She's wearing this weird, funky, flowered dress and a pair of beat-up cowboy boots, and she has cat-shaped granny eyeglasses on. Her lips are painted blood red. She looks amazing, even if she looks nothing like my Melanie.

At least when she hugs me, she still smells like Melanie: hair conditioner and baby powder. "God, you got skinny," she says. "You're supposed to gain your freshman fifteen, not lose it."

"Have you had dining hall food?"

"Yeah. Hello, all-you-can-eat ice-cream bar. That alone makes the tuition worthwhile!"

I pull back. Look at her again. Everything is new. Including the eyewear. "You need glasses?"

"They're fake. Look, no lenses." She pokes through the air right to her eyes to demonstrate. "It's part of my whole punk-rock librarian look. The musician guys love it!" She pulls off her glasses, sweeps down her hair. Laughs.

"And no more blond hair."

"I want people to take me seriously." She puts her glasses back on and grabs the handle of my suitcase. "So, how's almost-Boston?"

When I chose my college, Melanie made fun of the fact it was five miles outside of Boston, like the town we grew up in was twenty miles outside of Philadelphia. She'd said I was circling urban life. She meanwhile, dove right in. Her school is in downtown Manhattan.

"Almost good," I answer. "How's New York?"

"Beyond good! So much to do! Like tonight, we have options: There's a party at the dorm, a decent club with eighteen-and-over night on Lafayette, or a friend of a friend invited us to a loft party in Greenpoint, where this awesome band is playing. Or we could go to the last-minute tickets place in Times Square and see a Broadway show."

"I don't care. I'm just here to see you."

I feel the slightest pang when I say that. Even though it is technically true that I'm here to see her, it's not the whole story. I was going to see Melanie at home for Thanksgiving in a few days anyway, but when my parents booked my tickets, they said I had to take the train because flights were too unreliable and expensive on a holiday weekend.

When I imagined six hours on a train, I almost felt sick. Six hours of pushing back memories. Then Melanie mentioned that her parents were driving down the Tuesday before Thanksgiving to do some shopping and driving her back, so I got the brilliant idea to take the cheap Chinatown bus to New York and catch a lift back home with Melanie. I'll get the bus back to Boston too.

"Aww, I'm happy to see you as well. Have we ever gone this long without seeing each other?"

I shake my head. Not since we met.

"Okay, so dorm party, Broadway show, club, or really kick-ass band in Brooklyn?"

What I really want to do is go back to her room and watch movies and hang out like in the old days, but I suspect that if I suggested that, Melanie would accuse me of being adventure averse. The party in Brooklyn sounds the least appealing, and is probably what Melanie wants to do, so it's probably what I should choose. So I do.

It's like I picked the right answer on a test, the way her eyes light up. "Excellent! Some of my friends from school are going. We'll eat first, then go back and drop your stuff and get ready and trek out together. Sound good?"

"Great!"

"We're already in Chinatown, and my favorite Vietnamese place is nearby."

As we wind through the twisty, crowded streets, full of red

lanterns and paper umbrellas and fake pagodas, I try to keep my eyes on the sidewalk. There are signs everywhere. One of them will inevitably say double happiness. Paris is more than three thousand miles away, but the memories . . . One pops up, I push it away. But then another appears. I never know when one is going to jump out at me. They are buried every-where, like land mines.

We go into a tiny restaurant, all fluorescent lights and For-mica tables, and sit down at a corner table. Melanie orders us some spring rolls and a chicken dish and tea and then she folds up her glasses and puts them into a case (to better pro-tect the imaginary lenses?). After she pours us each a cup of tea, she looks at me and says, "So, you're doing better?"

It's not so much a question as a command. Melanie saw me at my absolute lowest. When I got back from Paris and completely lost it, she let me cry all night long, cursing Wil-lem for being a sleazy scoundrel just like she'd suspected all along. On the flight home, she cast scathing looks at anyone on the plane who looked at me funny when I kept crying for the entire eight-hour trip. When, somewhere over Green-land, I started hyperventilating, wondering if maybe I hadn't made an epic mistake, if maybe something hadn't happened, if maybe he hadn't got waylaid, she'd set me straight.

"Yeah. He did. He got *way laid*. By you! And then he got the hell out of Dodge."

"But what if . . . " I'd begun.

"Allyson, come on. In one day, you saw him get undressed by one girl, take a secret note from another, and God knows what happened on the train with those other girls; how you think he really got that stain on his jeans?"

I hadn't even thought of that.

She'd taken me into the tiny airplane bathroom and shoved the Sous ou Sur T-shirt in the garbage. Then we'd flushed the coin he'd given me down the toilet, where I imagined it falling all those thousands of feet, sinking into the ocean below.

"There, we've destroyed all evidence of him," she'd said.

Well, almost. I hadn't told her about the photo on my phone, the one Agnethe took of the two of us. I still haven't deleted it, though I haven't looked at it, not even once.

When we got back home, Melanie was ready to put the trip behind her and turn her attention to our next chapter: college. I understood. I should've been excited too. I just wasn't. Every day we schlepped to IKEA and Bed, Bath & Beyond, to American Apparel and J. Crew with our moms. But it was like I had a permanent case of jet lag; all I wanted to do was take naps on the display beds. When Melanie left for school two days before me, I burst into tears. Everyone else thought I was crying for the pending separation from my best friend, but Melanie knew better, which was maybe why she sounded a little impatient when she hugged me and whispered into my ear, "It was just one day, Allyson. You'll get over it."

So when Melanie asks me now if I'm better, I can't let her down. "Yes," I tell her. "I'm great."

"Good." She claps her hands together and pulls out her phone. She fires off a text. "There's a guy going tonight, a friend of my friend Trevor. I think you'll like him."

"Oh, no. I don't think so."

"You just said you're over the Dutch dickwad."

"I am."

She stares at me. "The first three months of college are the

most action you're supposed to get in your life. Have you so
much as blinked at a guy?"

"I've mostly kept my eyes closed during all the wild
orgies."

"Ha! Nice try. You forget I know you better than anyone.
I'll bet you haven't even kissed anyone."

I pull the weird innardy parts out of the spring roll, wiping the excess grease on a paper napkin. "So?"

"So the guy I want you to meet tonight. He's way more
your type."

"What's that supposed to mean?" Though I know what it
means. It was absurd to think that *he* was ever my type. Or
I his.

"Nice. Normal. I showed him your picture and he said
you looked dark and mysterious." She reaches out to touch
my hair. "Though you should cut your hair into the bob
again. Right now it's more of a blob."

I haven't cut my hair since London, and it hangs down my
neck in a messy curtain.

"That's the look I'm going for."

"Well, you're achieving it. But anyhow he's really nice,
Mason—"

"Mason? What kind of name is that?"

"You're getting hung up on a name? You sound just like
your mother."

I resist the urge to stab her through the eye with a chop-
stick.

"Anyhow, who cares? Maybe his name is really Jason but he
just wanted to call himself Mason," Melanie continues. "Speaking of, no one calls me Melanie here. They call me Mel or Lainie."

"Two names for the price of one."

"It's college, Allyson. No one knows who you were. There's never a better time to reinvent yourself. You should try it." She gives me a pointed look.

I want to tell her that I did. It just didn't take.

———

Mason actually turns out to be not that bad. He's smart and slightly nerdy, and from the South, which explains the name, I guess, and he speaks in a lilting accent, which he makes fun of. When we get to the party on a desolate stretch of windblown street, miles from the subway stop, he jokes that he's from the hipster police and do I have enough tattoos to be in this part of town. At which point Trevor shows off his tribal armband and Melanie starts talking about the "tat" she's thinking of getting on her ankle or butt or other places girls get them, and Mason looks at me and rolls his eyes a little.

At the party, an elevator opens up directly into a loft, which is both huge and decrepit, with giant canvases all over the walls and the smell of oil paint and turpentine. It smelled like this in the squat. Another land mine. I kick it away before it explodes.

Melanie and Trevor are going on and on about this kick-ass band, whose grainy video they show me on Melanie's phone. They're congratulating themselves on seeing them at a place like this, before the whole world discovers them. When the band fires up, Melanie—Mel, Lainie, whoever—and Trevor hop to the front and start dancing like crazy. Mason hangs back with me. It's too loud to attempt conversation, which I'm glad about, but I'm also glad that someone stayed with me. I feel my tourist sign flashing, and I'm on native soil.

After what seems like forever, the band finally takes a break; the ringing in my ears is so loud it's like they're still playing.

"Care for a libation?" Mason asks me.

"Huh?" I'm still half deaf.

He mimes drinking something.

"Oh, no thanks."

"I'll. Be. Right. Back," he says, exaggerating the words like we're lip-reading.

Meanwhile, Melanie and Trevor are doing a kind of lip-reading of their own. They're in a corner on a couch, making out. It's like they don't notice anyone else in the room. I don't want to watch them, but I can't seem to stop myself. Seeing them kiss makes me physically ill. It's hard to push that memory down. The hardest. It's why I keep it buried the deepest.

Mason comes back with a beer for himself and a water for me. He sees Melanie and Trevor. "It was bound to happen," he tells me. "Those two have been circling each other for weeks like a pair of dogs in heat. I wondered what was going to trip the wire."

"Alcohol and 'kick-ass' music," I say, making air quotes.

"Vacations. Easier to start something up when you know you don't have to see someone for a while. Takes the pressure off." He glances at them. "I give them two weeks, tops."

"Two weeks? That's pretty generous. Some guys wouldn't give it more than a night." Even over the din, I can hear my bitterness. I can taste it in my mouth.

"I'd give you more than a night," Mason says.

And, oh, it is so the right thing to say. And who knows?

Maybe he's even sincere, though by now I know that I cannot be trusted to discern sincerity from fakery.

But still, I want to be over this. I want all those memories to disappear or to be supplanted with something else, to stop haunting me. So when Mason leans in to kiss me, I close my eyes, and I let him. I try to lose myself in it, try not to worry if the bitterness in my mouth has actually given me bad breath. I try to be kissed by someone else, try to *be* someone else.

But then Mason touches my neck, to the spot on it where the cut from that night has since healed, and I pull away.

He was right, after all; it didn't leave a scar, though part of me wishes it had. At least I'd have some evidence, some justification of this permanence. Stains are even worse when you're the only one who can see them.

Seventeen

*I*t has become tradition when we arrive in Cancún for Melanie and me to strip to our bathing suits as soon as we get into the condo and run to the beach for an inaugural swim. It's like our vacation baptism. We've done it for every one of the last nine years we've come down here.

But this year, when Melanie digs through her suitcase for a bikini, I go to the little desk next to the kitchen that normally holds nothing but cookbooks and prop open my textbooks. Every day, from four to six, I am to have study hall. I get New Year's Day off, but that's it. These are the terms of my parole.

I kept my grades a secret throughout the entire semester, so when the report cards showed up at the end of the term, it was kind of a shocker. I'd tried. I really had. After my midterms were so dismal, I'd tried harder, but it wasn't like my bad grades were a result of slacking off. Or skipping classes. Or partying.

But I might as well have been partying, given how tired I was all the time. It didn't matter if I got ten hours of sleep the night before—once I set foot in the lecture hall and the professor started droning on about wave motion, writing up equations on the monitor, the numbers would start dancing before my eyes and then I'd feel my lids grow heavy, and I'd wake to other students tripping over my legs to get to their next class.

During Reading Week, I drank so much espresso that I got no sleep at all, as if I was using up all the credits from the class naps. I crammed as hard as I could, but by that point, I'd fallen so behind, I was beyond help.

Given all that, I thought it was miraculous I finished the semester with a 2.7.

Needless to say, my parents thought otherwise.

When my grades came through last week, they flipped out. And when my parents flip out, they don't yell—they get quiet. But their disappointment and anger is deafening.

"What do you think we should do about this, Allyson?" they asked me as we sat at the dining room table, as if they were truly soliciting my opinion. Then they presented two options. We could cancel the trip, which would be terribly unfair for the rest of them, or I could agree to go under certain conditions.

Melanie shoots me sympathy looks as she disappears to change into her suit. Part of me wishes she'd boycott the beach in solidarity, though I know that's selfish, but it seems like something the old Melanie would've done.

But this is the new Melanie. Or the new, new Melanie. In the month since Thanksgiving, she looks totally different.

Again. She cut her hair all asymmetrical and fringy, and she got a nose ring, which her parents gave her crap about until she told them it was between that and a tattoo. Now that she's changed into a bikini, I see that she's let her armpit hair grow, though her hair is so fine and blond, it barely shows.

"Bye," she mouths as she slips out the front door, her mom, Susan, thrusting a tube of SPF-40 into her hands. My mom is digging through a suitcase for her special magnifying glass so she can check all mattresses for bedbugs. When she finds it, she walks by me and pretends to look at my chem book with it. I snap the book shut. She gives me a pissy look.

"You think I want to be your warden? I thought I'd have all this free time now that you're in college, but it's like keeping you on track is its own full-time job."

Who asked you to keep me on track? I fume. In my head. But I bite my lip and open the chemistry textbook out and dutifully reread the first chapters as Mom has instructed me to do for catch-up. They make no more sense to me now than they did the first time I attempted them.

That night, we all six go out to dinner at the Mexican restaurant, one of the eight restaurants attached to the resort. We go here every year for our first night out. The waiters wear giant sombreros, and there's a traveling mariachi band, but the food tastes the same as it does at El Torrito back home. When the waiter takes our drink orders, Melanie asks for a beer.

The parents gawk at her.

"We're legal to drink here," she says casually.

Mom gives Susan a look. "I don't think that's wise," Mom says.

"Why not?" I challenge.

"If you want my opinion, it has to less to do with the age than the expectation. You've grown up with a drinking age of twenty-one, so you're not necessarily prepared for drinking now," is Susan's therapist answer.

"I'm sorry, but did you not go to college?" I ask. "I can't imagine it's changed that much. Do you not remember how all anyone does is drink?"

My parents look at each other, then at Susan and Steve.

"Is that's what going on with you? Have you been drinking too much at school?" Dad asks.

Melanie laughs so hard that the special bottled water Mom brings sprays through her nose. "I'm sorry, Frank, but do you not even know Allyson?" They continue to stare. "On the tour last summer, everyone drank." There is a moment of shocked silence. "Oh, spare me! The legal drinking age in Europe is eighteen! Anyhow, everyone drank but Allyson. She's totally straight and narrow. And you're asking if she's boozing it up at college? That's ludicrous."

My dad stares at me, then at Melanie. "We're just trying to understand what's going on with her. Why she got a two-seven GPA."

Now it's Melanie's turn to gawk. *"You got a two-seven?"* She clamps her hand over her lips and mouths, "Sorry." The look she gives me is one part surprise, one part respect.

"Melanie got a three-point-eight," Mom brags.

"Yes, Melanie is a genius, and I am an idiot. It's official."

Melanie looks wounded. "I go to the Gallatin School. Everyone gets As," she says apologetically.

"And Melanie probably drinks," I say, knowing full well she does.

She looks nervous for a second. "Of course I do. I don't pass out or anything. But it's college. I drink. Everyone drinks."

"I don't," I say. "And Melanie has the A average, and I have the C, so maybe I should go on a few benders and things will even out. Maybe that's a much better idea than this stupid study hall you have me in."

I'm really into this now, which is kind of crazy, because I don't even want a beer. One of the few things I like about this restaurant is the virgin margaritas—they're made with fresh fruit.

Mom turns to me, her mouth ready to catch some flies. "Allyson, do you have a drinking problem?"

I smack my hand to my head. "Mother, do you have a hearing problem? Because I don't know that you heard a word I said."

"I think she's saying that you might ease up a little and let them have a beer with dinner," Susan says.

"Thank you!" I say to Susan.

My mom looks to my dad. "Let the girls have a beer," he says expansively as he waves the waiter back over and asks for a couple of Tecates.

It's a victory of sorts. Except that I don't actually like beer, so in the end, I have to pretend to sip from mine as it grows sweaty on the table, and I don't order the virgin margarita I really wanted.

— — —

The next day, Melanie and I are sitting at the giant pool together. It's the first time we've managed to be alone since we got here.

"I think we should do something different," she says.

"Me too," I say. "Every year we come down here and we do the same things. We go to the same frigging ruins, even. Tulum is nice, but I was thinking we could branch out. Talk our parents into going somewhere new."

"Like swimming with the dolphins?" Melanie asks.

Dolphin swimming is different, but it's not what I'm after. Yesterday, I was looking at the map of the Yucatán Peninsula in the lobby, and some of the ruins are inland, more off the beaten path. Maybe we'd find a bit more of the real Mexico. "I was thinking we could go to Coba or Chichén Itzá. Different ruins."

"Oh, you're so wild," Melanie teases. She takes a slurp of iced tea. "Anyhow, I'm talking about New Year's Eve."

"Oh. You mean you don't want to do the Macarena with Johnny Maximo?" Johnny Maximo is this washed-up Mexican movie star who now has some job with the resort. All the mothers love him because he's handsome and macho and is always pretending to mistake them for our sisters.

"Anything but the Macarena!" Melanie puts down her book, something by Rita Mae Brown that looks like it's for school but Melanie says is not. "One of the bartenders told me about some big party on the beach in Puerto Morelos. It's a local thing, though he says lots of tourists come, but people like us. Young people. There's going to be a Mexican reggae band, which sounds bizarre. In a good way."

"You're just looking for a guy under sixty to make out with come midnight."

Melanie shrugs. "Under sixty, yes. A guy? Maybe not."
She gives me a look.

"What?"

"I've sort of being doing the girl thing."

"What?!" It comes out a shout. "Sorry. Since when?"

"Since right after Thanksgiving. There was this one girl
and we met in film theory class and we were friends and one
night we went out and it just happened."

I look at the new haircut, the nose ring, the hairy armpits.
It all makes sense. "So, are you a lesbian now?"

"I prefer not to label it," she says, somewhat sanctimo-
niously, the implication being that *I* need to label everything.
She's the one who's constantly branding herself: Mel, Mel 2.0.
Punk-rock librarian. I ask her girlfriend's name. She tells me
they're not into defining it like that, but her name is Zanne.

"Is that with an *X*?"

"*Z*. Short for Suzanne."

Doesn't anybody use a real name anymore?

"Don't tell my parents, okay? You know my mom. She'd
make us process it and talk about it as a phase of my development. I want to make sure this is more than a fling before I
subject myself to that."

"Please, you don't have to tell me about parental over-
analysis."

She pushes her sunglasses up her nose and turns to me.
"Yeah, so what's that all about?"

"What do you mean? You've met my parents. Is there a
part of my life they're *not* involved in? They must be freaking
out to not have their fingers literally in every aspect of what
I'm doing."

"I know. And when I heard about the study hall, I figured it was that. I thought maybe you had a low B average. But a two—point—seven? Really?"

"Don't *you* start on me."

"I'm not. I'm just surprised. You've always been such a kick-ass student. I don't get it." She takes a loud slurp of her mostly melted iced tea. "The Therapist says you're depressed."

"Your mom? She told you that?"

"I heard her mention it to your mom."

"What did my mom say?"

"That you weren't depressed. That you were pouting because you weren't used to being punished. Sometimes I really want to smack your mom."

"You and me both."

"Anyhow, later on my mom asked me if *I* thought you were depressed."

"And what'd you tell her?"

"I said lots of people have a hard time freshman year." She gives me a sharp look from behind her dark glasses. "I couldn't tell her the truth, could I? That I thought you were still pining for some guy you had a one-night stand with in Paris."

I pause, listening to the shriek of a little kid jumping off the high dive. When Melanie and I were little, we used to hold hands and jump together, over and over again.

"But what if it's not him? Not Willem." It's weird saying his name out loud. Here. After embargoing it for so long. *Willem.* I scarcely even allow myself to think it in my head.

"Don't tell me another guy dicked you over!"

"No! I'm talking about *me*."

"You?"

"It's, like, the me I was that day. I was different somehow."

"Different? How?"

"I was Lulu."

"But that was just a name. Just pretend."

Maybe it was. But still, that whole day, being with Willem, being Lulu, it made me realize that all my life I've been living in a small, square room, with no windows and no doors. And I was fine. I was happy, even. I thought. Then someone came along and showed me there was a door in the room. One that I'd never even seen before. Then he opened it for me. Held my hand as I walked through it. And for one perfect day, I was on the other side. I was somewhere else. Someone else. And then he was gone, and I was thrown back into my little room. And now, no matter what I do, I can't seem to find that door.

"It didn't feel pretend," I tell Melanie.

Melanie arranges her face in sympathy. "Oh, sweetie. It's because you were all hopped up on the fumes of infatuation. And Paris. But people don't change overnight. Especially you. You're Allyson. You're so solid. It's one of the things I love about you—how reliably *you* are."

I want to protest. What about transformations? What about the reinvention she's always going on about? Are those only reserved for her? Is there a different standard for me?

"You know what you need? Some Ani DeFranco." She pulls out her iPhone and shoves the buds in my ears, and as Ani goes on about finding your voice and making it heard, I feel so frustrated with myself. Like I want to pull my skin wide open and step out of it. I scrape my feet against the hot cement floor and sigh, wishing there was someone I could explain this to. Someone who might understand what I'm feeling.

And for one small second, I do imagine the person I could talk to, about finding this door, and losing it. He would understand.

But that's the one door that needs to stay shut.

Eighteen

Somehow, using the same we're-adults-you-have-to-treat-us-that-way argument from the Beer Dinner, plus promising to hire a hotel-approved taxi for the entire night, Melanie and I manage to procure parental permission to go to that New Year's Eve party. It's being held on a narrow crescent of sand, all lit up with tiki torches, and at ten o'clock, it's already slamming. There is a low stage on which the touted Mexican reggae band will play, though right now a d.j. is playing techno.

There are several giant piles of discarded shoes. Melanie tosses off her bright-orange flip-flops. I hesitate before taking off my less conspicuous black leather sandals, hoping I'll find them again, because if I lose anything else, I swear I will never hear the end of it.

"Quite the bacchanal," Melanie says approvingly, nodding to the guys in swim trunks holding bottles of tequila by the neck, the girls in sarongs with their hair freshly corn-rowed. There are even actual Mexicans here, the guys smartly dressed in sheer white shirts, hair slicked back, and the girls in fancy party dresses, cut up to there, legs long and brown.

"Dance first or drink first?"

I don't want to dance. So I say drink. We line up at the packed bar. Behind us is a group of French-speaking people, which makes me do a double take. There's hardly anyone but Americans at our hotel, but of course people from every-where come to Mexico.

"Here." Melanie shoves a drink into my hand. It's in a hollowed-out piece of pineapple. I take a sniff. It smells like suntan lotion. It is sweet and warm and burns slightly going down. "Good girl."

I think of Ms. Foley. "Don't call me that."

"Bad girl."

"I'm not that either."

She looks peeved. "Nothing girl."

We drink our drinks in silence, taking in the growing party. "Let's dance," Melanie says, yanking me toward the ring of sand that has been allocated as the dance floor.

I shake my head. "Maybe later."

And there's that sigh again. "Are you going to be like this all night?"

"Like what?" I think of what she called me on the tour—*adventure averse*—and what she said at the pool. "So like *me*? I thought that's what you *loved* about me."

"What is your problem? You've had a stick up your ass this whole trip! It's not my fault your mom is Study-Hall Nazi."

"No, but it is your fault for making me feel like crap because I don't want to dance. I hate techno. I have *always* hated techno, so you should know that, what with me being so reliably me."

"Fine. Why don't you be reliably you and sit on the side-lines while I dance."

"Fine."

She leaves me on the perimeter of the circle and goes off and just starts dancing with random people. First she dances with some guy with dreadlocks and then turns and dances with a girl with super-short hair. She seems to be having a fine time out there, swirling, twirling, and it strikes me that if I didn't already know her, she would no longer be someone I would know.

I watch her for at least twenty minutes. In between the monotonous techno songs, she talks to other people, laughs. After a half hour, I'm getting a headache. I try to catch her eye, but I eventually give up and slip away.

The party stretches all the way down the curve of the water—and into it—where a bunch of people are skinny-dipping in the moonlit sea. A little way's farther down, it gets more mellow, with a bonfire and people around it playing guitar. I plant myself a few feet away from the bonfire, close enough to feel its heat and hear the crackle of wood. I dig my feet into the sand; the top layer is cool, but underneath it's still warm from the day's sunshine.

Down the beach, the techno stops, and the reggae band takes the stage. The more mellow *bump-bump-thump* is nice. In the water, a girl starts dancing on a guy's shoulder, pulls off her bikini top, and stands there, half naked like a moonshine mermaid, before diving in with a quiet splash. Behind me, the guys on guitars start up with "Stairway to Heaven." It mingles strangely well with the reggae.

I lie down in the sand and look up at the sky. From this vantage point, it's like I have the beach all to myself. The band finishes a song, and the singer announces that it's a half hour until the New Year. "New Year. *Año nuevo.* It's a tabula rasa. Time to *hacer borrón y cuenta nueva,*" he chants. "One chance to wipe the board clean."

Can you really do that? Wipe the board clean? Would I even want to? Would I wipe all of last year away if I could?

"Tabula rasa," the singer repeats. "A new chance to start over. Start fresh, baby. Make amends. Make ch-ch-changes. To be who you want to be. Come the stroke of midnight, before you kiss your *amor,* save *un beso para tí.* Close your eyes, think of the year ahead. This is your chance. This can be the day it all changes."

Really? It's a nice idea, but why January first? You might as well say April nineteenth is the day that everything changes. A day is a day is a day. It means nothing.

"At the stroke of midnight, make your wish. *Qué es tu deseo?* For yourself. For the world."

It's New Year's. Not a birthday cake. And I'm not eight anymore. I don't believe in wishes coming true. But if I did, what would I wish for? To undo that day? To see him again?

Normally I have such willpower. Like a dieter resisting a cookie, I don't even let myself go there. But for the briefest second, I do. I picture him right here, walking down the beach, hair reflecting in the flames, eyes dark and light and full of teasing, and of so many other things. And for a second, I almost see him.

As I open myself to the fantasy, I wait for the accompanying clench of pain. But it doesn't come. Instead my breath slows and something warms inside me. I abandon caution and all good sense and wrap myself in thoughts of him. My own hands circle around my chest, as if he were holding me. For one brief moment, everything feels right.

"I thought I'd never find you!"

I look up. Melanie is striding toward me. "I've been right here."

"I've been looking for you for the last half hour! Up and down the beach. I had no idea where you were."

"I was right here."

"I looked everywhere for you. The party's getting totally out of control, like roofies-in-the-punch wild. Some girl just puked six inches from my feet, and guys are hitting on me with the worst pickup lines in the world. I've had my ass pinched more times than I can count, and one charming guy just asked me if I wanted a bite of his sandwich—and he wasn't talking about food!" She shakes her head as if trying to dislodge the memory. "We're supposed to have each other's backs!"

"I'm sorry. You were having fun, and I guess I just lost track of time."

"You lost track of time?"

"I guess so. I'm really sorry you were worried. But I'm fine. Do you want to go back to the party?"

"No! I'm over it. Let's leave."

"We don't have to." I look toward the bonfire. The flames are dancing, making it hard to pull my gaze away. "I don't mind staying." For the first time in a long while, I am having an okay time, I'm okay being where I am.

"Well, I do. I've spent the last half hour panicking, and now I'm sober, and I'm beyond over this place. It's like a Telemundo frat party."

"Oh, okay. Let's go then."

I follow her back to the shoe piles, where it takes ages for her to find her flip-flops, and then we get into our waiting taxi. By the time I think to look at the dashboard clock, it's twenty past twelve. I don't really believe what the singer said about midnight wishes, but now that I've missed mine, I feel like I should've tried before the window of opportunity closed.

We ride home in silence, save for the cab driver softly singing to his radio. When we pull into the gates of the resort, Melanie hands him some bills, and for a minute, I get an idea.

"Melanie. What if we hire this guy in a day or two and go off somewhere, away from the tourists?"

"Why would we want to do that?"

"I don't know. To see what would happen if we tried something different. Excuse me, señor, how much would it be for us to hire you for a whole day?"

"*Lo siento. No hablo inglés.*"

Melanie rolls her eyes at me. "I guess you have to be satisfied with your one big adventure."

At first I think she means this party, but then I realize she means the ruins. Because I did actually manage to get our families to visit a different ruin. We went to Coba instead of Tulum. And just as I'd hoped, we stopped at a small village along the way, and for a moment there, I'd gotten excited, thinking this was it, I had actually escaped into the real Mexico. Okay, my whole family was in tow, but it was a Mayan village. Except then Susan and my mom went crazy buying beaded jewelry, and the villagers came out and played drums for us, and we all were invited to dance in a circle and then there was even a traditional spiritual cleansing. But everyone was videoing everything, and after his cleansing, my dad "donated" ten dollars to a hat that was conspicuously put in front of us, and I realized that this was no different from being on the tour.

The condo is quiet. The parents are all in bed, though as soon as the door closes Mom pops out of her bedroom. "You're early," she says.

"I was tired," Melanie lies. "Good night. Happy New Year." She pads off toward our room, and Mom gives me a New Year's kiss and goes back to hers.

I'm nowhere near tired, so I sit out on the balcony and listen to the dwindling sounds of the hotel's party. On the horizon, a lightning storm is brewing. I reach into my purse for my phone and, for the first time in months, open the photo album.

His face is so beautiful, it makes my stomach twist. But he seems unreal, not someone I would ever know. But then I look at me, the me in the photo, and I hardly recognize her, either, and not just because the hair is different, but because she seems different. That's not me. That's Lulu. And she's just as gone as he is.

Tabula rasa. That's what the reggae singer said. Maybe I can't get my wish, but I can try to wipe the slate clean, try to get over this.

I allow myself look at the picture of Willem and Lulu in Paris for a long minute.

"Happy New Year," I tell them.

And then I erase them.

Nineteen

*T*wo feet of snow fall in Boston while I'm in Mexico, and the temperature never rises above freezing, so when I get back two weeks later, campus looks like a depressing gray tundra. I arrive a few days before classes start, with excuses of getting prepped for the new semester, but really because I could not handle being at home, under the watchful eye of the warden, one day longer. It had been bad enough in Cancún, but home, without Melanie to distract me—she took off for New York City the day after we got back, before we got a chance to ever resolve the weirdness that had settled between us—it was unbearable.

The Terrific Trio comes back from break full of stories and inside jokes. They spent New Year's together at Kendra's family's Virginia Beach condo and went swimming in the snow, and now they are ordering themselves Polar Bear T-shirts. They're nice enough, asking about my trip, but I find it hard to breathe with all that bonhomie, so I pile on my sweaters and parkas and trudge over to the U bookstore to pick up a new Mandarin workbook.

I'm in the foreign languages section when my cell phone rings. I don't even need to look at the caller ID. Mom has been calling at least twice a day since I got back.

"Hey, Mom."

"Allyson Healey." The voice on the other end is high and winsome, the opposite of Mom.

"Yes, this is Allyson."

"Oh, hello, Allyson. This is Gretchen Price from the guidance office."

I pause, breathing through the sickening feeling in my stomach. "Yes?"

"I'm wondering if you might like to stop by my office. Say hello."

Now I feel like I'm going to throw up right on the stacks of *Buon Giorno Italiano*. "Did my mother call you?"

"Your mother? I don't think so." I hear the sound of something knocking over. "Damn. Hang on." There's more shuffling and then she's back on the line. "Look, I apologize for the last-minute notice, but that seems to be my MO these days. I'd love for you to come in before the term starts."

"Umm, the terms starts the day after tomorrow."

"So it does. How about today, then?"

They are going to kick me out. I've blown it in one term. They know I'm not a Happy College Student. I don't belong in the catalog. Or here. "Am I in some kind of trouble?"

That tinkling laugh again. "Not with me. Why don't you

come by—hang on." There's more shuffling of paper. "How about four?"

"You're sure my mother didn't call?"

"Yes, Allyson, I'm quite sure. So four?"

"What's it about?"

"Oh, just getting-to-know-you stuff. I'll see you at four."

Gretchen Price's office is in a crowded corner of the ivy-covered administration buildings. Stacks of books and papers and magazines are scattered everywhere, on the round table and chairs by the window, on the love seat, on her messy desk.

She is on the phone when I'm ushered in, so I just stand there in the doorway. She gestures for me to come inside. "You must be Allyson. Just move a pile off the chair and take a seat. I'll be with you in a second."

I move a dirty Raggedy Ann doll with one of the braids chopped off and a stack of folders from one of the chairs. Some of the folders have sticky notes on them: *Yes. No. Maybe.* Paperwork slips out of one. It's a printout of a college application, like the one I sent in a year ago. I shove it back into the folder and put it on the next chair.

Gretchen hangs up the phone. "So, Allyson, how's it going?"

"It's going fine." I glance at all the applications, all the comers who want a spot like mine. "*Great* in fact."

"Really?" She picks up a file, and I have the distinct impression my goose is cooked.

"Yep," I say with all the chipperness I can muster.

"See, the thing is, I've been looking at your first-term grades."

I feel tears spring to my eyes. She lured me here under false pretenses. She said I wasn't in trouble, it was just a getting-to-know-you session. And I didn't fail. I just got Cs!

She looks at my stricken face and motions for me to calm down with her hands. "Relax, Allyson," she says in a soothing voice. "I'm not here to bust you. I just want to see if you need some help, and to offer it if that's the case."

"It's my first term. I was adjusting." I've used this excuse so much I've almost come to believe it.

She leans back in her chair. "You know, people tend think that college admissions is inherently unfair. That you can't judge people from paper. But the thing is, paper can actually tell you an awful lot." She takes a gulp from one of those coffee cups that kids paint. Hers is covered in smudgy pastel thumbprints. "Having never met you before, but judging just from what I'm seeing on paper, I suspect that you're struggling a bit."

She's not asking me *if* I'm struggling. She's not asking *why* I'm struggling. She just knows. The tears come, and I let them. Relief is more powerful than shame.

"Let me be clear," Gretchen continues, sliding over a box of tissues. "I'm not concerned about your GPA. First-term slides are as common as the freshman fifteen. Oh, man, you should've seen my first-semester GPA." She shakes her head and laughs. "Generally, struggling students here fall into two categories: Those getting used to the freedom, maybe spending a little too much time at the keg parties, not enough time in the library. They generally straighten out after a term or two." She looks at me. "Are you pounding too many shots of Jägermeister, Allyson?"

I shake my head, even though by the tone of her question, it seems like she already knows the answer.

She nods. "So the other pattern is a bit more insidious. But it's actually a predictor for dropouts. And that's why I wanted to see you."

"You think I'm going to drop out?"

She stares hard at me. "No. But looking at your records from high school and your first term, you fit a pattern." She waves around a file, which obviously contains my whole academic history. "Students like you, young women, in particular, do extraordinarily well in high school. Look at your grades. Across the board, they're excellent. AP, science classes, humanities classes, all As. Extremely high SAT scores. Then you get into college, which is supposedly why you've been working so hard, right?"

I nod.

"Well you get here, and you crumple. You'd be surprised how many of my straight-A, straight-and-narrow students wind up dropping out." She shakes her head in dismay. "I hate it when that happens. I help choose who goes here. It reflects badly on me if they crash and burn."

"Like a doctor losing a patient."

"Great analogy. See how smart you are?"

I offer a rueful smile.

"The thing is, Allyson, college is supposed to be . . ."

"The best years of my life?"

"I was going to say nourishing. An adventure. An exploration. I'm looking at you, and you don't seem nourished. And I'm looking at your schedule. . . ." She peers at her computer screen. "Biology, chemistry. Physics. Mandarin. Labs. It's very ambitious for your first year."

"I'm pre-med," I say. "I have to take those classes."

She doesn't say anything. She takes another gulp of coffee. Then she says. "Are those the classes you *want* to take?"

I pause. Nobody has ever asked me that. When we got the course catalog in the mail, it was just assumed I'd tackle all the pre-med requirements. Mom knew just what I should take when. I'd looked at some electives, had mentioned that I thought pottery sounded cool, but I may as well have said I was planning on majoring in underwater basket weaving.

"I don't know what I want to take."

"Why don't you take a look and see about switching things up a bit. Registration is still in flux, and I might be able to pull some strings." She stops and pushes the catalog clear across the desk. "Even if you do wind up pre-med, you have four years to take these classes, and you have a lot of humanities requisites to get in too. You don't need to jam everything together all at once. This isn't medical school."

"What about my parents?"

"What *about* your parents?"

"I can't let them down."

"Even if it means letting yourself down? Which I doubt they'd want for you."

The tears come again. She hands me another tissue.

"I understand about wanting to please your parents, to make them proud. It's a noble impulse, and I commend you for it. But at the end of the day, it's your education, Allyson. You have to own it. And you should enjoy it." She pauses, slurps some more coffee. "And somehow I imagine that your parents will be happier if they see your GPA come up."

She's right about that. I nod. She turns to her computer

screen. "So, let's just pretend we're going to jiggle some classes around. Any idea of what you might like to take?"

I shake my head.

She grabs the course catalog and flips through it. "Come on. It's an intellectual buffet. Archaeology. Salsa dancing. Child development. Painting. Intro to finance. Journalism. Anthropology. Ceramics."

"Is that like pottery?" I interrupt.

"It is." She widens her eyes and taps on her computer. "Beginning Ceramics, Tuesdays at eleven. It's open. Oh, but it conflicts with your physics lab. Shall we postpone the lab, and maybe physics, for another term?"

"Cut them." Saying it feels wonderful, like letting go of a bunch of helium balloons and watching them disappear into the sky.

"See? You're already getting the hang of it," Gretchen says. "How about some humanities, to balance you out? You're going to need those to graduate anyway as part of your core curriculum. Are you more interested in ancient history or modern history? There's a wonderful European survey. And a great seminar on the Russian Revolution. Or a fascinating American Pre-Revolution class that makes excellent use of our being so close to Boston. Or you could get started on some of your literature classes. Let's see. Your AP exams tested you out of the basic writing requirement. You know, we could be devilish and slip you into one of the more interesting seminar classes." She scrolls down her computer. "Beat Poetry. Holocaust Literature. Politics in Prose. Medieval Verse. Shakespeare Out Loud."

I feel something jolt up my spine. An old circuit-breaker

long since forgotten being tested out and sparking in the darkness.

Gretchen must see my expression, because she starts telling me about how this isn't just any Shakespeare class, how Professor Glenny has very strong opinions on how Shakespeare should be taught, and how he has a cult following on campus.

I can't help but think of *him*. And then I think of the tabula rasa. The resolution I made on New Year's. The fact that I am pre-med. "I don't think I'm supposed to take this class."

This makes her smile. "Sometimes the best way to find out what you're supposed to do is by doing the thing you're *not* supposed to do." She taps on her keyboard. "It's full, as usual, so you'll have to fight your way in off the wait list. Why not give it a shot? Leave it up to the fates."

The fates. I think that's another word for accidents.

Which I don't believe in anymore.

But I let her register me for the class just the same.

Twenty

Stepping into the classroom for Shakespeare Out Loud is like stepping into an entirely different school than the one I've attended for the past four months. Instead of a giant lecture hall, which is where all my science courses were located, or even a large classroom like Mandarin, it's in a tiny, intimate classroom, the kind we had in high school. There are maybe twenty-five desks arced into a U, around a lectern in the middle. And the students sitting at them, they look different too. Lip rings and hair dyed colors not found naturally on the human head. It's a sea of well-manicured alienation. The arty crowd, I guess. When I come in and look for a seat—they're all taken—no one looks at me.

I take a seat on the floor, near the door, for an easier escape. I may not belong in chemistry, but I don't belong here either. When Professor Glenny strides in five minutes late and looking like a rock star—shaggy graying hair, beat-up leather boots, he even has pouty Mick Jagger lips—he steps on me. As in, literally treads on my hand. As bad as my other classes have been, no one has ever stepped on me. Not an auspicious start, and I almost leave right then and there, but my way is now blocked by the overflow of other students.

"Show of hands," Professor Glenny begins after he has dropped his artfully worn leather satchel on top of the lectern. "How many of you have ever read a Shakespeare play for the sheer pleasure of it?" He has a British accent, though not the Masterpiece Theatre kind.

About half the hands in the class shoot up. I almost consider raising mine, but it's just too much of a lie, and there's no point in brown-nosing if I'm not staying.

"Excellent. Ancillary question: How many of you have fallen asleep while attempting to read a Shakespeare play by yourself?"

The class goes silent. No hands go up. Then Professor Glenny looks right at me, and I'm wondering how he knows, but then I realize he's not looking at me but the guy behind me, who is the only person who's raised a hand. Along with everyone else in the class, I turn and stare at him. He's one of two African American students in the room, though he's the only one sporting a huge halo of an afro covered in bejeweled barrettes, and bubble-gum-pink gloss on his lips. Otherwise, he's dressed like a soccer mom, in sweats and pink Uggs. In a field of carefully cultivated weirdness, he's a wildflower, or maybe a weed.

"Which play bored you to sleep?" Professor Glenny asks.

"Take your pick. *Hamlet. Macbeth. Othello.* I napped to the best of them."

The class titters, as if falling asleep while studying is so déclassé.

Professor Glenny nods. "So why, then, please—sorry, your name . . . ?"

"D'Angelo Harrison, but my friends call me Dee."

"I'll be presumptuous and call you Dee. Dee, why take this class? Unless you're here to catch up on your sleep."

Again, the class laughs.

"By my count, this class costs about five grand a semester," Dee says. "I can sleep for free."

I attempt the math. Is that how much one class costs?

"Quite prudent," Professor Glenny says. "So, again, why take this class, given the expenditure and given Shakespeare's soporific track record?"

"Well, I'm not actually in the class yet. I'm on your wait list."

At this point, I can't tell if he's stalling or parrying with the professor, but either way, I'm impressed. Everyone else here seems eager to give the right answer, and this guy is stringing the professor along. To his credit, Professor Glenny seems more amused than annoyed.

"My point is, Dee, why attempt it even?"

There's a long pause. You can hear the fluorescent lights humming, the throat-clearing of a few students who clearly have a ready answer. And then Dee says, "Because the movie of *Romeo and Juliet* makes me cry harder than just about anything else. Every damn time I see it."

Again, the class laughs. It's not a kind laugh. Professor Glenny turns back toward the lectern and pulls a paper and pen out of his satchel. It's a list. He stares at it ominously and then checks off a name—and I wonder if this Dee just got himself kicked off the wait list. What kind of class did Gretchen Price put me in? Gladiator Shakespeare?

Then Professor Glenny turns to a girl with weird pink Tootsie Roll twists who has her nose in a copy of the collected works of Shakespeare, the kind of girl who probably never deigned to watch Leo and Claire's version of *Romeo and Juliet* or fall asleep while reading *Macbeth*. He looms over her for a moment. She looks up at him and smiles bashfully, like, oh-you-caught-me-reading-my-book. He flashes a thousand-watt smile back at her. And then he slams her book shut. It's a big book. It makes a loud noise.

Professor Glenny returns to the lectern. "Shakespeare is a mysterious character. There is so much written about this man about whom we truly know so little. Sometimes I think only Jesus has had more ink spilled with less fruitful result. So I resist making any characterizations about the man. But I will go out on a limb and say this: Shakespeare did not write his plays so that you could sit in in a library carrel and read them in silence." He pauses, lets that sink in before continuing. "Playwrights are not novelists. They create works that need to be performed, interpreted. To be reinterpreted through the ages. It is credit to Shakespeare's genius that he gave us such great raw material that really could survive the ages, withstand the myriad reinterpretations we throw at it. But to truly appreciate Shakespeare, to understand why he has endured, you must hear it out loud, or better yet, see it performed, whether you see it performed in period costume or done naked, a dubious pleasure I've had. Though a good film production can do the trick, as our friend Dee has so aptly demonstrated. And Mr. Harrison," he looks at Dee again. "Thank you for your honesty. I too have fallen asleep while reading Shakespeare. My college textbook still bears some drool marks. You're off the wait list."

Striding back to the whiteboard, Professor Glenny scrawls *English 317—Shakespeare Out Loud* on it. "The name of this class is not accidental. It is quite literal. For in this class, we do not *read* Shakespeare quietly to ourselves or in the privacy of our bedrooms or libraries. We *perform* it. We *see* it performed. We read it aloud, in class or with partners. Every last one of us will become actors in this class, interpreters for one another, in front of one another. For those of you not prepared for this or who prefer a more conventional approach, this fine institution offers plenty of Shakespeare survey courses, and I suggest you avail yourself of one of them."

He pauses, as if to give people a chance to escape. Here would be my chance to go, but something roots me in place.

"If you know anything about this class, it's that I coordinate our readings to go with whatever Shakespeare is being performed during the term, be it by a community group or professional theater company. I expect attendance at all the plays, and I get us excellent group rates. As it happens, this winter and spring bring a delightful selection of plays."

He starts handing out the syllabus, and before one gets to me, before he finishes writing the order of plays on the board, I know it will be among them, even though Shakespeare wrote more than thirty plays, I know this one will be on our list.

It's midway through the syllabus, after *Henry V* and *The Winter's Tale* and before *As You Like It* and *Cymbeline* and

Measure for Measure. But there on the page, it seems to jump out at me like a billboard. *Twelfth Night.* And whether I want to take this class or not is irrelevant. I can't stand up here and read those lines. That is the opposite of tabula rasa.

Professor Glenny goes on for a while about the plays, pointing to them one by one with his hand, erasing the ink in his enthusiasm. "My absolute favorite thing about this class is that we, in effect, let the themes choose us by letting the plays choose us. The dean was skeptical at first of this academia via serendipity, but it always seems to work out. Take this sampling." He points to the list of plays again. "Can anyone surmise this semester's theme based on these particular plays?"

"They're all comedies?" the girl up front with the Tootsie Roll twists asks.

"Good guess. *The Winter's Tale,* *Measure for Measure,* and *Cymbeline,* though all have much humor, are not considered comedies so much as problem plays, a category we shall discuss later. And *Henry V,* though it has many funny bits, is quite a serious play. Any other takers?"

Silence.

"I'll give you a hint. It's most obvious in *Twelfth Night* or *As You Like It,* which *are* comedies—which isn't to say they're not also quite moving plays."

More silence.

"Come now. Some of you fine scholars must have seen one of these. Who here has seen *As You Like It* or *Twelfth Night?*"

I don't realize I've raised my hand until it's too late. Until Professor Glenny has seen me and nodded to me with those bright, curious eyes of his. I want to say that I've made a mistake, that it was some other version of Allyson who used to raise her hand in class who temporarily reappeared. But I can't, so I blurt out that I saw *Twelfth Night* over the summer.

Professor Glenny stands there, as if waiting for me to finish my thought. But that was it; that's all I have to say. There's an awkward silence, like I just announced I was an alcoholic—at a Daughters of the American Revolution meeting.

But Professor Glenny refuses to give up on me: "And, what was the main source of tension and humor in that particular play?"

For the briefest of seconds, I'm not in this overheated classroom on a winter's morning. It's the hot English night, and I'm at the canal basin in Stratford-upon-Avon. And then I'm in a Paris park. And then I'm back here. In all three places, the answer remains the same: "No one is who they pretend to be."

"Thank you. . . . ?"

"Allyson," I finish. "Allyson Healey."

"Allyson. Perhaps a slight overgeneralization, but for our purposes, it hits the nail right on the head." He turns to the board and scrawls *Altering Identity, Altering Reality* on it. Then he checks something else off on his sheet of paper.

Professor Glenny continues, "Now, before we part ways, one last piece of housekeeping. We won't have time to read each play completely in class, though we will make quite a dent. I believe I've made my point about reading alone to yourselves, so I'd like you to read the remaining sections aloud with partners. This is not optional. Please pair up now. If you're on the wait list, find a partner also on the wait list.

Allyson, you're no longer on the wait list. As you can see, class participation is rewarded in here."

There's bustle as everyone pairs off. I look around. Next to me is a normalish-girl with cat-eye glasses. I could ask her.

Or I could get up and walk out of the class. Even though I'm off the wait list, I could just drop the class, leave my spot for someone else.

But for some reason, I don't do either of those things. I turn away from the girl in the glasses and look behind me. That guy, Dee, is sitting there, like the unpopular and unathletic kid who always wound up the remainder during team picking for grade-school kickball games. He's wearing a bemused look, as if he knows no one will ask him and he's saving everyone the trouble. So when I ask him if he wants to be partners, his arch expression falls away for a moment and he appears genuinely surprised.

"Just so happens my dance card is none too full at the moment."

"Is that a yes?"

He nods.

"Good. I do have one condition. It's more of a favor. Two favors, actually."

He frowns for a moment, then arches his plucked eyebrow so high, it disappears into the halo of hair.

"I don't want to read *Twelfth Night* out loud. You can do all the parts, if you want, and I'll listen, and then I'll read one of the other plays. Or we can rent a movie version and read along. I just don't want to have to say it. Not a word of it."

"How you gonna get away with that in class?"

"I'll figure it out."

"What you got against *Twelfth Night*?"

"That's the other thing. I don't want to talk about it."

He sighs as if considering. "Are you a flake or a diva? Diva I can work with, but I got no time for flakes."

"I don't think I'm either." Dee looks skeptical. "It's just that one play, I swear. I'm sure there's a DVD for it."

He looks at me for a long minute, as if trying to X-ray my true self. Then he either decides I'm okay or recognizes he has no other options, because he rolls his eyes and sighs loudly. "There are several versions of *Twelfth Night*, actually." Suddenly, his voice and diction have completely changed. Even his expression has gone professorial. "There's a film version with Helena Bonham Carter, who is magnificent. But if we're going to cheat like this, we should rent the stage version."

I stare at him a moment, baffled. He stares back, then his mouth cracks into the smallest of grins. And I realize what I said before was right: *No one is who they pretend to be.*

Twenty-one

FEBRUARY
College

---

*F*or the first few weeks of class, Dee and I tried meeting in the library, but we got dirty looks, especially when Dee broke out into his voices. And he has lots of voices: a solemn English accent when doing Henry, a weird Irish brogue—his take on a Welsh accent, I guess—as Fluellen, exaggerated French accents when doing the French characters. I don't bother with accents. It's enough for me to get the words right.

After getting shushed in the library one too many times, we switched to the Student Union, but Dee couldn't hear me over the din. He projected so well, you'd think he was a theater major or something. But I think he's history or political science. Not that he's told me this; we don't talk aside from the reading. But I've glimpsed his textbooks, and they're all tomes about the history of the labor movement or treatises on government.

So right before we start reading the second play, *The Win-*

ter's Tale, I suggest that we move to my dorm, where it's generally quiet in the afternoons. Dee gives me a long look and then says okay. I tell him to come over at four.

That afternoon, I lay out a plate of the cookies that Grandma keeps sending me, and I make tea. I have no idea what Dee expects, but this is the first time I've ever entertained in my room, though I'm not sure what I'm doing qualifies as entertaining or if Dee is company.

But when Dee sees the cookies, he gives me a funny little smile. Then he takes off his coat and hangs it in the closet, even though mine is tossed over a chair. He kicks off his boots. Then he looks around my room.

"Do you have a clock?" he asks. "My phone's dead."

I get up and show him the box of alarm clocks, which I have since put back in the closet. "Take your pick."

He takes a long time choosing, finally settling on a 1940s mahogany deco number. I show him how to wind it. He asks how to set the alarm. I show him. Then he sets it for five fifty, explaining he has to be at his job at the dining hall at six. The reading usually doesn't take more than a half hour, so I'm not sure why he sets the alarm. But I don't say anything. About that. Or about his job, even though I'm curious about it.

He sits down on my desk chair. I sit on my bed. He picks up a tube of fruit flies from the desk, examining it with a slightly amused expression. "They're Drosophila," I explain. "I'm breeding them for a class."

He shakes his head. "If you run out, you can come get more in my mama's kitchen."

I want to ask him where that kitchen is. Where he's from.

But he seems guarded. Or maybe it's me. Maybe making friends is a specific skill, and I missed the lesson. "Okay, time for work. See you later, my dropsillas," he says to the bugs. I don't correct his pronunciation.

We read a really good scene at the beginning of *The Winter's Tale*, when Leontes freaks out and thinks that Hermione is cheating on him. When we get to the end point, Dee packs up his Shakespeare textbook, and I think he's going to leave, but instead he pulls out a book by someone called Marcuse. He gives me the quickest of looks.

"I'll make more tea," I say.

We study together in silence. It's nice. At five fifty, the alarm goes off and Dee packs up to go to work.

"Wednesday?" he says.

"Sure."

Two days later, we go through the same routine, cookies, tea, hello to the "dropsillas," Shakespeare out loud, and silent study. We don't talk. We just work. On Friday, Kali comes into the room. It's the first time she's seen Dee, seen anyone, in the room with me, and she looks at him for a long moment. I introduce them.

"Hi, *Dee*. Pleasure to *meet* you," she says in a strangely flirty voice.

"Oh, the pleasure is all mine," Dee says, his voice all exaggeratedly animated.

Kali looks at him and then smiles. Then she goes to her closet and pulls out a camel coat and a pair of tawny suede boots. "Dee, can I *ask* you something? What do you think of *these* boots with this jacket? Too *matchy matchy*?"

I look at Dee. He is wearing sky-blue sweats and a T-shirt

with sparkly lettering spelling out I BELIEVE. I'm not clear how this reads Fashion Expert to Kali.

But Dee gets right into it. "Oh, girl, those boots are fine. I might have to take them from you."

I look at him, sort of shocked. I mean I figured Dee was gay, but I've never heard him talk all sassy-gay-sidekick before.

"Oh, no, you won't," Kali replies, her strange ways of KO'ing words now blending with some latent Valley Girl tendencies. "They cost me, like, *four hundred* dollars. You can *borrow* them."

"Oh, you're a doll baby. But you got Cinderella feet, and ole Dee's like one of them ugly stepsisters."

Kali laughs, and they go on like this for some time, talking about fashion. I feel kind of bad. I guess I never realized Dee was so into this kind of thing. Kali got it right away. It's like she has some radar, the one that tells you how to pick up on things with people, how to be friends. I don't really care about fashion, but that night, when the alarm goes off and Dee packs up to leave, I show him the latest skirt my mom sent me and ask if he thinks it's too preppy. But he barely gives it half a glance. "It's fine."

After that, Kali starts showing up more often, and she and Dee go all *Project Runway*, and Dee always switches into that voice. I write it off as just a fashion thing. But then a few days after that, as we're leaving, Kendra walks in, and I introduce them. Kendra sizes Dee up, like she does with people, and puts on her flight-attendant smile and asks Dee where he's from.

"New York," he says. I make a note of that. I've known

him for almost three weeks, and I'm just now finding out the basics.

"Where in New York?"

"The city."

"Where?"

"The Bronx."

The flight attendant smile is gone, replaced by a tight line that looks penciled on.

"Oh, like the South Bronx? Well. You must be so glad to be living here."

Now it's Dee who gives Kendra the once-over. They're eyeing each other like dogs, and I wonder if it's because they're both black. Then, he switches to a different voice from the one he talks to Kali or me in. "You from the South Bronx?"

Kendra recoils a little. "No! I'm from Washington."

"Like where they got all the rain and shit?"

Rain and shit?

"No, not state. DC."

"Oh. I got some cousins in DC. Down in Anacostia. Shit, those are some nasty-ass projects. Even worse than where I came up. There's a shooting at their school every damn week."

Kendra looks horrified. "I've never even been to Anacostia. I live in Georgetown. And I went to Sidwell Friends, where the Obama girls go."

"I went to South Bronx High. Most wack school in America. Ever heard of it?"

"No, I'm afraid I haven't." She gives me a quick look. "Well, I have to go. I'm meeting Jeb soon." Jeb is her new boyfriend.

"Catch you later, homegirl," Dee calls as Kendra disappears into her room. As Dee picks up his backpack to leave, he is quaking with laughter.

I decide to walk him to the dining hall, maybe eat there for a change. Eating alone sucks, but there are only so many microwave burritos a girl can stomach. When we get downstairs, I ask him if he really went to South Bronx High School.

When he speaks again, he sounds like Dee. Or the Dee I know. "They closed South Bronx High School a year ago, not that I ever went there. I went to a charter school. Then I got snagged in Prep for Prep—scholarship thing—by a private school that's even more expensive than Sidwell Friends. Take that, Miss Thang."

"Why didn't you just tell her where you went?"

He looks at me and then, reverting to the voice he'd used with Kendra, says, "If homegirls wanna see me as ghetto trash"—he stops and switches to his lispy, sassy voice—"or big-ass queer"—now he switches to his deepest Shakespeare voice—"I shall not take it upon myself to disabuse them."

When we reach the dining hall, I feel like I should say something to him. But I'm not sure what. In the end, I just ask him if he wants chocolate chip or butter cookies next time. Grandma sent me both.

"I'll supply cookies. My mama sent up some homemade molasses spice ones."

"That's nice."

"Nothin' nice about it. She's throwing down. She wasn't about to be outdone by somebody's grandma."

I laugh. It's a strange sound, like an old car being started after a long time in the garage. "We won't tell my grandma that. If she accepts the challenge and bakes her own cookies, we might get food poisoning. She's the worst cook in the world."

— — —

It becomes a routine then. Every Monday, Wednesday, and Friday: cookies, tea, alarm clock, Shakespeare, study. We still don't talk much about ourselves, but little things slip through the cracks. His mother works at a hospital. He has no siblings, but five zillion cousins. He's on a full scholarship. He has a rather huge crush on Professor Glenny. He is double-majoring in history and literature, and maybe a minor in political science. He hums when he's bored, and when he's really into his reading, he twists his hair around his index finger so tight, it turns pink. And just as I suspected from that first day in class, he's smart. That he doesn't tell me, but it's obvious. He's the only one in the entire class to get an A on Glenny's first assignment, a paper on *Henry V*; Professor Glenny announces it to the class and reads snippets of Dee's paper to the class as an example of what the rest of us should strive for. Dee looks mortified, and I feel sort of bad, but the Glenny groupies regard Dee with such looks of naked envy that it's almost worth it. I, meanwhile, get a very solid B on my paper about Perdita and themes of lost and found.

I tell Dee little things about me too, but half the time, I find myself censoring what I want to say. I like him. I do. But I'm trying to make good on my tabula-rasa promise. Still, I sort of wish I could ask Dee's opinion about Melanie. I sent her the very first piece I made from ceramics class, along with a note about how I'd completely upended my schedule. I sent it Priority Mail, and then a week went by, and I didn't hear anything. So I'd called her up to make sure she'd gotten it— it was just a crappy, handmade bowl, but it had a beautiful crackly turquoise glaze—and she apologized for not responding, saying she was busy.

I told her all about my new classes, and about the crazy lengths I was going to so my parents wouldn't find out: sending them biology tests with improving scores (Dee's and my lengthy study sessions are paying off) but also sending them my old chemistry lab partner's tests, with my name on them. I figured she'd get a good laugh about this, but instead her voice had stayed flat, and she'd warned me about the kind of trouble I'd be in if I got caught—as if I didn't already know that. Then I'd switched gears, telling her all about Professor Glenny and Dee and reading out loud and how mortifying I'd thought it would be to read in front of the class but how everyone does it and it isn't so bad. I'd expected her to be excited for me, but her voice had been practically monotone, and I'd found myself getting so angry. We haven't talked or emailed in a couple of weeks, and I'm both upset about it and relieved too.

I'd kind of like to tell Dee about this, but I'm not sure how to do it. Aside from Melanie, I've never had a really close friend, and I'm unclear how you make one. It's silly, I know. I've seen other people do it. They make it seem so easy: Have fun, open up, share stories. But how am I supposed to do that when the one story I really want to tell is the very one I'm supposed to be wiping clean? And besides, the last time I did open up to somebody . . . well, that's precisely why I'm in need of a tabula rasa in the first place. It just seems safer to keep it like it is—friendly, cordial, nice and simple.

— — —

At the end of February, my parents come up for Presidents' Weekend. It's the first time they've been up since Parents' Weekend, and having learned my lesson, I go to elaborate lengths to keep up the image they expect of me. I put my clocks back out. I highlight pages in my unused chemistry textbook and copy labs out of my old lab partners' book. I make us lots of plans in Boston to keep us off campus, away from incriminating evidence and the Terrific Trio (who now have become more of a Dynamic Duo anyway because Kendra's always with her boyfriend). And I tell Dee, with whom I now study on weekends sometimes, that I won't be around and that I can't get together Friday and Monday.

"You throwing me over for Drew?" Drew is the second best Shakespeare reader in the class.

"No. Of course not," I reply, my voice all pinched and panicked. "It's just I have one of those trips with my ceramics class Friday." This isn't entirely untrue. My ceramics class does go on field trips occasionally. We're experimenting with glazes, using different kinds of organic materials in the kiln, and sometimes even firing our pottery outside in earthen furnaces we build. I *do* have field trips, just not in the next couple of days.

"And I'll probably work on a paper this weekend." Another lie; the only class I have papers for is Shakespeare. It's amazing how good at lying I've become. "I'll see you Wednesday, okay? I'll bring the cookies."

"Tell your grandma to send some more of those twisty ones with the poppy seeds."

"Rugelach."

"I can't say it. I just eat it."

"I'll tell her."

— — —

The weekend with my parents goes decently enough. We go to the Museum of Fine Arts, the Museum of Science. We go ice skating (I can't keep my blades straight). We go to the movies. We take tons of pictures. There's an awkward moment or two when Mom pulls out next year's course catalog and starts going over class schedules with me and then asks me about my summer plans, but I just listen to her suggestions like I always have and don't say anything. By the end of the weekend, I feel drained in the same way that I do after a marathon session of reading Shakespeare aloud and trying to be all those different people.

On Sunday afternoon, we're back at my dorm before dinner when Dee pops by. And though I haven't told him one single thing about my family, not even that they were coming, let alone what they believe about me, what they expect of me, he still shows up in a pair of plain jeans and a sweater, something I've never seen him wear before. His hair is pulled back into a cap and he's not wearing lip gloss. I almost don't recognize him.

"So, how do you two know each other?" Mom asks after I nervously introduce them.

I freeze, in a panic.

"We're biology lab partners," Dee says, not missing a

beat. "We're raising the Drosophila together." It's the first time I've ever heard him pronounce it correctly. He picks up the tube. "Breeding all kinds of genetic abnormalities here."

My dad laughs. "They had us do the same experiment when I went here too." He looks at Dee. "Are you pre-med also?"

Dee's eyebrows flicker up, the slightest ripple of surprise. "I'm still undeclared."

"Well, there's no rush," Mom says. Which almost makes me laugh out loud.

Dad turns to puts the tube back next to a cylinder of pottery I forgot to hide away. "What's this?"

"Oh, *I* made that," Dee says, picking up the piece. And then he starts explaining how he's taking a pottery class, and this year's class is experimenting with different kinds of glazes and firing methods, and for these pieces, they fired everything in an earthen kiln fueled by cow patties.

"Cow patties?" Mom asks. "As in . . . *feces?*"

Dee nods. "Yes, we went to local farms and asked if we could collect their cow manure. They actually don't smell that bad. They're grass-fed cows."

And it hits me then that Dee is using another voice, but this time, the person he's playing is me. I had told him all about the cow patties, the earthy smell, collecting them from the farms . . . though when I'd done it, he'd laughed his head off at the thought of all us rich kids at our forty-thousand-dollar-a-year school paying for a class in which we went to farms and picked up after cows. I've told Dee more about myself than I guess I realized. And he listened.

He paid attention, absorbed a bit of me. And now he's saving my ass with it.

"Cow feces. How fascinating," my mother tells him.

— — —

The next day, my parents leave, and on Wednesday, our Shakespeare class starts on *Twelfth Night*. Dee has checked out two different versions from the media center for us to watch. He feels that as penance for not doing our homework, we should at least watch several. He hands me the stage version as I fire up my laptop.

"Thank you for getting these," I say. "I would have done it."

"I was at the media center anyway."

"Well, thank you. Also, thank you for how completely awesome you were with my parents." I pause for a second, more than a little embarrassed. "How'd you know they were coming?"

"My girlfriend Kali. She tell me. She tell me *everything*, because we be *besties*." He narrows his eyes. "See? Wasn't no need to hide Miss Dee from the folks. I clean up real nice."

"Oh, right. I'm sorry about that."

Dee stares at me, waiting for more.

"Really. It's just my parents. There's a lot . . . well, it's complicated."

"Ain't so complicated. I gets it just fine. Okay to slum with Dee but not to bring out the good silver."

"No! You've got it wrong!" I exclaim. "I'm not slumming. I really like you."

He crosses his arms and stares at me. "How was your *field trip*?" he asks acidly.

I want to explain, I do. But how? How do I do that without giving myself away? Because I'm trying. I'm trying to be a new person here, a different person, a tabula rasa. But if I explain about my parents, about Melanie, about Willem, if I show who I really am, then aren't I just stuck back where I started?

"I'm sorry I lied. But I swear, it's not about you. I can't tell you how much I appreciate what you did."

"Ain't no *thang*."

"No, I *really* mean it. You were great. My parents loved you. And you were so smooth, about everything. They didn't suspect a thing."

He whips the lip gloss out of his pocket and, with painstaking precision, applies it first to his top lip, then his bottom. Then he smacks them together, noisily like some kind of rebuke. "What's to suspect? I don't know nothin' 'bout nobody. I just be the help."

I want to make it right. For him to know that I care about him. That I'm not ashamed of him. That he is safe with me. "You know," I begin, "you don't have to do that with me. The voices. You can just be yourself."

I mean it as a compliment, so he'll know that I like him as is. But he doesn't take it that way. He purses his lips and shakes his head. "This *is* myself, baby. All of my selves. I own each and every one of them. I know who I'm pretending to be and who I am." The look he gives me is withering. "Do you?"

I purposely tried to keep all of that from him, but Dee—smart, sharp Dee—he got it. All of it. He knows what a big fat fake I am. I'm so ashamed I don't even know what to say.

After a while, he slips *Twelfth Night* into my computer. We watch the entire thing in silence, no voices, no commentary, no laughing, just four eyeballs staring at a screen. And that's how I know I've blown it with Dee.

I'm so miserable about this that I forget to be upset about Willem.

Twenty-two

MARCH
College

$\mathcal{T}$he winter drags on, no matter what the groundhog says. Dee stops coming over in the afternoons, ostensibly because we're not reading *Twelfth Night* aloud, but I know that's not really it. The cookies from my grandmother pile up. I get a bad cold, which I can't seem to shake, though it does have the side benefit of getting me out of reading any of *Twelfth Night* in front of the class. Professor Glenny, who is stuffy himself, gives me a packet of something called Lemsips and tells me to get in shape so I can pull a double shift as Rosalind in *As You Like It*, one of his favorite plays.

We finish *Twelfth Night*. I thought I'd feel relieved, as if I'd dodged a bullet. But I don't. With Dee out of my life, I feel like I took the bullet, even without reading the play. Tabula rasa was the right move. Taking this class was the wrong move. Now I just have to buckle through. I'm getting used to that.

We move on to *As You Like It*. In his introductory spiel, Professor Glenny goes on about how this is one of Shakespeare's most romantic plays, his sexiest, and this gets all the Glenny groupies up front swooning. I take vacant notes as he outlines the plot: A deposed duke's daughter named Rosalind and a gentleman named Orlando meet and fall in love at first sight. But then Rosalind's uncle kicks her out of his house, and she flees with her cousin Celia to the Forest of Arden. There, Rosalind takes on the identity of a boy named Ganymede. Orlando, who has also fled to Arden, meets Ganymede, and the two strike up a friendship. Rosalind as Ganymede uses her disguise and their friendship to test Orlando's proclaimed love for Rosalind. Meanwhile, all sorts of people take on different identities and fall in love. As always, Professor Glenny tells us to pay attention to specific themes and passages, specifically how emboldened Rosalind becomes when she is Ganymede and how that alters both her and the courtship with Orlando. It kind of all sounds like a sitcom, and I have to work hard to keep it straight.

Dee and I start reading together again, but now we're back in the Student Union, and he packs up as soon as we finish our assignment. He's stopped doing all the crazy voices, which makes me realize just how helpful they were in "interpreting" the plays because now, with both of us reading in monotones, the words sort of drift over me like a foreign language. We may as well be reading it to ourselves for how boring it has become. The only time Dee uses his voices now is when he has to speak to me. I get a different voice, or two, or three, every day. The message is clear: I've been demoted.

I want to undo this. To make it right. But I have no idea how. I don't seem to know how to open up to people without getting the door slammed in my face. So I do nothing.

— — —

"Today we will read one of my favorite scenes in *As You Like It*, the beginning of act four," Professor Glenny says, one bone-chillingly cold March day that makes it seem like we're heading into winter, not out of it. "Orlando and Ganymede/Rosalind are meeting again in the Forest of Arden, and the chemistry between them reaches its boiling point. Which is kind of confusing and amusing, given that Orlando believes himself to be speaking to Ganymede, who is male. But it's equally confusing for Rosalind, who is in a kind of delicious torment, torn between two identities, the male and the female, and two desires: a desire to protect herself and remain Orlando's equal, and the exquisite desire to simply submit." Up in the front of the classroom, the groupies seem to emit a little joint sigh. If Dee and I were still friends, it would be the kind of thing that would make us look at each other and roll our eyes. But we're not, so I don't even look at him.

"So, Orlando comes to Ganymede in the forest, and the two perform a sort of Kabuki theater together, and in doing so, they fall deeper in love, even as they don't entirely know *whom* they're falling in love with," Professor Glenny continues. "The line between true self and feigned self is blurred on all sides. Which I think is a rather handy metaphor for falling in love. So, it's a good day to read. Who's up?" He scans the class. People are actually raising their hands. "Drew, why don't you read Orlando." There's a smattering of applause as

Drew walks up the front of the room. He's one of the best readers in the class. Normally, Professor Glenny pairs him with Nell or Kaitlin, two of the best girls. But not today. "Allyson, I believe you owe me a Rosalind."

I shuffle up to the front of the room, along with the other readers he's chosen. I've never loved this part of the class, but at least before, I could feel Dee cheering me on. Once we're assembled, Professor Glenny turns into a director, which apparently is what he used to do before becoming an academic. He offers us notes: "Drew, in these scenes, Orlando is ardent and steadfast, completely in love. Allyson, your Ganymede is torn: smitten, but also toying with Orlando, like a cat with a mouse. What makes this scene so fascinating to me is that as Ganymede questions Orlando, challenges him to prove his love, you can feel the wall between Rosalind and Ganymede drop. I love that moment in Shakespeare's plays. When the identities and false identities become a morass of emotion. Both characters feel it here. It gets very charged. Let's see how you two do."

The scene opens with Rosalind/Ganymede/me asking Orlando/Drew where he's been, why he's taken so long to come see me—I'm "pretending" to be Rosalind. That's the gimmick. Rosalind has been pretending to be Ganymede, who must now pretend to be Rosalind. And she tries to talk Orlando out of loving Rosalind, even though she really *is* Rosalind and even though she really does love him back. Trying to keep track of all the pretending makes my head spin.

Drew/Orlando replies that he came within an hour of his promised time. I say to be even an hour late when you've made a promise in love's name puts in question whether you're truly in love. He begs my forgiveness. We banter a bit more, and then I, as Rosalind as Ganymede feigning Rosalind, ask, "What would you say to me now, an I were your very very Rosalind?"

Drew pauses, and I find that I'm waiting, holding my breath, even, for his answer.

And then he replies, "I would kiss before I spoke."

Drew's eyes are blue, nothing like *his*, but for a second, it's his dark eyes I see. Electric and charged, right before he kissed me.

I'm kind of rattled as I deliver my next lines, advising Orlando that he should speak before he kisses. We go back and forth, and when we get to the part when Orlando says he would marry me—her—I don't know about Rosalind, but I'm feeling dizzy. Luckily, Rosalind has more grit than I do. She, as Ganymede, says, "Well, in her person, I say I will not have you."

Then Drew says, "Then in mine own person I die."

And then something in me just comes undone. I can't find the right line or the right page. And I seem to have lost something else too. My grip on myself, on this place. On time. I'm not sure how much of it elapses while I stand there frozen. I hear Drew clear his throat, waiting for me to say my next line. I hear Professor Glenny shift in his chair. Drew whispers my line to me, and I repeat it and somehow manage to regain my bearings. I continue to question Orlando. Continue to ask him to prove his love. But I am no longer acting, no longer pretending.

"Now tell me how long you would have her after you have possessed her?" I ask as Rosalind. My voice no longer sounds like mine. It is rich and resonant with emotion—full of the questions I should've asked back when I had the chance.

He answers, "For ever and a day."

All the breath whooshes out of me. This is the answer that I need. Even if it doesn't happen to be true.

I try to read the next line, but I can't speak. I can't breathe. I hear a roar of wind in my ears and blink to stop the words from dancing all over the page. After a few moments, I manage to choke out the next sentence, "Say 'a day' without the 'ever,'" before my voice breaks.

Because Rosalind understands. *Say a day without the ever.* That after the one day comes heartbreak. No wonder she won't tell him who she truly is.

I feel the hot tears in my eyes and through their veil see the class, silent, gaping at me. I drop my book to the floor and bolt toward the door. I run out into the hallway, past the classrooms, and into the ladies' room. Crouching in a corner stall, I gulp deep breaths and listen to the hum of the fluorescent lights, trying desperately to push back against this hollowness that threatens to swallow me alive.

I have a full life. How can I be this empty? Because of *one* guy? Because of *one* day? But as I hold back my tears, I see the days before Willem. I see myself with Melanie at school, feeling all cocooned and smug, gossiping about girls we didn't bother to get to know or, later on, on the tour, pantomiming a friendship sputtering on fumes. I see myself with my parents, at the dinner table, Mom with her ever-present calendar, scheduling dance class or SAT prep or some other enrichment activity, leafing through catalogs for a new pair of snow boots, talking at each other but not to each other. I see myself with Evan, after we slept together for the first time and he said something about how this meant we were the closest people to each other, and it had been a sweet thing to say, but it felt like something he'd gotten out of a book. Or maybe it was that I hadn't felt it because I'd begun to suspect that we'd only gotten together because Melanie had started dating his best friend. When I'd started to cry, Evan had mistaken my tears for joy, which had only made it worse. And, yet, I'd stayed with him.

I have been empty for a long time. Long before Willem entered and exited my life so abruptly.

I'm not sure how long I'm in there before I hear the squeak of the door. Then I see Dee's pink Ugg knockoffs under the stall.

"You in here?" he asks quietly.

"No."

"Can I come in?"

I unlock the stall. There's Dee, holding all my stuff.

"I'm so sorry," I tell him.

"Sorry? You were stupendous. You got a standing ovation."

"I'm sorry I didn't tell you my parents were coming. I'm sorry I lied to you. I'm sorry I bungled everything. I don't know how to be a friend. I don't know how to be anything."

"You know how to be Rosalind," he says.

"That's because I'm an expert faker." I swipe a tear with my hand. "I'm so good at faking I don't even know when I'm doing it."

"Oh, honey, have you learned nothing from these plays? Ain't such a line between faking and being." He opens his arms, and I step into them. "I'm sorry too," he says. "I might've overreacted a hair. I can be dramatic, in case you haven't noticed."

I laugh. "Really?"

Dee holds my coat, and I slip into it. "I don't like being lied to, but I do appreciate what you tried to say to me. People have never known what to make of me—not in my neighborhood, not at high school, not here—so they're always trying to figure it out and tell me what I am."

"Yeah, I know something about that."

We look at each other for a long minute. A whole lot gets said in that silence. Then Dee asks, "You wanna tell me what all that was about in there?"

And I do. So much it's squeezing my chest. I've been wanting to tell him this, everything about me, for weeks now. I nod.

Dee offers me his arm, and I loop mine through it, and we leave the bathroom as a pair of girls come in, giving us a strange look.

"Well, there was this guy . . ." I begin.

He shakes his head and gently clucks his tongue like a sweetly scolding grandmother. "There always is."

— — —

I take Dee back to my dorm. I serve him a backlog of cookies. And I tell him everything. When I finish, we've munched our way through black-and-whites and peanut butter. He wipes the crumbs off his lap and asks me if I ever thought about *Romeo and Juliet*.

"Not *everything* tracks back to Shakespeare."

"Yes it does. Did you ever think what might've happened if

they weren't so damn impatient? If maybe Romeo had stopped for a second and gotten a doctor, or waited for Juliet to wake up? Not jumped to conclusions and gone and poisoned himself thinking she was dead when she was *just sleeping*?"

"I can see you have." And I can. He's pretty worked up.

"I've seen that movie so many times, and every damn time, it's like screaming at the girl in the horror movie. *Stop. Don't go in the basement. The killer's down there.* With Romeo and Juliet, I yell, 'Don't jump to conclusions.' But do those fools ever listen to me?" He shakes his head in dismay. "I always imagine what might've happened if they'd waited. Juliet would've woken up. They'd already be married. They might've moved away, far away from the Montagues and the Capulets, gotten themselves a cute castle of their own. Decorated it up nice. Maybe it would've been like *The Winter's Tale*. By thinking Hermione was dead, Leontes had time to stop acting like a fool and then later he was so happy to find out she was alive. Maybe the Montagues and Capulets would find out later that their beloved kids weren't dead, and wasn't it stupid to feud, and everyone would be happy. Maybe it would've turned the whole tragedy into a comedy."

"*The Winter's Tale* isn't a comedy; it's a problem play."

"Oh, you hush up. You see where I'm going with this."

And I do. And maybe I hadn't thought about this with *Romeo and Juliet*, but I had briefly gone to the what-if place with me and Willem. On the train back to England and then on the flight home, I'd had second thoughts. What if something had happened to him? But both times, I'd voiced my doubts—first to Ms. Foley and then to Melanie—and both times I'd been set straight. Willem wasn't Romeo. He was *a* romeo. And I'm no Juliet. I tell Dee this. I enumerate all the examples of him being a player, beginning with the fact that he picked up a random girl on a train and, an hour later, invited her to Paris for the day.

"Normal people don't do that," I say.

"Who said anything about normal? And maybe you weren't random. Maybe you were something to him too."

"But he didn't even know *me*. I was someone else that day. I was Lulu. That's who he liked. And besides, let's pretend something did happen, he didn't ditch me. I only know his first name. He doesn't even know my name. He lives a continent away. He's irretrievably lost. How do you find someone like that?"

Dee looks at me as if the answer is obvious. "You look."

Twenty-three

NAME: Willem
NATIONALITY: Dutch
AGE: 20 as of last August
GREW UP IN AMSTERDAM.
PARENTS: Yael and Bram. Mom isn't Dutch
Mom is a naturopathic doctor
1.9 meters, which is about 6'3"; 75 kilos,
    which is about 165 pounds.
Acted with the theater troupe Guerrilla Will
    last summer

*T*his is the complete list of hard biographical facts that I have on Willem. It takes up barely a third of a page in one of my abandoned lab notebooks. When I finish, the list is like a taunt, reality's bitchslap. *You think you fell in love with someone, and* this *is what you know about him? Eight things?* And how would I find him with these eight things? Forget looking for a needle in a haystack. That's easy. At least it would stand out. I'm looking for one specific needle in a needle factory.

Eight things. It's humiliating. I stare at the page and am about to tear it out and crumple it up.

But instead, I turn the page and start writing a different list. Random things. Like the amused look on his face when I admitted I'd thought he was a kidnapper. And the way he looked at the café when he found out I was an only child and asked if I was alone. The goofy happiness as he bounded around the barge with Captain Jack. How good it felt to know that I was responsible for him looking that way. The way Paris sounded under the canal. The way it looked from the back of the bike. The way his hand felt in the crook of my hip. The fierceness in his eyes when he jumped up to help those girls in the park. The reassurance of his hand, grasping mine as we ran through the streets of Paris. The raw expression on his face at the dinner table when I'd asked him why he'd brought me there. And later, at the squat, how he looked at me and I felt so big and strong and capable and brave.

I let the memories flood me as I fill one page. Then another. And then I'm not even writing about him anymore. I'm writing about me. About all the things I felt that day, including panic and jealousy, but more about feeling like the world was full of nothing but possibility.

I fill three pages. None of what I'm writing will help me find him. But in writing, I feel good—no, not just good, but full. Right, somehow. It's a feeling I haven't experienced in a long, long time, and it's this more than anything that convinces me to look for him.

— — —

The most concrete thing on the list is Guerrilla Will, so I start there. They have a bare-basics website, which gets me pretty excited—until I see how out of date it is. It's advertising plays from two summers ago. But still, there's a contact tab with an email address. I spend hours composing ten different emails and then finally just delete them in favor of a simple one:

> Hello:
> I am trying to find a Dutch guy named Willem, age
> 20, who performed in last summer's run of Twelfth
> Night. I saw it and met him, in Stratford-upon-
> Avon, and went to Paris with him last August. If
> anyone knows where he is, please tell him that
> Lulu, also known as Allyson Healey, would like him
> to get in touch with her. This is very important.

I list all my contact info and then I pause there for a moment, imagining the ones and zeros or whatever it is that emails are made of, traveling across oceans and mountains, landing somewhere in someone's inbox. Who knows? Maybe even his.

And then I press Send.

Thirty seconds later, my inbox chimes. Could it be? Could it be that fast? That easy? Someone knows where he is. Or maybe he's been looking for me all this time.

My hand shakes as I go to my inbox. Only all that's there is the message I just sent, bounced. I check the address. I send it again. It bounces again.

"Strike one," I tell Dee before class the next day. I explain about the bounced email.

"I don't do sports metaphors, but I'm pretty sure baseball games are generally nine innings."

"Meaning?"

"Dig in for the long haul."

Professor Glenny sweeps in and starts talking about *Cymbeline*, the play we're about to start, and announcing last call for tickets for *As You Like It* before giving a brief warning to start thinking about oral presentations at the end of the year. "You can either work alone or with your partners, do a regular presentation or something more theatrical."

"We'll do theatrical," Dee whispers.

"It's the Glenny way."

And then we look at each other as if both getting the same idea. After class, we go up to the lectern where the usual coterie of groupies are simpering.

"Well, Rosalind, here to buy your *As You Like It* tickets?"

I blush. "I already bought mine. I'm actually trying to get ahold of someone I lost touch with, and I don't have very many leads, but the one I do have is through this Shakespeare troupe that I saw in Stratford-upon-Avon last year, and they have a website, but the email bounced, but I saw them do a play less than a year ago . . . "

"In Stratford-upon-Avon?"

"Yeah. But not at a theater. It was sort of an underground thing. It was called Guerrilla Will. They performed at the canal basin. They were really good. I actually ditched the RSC's *Hamlet* to watch them do *Twelfth Night*."

Professor Glenny likes this. "I see. And you've lost a Sebastian, have you?" I gasp and I blush but then I realize he's just referring to the play. "I have an old mate in the tourist bureau there. Guerrilla Will, you say?"

I nod.

"I'll see what I can dig up."

The following week, right before spring break, Professor Glenny hands me an address. "This is what my friend found. It's from police records. Apparently your Guerrilla Will friends have a habit of performing without permits, and this is from an old arrest. Not sure how current it is." I look at the address. It's for a city in England called Leeds.

"Thank you," I say.

"You're welcome. Let me know how it ends."

That night, I print out the copy of the email I sent to Guerrilla Will but then I change my mind and write a handwritten letter to Willem.

> *Dear Willem:*
>
> *I've been trying to forget about you and our day in Paris for nine months now, but as you can see, it's not going all that well. I guess more than anything, I want to know, did you just leave? If you did, it's okay. I mean it's not, but if I can know the truth, I can get over it. And if you didn't leave, I don't know what to say. Except I'm sorry that I did.*
>
> *I don't know what your response will be at getting this letter, like a ghost from your past. But no matter what happened, I hope you're okay.*

I sign Lulu and Allyson and leave all my various contact details. I put it inside an envelope and write Forward to Willem, in care of Guerrilla Will. The night before I leave for spring break, I mail it.

— — —

I spend a boring break at home. Melanie's vacation doesn't coincide with mine, and I both miss her and feel relieved not to have to see her. I hole up in my room and prop my old science books all around me and spend the time doing Facebook searches and Twitter searches and every imaginable social networking search, but it turns out, only having a first name is kind of a problem. Especially because Willem is a pretty common Dutch name. Still, I go through hundreds of pages, staring at pictures of all different Willems, but none of them are him.

I post a Facebook page as Lulu with pictures of Louise Brooks and of me. I change the status every day, to something only he'd understand. *Do you believe in accidents of the universe? Is Nutella chocolate? Is falling in love the same as being in love?* I get friend requests from New Age freaks. I get requests from perverts. I get requests from a Nutella fan club in Minnesota (who knew?). But nothing from him.

I try searching for his parents. I do combination searches: Willem, Bram, Yael and then just Bram, Yael. But without a last name, I get nothing. I search every Dutch naturopathic site I can find for a Yael but come up with nothing. I Google the name Yael, and it's a Hebrew name. Is his Mom Jewish? Israeli? Why didn't I think to ask him any of these questions when I had the chance? But I know why. Because when I was with him, I felt like I already knew him.

Twenty-four

Spring break ends, and in Shakespeare class we start read-ing *Cymbeline*. Dee and I are halfway through, at the really juicy part where Posthumus, Imogen's husband, sees Iachimo with the secret bracelet that he gave Imogen and decides this is proof that she cheated on him, though of course, the brace-let was stolen by Iachimo, precisely so he could win his bet with Posthumus that he could get Imogen to cheat.

"Another jumped conclusion," Dee says, looking at me pointedly.

"Well, he did have good reason to suspect," I say. "Iachimo totally knew things about her, what her bedroom looked like, that she had a mole on her boob."

"Because he spied on her when she was sleeping," Dee says. "There was an explanation."

"I know. I know. Just like you say there might be a good explanation for Willem disappearing. But you know, sometimes you do have accept the evidence at face value. In one day, I saw Willem flirt with, get undressed by, and get a telephone number from a minimum of three girls, not counting me. That says 'player' to me. And I got played."

"For a player, boy talked a lot about falling in love."

"Falling in love, not being in love," I say. "And with Céline." Though when he spoke of his parents, of being stained, I recall the look on his face, one of unmasked yearning. And then I feel the heat on my wrist, as if his saliva were still wet there.

"Céline," Dee says, snapping his fingers. "The hottie French girl."

"She wasn't *that* hot."

Dee rolls his eyes. "Why didn't we think of this? What's the name of the club she worked at? Where you left your bag?"

"I have no idea."

"Okay. Where was it?"

"Near the train station."

"Which train station?"

I shrug. I've sort of blocked it all out.

Dee grabs my laptop. "Now you're just being ornery." He taps away. "If you came from London, you arrived at Gare du Nord." He pronounces it Gary du Nord.

"Aren't you clever?"

He pulls up Google Maps and then types something in. A cluster of red flags appear. "There."

"What?"

"Those are the nightclubs near Gare du Nord. You call them. Presumably Céline works in one of them. Find her, find him."

"Yeah, maybe in the same bed."

"Allyson, you just said you had to have your eyes wide open."

"I do. I just don't ever want to see Céline again."

"How bad do you want to find him?" Dee asks.

"I don't know. I guess, more than anything, I want to find out what happened."

"All the more reason to call this Céline person."

"So I'm supposed to call all these clubs and ask for her? You forget, I don't speak French."

"How hard can it be?" He stops and arranges his face into a puckered expression. "*Bon lacroix monsoir oui, tres, chic chic croissant French Ho-bag.*" He smirks. "See? Easy peasy lemon squeezy."

"Is that French too?"

"No, that's Latin. And you can ask for the other guy too, the African."

The Giant. Him I wouldn't mind talking to, but of course, I don't even know his name.

"You do it. You're better at all that than me."

"What you on about? I studied Spanish."

"I just mean you're better at voices, pretending."

"I've seen you do Rosalind. And you spent a day playing Lulu, and you're currently masquerading as a pre-med student to your parents."

I look down, pick at my nail. "That just makes me a liar."

"No it doesn't. You're just trying on different identities, like everyone in those Shakespeare plays. And the people we pretend at, they're already in us. That's why we pretend them in the first place."

— — —

Kali is taking first-year French, so I ask her, as casually as possible, how one might ask for Céline or a Senegalese bartender whose brother lives in Rochester. At first she looks at me, shocked. It's probably the first time I've asked her something more involved than "Are these socks yours?" since school started.

"Well, that would *depend* on lots of *factors*," she says. "Who *are* these people? What is your *relationship* to them? French is a language of *nuance*."

"Um, can't they just be people I'm wanting to get on the phone?"

Kali narrows her eyes at me, turns back to her work. "Try an *online* translation program."

I take a deep breath, sigh out a gust. "Fine. They are, respectively, a total bitchy beauty and a really nice guy I met once. They both work at some Parisian night club, and I feel like they might hold the key to my . . . my happiness. Does that help you with your nuance?"

Kali closes her textbook and turns to me. "Yes. And no." She grabs a piece of paper and taps it against her chin. "Do you happen to *know* the brother from *Rochester*'s name?"

I shake my head. "He told it to me once, really fast. Why?"

She shrugs. "Just seems if you *had* it, you could *track* him down in Rochester and *then* find his brother."

"Oh, my God, I didn't even think of that. Maybe I can remember it and try that too. Thank you."

"*Amazing* things happen when you *ask* for help." She gives me a pointed look.

"Do you want to know the whole story?"

Her raised eyebrow says *Do pigs like mud?*

So I tell her, Kali, the unlikeliest of confidantes, a brief version of the saga.

"Oh. My. God. So *that* explains it."

"Explains what?"

"Why you have been such a *loner*, always saying *no* to us. We thought you *hated* us."

"What? No! I don't hate you. I just felt like a reject and felt so bad you guys got stuck with me."

Kali rolls her eyes. "I broke up with my *boyfriend* right before I *got* here, and Jenn split with her *girlfriend*. Why do you think I have so many pictures of *Buster*? *Everyone* was feeling sad and homesick. That's why we *partied* so much."

I shake my head. I didn't know. I didn't think to know. And then I laugh. "I've had the same best friend since I was seven. She's the only girlfriend I've ever really hung out with, so it's like I missed the integral years of learning how to be friends with people."

"You missed *nothing*. Unless you missed *kindergarten* too."

I stare at her helplessly. Of course I went to kindergarten.

"If you went to *kindergarten*, you learned how to make *friends*. It's like the *first* thing they teach you." She stares at me. "To *make* a friend . . ." she begins.

"You have to *be* a friend," I finish, remembering the saying I was taught in Mrs. Finn's class. Or maybe it was from *Barney*.

She smiles as she picks up the pen. "I think it'll be *simpler* if you just ask for this *Céline* chick and the *bartender* from Senegal, leave out the *brother*, because how many Senegalese *bartenders* are there? Then if you get the *bartender*, you can ask if he has a *brother* in Rochester."

"Roché Estair," I correct. "That's what he called it."

"I can *see* why. It sounds much *classier* that way. Here." She hands me a piece of paper. *Je voudrais parler à Céline ou au barman qui vient du Senegal, s'il vous plait.* She has written both the French and the phonetic translations. "That's how you ask for them in *French*. If you want *help* making the calls, let me *know*. *Friends* do that."

Je voudrais parler à Céline ou au barman qui vient du Senegal, s'il vous plait. One week later, I've uttered this phrase so many times—first to practice, then in a series of increasingly depressing phone calls—that I swear I'm saying it in my sleep. I make twenty-three phone calls. *Je voudrais parler à Céline ou au barman qui vient du Senegal, s'il vous plait.* . . . That's what I say. And then one of three things happens: One, I get hung up on. Two, I get some form of *non*—and then hung up on. Those I cross off the list, a definitive no. But three is when the people launch into turbo-French, to which I am helpless to respond. *Céline? Barman? Senegal?* I repeat into the receiver, the words sinking like defective life rafts. I have no idea what these people are saying. Maybe they're saying Céline and the Giant are at lunch but will be back soon. Or maybe they're saying that Céline is here but she's downstairs having sex with a tall Dutchman.

I take Kali up on her offer of help, and sometimes she can suss out that there is no Céline, no Senegalese bartender, but more often than not, she's as baffled as I am. Meanwhile, she and Dee start Googling every potential Senegalese name in Rochester. We make a few embarrassing calls but come up empty.

After the twenty-fourth miserable phone call, I run out of nightclubs anywhere in the vicinity of Gare du Nord. Then I remember the name of the band on the T-shirt Céline had in the club, the one she gave to Willem—and me. I Google Sous ou Sur and look up all their tour dates. But if they played at Céline's nightclub, it was a long time ago, because now they're apparently broken up.

By this point, more than three weeks have passed since I mailed my letter, so I'm losing hope on that front too. The chances of finding him, never all that great, dim. But the strangest thing is, that feeling of rightness, it doesn't. If anything, it grows brighter.

— — —

"How's your search for Sebastian going?" Professor Glenny calls after class one day as we're lining up to get our *Cymbeline* papers back. The groupies all look at me with envy. Ever since I told him about Guerrilla Will, he has a newfound respect for me. And, of course, he's always loved Dee.

"Sort of dried up," I tell him. "No more leads."

He grins. "Always more leads. What is it the detectives in film always say? 'Gotta think outside the box.'" He says the last part in a terrible New York accent. He hands me my paper. "Nice work."

I look at the paper, at the big red A minus on it, and feel a huge rush of pride. As Dee and I walk to our next classes, I keep peeking at it, to make sure it doesn't shape-shift into a C, though I know it won't. I still can't stop looking. And grinning. Dee catches me and laughs.

"For some of us, these A grades are novel," I say.

"Oh, cry me a river. See you at four?"

"I'll be counting the moments."

When Dee comes in at four, he's bouncing off the walls. "Never mind thinking outside the box—we got to look inside the box." He holds up two DVDs from the media center. The title on one reads *Pandora's Box,* and there's a picture of a beautiful woman with sad, dark eyes and a sleek helmet of black hair. I immediately know who she is.

"How are these going to help us?"

"I don't know. But when you open up Pandora's Box, you never know what's gonna fly out. We can watch them tonight. After I get off work."

I nod. "I'll make popcorn."

"I'll take some leftover cakes from the dining hall."

"We know how to party on a Friday night."

Later, as I'm getting ready for Dee, I see Kali in the lounge. She looks at the popcorn. "Having a *snack attack?*"

"Dee and I are watching some movies." I've never invited Kali anywhere. And she almost always goes out on weekend nights. But I think of the help she's offered, and what she said about being a friend, and so I invite her to join us. "It's sort of a movie/fact-finding mission. We could use your help. You were so smart with your idea of trying to find the brother in Rochester."

Her eyes widen. "I'd *love* to help. I'm so *over* keg parties. Jenn, wanna watch a *movie* with *Allyson* and *Dee?*"

"Before you say yes, be warned, they're silent movies."

"Cool," Jenn says. "I've never seen one before."

Neither have I, and turns out to be a little like watching Shakespeare. You have to adjust to it, to get into a rhythm.

There are no words, but it's not like a foreign film, either, where all the dialogue is subtitled. Only major pieces of dialogue are shown with words. The rest you sort of have to figure out from the actors' expressions, from the context, from the swell of the orchestral music. You have to work a little bit.

We watch all of *Pandora's Box*, which is about a beautiful party girl named Lulu, who goes from man to man. First she marries her lover, then shoots him on the eve of her wedding. She's tried for murder but escapes jail, going into exile with her murdered husband's son. She winds up sold into prostitution. It ends with her getting killed on Christmas Eve, by Jack the Ripper, no less. We all watch it like you'd watch a slow-motion train wreck.

After we finish, Dee pulls out the next one, *Diary of a Lost Girl*. "This one's a comedy," he jokes.

It's not quite as bad. Lulu, though she's not called that in this one, doesn't die in the end. But she does get seduced, have a baby out of wedlock, get the baby taken away from her, wind up cast out and dumped in a horrible reform school. She too dabbles in prostitution.

It's almost two in the morning when we flick on the lights. We all look at each other, bleary-eyed.

"So?" Jenn asks.

"I like her *outfits*," Kali says.

"The outfits were indeed extraordinary, but not exactly enlightening." Dee turns to me. "Any clues?"

I look around. "I got nothin'." And really, I don't. All this time, I've been thinking I was like Lulu. But I'm *nothing* like the girl in those movies. I wouldn't want to be.

Jenn yawns and opens a laptop and pulls up a page on

Louise Brooks, who apparently had a life as tumultuous as Lulu's, going from A-list movie star to a shopgirl at Saks, winding up a kept woman, and finally a recluse. "But it says here she was always a rebel. She always did things her own way. And she had a lesbian affair with Greta Garbo!" Jenn smiles at that.

Kali grabs the computer and reads. "Also, she *pioneered* the short bobbed haircut."

"My hair was cut into a bob when we met. I probably should've mentioned that."

Kali puts the computer down and takes my hair out of its ponytail and folds it up to my chin. "Hmm. With your hair *bobbed*, you *do* sort of look like her."

"Yeah, that's what he said. That I looked like her."

"If he saw you that way," Jenn says, "it means he thought you were very beautiful."

"Yeah. Maybe. Or maybe this is all some game to him. Or calling me Lulu was a way to distance me, so he never had to learn anything about me." But as I throw out the less romantic scenarios—and let's be honest, the more likely ones—I don't feel that usual clutch of shame and humiliation. With these guys at my back, nothing feels quite so fraught.

Kendra's staying over at Jeb's, so Kali offers her bed to Dee, and she crashes on Kendra's bed. When all of us nestle under our covers, we call out good night to each other, like we're in summer camp or something, and I feel that sense of rightness, stronger than ever.

Dee starts snoring straightaway, but it takes me a long time to drift off, because I'm still wondering about Lulu. Maybe it was just a name. Maybe it was just pretend. But at some point, it stopped being pretend. Because for that day, I really did become Lulu. Maybe not the Lulu from the film or the real Louise Brooks, but my own idea of what Lulu represented. Freedom. Daring. Adventure. Saying yes.

I realize it's not just Willem I'm looking for; it's Lulu, too.

Twenty-five

*M*om and Dad are waiting for me at my gate in the Miami airport, Mom having arranged for their flight to get in a half hour before mine. I'd hoped I might have gotten out of this year's Passover Seder. I just saw Mom and Dad for spring break a few weeks ago, and coming down for Seder means taking a day off from school. But no such luck. Tradition is tradition, and Passover is the one time of year we go to Grandma's.

I love Grandma, and even if the Seders are always mind-numbingly dull and you take your life in your own hands eating so much of Grandma's home cooking, that's not why I dread them.

Grandma makes Mom crazy, which means that whenever we're visiting, Mom makes *us* crazy. When Grandma visits us at home, it's dealable. Mom can get away, go vent to Susan, play tennis, organize the calendar, go to the mall to buy me a new wardrobe I don't need. But when we're at Grandma's old-people condo in Miami Beach, it's like being trapped on a geriatric island.

Mom starts in on me at the baggage claim, sniping at me for not sending thank-you notes out for my birthday presents, which means she must have asked Grandma and Susan if they'd gotten theirs. Because other than Jenn and Kali—who baked me a cake—and Dee—who took me out to his favorite food truck in Boston for dinner—and Mom and Dad, of course, there was no one else to send thank-you cards to this year. Melanie didn't send anything. She just posted a greeting on my Facebook page.

Once we get into a cab (the second one, Mom having rejected the first one because the AC was too weak—no one is safe from Mom when she's on a Grandma trajectory)—she starts in on me about my summer plans.

Back in February, when she first brought this up, asking what I was going to do over the summer, I told her I had no idea. Then, a few weeks later, at the end of spring break, she announced that she had made some inquiries on my behalf and used some connections and now had two promising offers. One is working in a lab at one of the pharmaceutical companies near Philadelphia. The other is working in one of Dad's doctor friend's offices, a proctologist named Dr. Baumgartner (Melanie used to call him Dr. Bum-Gardner). Neither job would be paid, she explained, but she and Dad had discussed it and decided they'd counter the loss with a generous allowance. She looked so pleased with herself. Both jobs would look excellent on my résumé, would go a long way toward offsetting what she referred to as the "debacle" of my first term.

I'd been so irritated, I'd almost told her that I couldn't

take those internships because I wasn't qualified; I wasn't pre-med. Just to spite her. Just to see the look on her face. But then I'd gotten scared. I was getting an A in Shakespeare Out Loud. An A minus in Mandarin, which was a first for me. A solid B in my biology class and labs, and an A in ceramics. I realized I was actually proud of how well I was doing in my classes and I didn't want Mom's inevitable and perennial disappointment to poison that. But that was going to happen no matter what, though I was sticking to my plan A—to show her my final grades when I made the announcement.

But finals are still three weeks away, and Mom is breathing down my neck right now about these jobs. So as we pull into Grandma's high-rise, I tell her that I'm still mulling it over and then I skip out of the cab to help Dad with the bags.

It's so strange. Mom is the most formidable person I know, but when Grandma opens the door, Mom seems to shrink, as if Grandma is some ogre instead of a five-foot bottle blonde in a yellow tracksuit and a KISS THE MESHUGGENEH COOK apron. Grandma grabs me in a fierce hug that smells of Shalimar and chicken fat. "*Ally!* Let me look at you! You're doing something different with your hair! I saw the pictures on Facebook."

"You're on Facebook?" Mom asks.

"Ally and I are friends, aren't we?" She winks at me.

I see Mom wince. I'm not sure if it's because Grandma and I are FB friends or because Grandma insists on shortening my name.

We step inside. Grandma's boyfriend, Phil, is asleep on the big floral couch. A basketball game blares from the giant television.

Grandma touches my hair. It's to my shoulders now. I haven't cut it since last summer. "It was shorter before," I say. "It's sort of in between."

"It's better than it was. That bob was awful!" Mom says.

"It was a bob, Mom. Not a Mohawk."

"I know what it was. But it made you look like a boy."

I turn to Grandma. "Was she traumatized by a bad haircut in her youth? Because she seems unwilling to let this go."

Grandma claps her hands. "Oh, Ally, you might be right. When she was ten, she saw *Rosemary's Baby* and begged me to take her to the children's beauty parlor. She kept making the lady go shorter until it was all off, and as we were leaving the salon, another mother pointed Ellie out to her son and said, 'Why don't you get a haircut like that nice little boy?'" She looks at Mom, smiling. "I didn't realize that still upset you, Ellie."

"It doesn't upset me, because it never happened, Mother. I never saw *Rosemary's Baby*. And if I had, at ten, that would've been entirely inappropriate, by the way."

"I can show you the pictures!"

"That won't be necessary."

Grandma eyes Mom's hair. "You might think of trying that pixie again now. I think you've been wearing the same style since Bill Clinton was president." Grandma gives another wicked grin.

Mom seems to shrink another inch as she touches her hair—straight, brown, in a low ponytail. Grandma leaves her like that, pulling me into the kitchen. "You want some cookies? I have some macaroons."

"Macaroons are not cookies, Grandma. They're coconut cookie substitutes. And they're disgusting." Grandma doesn't keep anything in the house with flour during Passover.

"Let's see what else I have." I follow Grandma into the kitchen. She pours me some of her diet lemonade. "Your mom is having such a hard time," Grandma says. When Mom's out of sight, she's sympathetic, almost defending her, like I was the one who riled her up.

"I don't see why. She has a charmed life."

"Funny, that's what she says about you whenever she thinks you're being ungrateful." Grandma opens the oven door to check on something. "She's having a hard time adjusting, with you being gone. You're all she's got."

I feel a pit in my stomach. Another way I've let Mom down.

Grandma puts out a plate of those gross jelly candies I can never resist. "I told her she should have another child, give her something to do with herself."

I spit out my lemonade. "She's forty-seven."

"She could adopt." Grandma waves her hand. "One of those Chinese orphans. Lucy Rosenbaum got a cute one as a granddaughter."

"They're not dogs, Grandma!"

"I know that. Still, she could get an older one. It's a real mitzvah then."

"Did you tell Mom that?"

"Of course I did."

Grandma always brings up things the rest of us don't. Like she lights a memorial candle on the anniversary of when Mom had her miscarriage all those years ago. This, too, drives Mom crazy.

"She needs to do something if she's not going back to work." She glances out toward the living room. I know Mom and Grandma fight about Mom not working. Once, Grandma sent a clipping from a news magazine about how badly the ex-wives of doctors fared financially in the event of divorce. They didn't speak for months after that.

Mom comes into the kitchen. She glances at the jelly candy. "Mother, can you feed her some real food, please?"

"Oh, cool your jets. She can feed herself. She's nineteen now." She winks at me, then turns to Mom. "Why don't you take some cold cuts out?"

Mom pokes in Grandma's refrigerator. "Where's the brisket? It's almost two now. We should put it in soon."

"Oh, it's already cooking," Grandma says.

"What time did you put in?"

"Don't you worry. I got a nice recipe from the paper."

"How long has it been in?" Mom peeks in the oven. "It's not that big. It shouldn't take longer than three hours. And you have to cover it in foil. Also you have the heat way up. Brisket's meant to slow-cook. We're starting the Seder at five? When did it go in?"

"Never you mind."

"It'll be like leather."

"Do I tell you how to cook in your kitchen?"

"Yes. All the time. But I don't listen. And we've dodged many a case of food poisoning because of it."

"Enough of your smart mouth."

"I think I'll go change," I announce. But neither one is paying attention to me anymore.

I go into the spare room and find Dad hiding in there, looking wistfully at a golf shirt. "What are the chances I can escape for a round?"

"You'd have to throw down some plagues at the Pharaoh first." I look out the window to the silver-blue strip of sea.

He puts the golf shirt back in the suitcase. How quickly we all give in to her. This Seder means nothing to him. Dad's not even Jewish, though he celebrates all the holidays with Mom. Grandma was supposedly furious when Mom got engaged to him, though after Grandpa died, she took up with Phil, who's not Jewish, either.

"I was just kidding," I say, even though I wasn't. "Why don't you just go?"

Dad shakes his head. "Your mom needs backup."

I scoff, as if Mom needs anything from anyone.

Dad changes the subject. "We saw Melanie last weekend."

"Oh, really?"

"Her band had a gig in Philadelphia, so she made a rare appearance."

She's in a *band* now? So she can become Mel 4.0—and I'm supposed to stay reliably me? I smile tightly at my dad, pretending like I know this.

"Frank, I can't find my Seder plate," Grandma calls. "I had it out for a polish."

"Just visualize the last place you had it," Dad says. Then he gives me a little shrug and heads off to help. After the Seder plate is located, he helps Grandma get down serving bowls, and then I hear Mom tell him to keep Phil company, so he sits and watches the basketball with napping Phil. So much for golf. I go out onto the balcony and listen to the competing sounds of Mom and Grandma's bickering and the game on the TV. My life feels so small it itches, like a too-tight wool sweater.

"I'm going for a walk," I announce, even though there's no one on the balcony but me. I put on my shoes and slip out the door and walk down to the beach. I take off my shoes and run up and down the shore. The rhythmic beat of my feet on the wet sand seems to churn something out of me, pushing it through the sweat on my sticky skin. After a while, I stop and sit down and look out over the water. On the other side is Europe. Somewhere over there is him. And somewhere over there, a different version of me.

— — —

When I get back, Mom tells me to shower and set the table. At five, we sit down, settling in for a long night of reenacting the Jews' escape from slavery in ancient Egypt, which is supposed to be an act of liberation, but somehow with Mom and Grandma glowering at each other, it always winds up feeling just like more oppression. At least the adults can get drunk. You have to down, like, four glasses of wine during the night. I, of course, get grape juice, in my own crystal carafe. At least I usually do. This time when I go to drink my first sip of juice after the first blessing, I almost choke. It's wine. I think it's a mistake, except Grandma catches my eye and winks.

The Seder carries on as usual. Mom, who, in every other part of her life, is respectful, assumes the mantle of rebellious teenager. When Grandma reads the part about the Jews wandering through the desert for forty years, Mom cracks it's because Moses was a man who refused to ask directions. When the talk to turns to Israel, Mom harps on about politics, even though she knows this gets Grandma crazy. When we eat matzo-ball soup, they argue about the cholesterol content of matzo balls.

Dad knows enough to keep quiet. And Phil plays with his hearing aids and dozes in and out of consciousness. I refill my "juice" glass many, many times.

After two hours, we get to the brisket, which means we get to stop talking about Exodus for a while, which is a relief, even if the brisket isn't. It's so dry it looks like beef jerky and tastes charred. I move it around my plate, while Grandma chitchats about her bridge club and the cruise she and Phil are taking. Then she asks about our annual summer trip to Rehoboth Beach, which she usually comes up for a portion of.

"What else do you have planned for the summer?" she asks me casually.

It's a throwaway question, really. Along the lines of *how are you*? Or *what's new*? I'm about to say, "Oh, this and that," when Mom interrupts to say that I'm working in a lab. Then she tells Grandma all about it. A research lab at a pharmaceutical company. Apparently, I accepted the position just today.

It's not like I didn't know she would do this. It's not like she hasn't done this my entire life. It's not like I haven't let her.

The fury that fills me feels hot and cold, liquid and metal, coating my insides like a second skeleton, one stronger than my own. Maybe this is what allows me to say, "I'm not working in a lab this summer."

"Well, it's too late," Mom snaps back. "I already called Dr. Baumgartner to decline his offer. If you'd had a preference, you had three weeks to make it known."

"I'm not working at Dr. Baumgartner's, either."

"Did you line up something else?" Dad asks.

Mom scoffs, as if that's unthinkable. And maybe it is. I've never had a job. Never had to get one. Never had to do anything for myself. I am helpless. I am a void. A disappointment. My helplessness, my dependency, my passivity, I feel it whorling into a little fiery ball, and I harness that ball, somewhere wondering how something made of weakness can feel so strong. But the ball grows hotter, so hot, the only thing I can do with it is hurl it. At her.

"I don't think your lab would want me anymore, given that I've dropped most of my science courses and am going to drop the rest of them come fall," I say, spite dripping from my voice. "See, I'm not pre-med anymore. So sorry to *disappoint* you."

My sarcasm hangs in the humid air—and then, like a vapor, it floats away as I realize that, for the first time in my life, I'm *not* sorry to disappoint her. Maybe it's the spite talking, or maybe Grandma's secret wine, but I'm almost glad of it. I'm so tired of avoiding the unavoidable, because I feel like I've been disappointing her for such a long time.

"You've dropped pre-med?" Her voice is quiet, that lethal mix of fury and woundedness that could always take me down like a bullet to the heart.

"That was always *your* dream, Ellie," Grandma says, shielding me. She turns to me. "You still haven't answered my question, Ally. What are *you* doing this summer?"

Mom is looking so fragile and so angry, and I feel my will starting to break, feel myself starting to give in. But then I hear a voice—my voice—announcing this:

"I'm going back to Paris."

It comes out, as if the idea were fully formed, something plotted for months, when in fact, it just slipped out, the same way all those admissions to Willem did. But when it does, I feel a thousand pounds lighter, my anger now fully dissipated, replaced by exhilaration flowing through me like sunlight and air.

This is how I felt that day in Paris with Willem. And *this* is how I know that it's the right thing to do.

"Also, I'm learning French," I add. And for some reason, this announcement makes the table erupt into pandemonium. Mom starts screaming at me about lying to her and throwing my whole future away. Dad is yelling about switching majors and who's going to pay for my exchange program to Paris. Grandma is yelling at Mom for ruining yet another Seder.

So with all the commotion, it's a little strange that anyone can hear Phil, who has barely said a word since the soup, when he pipes up, "*Back* to Paris, Ally? I thought Helen said your trip to Paris got canceled because they were striking." He shakes his head. "They always seem to be striking over there."

The table goes silent. Phil picks up a piece of matzo and starts munching on it. Mom, Dad, and Grandma all stare at me.

I could so easily cover this up. Phil's hearing aid was turned down. He heard wrong. I could say that I want to go *to* Paris because I never made it there on the last trip. I've told so many lies. What's one more?

But I don't want to lie. I don't want to cover up. I don't want to pretend anymore. Because that day with Willem, I may have pretended to be someone named Lulu, but I had never been more honest in my life.

Maybe that's the thing with liberation. It comes at a price. Forty years wandering through the desert. Or incurring the wrath of two very pissed-off parents.

I take a breath. I brave up.

"*Back* to Paris," I say.

Twenty-six

MAY

Home

I make a new list.

- Airfare to Paris: $1200
- French class at community college: $400
- Spending money for two weeks in Europe: $1000.

All together that's $2,600. That's how much money I'll need to save to get to Europe. Mom and Dad are not helping with the trip, obviously, and they're refusing to let me use any of the money in my savings account, from gifts through the years, because that's supposed to be for educational purposes, and they're the trustees on the account, so I can't argue. Besides, it's only through Grandma's intervention, coupled with my threat to go live at Dee's for the summer that Mom has even agreed to let me live at home. She's that mad. She's that mad without even knowing the entire story. I told them

I went to Paris. I didn't tell them why. Or with whom. Or why I need to go back, except that I left something important there—they think it's the suitcase.

I'm not sure what infuriates her more. Last summer's deceit or the fact that I won't tell her everything about it. She refused to speak to me after the Seder and then four weeks went by with barely a word from her. Now that I'm back home for the start of the summer she basically avoids me. Which is both a relief and also kind of scary, because she's never done anything like this before.

Dee says that twenty-six hundred dollars is a lot for two months, but not impossible. He suggests skipping the French class. But I feel like I need to do that. I've always wanted to learn French. And I'm not going back to Paris—not facing down Céline—without it.

So, twenty-six hundred bucks. Doable. If I get a job. But the thing is, I've never had a job before. Nothing remotely job-like, beyond babysitting and filing at Dad's office, which hardly fills the spiffy new résumé that I've printed on beautiful card stock. Maybe this explains why, after dropping it off at every business in town with a job opening, I get zero response.

I decide to sell my clock collection. I take them to an antique dealer in Philadelphia. He offers me five hundred bucks for the lot. I've easily spent double that on the clocks over the years, but he just looks at me and says that maybe I'll do better on eBay. But that would take months, and I just want to be rid of them. So I hand over the clocks, except for a Betty Boop one, which I send to Dee.

When Mom finds out what I've done, she shakes her head

with such profound disgust, like I have just sold my body, not my clocks. The disapproval intensifies. It wafts through the house like a radiation cloud. Nowhere is safe to hide.

I *have* to get a job. Not just to earn the money but to get out of this house. Escaping to Melanie's isn't an option. Number one, we're not speaking, and number two, she's at a music program in Maine for the first half of summer—this according to my dad.

"You just gotta keep trying," Dee advises when I call him for job advice from our landline. As part of my punishment, my cell phone has been turned off, and the family Internet password protected, so I have to ask them to log me onto the web or else go to the library. "Drop your résumé at every business in town, not just the ones saying they're hiring, 'cause usually places that are desperate enough to hire someone like you don't have time to advertise."

"Thanks a lot."

"You want a job? Swallow your pride. And drop off a résumé everywhere."

"Even the car wash?" I joke.

"Yeah. Even the car wash." Dee isn't kidding. "And ask to speak to the manager of the car wash and treat him like the King of All Car Washes."

I imagine myself scrubbing hubcaps. But then I think of Dee, working in a pillow factory this summer or hosing off dishes in the dining hall. He does what he has to do. So the next day, I print out fifty new résumés and just go door to door, from bookstore to sewing shop to grocery store, CPA firm to the liquor store to, yes, the car wash. I don't just drop my résumé. I ask to speak to managers. Sometimes the managers come out. They ask me about my experience. They ask me how long I want to be employed for. I listen to my own answers: No real job experience to speak of. Two months. I get why nobody's hiring me.

I'm almost out of résumés when I pass by Café Finlay. It's a small restaurant on the edge of town, all done up in 1950s décor, with black-and-white-checked floors and a mishmash of Formica tables. Every other time I've gone past, it seemed to be closed.

But today music is blasting from inside so loud the windows are vibrating. I push the door, and it nudges open. I shout "hello." No one replies. The chairs are all stacked up on the tables. There's a pile of fresh linens on one of the booths. Yesterday's specials are scrawled on a chalkboard on the wall. Things like halibut with an orange tequila jalapeño beurre blanc with kiwi fruit. Mom calls the food here "eclectic," her code for weird, which is why we've never eaten here. I don't know anyone who eats here.

"You here with the bread?"

I spin around. There's a woman, Amazon tall and just as broad, with wild red hair poking out from under a blue bandanna.

"No," I say.

"Mother*fucker*!" She shakes her head. "What do you want?" I hold out a résumé. She waves it away. "Ever work in a kitchen?" I shake my head.

"Sorry. No," she says.

She looks at the Marilyn Monroe wall clock. "I'm going to kill you, Jonas!" She shakes her fist at the door.

I turn to leave, but then I stop. "What's the bread order?" I ask. "I'll run and get it for you."

She glances at the clock again and sighs dramatically. "Grimaldi's. I need eighteen French baguettes, six loaves of the Harvest. And a couple of day-old brioche. You got that?"

"I think so."

"*Think so*'s not gonna butter the bread, honey."

"Eighteen baguettes. Six loaves of Harvest and a couple of day-old brioche."

"Make sure it's *stale* brioche. Can't make bread pudding with fresh bread. And ask for Jonas. Tell him it's for Babs and tell him he can throw in the brioche for free and knock twenty percent off the rest because his damn delivery guy was a no-show again. Also, make sure I don't get any sourdough. I hate that shit."

She grabs a wad of cash from the vintage register. I take it from her and sprint to the bakery as fast as I can, get Jonas, bark the order, and run back with it, which is harder than it sounds, carrying thirty loaves of bread.

I pant as Babs looks over the bread order. "You know how to wash dishes?"

I nod. That much I can do.

She shakes her head in resignation. "Go to the back and ask Nathaniel to introduce you to Hobart."

"Hobart?"

"Yep. You two'll be getting intimate."

Hobart turns out to be the name of the industrial dish washer, and once the restaurant opens, I spend hours with it, rinsing dishes with a giant hose, loading them in Hobart, unloading them while they're still scalding hot and repeating the whole enterprise. By some miracle, I manage to stay on top of the never-ending flow of dishes and not drop anything or burn my fingers too badly. When there's a lull, Babs orders me to cut bread or whip cream by hand (she insists it tastes better that way) or mop the floor or find the tenderloins from one of the walk-in coolers. I spend the night in an adrenaline panic, thinking I'm about to screw up.

Nathaniel, the prep cook, helps me as much as he can, telling me where things are, helping me scrub sauté pans when I get too slammed. "Just wait till the weekend," he warns.

"I thought no one ever ate here." I put my hand over my mouth, instinctually knowing Babs would be mad to hear that.

But Nathaniel just laughs. "Are you kidding? Babs is worshipped by the Philadelphia foodies. They make the trek out here just for her. She'd make way more money if she moved to Philly, but she says her dogs would hate it in the city. And by dogs, I think she means us."

When the last of the diners leave, the kitchen staff and the waiters seem to all exhale at once. Someone blasts some old Rolling Stones. A bunch of tables are pushed together and everyone sits down. It's well past midnight, and I have a long walk home. I start to pack up my things, but Nathaniel motions for me to join them. I sit at the table, feeling shy even though I've been bumping hips with these people all night.

"You want a beer?" he asks. "We have to pay for them, but only cost."

"Or you can have some of the reject wine the distributors bring by," a waitress named Gillian says.

"I'll take some wine."

"It looks like someone died on you," says one of the waiters. I look down. My nice skirt and top—my good job-hunting outfit—are covered in sauces that look vaguely like bodily fluids.

"I feel like I'm the one who died," I say. I don't think I've ever been this tired. My muscles ache. My hands are red from the near-scalding water. And my feet? Don't get me started.

Gillian laughs. "Spoken like a true kitchen slave."

Babs appears with the big bowls of steaming pasta and small chunks of leftover fish and steak. My stomach lets out a gurgle. The platters get passed around. I don't know if her cooking is "eclectic," but the food is amazing, the orange tequila jalapeño sauce is only faintly orange, and it's smoky rather than spicy. I clear my plate, and then sop up any remaining sauce with a hunk of Jonas's not-sourdough bread.

"So?" Babs asks me when I've finished.

All eyes turn to me. "It's the second best meal I've ever had," I say. Which is the truth.

Everyone else oohs, like I've just insulted Babs. But she just smirks. "I'll bet your first best was with a lover," she says, and I go as red as her hair.

Babs instructs me to return the next day at five, and the routine starts all over again. I work harder than I ever have, eat an amazing meal, and pour myself into bed. I have no idea if I'm filling in for someone or maybe being auditioned. Babs screams at me constantly, for using soap on her cast-iron sauté pan or not getting the lipstick off the coffee cups before they go into Hobart or making the whipped cream too stiff or not stiff enough or not adding the exact right amount of vanilla extract. But by the fourth night, I'm learning not to take it so personally.

On the fifth night, before the dinner rush, Babs calls me to the back near the walk-in refrigerator. She's sucking on a bottle of vodka, which is what she does before the rush begins. Her lipstick leaves smudges on the rim. For a second, I think this is it, that she's going to fire me. But instead she hands me a sheaf of documents.

"Tax forms," she explains. "I pay minimum wage, but you'll get tips. Which reminds me. You keep forgetting to collect yours." She reaches under the counter for an envelope with my name on it.

I open up the envelope. There's a wad of cash in there. Easily a hundred dollars. "This is *mine*?"

She nods. "We pool tips. Everyone gets a cut."

I run my fingers over the money. The bills snag on my ragged hangnails. My hands are beyond thrashed, but I don't care because they're thrashed from my job. Which has earned me this money. I feel something well up inside me that has nothing to do with airplane tickets or Paris trips or money at all, really.

"It'll go up in the fall," Babs says. "Summer's our slow season."

I hesitate. "That's great. Except I won't be here in the fall."

She wrinkles her red brows. "But I just broke you in."

I feel bad, guilty, but it was right there on my résumé, the first line—Objective: To obtain short-term employment. Of course, Babs never read my résumé.

"I go to college," I explain.

"We'll work around your schedule. Gillian's a student too. And Nathaniel, on and off."

"In Boston."

"Oh." She pauses. "Oh, well. I think Gordon's coming back after Labor Day."

"I'm hoping to leave by the end of July. But only if I can save two thousand dollars by then." And as I say it, I do the math. More than a hundred bucks a week in tips, plus wages—I actually might be able to pull it off.

"Saving for a car?" she asks absentmindedly. She takes another swig of her vodka. "You can buy mine. That beast'll be the death of me." Babs drives an ancient Thunderbird.

"No. I'm saving for Paris."

She puts her bottle down. "Paris?"

I nod.

"What's in Paris?"

I look at her. I think of him for the first time in a while. In the craziness of the kitchen, he became a little abstract. "Answers."

She shakes her head with such vehemence her auburn curls come loose from her bandanna. "You can't go to Paris looking for answers. You have to go looking for questions— or, at the very least, macarons."

"Macaroons? The coconut things?" I think of the gross cookie replacements we eat on Passover.

"Not macaroons. Macarons. They're meringue cookies in pastel colors. They are edible angel's kisses." She looks at me. "You need two thousand bucks by when?"

"August."

She narrows her eyes at me. They're always a little bit bloodshot, though, oddly, more so at the beginning of a shift than at the end, when they take on a sort of manic gleam. "I'll make you a deal. If you don't mind working some doubles for weekend brunch, I'll make sure you earn your two grand by July twenty-fifth, which is when I close the restaurant for two weeks for *my* summer vacation. On one condition."

"Which is?"

"Every day in Paris, you eat a macaron. They have to be fresh, so no buying a pack and eating one a day." She stops and closes her eyes. "I ate my first macaron in Paris on my honeymoon. I'm divorced now, but some loves are enduring. Especially if they happen in Paris."

A tiny chill prickles up my neck. "Do you really believe that?" I ask her.

She takes a slug of vodka, her eyes glinting knowingly. "Ahh, it's those kind of answers you're after. Well, I can't help you with that, but if you hustle into the walk-in and find the buttermilk and the cream, I can give you the answer to the proverbial question of how to make the perfect crème fraîche."

Twenty-seven

JUNE
Home

*I*ntro to French runs three days a week for six weeks, from eleven thirty to one, giving me yet another reason to be out of the House of Disapproval. Though I'm at Café Finlay five nights a week these days, and all day on weekends, on weekdays, I still don't go in until five. And the restaurant is closed on Monday and Tuesday, so there's a lot of dead time for Mom and me to avoid each other in.

On the first day of class, I arrive a half hour early and grab an iced tea from the little kiosk and find the classroom and start looking through my book. There's lots of pictures of France, many from Paris.

The other students start to filter in. I expected college kids, but everyone except me is my parents' age. One woman with frosted blond hair plops down at the desk next to mine and introduces herself as Carol and offers me a piece of gum. I gladly accept her handshake but

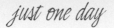

decline the gum—it doesn't seem very French to chew gum in class.

A birdlike woman with cropped gray hair strides in. She looks like she stepped out of a magazine in her tight linen pencil skirt and little silk blouse, both perfectly pressed, which seems impossible, given the ninety percent humidity outside. Plus, she's wearing a scarf, also strange, given the ninety percent humidity.

Clearly, she is French. And if the scarf wasn't a giveaway, then there's the fact that she marches up to the front of the room and starts speaking. In French.

"*Are we in the wrong class?*" Carol whispers. Then the teacher goes to the board and writes her name, Madame Lambert, and the name of the class, Intro to French. She also writes it in French. "Oh, no such luck," Carol says.

Madame Lambert turns to us and in the thickest accent imaginable tells us in English that this is beginning French, but that the best way to learn French is to speak and hear it. And that is about the only English I hear for the next hour and a half.

"*Je m'appelle Thérèse Lambert,*" she says, making it sound like this: Teh-rez. Lomb-behr. "*Comment vous appelez-vous?*"

The class stares at her. She repeats the question, gesturing to herself, then pointing to us. Still no one answers. She rolls her eyes and does this clicking with her teeth. She points to me. Clicks again, gestures for me to stand up. "*Je m'appelle Thérèse Lambert,*" she repeats, enunciating slowly and tapping her chest. "*Comment t'appelles-tu?*"

I stand there for a second frozen, feeling like it's Céline again jabbering away at me disdainfully. Madame Lambert repeats the question. I get that she's asking me my name. But I don't speak French. If I did, I wouldn't be here. In *Intro* to French.

But she's just waiting now. She's not letting me sit down.

"Je m'appelle Allyson?" I try.

She beams, as though I've just explained the origins of the French Revolution, in French. *"Bravo! Enchantée, Allyson."*

And she goes around the class asking everyone else's name the same way.

That was round one. Then comes round two: *"Pourquoi voulez-vous apprendre le français?"*

She repeats the question, writing it down on the board, circling certain words and writing their English translations. *Pourquoi*: why. *Apprendre*: learn. *Voulez-vous*: do you want. Oh, I see. She's asking why we want to learn French.

I have no clue how to begin to answer that. That's why I'm here.

But then she continues.

"Je veux apprendre le français parce que . . ." She circles *Je veux*: I want. *Parce que*: because. She repeats it three times. Then points to us.

"I can do this one. I know this word from the movie," Carol whispers. She raises her hand. *"Je veux apprendre le français parce que,"* she stumbles over the words and her accent is awful, but Madame just watches her expectantly. *"Parce que le divorce!"*

"Excellent," Madame Lambert says, only she says it in the French way, which makes it sound even more excellent. *Le divorce,* she writes on the board. *"Divorce. La même,"* she says. *The same,* she writes. Then she writes down *le mariage* and explains that this is the antonym.

Carol leans in. "When I divorced my husband, I told myself I was going to let myself get fat and I was going to learn French. If I do as well with the French as I'm doing with the fat, I'll be fluent by September!"

Madame Lambert goes around the room, and people stumble to explain why they want to learn French. Two of the people are going on vacation in France. One is going to study art history and needs some French. One thinks it's pretty. In each case, Madame writes down the word, its translation, and its opposite. Vacation: *vacances*. Work: *travail*.

I went first last time, and this time I'm last. I'm in a bit of panic by then, trying to think of what to say. How do you say *accidents* in French? Or because I think I might have made a mistake. Or *Romeo and Juliet*. Or to find a lost thing. Or because I don't want to compete, I just want to speak French. But I don't know how to say that in French. If I did, I wouldn't be here.

Then I remember Willem. The Nutella. Falling in love versus being in love. How did he say it? *Stain* in French? *Sash*? *Tache*?

"Allyson," she says. "*Pourquoi veux-tu apprendre le français?*"

"*Je veux apprendre le français*," I begin, mimicking what I've just heard everyone else say. I've got that part down. "*Parce que . . .*" I stop to think. "*Le tache*," I say finally.

It's such a weird thing to say, if that's what I've said. A stain. It doesn't make any sense. But Madame Lambert gives a stern nod and writes *la tâche* on the board. Then she writes *task*. I wonder if I remembered the word wrong. She looks at me, at my confusion. And then she writes another word on the board. *La tache*: stain.

I nod my head. Yes, that's it. She doesn't write down an opposite. There is no opposite of stain.

When we're all done, Madame smiles and claps. *"C'est courageux d'aller dans l'inconnu,"* she says, writing it down on the board. She has us write it down and deconstruct it with a dictionary. *Courageux* we get is courageous. *Dans* is into. *L'inconnu* is the unknown. *D'aller*. It takes us twenty minutes, but we finally get it: It's courageous to go into territory unknown. When we figure this out, the class is as proud as Madame.

Still, I spend the first week of class living in a state of half terror of being called on—because everyone gets called on a lot; there are only six of us, and Madame is a big fan of class participation. Whenever we get shy, she reminds us, *"C'est courageux d'aller dans l'inconnu."* Eventually, I just sort of get over myself. I blunder every time I speak, and I know I'm butchering the grammar, and my pronunciation is awful, but then we're all in the same boat. The more I do it, the less self-conscious I get and the easier it is to just try.

"I feel like a damn fool, but it might just be working," Carol says one afternoon after class.

She and I and a few of the other students have started getting together for coffee or lunch after class to practice, to recover from Madame Lambert's verbal barrages, and to deconstruct what she really means when she goes "pff" and blows air through her lips. There's a whole language in her *pff*s.

"I think I had a dream in French," Carol says. "I was telling my ex terrible things in perfect French." She grins at the memory.

"I don't know if I'm that advanced, but I'm definitely getting the hang of it," I reply. "Or maybe I'm just getting the hang of feeling like an idiot."

"*Un idiot,*" Carol says it in French. "Half the time, you add a French accent and it works. But getting over feeling like *un idiot* might just be half the battle."

I imagine myself, alone in Paris. There are so many battles I'm going to have to fight, traveling alone, facing Céline, speaking French—all of it is so daunting, some days I can't believe I'm actually even attempting it. But I think Carol might be right about this, and the more I flub and get over it in class, somehow, the better prepared I feel for the trip. Not just the French. All of it. *C'est courageux d'aller dans l'inconnu.*

— — —

At the restaurant, Babs blabs to the entire staff that I'm saving to go to Paris to meet my lover, and I'm learning French because he speaks no English, so now Gillian and Nathaniel have taken it upon themselves to tutor me. Babs is doing her part by adding a bunch of French items to the specials menu, including macarons, which apparently take hours to make, but when I eat them—oh, my God, I get what all the fuss is about. Pale pink, hard outside, but spongy and light and delicate inside, with a raspberry deliciousness filling.

In between classes, hanging with my fellow students, and being at work, I'm spending a fair amount of time, if not speaking French, then thinking about it. When Gillian buses plates into the kitchen, she'll drill me on verbs. "Eat," she'll call out. *"Je mange, tu manges, il mange, nous mangeons, vous mangez, ils mangent,"* I'll call back. Nathaniel, who doesn't actually speak French but used to have a French girlfriend, teaches me how to swear. Specifically, how to fight with your girlfriend.

T'es toujours aussi salope? Are you always such a bitch?

T'as tes règles ou quoi? Are you on the rag or what?

And *ferme ta gueule!* Which he claims means: Shut your piehole!

"They can't say 'shut your piehole' in France," I say.

"Well, maybe it's not a direct translation, but it's pretty damn close," he replies.

"But it's so crass. The French are tasteful."

"Dude, those people sainted Jerry Lewis. They're human just like you and me." He pauses, then grins. "Except for the women. They're superhuman."

I think of Céline and get a bad feeling in my stomach.

Another one of the waiters loans me his Rosetta Stone CDs, and I start practicing with those too. After a few weeks, I start to notice that my French is improving, that when Madame Lambert calls on me to describe what I'm eating for lunch, I can handle it. I start to speak in phrases, then sentences, sentences I don't have to map out beforehand like I do with Mandarin. Somehow, it's happening. I'm doing it.

— — —

One morning, toward the end of the month, I come downstairs to find Mom at the kitchen table. In front of her is the catalog from the community college and her checkbook. I say good morning and go the fridge for some orange juice. Mom just watches me. I'm about to take my juice out to the back patio, which is sort of what we've done if Dad's not home as a buffer—if she's in one room, I go into another—when she tells me to sit down.

"Your father and I have decided to reimburse you for your French class," she says, ripping off the check. "It doesn't mean we condone any part of this trip. Or condone your duplicity. We absolutely don't. But the French class is part of your education, and you're obviously taking it seriously, so you shouldn't have to pay for it."

She hands me the check. It's for four hundred dollars. It's a lot of money. But I've already saved nearly a thousand dollars, even with the money I paid for my class, and I just put a deposit down on an airplane ticket to Paris, and Babs is advancing me a week's wages so I can buy it next week. And I have a month yet to save. The four hundred dollars would take the edge off. But the thing is, maybe I don't need the edge to be off.

"It's okay," I tell Mom, handing back the check. "But thank you."

"What, you don't want it?"

"It's not that. I don't need it."

"Of course you need it," she retorts. "Paris is expensive."

"I know, but I'm saving a lot of money from my job, and I'm hardly spending anything this summer. I don't even have to pay for gas." I try to make a joke out of it."

"That's another thing. If you're going to be working until all hours, you should take the car at night."

"That's okay. I don't want to leave you stranded."

"Well, call me for a ride."

"It's late. And I usually get a lift home from someone."

She takes the check back and with a violence that surprises me, rips it up. "Well, I can't do anything for you anymore, can I?"

"What does that mean?"

"You don't want my money or my car or my ride. I tried to help you get a job, and you don't need me for that."

"I'm nineteen," I say.

"I am aware of how old you are, Allyson. I did give birth to you!" Her voice cracks like a whip, and the snap of it seems to startle even her.

Sometimes, you can only feel something by its absence. By the empty space it leaves behind. As I look at Mom, all pissed and pinched, I finally get that she's not just angry. She's hurt. A wave of sympathy washes over me, taking away a chink of my anger. Once it's gone, I realize how much of it I have. How angry I am at her. Have been for this past year. Maybe a lot longer.

"I know you gave birth to me," I tell her.

"It's just I've spent nineteen years raising you, and now I'm being shut out of your life. I can't know anything about you. I don't know what classes you're taking. I don't know who you're friends with anymore. I don't know why you're going to Paris." She lets out something between a shudder and a sigh.

"But *I* know," I tell her. "And for now, can't that be enough?"

"No, it can't," she snaps.

"Well, it'll have to be," I snap back.

"So you dictate the rules now, is that it?"

"There aren't any rules. I'm not dictating anything. I'm just saying you have to trust the job you did raising me."

"*Did*. Past tense. I wish you'd stop talking like you're laying me off from my job."

I'm startled by that, not by her thinking of me as a job, so much as by the implication that I am in a position to do the firing. "I thought you were going to go back to some kind of PR job."

"I was, wasn't I?" She guffaws. "I said I'd do it when you started middle school. When you started high school. When you got your driver's license." She rubs her eyes with the heels of her hands. "Don't you think if I'd wanted to go back, I'd have done it by now?"

"So why haven't you?"

"It wasn't what I wanted."

"What *do* you want?"

"For things to be how they were."

For some reason, this makes me angry. Because it's both true—she wants to keep me fossilized—and such a lie. "Even when things were 'how they were,' it was never enough. I was never enough."

Mom looks up, her eyes tired and surprised at the same time. "Of course you were," she says. "You are."

"You know what bothers me? How you and Dad always say you quit while you were ahead. There's *no such thing* as quitting while you're ahead. You quit while you were *behind*. That's *why* you quit!"

Mom frowns, exasperated; it's her dealing-with-a-crazy-teenager look, one I've gotten to know well this past year, my last year of actually being a teenager. Oddly enough, it wasn't something she had to zing me with much before. Which I now realize was maybe part of the problem.

"You wanted more kids," I continue. "And you had to settle for just me. And you've spent my whole life trying make me be enough."

That gets her attention. "What are you talking about? You are enough."

"No, I'm not. How can I be? I'm the one shot, the heir *and* the spare, so you have to make damn sure your one investment pays off because there's no backup."

"That's ridiculous. You're not an investment."

"You treat me like one. You've poured all your expectations into me. It's like I have to carry the load of hopes and dreams for all the kids you didn't get to have."

She shakes her head. "You don't know what you're talking about," she says in a quiet voice.

"Really? Medical school at thirteen. *Come. On!* What thirteen-year-old wants to go to medical school?"

For a moment, Mom looks likes she's been punched in the gut. Then she places her hand on her stomach, as if covering the place of impact. "*This* thirteen-year-old."

"*What?*" I'm totally confused now. But then I remember how in high school, Dad always sent me to Mom when I needed help with chem or bio, even though he was the doctor. And I can hear Mom reciting the pre-med requisites by heart when the college catalog came. And I think about the job she once had, doing public relations, but for a drug company. Then I remember what Grandma said to her at the disastrous Seder: *That was always your dream.*

"You?" I ask. "*You* wanted to be a doctor."

She nods. "I was studying for the MCATs when I met your father. He was just in his first year of medical school and somehow found the time to tutor in his spare time. I took the tests, applied to ten schools, and didn't get into one. Your father said it was because I didn't have any lab experience. So I went to work at Glaxo, and I thought I'd apply again, but then your father and I got married, and I wound up moving over to PR, and then a few years went by, and we decided to start a family, and I didn't want your father and me to both be in the midst of school and residencies with a small baby and then we had all the fertility issues. When we gave up on having another child, I quit working—because we could afford to live on your father's income. I thought about applying again, but then I discovered I liked spending time with you. I didn't want to be away from you."

My head is spinning. "You always said you and Dad were set up."

"We were. By the campus tutoring center. I never told you everything because I didn't want you to feel like I'd given up on account of you."

"You didn't want me to know you'd quit when you were behind," I clarify. Because isn't that exactly what she did do?

Mom reaches out to grab my wrists. "No! Allyson, you're wrong about quitting while you're ahead. It means being grateful. Stopping when you realize what you have is enough."

I don't entirely believe her. "If that's true, maybe you should quit while you're ahead now—before things between us get really messed up."

"Are you asking me to quit being your mother?"

At first I think the question is rhetorical, but then I see her looking at me, her eyes wide and fearful, and a little bit of my heart breaks to think she'd ever truly think that.

"No," I say quietly. There's a moment of silence as I steel myself to say the next thing. Mom stiffens, like she's maybe steeling herself too. "But I am asking you to be a different kind of mother."

She slumps back in her chair, I can't tell if it's in relief or defeat. "And what do I get out of this?"

For a brief second, I can picture us one day, having tea, me telling her all about what happened in Paris last summer, what will happen on this trip I'm about to take. One day. Just not yet.

"A different kind of daughter," I say.

Twenty-eight

I've bought my airplane ticket. I've paid for my French class, and even with both of those expenditures, I still have five hundred dollars saved by the end of a surprisingly busy and lucrative July Fourth weekend. Café Finlay closes on July 25, but unless things go disastrously in the next three weeks, I should have enough money saved by then.

Right after the Fourth of July, Melanie comes home. My parents told me she'd be back from camp for a week before heading off to a rafting trip in Colorado. By the time she gets back from that, I'll be gone. And by the time I come back from Europe, it'll be time for school. I wonder if the entire summer is going to pass, as the last six months have, as if our friendship never existed. When I see Melanie's car in her driveway, I don't say anything. Mom doesn't either, which is how I know that she and Susan have discussed our falling-out.

French class comes to an end. During the last week, each

of us has to give an oral presentation about something particularly French. I give mine on macarons, explaining their origins and how they're made. I dress up in one of Babs's chef aprons and wear a beret, and when I'm done, I hand out macarons that Babs made special for the class, along with Café Finlay postcards.

I am coming home from class in Mom's car, which I've borrowed to lug all my presentation stuff, when I see Melanie in her driveway. She sees me too, and we look at each other for a moment. It's like we're asking each other, Are we both going to pretend the other doesn't exist? That *we* don't exist?

But we do exist. At least we used to. And so I wave to her. Then I walk toward the neutral territory of the sidewalk. Melanie does too. When she gets closer, her eyes widen. I look at my silly costume.

"French class," I explain. "Here, do you want a macaron?" I pull out one of the extras that I was bringing home for Mom and Dad.

"Oh, thanks." She takes a bite, and her eyes widen. I want to say, *I know.* But with all the months gone by, I don't. Because maybe I don't know. Not anymore.

"So French class?" she says. "We both did the summer-school thing this year, huh?"

"Right, you were in Portland. At a music program?"

Her eyes light up. "Yeah. It was intense. Not just playing, but composing and learning about different facets of the industry. We had these professionals come in to work with us. I composed an experimental piece that I'm going to produce at school next year." Her whole face glows. "I think I'm going to major in music theory. What about you?"

I shake my head. "I'm not sure. I think I like languages." In addition to Mandarin, this fall, I'll take French, along with another Shakespeare class with Professor Glenny. Intro to Semiotics. And African Dance.

She looks up, hesitates for a second. "So, no Rehoboth Beach this summer?"

We've gone to the same summer house since I was five. But not this year. "Dad was invited to a conference in Hawaii, and he convinced Mom to go with him. As a personal favor to me, I think."

"Because you're going to Paris."

"Right. I'm going to Paris."

There's a pause. In the background, I can hear the neighbor kids splashing around in the sprinklers. Just like Melanie and I used to.

"To find him."

"I have to know. If something happened. I just need to find out."

I brace myself for Melanie's derision, for her to scoff or laugh at me. But she just considers what I've said. And when she says the next thing, it's not snide so much as matter-of-fact: "Even if you find him. Even if he didn't leave you on purpose, he can't possibly live up to the person you've built him into."

It's not like the thought hasn't occurred to me. I get that the chances of finding him are small, but the chances of finding him as I remember him are even smaller. But I just keep going back to what my dad always says, about how when you lose something, you have to visualize the last place you had it. And I found—and then lost—so many things in Paris.

"I know," I tell Melanie. And it's weird because I don't feel defensive. I feel a little bit relieved because it almost seems like Melanie is worrying about me again. And also relieved because I'm *not* worrying about me. Not about this, anyhow. "I don't know that it matters."

Her eyes widen at that. Then she narrows them, looks me up and down. "You look different."

I laugh. "No. I still look like me. It's just this outfit."

"It's not the outfit," Melanie says, almost harshly. "You just seem different."

"Oh. Well . . . *thanks*?"

I look at Melanie, and for the first time, I notice how she seems. Which is utterly familiar. Like Melanie again. Her hair is growing out and is back to its natural color. She's wearing cutoff shorts, a cute embroidered tee. No nose rings. No tats. No multicolored hair. No slutty-chic outfits. Of course, just because she looks the same has no bearing on whether she actually is the same. It hits me that Melanie's year was probably was just as tumultuous as mine in ways that I didn't understand, either.

Melanie is still staring at me. "I'm sorry," she says at last.

"For what?" I ask.

"For forcing you to cut your hair in London when you weren't ready. I felt so bad when you cried like that."

"It's okay. And I'm glad I did it." And I am. Maybe he never would've stopped me had I not had the Louise Brooks hair. Or maybe he would've, and we would've exchanged actual names. I'll never know. Once accidents happen, there's no backtracking.

We both just stand there on the sidewalk, hands at our

sides, unsure of what to say. I hear the neighbor kids yelp in the sprinklers. I think of me and Melanie when we were younger, on the high dive at the pool in Mexico. We would always hold hands as we jumped, but by the time we swam back up to the surface, we'd have let go. No matter how we tried, once we started swimming, we always let go. But after we bobbed to the surface, we'd climb out of the pool, clamber up the high-dive ladder, clasp hands, and do it again.

We're swimming separately now. I get that. Maybe it's just what you have to do to keep above water. But who knows? Maybe one day, we'll climb out, grab hands, and jump again.

Twenty-nine

New York City

My parents want to drive me to JFK, but I've made plans to spend the day with Dee before I go, so they drop me off at 30th Street Station in Philadelphia. I'm going to take the train—my first train in a year—to Manhattan, and Dee will meet me at Penn Station. Tomorrow night, I catch my flight to London and then onward to Paris.

When my train is announced, we walk toward the platform. Dad taps his toes impatiently, visions of Maui golf courses dancing through his head. They leave on Monday. Mom just paces. Then when my train's headlights are visible in the distance, she pulls a box out of her purse.

"I thought we weren't doing presents this time." Last year, there'd been the big dinner out, lots of little last-minute gadgets. Last night was more low-key. Homemade lasagna in the dining room. Both Mom and I pushed it around our plates.

"It's less for you than for me."

I open the box. Inside is a small cell phone with a charger and a plug adapter.

"You got me a new phone?"

"No. I mean yes. I mean, your old phone, we'll unfreeze the plan when you get back. But this is a special quad-band phone. It *definitely* works in Europe. You just have to buy a . . . what are they called?" she asks Dad.

"SIM card."

"Right." She fumbles to flick open the back. "They're very inexpensive, apparently. So you can get a local number anywhere you go and have a phone if you need one, and you can call us in an emergency or text us—but only if you choose to. It's more for you, so you have a way to reach us. If you need to. But you don't have to—"

"Mom," I interrupt, "it's okay. I'll text you."

"Really?"

"Well, yeah! And you can text me back from Hawaii. And does this thing have a photo function?" I peer at the camera. "I'll send you pictures."

"You will?"

"Of course I will."

By the look on her face, you'd think I'd given her the present.

— — —

Penn Station is mobbed, but I find Dee right away, under the departure board, wearing a pair of lemon-lime paneled nylon shorts and a tank top with UNICORNS ARE REAL emblazoned on it. He scoops me up in a big hug.

"Where's your suitcase?" he asks.

I turn around, show off the olive backpack I got from the Army-Navy surplus store in Philadelphia.

Dee whistles. "How'd you fit your ball gown?"

"It folds down really small."

"I thought you'd have a bigger bag, and I told Mama we'd come back home before we went out exploring, so she made lunch."

"I like lunch."

Dee throws up his hands. "Actually, Mama planned a surprise party for you. Don't tell her I told."

"A party? She doesn't even know me."

"She thinks she does by how much I talk about you, and she'll use any excuse to cook. My family's coming, including my cousin Tanya. I told you about her?"

"The one who does hair?"

Dee nods. "I asked her if she'd do yours. She does white-girl hair too, works in a fancy salon in Manhattan. I thought maybe you could get a bob again, go all Louise Brooks. Look just like you did when you met. You gotta do something with that mop." He fingers my hair, up, as usual, in a clip.

We take the subway all the way uptown, to the last stop on the train. We get out and transfer to a bus. I look out the window, expecting the rough-and-tumble streets of the South Bronx, but the bus passes a bunch of pretty brick buildings all shaded by mature trees.

"*This* is the South Bronx?" I ask Dee.

"I never said I lived in the South Bronx."

I look at him. "Are you serious? I've heard you say a bunch of times that you're from the South Bronx."

"I only said that I was from the Bronx. This is the Bronx, technically. It's Riverdale."

"But you told Kendra you were from the South Bronx. You told her you went to South Bronx High School. . . ." I pause, remembering that first conversation. "Which does not even exist."

"I left the girl to her own jumped conclusions." He gives me a knowing smirk. He rings the bell to get off the bus. We exit onto a busy street full of tall apartment buildings. It's not fancy, but it's nice.

"You are a master pretender, D'Angelo Harrison."

"Takes one to know one. I *am* from the Bronx. And I *am* poor. If people want to translate that as ghetto boy, that's their choice." He smiles. "Especially if they want to throw scholarship money my way."

We arrive at a pretty brick building with cracked gargoyles hanging over the front entrance. Dee rings the buzzer—"so they know we're coming"—and then we take one of those ancient caged-in elevators to the fifth floor. Outside the front door, he looks at me and tucks some strands of stray hair behind my ear.

"Act surprised," he whispers and opens the door.

We step into a party, about a dozen people crowded into the small living room where there's a BON VOYAGE ALLYSON sign tacked up over a table laden with food. I look at Dee, eyes wide in shock.

"Surprise!" he says, twinkling jazz hands.

Dee's mother, Sandra, comes up to me and wraps me in a gardenia-scented bear hug. "He told you, didn't he? That was the worst look of surprise I ever saw. My baby couldn't keep a secret if was stapled to him. Well, come on, then, meet the folk, have some food."

Sandra, introduces me to various aunts and uncles and cousins and gives me a plate of barbecued chicken and mac and cheese and some greens and sits me down at a table. "Now you hold court."

Dee has pretty much told everyone about Willem, so they all have advice on how to track him down. Then they start peppering me with questions about the trip. How I'm getting there—a flight from New York to London and then on to Paris—and where I'm staying—a youth hostel in the Villette area Willem and I hung out in, twenty-five bucks a night for a dorm—and how I'll get around—with the help of a guidebook, and I will brave the Metro. And they ask about Paris, and I tell them about what I saw last year, and they're very interested to hear how diverse it was, about the sections that were full of Africans and then this starts a big debate about which African countries France colonized until someone goes for a map to figure it out.

While everyone pores over the atlas, Sandra comes up with a plate of peach cobbler. "I got you a little something," she says, handing me a thin package.

"Oh, you shouldn't—"

She waves away my objections like stale air. I open the package. Inside is a laminated map of Paris. "The man at the store said this would be 'indispensable.' It has all the subway stops and an index of major streets." She opens the map to show me. "And D'Angelo and I spent so many hours looking at it, it has our good blessings coursing through it."

"Then I'll never get lost again."

She folds the map up and puts it in my hands. She has the same eyes as Dee. "I want to thank you for helping my boy this year."

"Me helping Dee?" I shake my head. "I think you have it the other way around."

"I know exactly the way I have it," she says.

"No, seriously. All Dee has done is help me. It's almost embarrassing."

"Stop with such nonsense. D'Angelo is both brilliant and blessed with the road life has taken him on. But it's not been easy for him. In his four years of high school and one year of college, you are the first friend from school he's ever talked about, much less brought home."

"You two are talking about me, aren't you?" Dee asks. He puts an arm around each of us. "Extolling my brilliance?"

"Extolling your something," I say.

"Don't either of you believe a word!" He turns around to introduce a tall, regal girl with a head full of intricate twists. "I was telling you about Tanya."

We exchange hellos, and Sandra goes off to fetch some more cobbler. Tanya reaches out to free my hair from its clip. She fingers the ends and shakes her head, clucking her tongue the same disapproving way Dee so often does.

"I know. I know. It's been a year," I say. And then I realize it has. A year.

"Was it short or long?" Dee asks. He turns to Tanya. "You have to make her look just the same. For when she finds him."

"*If* I find him," I clarify. "It was to here." I point to the base of my skull, where the stylist in London had cut my hair to last year. But then I drop my hand. "You know, though. I don't think I want the bob."

"You don't want a haircut?" Tanya asks.

"No, I would *love* a haircut," I tell her. "But not a bob. I want to try something totally new."

Thirty

Paris

It takes approximately thirteen hours and six time zones for me to freak out.

It happens when I stumble into the arrivals hall of Charles de Gaulle airport. All around me, other passengers are being greeted by hugging relatives or drivers with signs. I'm not being met by anyone. No one is expecting me. No one is watching out for me. I know I have people out there in the world who love me, but right now, I've never felt so alone. I feel that flashing sign click on over my head, the one that used to read TOURIST. Only now it also reads WHAT HAVE YOU DONE?

I pull my backpack straps tighter around my chest, like they could hug me. I take a deep breath. I pick up one leg and put it in front the other. A step. I take another. And another. I pull out the to-do list I made on the plane. Number one: exchange money.

I go to one of the many foreign exchange bureaus and in

halting French ask if I can exchange my dollars. "Of course. This is a bank," the man behind the counter answers in French. I hand over a hundred dollars and am too relieved to bother to count the euros I get in return.

Next on the list: find youth hostel. I've mapped the route, a train to the city, then a Metro to the Jaurès stop. I follow the signs for the RER, the train to central Paris, but it turns out I have to take an airport train to get to the RER station, and I go the wrong way and wind up at a different terminal and have to double back around, so it takes me almost an hour just to get to the airport train station.

When I get up to the automated ticket machines, it's like facing off against an enemy. Even with choosing English as the language, the instructions are bewildering. Do I need a Metro ticket? A train ticket? Two tickets? I feel that neon sign over my flash brighter. Now it says WHAT THE *HELL* HAVE YOU DONE?

I open the guidebook again to the section about getting into Paris. Okay, one ticket will get me into Paris and transfer to the Metro. I look at the map of the Paris Metro. The different lines knot together like snakes. Finally, I locate my stop, Jaurès. I trace the RER line to the airport to the transfer point and realize with a start that it's at Gare du Nord. Someplace familiar, someplace to tie me to that day.

"Okay, Allyson, no way through it but through it," I tell myself. And then I face the ticket machine, shoulders back, like we are competitors in a duel. I punch the touch screen, feed it a ten-euro note and then it spits me back some change and a tiny ticket. A small victory against an impassive opponent, but I am flush with satisfaction.

I follow the throngs to the gates, which work like the Tube gates, though it turns out, it's much easier to get through them when you're not lugging a giant suitcase. Ha! Another enemy foiled.

In the Metro/RER interchange beneath Gare du Nord, I get lost again trying to find the right Metro line, and then I misplace my little ticket, which you need not only to get out of RER but into the Metro. Then I almost get on the Metro going the wrong direction but figure it out right before the doors close and jump off. When I finally arrive at my stop, I'm completely exhausted and totally disoriented. It takes about fifteen minutes poring over the map just to figure where I am. I take a half dozen more wrong turns until I hit the canals, which is the first sign that I'm in the right area.

But I still have no idea where the hostel is, and I'm exhausted, frustrated, and near tears. I can't even find the hostel. And I have an address. And a map. What in the world makes me think I can find him?

But then just when I'm about to lose it, I stop, look out at the canals, and I just breathe. And my panic subsides. Because this place, it feels familiar. It *is* familiar, because I've been here before.

I fold up my map and put it away. I breathe some more. I look around. There are the same gray bicycles. There are the same stylish women, teetering across the cobblestones on heels. The cafés, crowded, as though no one ever has to work. I take another deep breath, and a sort of sense memory takes over. And somehow I just know where I am. To the left is the park with the lake where we met Jacques and the Danes. To my right, a few blocks back, is the cafe where we had crêpes.

I take the map out again. I find myself. Five minutes later, I'm at the youth hostel.

My room is on the sixth floor, and the elevator is out of order, so I walk up a winding stairway. A guy with a tattoo of some sort of Greek god on his arm points out the breakfast room, the communal bathrooms (coed), and then my room, with seven beds. He gives me a lock and shows me where I can store my stuff when I go out. Then he leaves me with a *bonne chance*, which means good luck, and I wonder if he says that to everyone or if he senses that I'll need it.

I sit down on the bed and unhook the sleeping bag from the top of my backpack, and as I slump into the springy mattress, I wonder if Willem has stayed here. Has slept in this very bed. It's not likely, but it's not impossible either. This is the neighborhood he introduced me to. And everything seems possible right now, this feeling of rightness, throbbing right alongside my heartbeat, soothing me to sleep.

I wake up a few hours later with drool on my pillow and static in my head. I take a lukewarm shower, shampooing the jet lag out of my hair. Then I towel it try and put in the gel like Tanya showed me—wash and wear, she said. It's very different, all chunks and layers, and I like it.

Downstairs, the clock on the lobby wall behind the giant spray-painted peace sign reads seven o'clock; I haven't eaten anything since the hard roll and yogurt they gave me on the plane over from London, and I'm woozy with hunger. The little café in the lobby only serves drinks. I know that part of traveling alone means eating alone and ordering in French, and I practiced that a lot with Madame Lambert. And it's not like I haven't eaten alone plenty of times in the dining hall this past year. But I decide I've conquered enough things for one day. Tonight, I can get a sandwich and eat in my room.

In front of the hostel, a bunch of people are hanging out in the drizzle. They're speaking English in what I think are Australian accents. I take a breath and walk over and ask them if they know of a place to get a good sandwich nearby.

One muscular girl with streaky brown hair and a ruddy face turns to me and smiles brightly. "Oh, there's a place over the canal that makes gorgeous smoked salmon sandwiches," she says. She points out the way and then she resumes talking to her friend about a bistro that supposedly sells a prix fixe for twelve euro, fifteen with a glass of wine.

My mouth waters at the mere thought of it, the food, the company. It seems incredibly presumptuous to invite myself, the kind of thing I would never do.

But then again, I'm alone in Paris, so this is all virgin territory. I tap the Australian girl on her sunburnt shoulder and ask if I can tag along with them for dinner. "It's my first day traveling, and I'm not sure where to go," I explain.

"Good on you," she replies. "We've all been at it for ages. We're on our OAs."

"OAs?"

"Overseas Adventures. It's so bloody expensive to get out of Australia that once you go, you stay gone. I'm Kelly, by the way. This is Mick, that's Nick, that's Nico, short for Nicola, and that's Shazzer. She's from England, but we love her anyway."

Shazzer sticks her tongue out at Kelly, smiles at me.

"I'm Allyson."

"That's my mum's name!" Kelly says. "And I was just saying I was missing my mum! Wasn't I? It's karma!"

"Kismet," Nico corrects.

"That too."

Kelly looks at me, and for half a second, I stand there, because she hasn't said yes and I'm going to feel like an idiot if she says no. Still, maybe it's all that prep in French class, but I'm kind of okay with feeling like an idiot. The group starts to walk off, and I start to turn toward the sandwich place. Then Kelly turns around.

"Come on, then," she says to me. "Don't know about you, but I could eat a horse."

"You might do. They eat those here," Shazzer says.

"No they don't," one of the guys says. Mick or Nick. I'm not quite sure who's who.

"That's Japan," Nico says. "It's a delicacy there."

We start walking, and I listen as the rest of them argue over whether or not the French eat horse meat, and as I amble along, it hits me that I'm doing it. Going to dinner. In Paris. With people I met five minutes ago. Somehow, more than anything else that's happened in the last year, this blows my mind.

On the way to the restaurant, we stop so I can get a SIM card for my phone. Then, after getting slightly lost, we find the place and wait for a table big enough to seat us all. The menu's in French, but I can understand it. I order a delicious salad with beets that's so beautiful I take a picture of it to text my mom. She immediately texts me back the less artful look-ing loco moco that Dad is having for breakfast. For my entrée, it's some kind of mystery fish in a peppery sauce. I'm having such a nice time, mostly listening to their outrageous travel tales, that it's only when it's time for dessert that I remember my promise to Babs. I check out the menu, but there are no macarons on it. It's already ten o'clock, and the shops are closed. Day one, and I've already blown my promise.

"Shit," I say. "Or make that *merde*!"

"What's wrong?" Mick/Nick asks."

I explain about the macarons, and everyone listens, rapt.

"You should ask the waiter," Nico says. "I used to work at a place in Sydney, and we had a whole menu that wasn't on the menu. For VIPs." We all give her a look. "It never hurts to ask."

So I do. I explain, in French that would make Madame Lambert proud, about *ma promesse du manger des macarons tous les jours*. The waiter listens intently, as though this is serious business and goes into the kitchen. He returns with everyone else's dessert—crèmes brûlée and chocolate mousse—and, miraculously, one perfect creamy macaron just for me. The inside is filled with brown, sweet, gritty paste, figs I think. It's dusted with powdered sugar so artfully it's like a painting. I take another picture. Then I eat it.

By eleven o'clock, I'm falling asleep into my plate. The rest of the group drops me off back at the hostel before going out to hear some French all-girl band play. I fall into a dead sleep and wake up in the morning to discover that Kelly, Nico, and Shazzer are my dorm mates.

"What time is it?" I ask.

"Late! Ten o'clock," says Kelly. "You slept ages. And through such a racket. There's a Russian girl who blow-dries her hair for an hour every day. I waited for you to see if you wanted to come with us. We're all going to Père Lachaise Cemetery today. We're going to have a picnic. Which sounds bloody morbid to me, but apparently French people do it all the time."

It's tempting: to go with Kelly and her friends and spend my two weeks in Paris being a tourist, having fun. I wouldn't have to go to dank nightclubs. I wouldn't have to face Céline. I wouldn't have to risk getting my heart broken all over again.

"Maybe I'll meet up with you later," I tell her. "I've got something to do today."

"Right. You're on an epic quest for macarons."

"Right," I say. "That."

At breakfast, I spend a little time with my map, figuring out the route between the hostel and Gare du Nord. It's walking distance, so I set out. The route seems familiar, the big wide boulevard with the bike paths and sidewalks in the middle. But as I get closer to the station, I start to feel sick to my stomach, the tea I had a while ago coming back to my mouth, all acidic with fear.

At Gare du Nord, I stall for time. I go in the station. I wander over to the Eurostar tracks. There's one there, like a horse waiting to leave the gate. I think of when I was here a year ago, broken, scared, running back to Ms. Foley.

I force myself to leave the station, letting my memory guide me again. I turn. I turn again. I turn once more. Over the train tracks and into the industrial neighborhood. And then, there it is. It's kind of shocking, after all that searching online, how easy it is to find. I wonder if this one wasn't listed on Google, or if it was and maybe my French was so mangled that no one understood me.

Or maybe that's not it at all. Maybe I was perfectly understood and Céline and the Giant simply don't work here anymore. A year is a long time. A lot can change!

When I open the door and see a younger-looking man

with hair in a ponytail behind the bar, I almost cry out in disappointment. Where is the Giant? What if he's not here? What if she's not here?

"Excusez moi, je cherche Céline ou un barman qui vient du Sénégal."

He says nothing. Doesn't even respond. He just continues washing glasses in soapy water.

Did I speak? Was it in French? I try again: I add a *s'il vous plaît* this time. He gives me a quick look, pulls out his phone, texts something, and then goes back to dishes.

Con, I mutter in French, another of Nathaniel's teachings. I shove open the door, adrenaline pushing through me. I'm so angry at that jerk behind the counter who wouldn't even answer me, at myself, for coming all this way for nothing.

"You came back!"

And I look up. And it's him.

"I knew you would come back." The Giant takes my hand and kisses me on each cheek, just like the last time. "For the suitcase, *non?*"

I'm speechless. So I just nod. Then I throw my arms around him. Because I'm so happy to see him again. I tell him so.

"As am I. And so happy I save your suitcase. Céline insist to take it away, but I say no, she will come back to Paris and want her things."

I find my voice. "Wait, how'd you know I was here? I mean, today?"

"Marco just text me an American girl was looking for me. I knew it had to be you. Come."

I follow him back inside the club, where this Marco is now mopping the floor and refusing to look at me. I have a hard time looking at him after calling him an asshole in French.

"Je suis très désolée," I apologize as I shuffle past him.

"He's Latvian. His French is new, so he's timid to speak," Yves says. "He is the cleaner. Come downstairs, that is where your suitcase is." I glance at Marco and think of Dee, and Shakespeare, and remind myself that things are rarely what they appear. I hope he didn't understand my French curses, either. I apologize again. The Giant beckons downstairs to the storeroom. In a corner, behind a stack of boxes, is my suitcase.

Everything is as I left it. The Ziploc with the list. The souvenirs. My travel diary with the bag of blank postcards inside. I half expect it all be covered in a layer of dust. I finger the diary. The souvenirs from last year's trip. They're not the memories that matter, the ones that lasted.

"It is very nice suitcase," the Giant says.

"You want it?" I ask. I don't want to lug it around with me. I can ship the souvenirs home. The suitcase is just extra baggage.

"Oh, no, no, no. It is for you."

"I can't take it. I'll take the important things, but I can't carry all this with me."

He looks at me seriously. "But I save it for you."

"The saving is the best part, but I really don't need it anymore."

He smiles, the whites of his teeth gleaming. "I *am* going to Roché Estair in the spring, to celebrate my brother's graduation."

I fish out the important things—my diary, my favorite

T-shirt, earrings I've missed—and put them in my bag. I put all the souvenirs, the unwritten postcards in a cardboard box to ship home. "You take this to Roché Estair for the graduation," I tell him. "It would make me happy."

He nods solemnly. "You did not come back for your suitcase."

I shake my head. "Have you seen him?" I ask.

He looks at me for a long moment. He nods again. "One time. The day after I meet you."

"Do you know where I might find him?"

He strokes the goatee on his chin and looks at me with a sympathy I could really do without. After a long moment, he says, "Maybe you should better speak with Céline."

And the way he says it, it implies all the things I already know. That Willem and Céline have a history. That I might've been right to doubt him all along. But if the Giant knows any of that, he's not saying. "She is off today, but sometimes she comes to the shows at night. Androgynie is playing, and she is very good friends with them. I will see if she is coming and let you know. Then you can find out what you need. You can call me later, and I will let you know if she will be here."

"Okay." I pull out my Paris phone, and we exchange numbers. "You never told me your name, by the way?"

He laughs at that. "No, I didn't. I am Modou Mjodi. And I never learned your name. I looked on the suitcase but there was nothing."

"I know. My name is Allyson, but Céline will know me as Lulu."

He looks perplexed. "Which is correct?"

"I'm beginning to think they both are."

He shrugs a little, takes my hand, kisses my cheeks twice, and then he bids me adieu.

— — —

It's only lunchtime when I leave Modou, and with no idea when I will see Céline, I feel oddly relieved, like I've been given a reprieve. I hadn't really planned on being a tourist in Paris, but I decide to do it. I brave the Metro and get off in the Marais quarter and go to one of the cafés along the beautiful Place des Vosges, where I order a salad and a *citron pressé*, adding plenty of sugar this time. I sit there for hours, waiting for the waiter to kick me out, but he leaves me alone until I ask for my check. At a patisserie, I get a ridiculously expensive macaron—this one a pale tangerine, like the last whispers of a sunset. I eat it and walk, in and out of the narrow streets, through a lively Jewish section, full of Orthodox men with black hats and stylish skinny suits. I snap a few pictures for my mom and text them to her and tell her to forward them to Grandma, who'll get a kick out of it. Then I wander around looking at the boutiques, gazing at clothing I can barely afford to touch. When the salesladies ask me in French if I need help, I answer in French that I am just browsing.

I buy some postcards and go back to Place des Vosges and sit down in the park inside the square. Amid the mothers playing with their babies and the old men reading their newspapers, puffing away on cigarettes, I write them out. I have a lot to send. One to my parents, one to my grandmother, one to Dee, one to Kali, one to Jenn, one to Café Finlay, one to Carol. And then, at the last minute, I decide to write one to Melanie too.

It's kind of a perfect day. I feel totally relaxed, and though I'm undoubtedly a tourist, I also feel like a Parisian. I'm almost relieved that I haven't heard from Modou. Kelly sends me a text about meeting up for dinner, and I'm getting ready to make my way back to the hostel when my phone chirps. It's from Modou. Céline will be at the club after ten o'clock.

I feel like the mellow relaxing vibe of the afternoon disappears behind a storm cloud. It's only seven. I have several hours to kill, and I could go meet the Oz gang for dinner, but I'm too nervous. So, I walk the city in my nervousness. I get to the club at nine thirty and stand outside, the heavy bass thump of live music making my heart pound. She's probably already there, but it feels like being early is some kind of faux pas. So I linger outside, watching the stylishly edgy Parisians with razored haircuts and angular clothes filter into the club. I look down at myself: khaki skirt, black T-shirt, leather flip-flops. Why didn't I dress for battle?

At ten fifteen, I pay my (ten-euro) entry and go in. The club is packed, and there's a band on the stage, all heavy guitars and a violin screeching feedback, and the tiniest Asian girl singing in this high, squeaky voice. All alone, surrounded by these hipsters, I don't think I've ever felt so out of place, and every part of me is telling me to leave before I make a fool of myself. But I don't. I haven't come this far to chicken out. I fight my way to the bar, and when I see Modou, I greet him like a long-lost brother. He smiles at me and pours me a glass of wine. When I try to pay, he waves the bill away, and immediately, I feel better.

"Ahh, Céline is there," he says, pointing to a table up front. She sits, alone, watching the band with a strange intensity, the smoke from her cigarette curling witchily around her.

I walk over to her table. She doesn't acknowledge me, though I can't tell if it's because she's snubbing me or concentrating on the band. I stand next to the open chair waiting for her to invite me to sit down, but then I just give up. I pull the chair out and sit. She gives me the slightest of nods, takes a puff of the cigarette, and blows smoke all over me, which I suppose counts as a greeting. Then she turns back to the band.

We sit there, listening. We are sitting right up close to the speakers, so the sound is extra deafening; my ears are already beginning to ring. It's hard to tell if she's enjoying the music. She doesn't tap her toes or sway or anything. She just stares and smokes.

Finally, when the band takes a break, she looks at me. "Your name is Allyson." She pronounces it *Aleeseesyoohn*, which makes it sound ridiculous somehow, an SUV of an American name with too many syllables.

I nod.

"So, not French at all?"

I shake my head. I never claimed it was.

We stare at each other, and I realize she won't give me a thing. I have to take it. "I'm looking for Willem. Do you know where I can find him?" I'd meant to come in guns blazing, French spouting, but my nerves have sent me scurrying back to the comforts of my mother tongue.

She lights a new cigarette and blows more smoke on me. "No."

"But, but he said you were good friends."

"He said that? No. I am just like you."

I cannot imagine in what way she would think she is even remotely like me, aside from us both possessing two X chromosomes. "How, how are we anything alike?"

"I am just one of the girls. There are many of us."

It's not like I didn't know this about him. Not like he hid it. But hearing it out loud, from her, I feel exhausted, jet lag dropping me like a plummeting elevator.

"So you don't know where he is?"

She shakes her head.

"And you don't know where I can find him?"

"No."

"And would you even tell me if you did?"

Her eyebrow goes up into that perfect arch as smoke curls out of her mouth.

"Can you even tell me his last name? Can you tell me that much?"

And here she smiles. Because in this little game we are playing, have been playing since last summer, I just showed my hand. And what a rotten hand it is. She takes a pen and a scrap of paper and writes something down. She slides the paper over to me. His name is on there. His full name! But I won't give her the satisfaction of my eagerness, so I casually tuck it in my pocket without even glancing at it.

"Do you need anything else?" Her tone, haughty and gloating, manages to carry over the sounds of the band, who have started playing again. I can already hear her laughing about me with all her hipster pals.

"No, you've done quite enough."

She eyes me for a long second. Her eyes aren't so much blue as violet. "What will you do now?"

I force a bitchy smile, which I expect doesn't look bitchy so much as constipated. "Oh, you know, see the sights."

She blows more smoke on me. "Yes, you can be a *touriste*," she says, as though tourist were an epithet. Then she begins ticking off all the places lowly people like us go. The Eiffel Tower. Sacré-Coeur. The Louvre.

I search her face for hidden meaning. Did he tell her about our day? I can just picture them laughing about me throwing the book at the skinheads, telling Willem I'd take care of him.

Céline is still talking about all the things I can do in Paris. "You can go shopping," she is saying. Buy a new handbag. Some jewelry. Another watch. Some shoes. I can't quite fathom how someone spouting off Ms. Foley–like advice can be so condescending.

"Thank you for your time," I say. In French. Annoyance has made me bilingual.

Thirty-one

---

*W*illem de Ruiter.

His name is Willem de Ruiter. I rush to an Internet café and start Googling him. But Willem de Ruiter turns out to be a popular name in Holland. There's a Dutch cinematographer with that name. There's some famous diplomat with that name. And hundreds of other nonfamous people who nevertheless have some reason to be on the Internet. I go through hundreds of pages, in English, in Dutch, and I find not one link to him, not one piece of evidence that he actually he exists. I Google his parents' names Bram de Ruiter. Yael de Ruiter. Naturopath. Actor. Anything I can think of. All these combinations. I get vaguely excited when some weird theater thing comes up, but when I click through, the website is down.

How can it be this hard to find someone? It occurs to me that maybe Céline intentionally gave me the wrong name.

But then I Google myself, "Allyson Healey," and I don't come up, either. You have to add the name of my college before you get my Facebook page.

I realize then it's not enough to know what someone is called.

You have to know who they are.

Thirty-two

The next morning, Kelly and her friends ask me if I want to join them for a trip to the Rodin Museum, followed by some shopping. And I almost say yes. Because that's what I would like. But there is still one more stop. It's not even that I think I'll find anything; it's just that, if I'm facing down demons, I have go to there too.

I'm not sure where it is, exactly, but I do know the intersection where Ms. Foley had me picked up. It is seared into my brain. Avenue Simon Bolivar and Rue de l'Equerre, the cross streets of Humiliation and Defeat.

When I get out of the Metro, nothing seems familiar. Maybe because the last time I was here, I was flipping out in such a panic. But I know I didn't run that far before finding the pay phone, so I know it can't be that far to the art squat. I methodically go up one block. Down the next. Up and back. But nothing seems familiar. I attempt to ask directions, but how do you say "art squat" in French? Old building with art-ists? That doesn't work. I remember the Chinese restaurants in the vicinity and ask for them. One young guy gets really excited and, I think, offers a recommendation to one sup-posedly good place across on Rue de Belleville. I find it. And from there, I find a sign for double happiness. It could be one of many, but I have a feeling it's the one.

I wander around for fifteen more minutes and, on a quiet triangle of streets, find the squat. It has the same scaffolding, same distorted portraits, maybe a little more weather-beaten. I knock on the steel door. No one answers, but there are obvi ously people inside. Music wafts out from the open windows. I give the door a push. It creaks open. I push it farther. I walk inside. No one pays me any notice. I go up the creaking stair-case, to the place where it all happened.

I see the clay first, bright white, yet at the same time, golden and warm. Inside, a man is working. He is petite, Asian, a study in contrasts: His hair white with black roots, his clothes all black and strangely antiquated, like he stepped out of a Charles Dickens novel, and all covered in the same white dust that covered me that night.

He is carving at a piece of clay with a scalpel, his atten-tion so focused I'm afraid he'll startle with the merest sound. I clear my throat and knock quietly on the door.

He looks up and rubs his eyes, which are bleary with con-centration. "*Oui.*"

"*Bonjour,*" I begin. And then I sputter. My limited French is no match for what I need to explain to him. I crashed your squat, with a guy. I had the most intimate night of my life, and I woke up utterly alone. "Umm, I'm looking for a friend who I think you might know. Oh, I'm sorry—*parlez-vous anglais?*"

He lifts his head and nods, slightly, with the delicacy and control of a ballet dancer. "Yes," he says.

"I'm looking for a friend of mine, and I wonder if you might know him. His name is Willem de Ruiter. He's Dutch?" I watch his face for a flicker of recognition, but it remains impassive, as smooth as the clay sculptures that surround us.

"No? Well, he and I stayed here one night. Not exactly *stayed* here . . ." I trail off, looking around the studio, and it all comes back to me: the smell of the rain against the thirsty pavement, the swirl of dust, the smooth wood of his work-table pressing into my back. Willem towering over me.

"What did you say your name was?"

"Allyson," I hear myself say as if from a distance away.

"Van," he says, introducing himself while fingering an old pocket watch on a chain.

I'm staring at the table, remembering the intense sharpness of it against my back, the ease with which Willem hoisted me onto it. The table is, as it was then, meticulously clean, the neat pile of papers, the half-finished pieces in the corner, the mesh cup of charcoals, and pens. Wait, what? I grab for the pens.

"That's my pen!"

"I'm sorry?" Van asks.

I reach over to grab the pen out of the cup. The Rollerball, inscribed BREATHE EASY WITH PULMOCLEAR. "This is my pen! From my dad's practice."

Van is looking at me, perplexed. But he doesn't understand. The pen was in my bag. I never took it out. It just went missing. I had it on the barge. I wrote double happiness with it. And then the next day, when I was on the phone with Ms. Foley, it was gone.

"Last summer, my friend Willem and I, well, we came here hoping someone might put us up for the night. He said that squats will do that." I pause. Van nods slightly. "But no one was here. Except a window was open. So we slept here, in your studio, and when I woke up the next morning, my friend, Willem, he was gone."

I wait for Van to get upset about our trespassing, but he is looking at me, still trying to understand why I'm gripping the Pulmoclear pen in my hand like it's a sword. "This pen was in my purse and then it was gone and now it's here, and I'm wondering, maybe there was a note or something. . . ."

Van's face remains blank, and I'm about to apologize, for trespassing before, and now again, but then I see something, like the faint glimmers of light before a sunrise, as some sort of recognition illuminates his face. He taps his index finger to the bridge of his nose.

"I did find something; I thought it was a shopping list."

"A shopping list?"

"It said something about, about . . . I don't recall, perhaps chocolate and bread?"

"Chocolate and bread?" Those were Willem's staple foods. My heart starts to pound.

"I don't remember. I thought it came in from the garbage. I had been away for holiday, and when I came back, everything was disarrayed. I disposed of it. I'm so sorry." He looks stricken.

We snuck into his studio, made a mess of it, and *he* looks guilty.

"No, don't be sorry. This is so helpful. Would there have been any reason for a shopping list to be in here? I mean, might you have written it?"

"No. And if I did, it would not have contained bread and chocolate."

I smile at that. "Could the list have been, maybe, a note?"

"It is possible."

"We were supposed to have bread and chocolate for breakfast. And my pen is here."

"Please, take your pen."

"No, you can *have* the pen," I say, and out escapes a whoop of laughter. A note. Could he have left me a note?

I throw my arms around Van, who stiffens for a moment in surprise but then relaxes into my embrace and reaches around to hug me back. It feels good, and he smells nice, like oil paint and turpentine and dust and old wood—smells that, like every-thing from that day, are stitched into the fabric of me now. For the first time in a long time, this doesn't seem like a curse.

— — —

When I leave Van, it's mid-afternoon. The Oz crew is prob-ably still at the Rodin Museum; I could meet up with them. But instead, I decide to try something else. I go to the nearest Metro station and close my eyes and spin around and then I pick a stop. I land on Jules Joffrin and then I figure out the series of trains that will take me there.

I wind up in a very Parisian-seeming neighborhood, lots of narrow, uphill streets and everyday shops: shoe stores, barbershops, little neighborhood bars. I meander a ways, no idea where I am, but surprisingly enjoying the feeling of being lost. Eventually, I come across a broad staircase, carved into the steep hillside, forming a little canyon between the apartment buildings and green foliage hanging down on either side. I have no idea where the stairs lead. I can practically hear Willem's voice: *All the more reason to take them.*

So I do. And take them, and take them. No sooner do I reach one landing than I find another set of stairs. At the top of the stairs, I cross a small cobblestoned medieval street and then, *boom*, it's like I'm back in the world of the tour. There are idling coaches and sardine-packed cafés, and an accordion player doing Edith Piaf covers.

I follow the crowds around the corner, and at the end of a street full of cafés advertising menus in English, Spanish, French, and German is a huge white-domed cathedral.

"Excusez-moi, qu'est-ce que c'est?" I ask a man standing outside of one of the cafés.

He rolls his eyes. *"C'est Sacré-Coeur!"*

Oh, Sacré-Coeur. Of course. I walk closer and see three domes, two smaller ones flanking the big one the middle, reigning regal over the rooftops of Paris. In front of the cathedral, which is glowing golden in the afternoon sun, is a grassy hillside esplanade, bisected by marble staircases leading down the other side of the hill. There are people everywhere: the tourists with their video cameras rolling, backpackers lolling in the sun, artists with easels out, young couples leaning into each other, whispering secrets. Paris! Life!

At the end of the tour, I'd sworn off setting foot in another moldering old church. But for some reason, I follow the crowds inside. Even with the golden mosaics, looming statues and swelling crowds, it somehow still manages to feel like a neighborhood church, with people quietly praying, fingering rosaries, or just lost in thought.

There's a stand of candles, and you can pay a few euros and light one yourself. I'm not Catholic, and I'm not entirely clear on this ritual, but I feel the need to commemorate this somehow. I hand over some change and am given a candle, and when I light it, it occurs to me that I should say a prayer. Should I pray for someone who's died, like my grandfather? Or should I pray for Dee? For my mom? Should I pray to find Willem?

But none of that feels right. What feels right is just *this*. Being here. Again. By myself, this time. I'm not sure what the word for *this* is, but I say a prayer for it anyway.

I'm getting hungry, and the long twilight is starting. I decide to go down the back steps into that typical neighborhood and try to find an inexpensive bistro for dinner. But first, I need to get a macaron before all the patisseries close for the day.

At the base of the steps, I wander for a few blocks before I find a patisserie. At first I think it's closed because a shade is drawn down the door, but I hear voices, lots and lots of voices, inside, so hesitantly, I push the door open.

It seems like a party is going on. The air is humid with so many people crammed together, and there are bottles of booze and bouquets of flowers. I begin to edge back out, but there is a huge booming protest from inside, so I open it up again, and they wave me in. Inside, there are maybe ten people, some of them still in bakers' aprons, others in street clothes. They all have cups in hands, faces flushed with excitement.

In halting French, I ask if it might be possible to buy a macaron. There is much shuffling, and a macaron is produced. When I reach for my wallet, my money is refused. I start to head for the door, but before I get to it, I'm handed some Champagne in a paper cup. I raise the cup and everyone clinks with me and drinks. Then a burly guy with a handlebar mustache starts to cry and everyone pats him on the back.

I have no idea what's going on. I look around questioningly, and one of the women starts talking very fast, in a very strong accent, so I don't catch much, but I do catch *bébé*.

"Baby?" I exclaim in English.

The guy with the handlebar mustache hands me his telephone. On it is a photo of a puckered, red-faced thing in a blue cap. "Rémy!" he declares.

"Your son?" I ask. *"Votre fils?"*

Handlebar Mustache nods, then his eyes fill with tears.

"Félicitations!" I say. And then Handlebar Mustache embraces me in a huge hug, and the crowd claps and cheers.

A bottle of amber booze is passed around. When all our paper cups have been filled, people hold them up and offer different toasts or just say some version of cheers. Everyone takes a turn, and when it gets to me, I shout out what Jewish people say at times like this: *"L'chaim!"*

"It means 'to life,'" I explain. And as I say it, I think that maybe this is what I was saying a prayer for back in the cathedral. To life.

"L'chaim," the rowdy bakers repeat back to me. And then we drink.

Thirty-three

The next day, I accept Kelly's invitation to join the Oz crew. Today they're going to brave the Louvre. Tomorrow they're going to Versailles. The day after that, they're taking the train to Nice. I'm invited to come with them for all of it. I have ten days left on my ticket, and it feels like I've found as much as I'm going to find. I found out that he left me a note. Which is almost more than I could've hoped for. I am considering going with them to Nice. And, after my wonderful day yesterday, I'm also considering going off on my own somewhere.

After breakfast, we all get onto the Metro toward the Louvre. Nico and Shazzer are showing off some of their new clothes, which they got from a street market, and Kelly is making fun of them for coming to Paris to buy clothes made in China. "At least I got something local." She thrusts out her wrist to show off her new high-tech digital Frenchmanufactured watch. "There's this huge store near Vendôme, all they sell is watches."

"Why do you need a watch when you're traveling?" Nick asks.

"How many bloody trains have we missed because someone's phone alarm failed to go off?"

Nick gives her that one.

"You should see this place. It's bloody enormous. They sell watches from all over; some of them cost a hundred thousand euros. Imagine spending that on a watch," Kelly goes on, but I've stopped listening because I'm suddenly thinking of Céline. About what she said. About how I could get *another* watch. Another. Like she knew I lost my last one.

The Metro is pulling into a station, "I'm sorry," I tell Kelly and the gang. "I've gotta go."

———

"Where's my watch? And where's Willem?"

I find Céline in the club's office, surrounded by stacks of paperwork, wearing a thick pair of eyeglasses that somehow makes her both more and less intimidating.

She looks up from her papers, all sleepy-eyed and, maddeningly, unsurprised.

"You said I could get *another* watch, which means you knew Willem had *my* watch," I continue.

I expect her to deny it, to shoot me down. Instead, she gives me a dismissive little shrug. "Why would you do that? Give him such an expensive watch after one day? It is a little desperate, no?"

"As desperate as lying to me?"

She shrugs again, lazily taps on her computer. "I did not lie. You asked if I knew where to find him. I do not."

"But you didn't tell me everything, either. You saw him, after . . . after he, he left me."

She does this thing, neither a nod nor a shake of the head, somewhere in between. A perfect expression of ambiguity. A diamond-encrusted stonewall.

And at just that moment, another one of Nathaniel's French lessons comes back to me: *"T'es toujours aussi salope?"* I ask her.

One eyebrow goes up, but her cigarette goes into the ashtray. "You speak French now?" she asks, in French.

"Un petit peu." A little bit.

She shuffles the paperwork, stubs out the smoldering cigarette. *"Il faut mieux être salope que lâche,"* she says.

I have no idea what she said. I do my best to keep a straight face as I try to find keywords to unlock the sentence like Madame taught us, *salope*, bitch; *mieux*, better. *Lâche*. Milk? No, that's *lait*. But then I remember Madame's refrain about venturing into the unknown being an act of bravery and her teaching us, as always, the opposite of *courageux*: lâche.

Did Céline just call me a coward? I feel the indignation travel from the back of my neck up to my ears to the top of my head. "You can't call me that," I sputter in English. "You don't *get* to call me that. You don't even know me!"

"I know enough," she replies in English. "I know that you forfeited." Forfeit. I see myself waving a white flag.

"Forfeit? How did I forfeit?"

"You ran away."

"What did the note say?" I am practically screaming now.

But the more excited I become, the more aloof she becomes. "I don't know anything about it."

"But you know *something*."

She lights another cigarette and blows smoke on me. I wave it away. "Please, Céline, for a whole year, I've assumed the worst, and now I'm wondering if I assumed the wrong worst."

More silence. Then "He had the, how do you say it, sue-tours."

"Sue-tours?"

"Like with sewing on skin." She points to her cheek.

"Sutures? Stitches? He had stitches?"

"Yes, and his face was very swollen, and his eye black."

"*What happened?*"

"He would not tell me."

"Why didn't you tell me this yesterday?"

"You did not ask me this yesterday."

I want to be furious with her. Not just for this, but for being such a bitch that first day in Paris, for accusing me of cowardice. But I finally get that none of this is about Céline; it never was. I'm the one who told Willem I was in love with him. I'm the one who said that I'd take care of him. I'm the one who bailed.

I look up at Céline, who is watching me with the cagey expression of a cat eyeing a sleeping dog. *"Je suis désolée,"* I apologize. And then I pull the macaron out of my bag and give it to her. It's raspberry, and I was saving it as a reward for confronting Céline. It is cheating Babs's rule to give it to someone else, but somehow, I feel she'd approve.

She eyes it suspiciously, then takes it, pinching it between her fingers as though it were contagious. She gingerly lays it on a stack of CD cases.

"So, what happened?" I ask. "He came back here all banged up?"

She nods, barely.

"Why?"

She frowns. "He would not say."

Silence. She looks down, then quickly glances at me. "He looked through your suitcase."

What was in there? A packing list. Clothes. Souvenirs. Unwritten postcards. My luggage tag? No, that snapped off in the Tube station back in London. My diary? Which I now have. I grab it out of my bag, leaf through a few entries. There's something about Rome and feral cats. Vienna and the Schönbrunn Palace. The opera in Prague. But there is nothing, nothing of me. Not my name. My address. My email address. Not the addresses of any of the people I met on the tour. We didn't even bother with the pretense of keeping in touch. I shove the diary back in my bag. Céline is peering through narrowed eyes, watching while pretending not to.

"Did he take anything from my bag? Find anything?"

"No. He only smelled. . . ." She stops, as if in pain.

"He smelled what?"

"He smelled terrible," she says solemnly. "He took your watch. I told him to leave it. My uncle is a jeweler, so I know it was expensive. But he refused."

I sigh. "Where can I find him, Céline? Please. You can help me with that much."

"*That much?* I help you with so much already," she says, all huffy with her own indignation. "And I don't know where to find him. I don't lie." She looks hard at me. "I tell you the truth, and that is that Willem is the kind of man who comes when he comes. And mostly, he doesn't."

I wish I could tell her that she's wrong. That with us, it was different. But if he didn't stay in love with Céline, what makes me think that after one day, even if he did like me, I haven't been completely licked clean?

"So you did not have any luck? On the Internet?" she asks.

I start to gather my things. "No."

"Willem de Ruiter is a common name, *n'est-ce pas?*" she says. Then she does something I wouldn't have thought her capable of. She blushes. And that is how I know she's looked for him too. And she didn't find him, either. And all at once, I wonder if I haven't gotten Céline, if not altogether wrong, then a little bit wrong.

I take one of my extra Paris postcards. I write my name, address, all my details on it, and hand it to her. "If you see Willem. Or if you're ever in Boston and need a place to crash—or store your stuff."

She takes the postcard and looks at it. Then she shoves it in a drawer. "Boss-tone. I think I prefer New York," she sniffs. I'm almost relieved that she's sounding like her haughty self again.

I think of Dee. He could handle Céline. "That can probably be arranged."

When I get to the door, Céline calls out my name. I turn around. I see that she's taken a bite of the macaron, the round cookie now a half moon.

"I am sorry I called you a coward," she says.

"That's okay," I say. "I am sometimes. But I'm trying to be braver."

"*Bon.*" She pauses, and if I didn't know better, I'd think she maybe almost was considering a smile. "If you find Willem again, you will need to be brave."

— — —

I go sit down on the edge of a fountain to consider what Céline said. I can't quite make out if it was meant in support or warning, or maybe both. But it all seems academic, anyhow, because I've reached a dead end. She doesn't know where he is. I can try some more Internet searching and send another letter to Guerrilla Will, but other than that, I'm tapped.

You will need to be brave.

Maybe it's all for the best. Maybe I end here. Tomorrow I will go to Versailles with the Oz crew. And that feels okay. I pull out the map Dee and Sandra gave me to plot my route back to the hostel. It's not too far. I can walk. I trace the route with my finger. When I do, my finger runs over not one but two big pink squares. The big pink squares on this map are hospitals. I pull the map closer to my face. There are pink squares all over the place. Paris is crazy with hospitals. I run my finger to the art squat. There are several hospitals within a thumb's width of the squat too.

If Willem got hurt near the art squat, and he got stitches, there's a good chance it happened at one of these hospitals. "Thank you, Dee!" I call out into the Paris afternoon. "And thank you, Céline," I add a bit more quietly. And then I get up and go.

— — —

The next day, Kelly greets me coolly, which I can tell is hard work for her. I apologize for going MIA yesterday.

"S'okay," she says, "but you're coming with us today to Versailles?"

I grimace. "I can't."

Her face hardens into hurt. "If you don't want to hang with us, it's fine, but don't make plans to spare our feelings."

I'm not sure why I haven't told her. It feels sort of silly, being over here, going to all this trouble, for a guy I knew for a day. But as I tell Kelly a short version of the long story, including today's mad quest, her face grows serious. When I'm done, she just gives a little nod of her head. "I understand," she says solemnly. "I'll see you down at brekkie."

When I get down to the breakfast room, Kelly and the group are huddled around one of the big wooden tables, maps spread out in front of them. I take my croissant and tea and yogurt and join them.

"We're coming with you," she declares. "All of us."

"What? Why?"

"Because you need an army for this." The rest of the group sloppy salute me, and then they all start talking at once. Very loudly. People look over at us, but these guys are irrepressible. Only the pale petite girl at the edge of our table ignores us, keeping her nose in a book.

"Are you sure you guys want to miss Versailles?"

"Versailles is a relic," Kelly insists. "It's not going anywhere. But this is real life. Real romance. What could be more French than that?"

"We're coming with you, like it or not. If we have to follow you to every French hospital between here and Nice," Shazzer says.

"I don't think that'll be necessary," I say "I've looked on the map. I've narrowed it down to three likely hospitals."

The elfin girl looks up. Her eyes are so pale they seem to be made of water. "I'm sorry, but did you say you were going to a hospital?" she asks.

I look at the Australians, my ragtag army, all of them gung ho. "Apparently so."

The elfin girl looks at me with a weird intensity. "I know hospitals," she says in a quiet voice.

I look back at her. Really, I can't think of anything more boring than this, except maybe a visit to a French unemployment office. I can't imagine that she would want to come along. Except maybe she's lonely. And that I understand.

"Do you, do you want to go with us?" I ask.

"Not particularly," she says. "But I think I should."

The first hospital on the map turns out to some sort of private hospital, where, after an hour of being sent from one office to the next, we find out that, while there is an emergency room, it does not take most cases off the street, but rather sends them to the public hospitals. They send us to Hôpital Lariboisière. We head straight for the *urgences*, the French version of the emergency room, and after being given a number and told to wait, we sit for ages in uncomfortable chairs, along with all the people with broken elbows and coughs that sound really ugly and contagious.

The initial enthusiasm of the group starts to flag when they realize that going to an emergency room is as boring in

France as it is anywhere else. They are reduced to entertaining themselves with spitballs and card games of War, which does not endear the nurses to them. Wren, the strange, pale, pixie girl we've picked up, participates in none of the silliness. She just keeps reading her book.

By the time we are called to the front counter, the nurses are hating us, and the feeling is pretty much mutual. Shazzer, who apparently speaks the best French, is anointed ambassador, and I don't know if it's her French skills or her diplomatic ones that are lacking, but within five minutes, she is heatedly arguing with the nurse, and within ten, we are being escorted to the street.

It's now three o'clock. The day is half gone, and I can see the group is antsy, tired, hungry, wishing that they'd gone to Versailles. And now that I think about it, I realize how ridiculous this is. The front desk at my father's practice is manned by a nurse named Leona, who won't let even me go back into the office unless my father is in there and waiting for me. Leona would never give out a record to me—her boss's daughter, who speaks the same language as she does—let alone a foreign stranger.

"That was a bust," I tell them when we come out onto the pavement. The cloud layer that has been sitting over Paris for the last few days has burned off while we were waiting inside, and the day has turned hot and clear. "At least you can salvage the rest of the afternoon. Get some food and have a picnic in the Luxembourg Gardens."

I can see the idea is tempting. No one rebuffs it. "But we promised we'd be your wingmen," Kelly says. "We can't let you do this alone."

I hold up my hands in surrender. "You're not. I'm done. This is a lost cause."

Maps are taken out. Metro routes are debated. Picnic items are discussed.

"People mix up their patron saints, you know?" I look up. Wren, our pixie tagalong, who has been all but silent all day, has finally spoken.

"They do?"

She nods. "Saint Anthony is the patron saint of lost things. But Saint Jude is the patron saint of lost causes. You have to make sure you ask the right saint for help."

There's a moment as everyone looks at Wren. Is she some kind of religious nut?

"Who would be in charge of a lost person?" I ask.

Wren stops to consider. "That would depend. What kind of lost?"

I don't know. I don't know if he's lost at all. Maybe he's exactly where he wants to be. Maybe I'm the lost one, chasing someone who has no desire to be found. "I'm not sure."

Wren twirls her bracelet, fingering the charms. "Perhaps you should just pray to both." She shows me the little charms with each patron saint. There are many more charms, one with a date, another with a clover, one with a bird.

"But I'm Jewish."

"Oh, they don't care." Wren looks up at me. Her eyes don't seem blue so much as the absence of blue. Like the sky just before dawn. "You should ask the saints for help. And you should go to that third hospital."

— — —

Hôpital Saint-Louis turns out to be a four-hundred-year-old hospital. Wren and I make our way into the modern wing that sits adjacent. I've sent the others on to Luxembourg Gardens without much of an argument. Sunlight filters in through the glass atrium, throwing prisms of light onto the floor.

It's quiet in the ER, only a few people sitting among rows of empty chairs. Wren goes right up to the two male nurses behind the desk and that weirdly mellifluous voice of hers breaks out in perfect French. I stand behind her, catching enough of what she says to get that she is telling my story, mesmerizing them with it. Even the people in the chairs are leaning in to hear her quiet voice. I have no idea how Wren even knows the story; I didn't tell her. Maybe she picked it up at breakfast or among the others. She finishes, and there is silence. The nurses stare at her, then look down and start typing.

"*How do you speak French so well?*" I whisper.

"I'm from Quebec."

"Why didn't you translate at the other hospital?"

"Because it wasn't the right one."

The nurses ask me his name. I say it. I spell it. I hear the tap of the computer keys as they input it.

"*Non,*" one nurse says. "*Pas ici.*" He shakes his head.

"*Attendez,*" the other says. *Wait.*

He types some more. He says a bunch of things to Wren, and I lose track, but then one phrase floats to the top: a date. The day after the day Willem and I spent together. The day we got separated.

My breath stops. He looks up, repeats the date to me.

"Yes," I say. That would've been when he was here. "*Oui.*"

The nurse says something and something else I don't understand. I turn to Wren. "Can they tell us how to find him?"

Wren asks a questions, then translates back. "The records are sealed."

"But they don't have to give us anything written. They must have something on him."

"They say it's all in the billing department now. They don't keep much here."

"There has to be something. Now's the time to ask Saint Jude for help."

Wren fingers the charm on her bracelet. A pair of doctors in scrubs and lab coats come through the double doors, coffee cups in hand. Wren and I look at each other, Saint Jude apparently deciding to bestow twin inspiration.

"Can I speak to a doctor?" I ask the nurses in my horrible French. "Maybe the . . ." I turn to Wren. "How do you say 'attending physician' in French? Or the doctor who treated Willem?"

The nurse must understand some English because he rubs his chin and goes back to the computer. "Ahh, Dr. Robinet," he says, and picks up a phone. A few minutes later, a pair of double doors swing open, and it's like this time Saint Jude decided to send us a bonus, because the doctor is TV-handsome: curly salt-and-pepper hair, a face that's both delicate and rugged. Wren starts to explain the situation, but then I realize that, lost cause or not, I have to make my own case. In the most labored French imaginable, I attempt to explain: *Friend hurt. At this hospital. Lost friend. Need to find.* I'm frazzled, and with my bare-basics phrases, I must sound like a cavewoman.

Dr. Robinet looks at me for a while. Then he beckons for us to follow him through the double doors into an empty examination room, where he gestures for us to sit on the table while he settles on a rolling stool.

"I understand your dilemma," he replies in perfect British-accented English. "But we can't just give out files about a patient." He turns to look directly at me. His eyes are bright green, both sharp and kind. "I understand you've come all the way from America, but I am sorry."

"Can you at least *tell* me what happened to him? Without actually looking into his chart? Would that be breaking protocol?"

Dr. Robinet smiles patiently. "I see dozens of patients a day. And this was, you say, a year ago?"

I nod. "Yes." I bury my head in my hands. The folly of it hits me anew. One day. One year.

"Perhaps if you described him." Dr. Robinet feeds me some rope.

I snatch it up. "He was Dutch. Very tall, six foot three—it's one point nine in metric. Seventy-five kilos. He had very light hair, almost like straw, but very dark eyes, almost like coals. He was skinny. His fingers were long. He had a scar, like a zigzag, right on the top of his foot." As I continue to describe him, details I thought I'd forgotten come back to me, and an image of him emerges.

But Dr. Robinet can't see it. He looks puzzled, and I realize that from his point of view, I've described a tall blond guy, one person among thousands.

"Perhaps if you had a photograph?"

I feel as if the image I've created of Willem is alive in the room. He'd been right about not needing a camera to record the important things. He'd been there inside me all this time.

"I don't," I say. "Oh, but he had stitches. And a black eye."

"That describes a majority of the people we treat," Dr. Robinet says. "I am very sorry." He stands up off the stool; something clinks to the ground. Wren retrieves a euro coin off the floor and starts to hand it back to him.

"Wait! He did this thing with coins," I say. "He could balance a coin along his knuckles. Like this. May I?" I reach out for the euro and show how he flipped a coin across his knuckles.

I hand Dr. Robinet back his euro, and he holds it in his hand, examining it as if it were a rare coin. Then he flips it up in the air and catches it. *"Commotion cérébrale!"* he says.

"What?"

"Concussion!" Wren translates.

"Concussion?"

He holds up his index finger and turns it around slowly, like he's spooling information from a deep well. "He had a concussion. And if I recall, a facial laceration. We wanted him to stay for observation—concussions can be serious—and we wanted to report it to the police because he'd been assaulted."

"*Assaulted?* Why? By whom?"

"We don't know. It is customary to file a police report, but he refused. He was very agitated. I remember now! He wouldn't stay beyond a few hours. He wanted to leave straight away, but we insisted he stay for a CT scan. But as soon as we stitched him up and saw there was no cerebral bleeding, he insisted he had to go. He said it was very important. Someone he was going to lose." He turns to me, his eyes huge now. "*You*?"

"You," Wren says.

"Me," I say. Black spots dance in my vision, and my head feels liquid.

"I think she's going to faint," Wren says.

"Put your head between your legs," Dr. Robinet advises. He calls out into the hall, and a nurse brings me a glass of water. I drink it. The world stops spinning. Slowly, I sit back up. Dr. Robinet is looking at me now, and it's like the shade of professionalism has dropped.

"But this was a year ago," he asks in a blanket-soft voice. "You lost each other a year ago?"

I nod.

"And you've been looking all this time?"

I nod again. In some way, I have.

"And do you think he's been looking for you?"

"I don't know." And I don't. Just because he tried to find me a year ago doesn't me he wants to find me now. Or wants me to find him.

"But you *must* know," he replies. And for a minute I think he's reprimanding me that I ought to know, but then he picks up the phone and makes a call. When he's done, he turns to me. "You must know," he repeats. "Go to window two in the billing office now. They cannot release his chart, but I have instructed them to release his address."

"They have it? They have his address?"

"They have *an* address. Go collect it now. And then find him." He looks at me again. "No matter what, you must know."

I walk out of the hospital, past where the cancer patients are taking their chemotherapy treatments in the late afternoon sun. The printout with Willem's address is clenched in my fist. I haven't looked at it yet. I tell Wren that I need a moment alone and make my way toward the old hospital walls.

I sit down on a bench alongside the quadrangle of grass, between the old brick buildings. Bees dance between the flower bushes, and children play—there's so much life in these old hospital walls. I look at the paper in my hand. It could have any address. He could be anywhere in the world. How far am I willing to take this?

I think of Willem, beaten—*beaten!*—and still trying to find me. I take a deep breath. The smell of fresh-cut grass mingles with pollen and the fumes from trucks idling on the street. I look at the birthmark on my wrist.

I open the paper, not sure where I'm going next, only sure that I'm going.

Thirty-four

AUGUST

Utrecht, Holland

My guidebook has all of two pages on Utrecht, so I expect it to be tiny or ugly or industrial, but it turns out to be a gorgeous, twisting medieval city full of gabled row houses and canals with houseboats, and tiny little alley streets that look like they might house humans or might house dolls. There aren't many youth hostels, but when I turn up at the only one I can afford, I learn that before it was a hostel, it was a squat. And I get that sense, almost like a radar communicating from some secret part of the world just to me: *Yes, this is where you're meant to be.*

The guys at the youth hostel are friendly and helpful and speak perfect English, just like Willem did. One of them even looks like him—that same angular face, those puffy red lips. I actually ask him if he knows Willem; he doesn't and when I explain that he looks like someone I'm looking for, he laughs and says he and half of Holland. He gives me a map of Utrecht and shows me how to get to the address the hospital gave me, a few kilometers from here, and suggests I rent a bike.

I opt for the bus. The house is out of the center, in an area full of record stores, ethnic restaurants with meat turning on spits, and graffiti. After a couple of wrong turns, I find the street, opposite some railroad tracks, on which sits an abandoned freight car, almost completely graffitied over. Right across the street is a skinny town house, which according to my printout, is the last known address of Willem de Ruiter.

I have to push my way past six bikes locked to the front rail to get to the door, which is painted electric blue. I hesitate before pressing the doorbell, which looks like an eyeball. I feel strangely calm as I press. I hear the ring. Then the heavy clump of feet. I've only known Willem for a day, but I recognize that those are not his footsteps. His would be lighter, somehow. A pretty, tall girl with a long brown braid opens the door.

"Hi. Do you speak English?" I ask.

"Yes, of course," she answers.

"I'm looking for Willem de Ruiter. I'm told he lives here." I hold up the piece of paper as if in proof.

Somehow I knew he wasn't here. Maybe because I wasn't nervous enough. So when her expression doesn't register, I'm not all that surprised. "I don't know him. I'm just renting here for the summer," she says. "I'm sorry." She starts to close the door.

By now, I've learned *no* or *sorry* or *I can't help you*—these are opening offers. "Is there someone else here who might know him?"

"Saskia," she calls. From the top of a stairway so narrow it looks like a ladder, a girl appears. She climbs down. She has blond hair and rosy cheeks and blue eyes, and there's something vaguely farm-fresh about her, as though she just this minute finished riding a horse or plowing a field, even though her hair is cut in spikes and she's dressed in a woven black sweater that is anything but traditional.

Once again I explain that I'm looking for Willem de Ruiter. Then, even though she doesn't know me, Saskia invites me in and offers me a cup of coffee or tea.

The three of us sit down at a messy wooden table, piled high with stacks of magazines and envelopes. There are clothes strewn everywhere. It's clear a lot of people live here. But apparently not Willem.

"He never really lived here," Saskia explains after she serves me tea and chocolates.

"But you know him?" I ask.

"I've met him a few times. I was friends with Lien, who was the girlfriend of one of Robert-Jan's friends. But I don't really know Willem. Like Anamiek, I just moved in over the summer."

"Do you know why he would use this as his address?"

"Probably because of Robert-Jan," Saskia says.

"Who's Robert-Jan?"

"He goes to the University of Utrecht, same as me. He used to live here," Saskia explains. "But he moved out. I took over his room."

"Of course you did," I mutter to myself.

"In student houses, people come and go. But Robert-Jan will be back to Utrecht. Not here but to a new flat. Unfortunately, I don't know where that will be. I just took over his room." She shrugs as if to say, that's all.

I drum my fingers on the old wooden table. I look at the pile of mail. "Do you think maybe I could look through the mail? See if there's anything with a clue?"

"Go ahead," Saskia says.

I go through the piles. They are mostly bills and magazines and catalogs, addressed to various people who live or have lived at this address. I count at least a half dozen names, including Robert-Jan. But Willem doesn't have a single piece of mail.

"Did Willem *ever* get mail here?"

"There used to be some," Saskia replies. "But someone organized the mail a few days ago, so maybe they threw his away. Like I said, he hasn't been around in months."

"Wait," Anamiek says. "I think I saw some new mail with his name on it. It's still in the box by the door."

She returns with an envelope. This one isn't junk mail. It's a letter, with the address handwritten. The stamps are Dutch. I want to find him, but not enough to open his personal correspondence. I put the envelope down on the piles, but then I double-take. Because the return address in the upper left-hand corner, written in a swirling unfamiliar script, is mine.

I take the envelope and hold it up to the lamp. There's another envelope inside. I open the outer envelope and out of that spills my letter, the one I sent to Guerrilla Will in England, looking for Willem. From the looks of the stamps and crossed-out addresses and tape on the envelope, it's been forwarded a few times. I open up the original letter to see if anyone has added anything to it, but they haven't. It's just been read and passed on.

Still, I feel overjoyed somehow. All this time, my scrappy

little letter has been trying to find him too. I want to kiss it for its tenacity.

I show the letter to Saskia and Anamiek. They read it and look at me confused. "I wrote this letter," I say. "Five months ago. When I first tried to find him. I sent it to an address in England, and somehow it found its way here. Same as me." As I say it, I get that sense again. I'm on the right path. My letter and I landed in the same place, even if it's the wrong place.

Saskia and Anamiek look at each other.

"We will make some calls," Saskia says. "We can certainly help you find Robert-Jan."

The girls disappear up the stairs. I hear a computer chime on. I hear the sounds of one-sided conversations, Saskia on the phone. About twenty minutes later, they come back down. "It's August, so almost everyone is away, but I am sure I can get you contact information for Robert-Jan in a day or two."

"Thank you," I say.

Her eyes flicker up. I don't like the way they look at me. "Though I might have found a faster way to find Willem."

"Really? What?"

She hesitates. "His girlfriend."

Thirty-five

Ana Lucia Aureliano. That's her name. Willem's girlfriend. She goes to some honors college connected to the University of Utrecht.

In all the time I've been looking, I never dreamed of getting this far. So I didn't let myself imagine actually finding him. And while I have imagined him having *lots* of girls, I hadn't thought of him having just one. Which, in retrospect, seems awfully stupid.

It's not like I'm here to get back together. It's not like there's a together to get back to. But if I came this close, only to leave, I think I'd regret it for the rest of my life.

Ironically, it's Céline's words that finally convince me to go find the girlfriend: *You will need to be brave.*

University College's campus is small and self-contained, unlike the University of Utrecht, which sprawls through the city center, Saskia explained. It's on the outskirts of town, and as I ride out there on a pink bike that Saskia insisted I borrow, I practice what I'm going to say if I find her. Or find him.

The school has very few students, and they all live on campus, and it's also an international school, drawing students from all over the world, with all the classes taught in English. Which means it only takes asking two people about Ana Lucia before I'm given directions to her dorm.

A dorm that seems less like a college residence than an IKEA showroom. I peer inside the sliding-glass door; it's all sleek wood and modern furniture, a million miles away from the industrial blah of the room I shared with Kali. The lights are out, and when I knock, no one answers. There's a little cement landing outside the door that has some embroidered cushions, so I sit down and wait.

I must have dozed off because I wake up falling backward. Someone has opened the door behind me. I look up. The girl—Ana Lucia, I assume—is beautiful, with long wavy brown hair and rosebud lips, accentuated with red lipstick. Between her and Céline, I should feel flattered to be in such company, but that's not what I'm feeling at the moment.

"Can I help you?" she asks, hovering over me, eyeing me as you might eye a vagrant you caught sleeping on your stoop.

The sun has come out from behind the clouds and it reflects off the glass window, creating a glare. I shield my eyes with my hands and heave myself up. "I'm sorry. I must've fallen asleep. I'm looking for Ana Lucia Aureliano."

"I'm Ana Lucia," she says, emphasizing the correct pronunciation with the strength of her Spanish lisp: *Ana Lu-thee-uh*. She squints her eyes, studying me. "Have we met before?"

"Oh, no. I'm Allyson Healey. I'm . . . I'm sorry. This is weird. I'm from America, and I'm trying to find someone."

"Is this your first term here? There is an online student directory."

"What? Oh, no. I don't go here. I go to school in Boston."

"Who do you search for?"

I almost don't want to say his name. I could make up a name and then she'd be none the wiser. I wouldn't have to hear her ask in that adorable accent of hers why I want to know where her boyfriend is. But then I would go home, and I'd have come this far and would never know. So I say it.

"Willem de Ruiter."

She looks at me for a long moment and then her pretty face puckers, her cosmetic-ad lips part. And then out of those perfect lips comes a spew of what I assume is invective. I can't be sure. It's in Spanish. But she's waving her arms and talking a mile a minute, and her face has gone red. *Vate! Déjame, puta!* And then she picks me up by my shoulders and throws me off the stoop, like a bouncer ejecting a drunk. She throws my backpack after me, so that everything spills out. Then she slams the door shut, as much as you can slam a sliding-glass door. Locks it. And draws the shades.

I sit there agape for a moment. Then, in a daze, I start putting my things back in my bag. I examine my elbow, which has a scrape from where I landed, and my arm, which bears the half-moons of her nail marks.

"Are you okay?" I look up and see a pretty girl with dreadlocks who has bent down beside me and is handing me my sunglasses.

I nod.

"You don't need ice or anything? I have some in my room." She starts to walk back to her stoop.

I touch my head. There's a bump there too, but nothing serious. "I think I'm okay. Thanks."

She looks at me and shakes her head. "You were not, by any chance, asking about Willem?"

"You know him?" I ask. "You know Willem?" I come over to her stoop. There's a laptop and a textbook sitting there. It's a physics book. She has it open to the section on quantum entanglement.

"I've seen him around. This is only my second year, so I didn't know him when he went here. But only one person makes Ana Lucia crazy like that."

"Wait. *Here?* He went to college? Here?" I try to reconcile the Willem I met, the itinerant traveling actor, with an honors college student, and it hits me again how little I know this person.

"For one year. Before I got here. He studied economics, I think."

"So what happened?" I meant with the college, but she starts telling me about Ana Lucia. About how she and Willem got back together last year but then how she found out that he'd been cheating on her with some French girl the whole time. She's very casual about it, like none of it is all that surprising.

But my head is reeling. Willem went *here*. He studied *economics*. So it takes a minute to finally digest the last part. The cheating-on-Ana-Lucia-with-a-French-girl part.

"A French girl?" I repeat.

"Yes. Apparently, Willem was going to meet her for some secret tryst, in Spain, I think. Ana Lucia saw him shopping for flights on her computer, and thought he was planning to take her as a surprise because she has relatives there. So she canceled her vacation to Switzerland, and then told her family all about it, and they planned a big party, only to discover that the tickets were never for her. They were for the French girl. She freaked out, confronted him right in the middle of the campus—it was quite a scene. He hasn't been around since, obviously. Are you sure you don't need some ice for your head?"

I sink onto the stoop next to her. Céline? But she claimed she hadn't seen him since last year. But then she'd said a lot of things. Including that we were both just ports that Willem visited. Maybe there were a bunch of us out there. A French girl. Or two or three. A Spaniard. An American. A whole United Nations of girls waving from their ports. I think of Céline's parting words to me, and now they seem ominous.

I always knew that Willem was a player and that I was one of many. But now I also know that he didn't ditch me that day. He wrote me a note. He tried, however halfheartedly, to find me.

I think of what my mom said. About being grateful for what you have instead of yearning for what you think you want. Standing here, on the campus where he once walked, I think I finally get what she was talking about. I think I finally understand what it truly means to quit while you're ahead.

Thirty-six

*F*orward momentum. That's my new motto. No regrets. And no going back.

I cancel the Paris-London portion of my flight home so I can fly home straight from London. I don't want to go back to Paris. I want to go somewhere else. I have five more days in Europe, and there are all these low-cost airlines. I could go to Ireland. Or Romania. I could take a train to Nice and hook up with the Oz crew. I could go anywhere.

But to get to any of those places, I have to go to Amsterdam. So that's where I'm going first. On the pink bike.

When I went to deliver the bike to Saskia, along with a box of chocolates to say thank you, I told her that I didn't need her to find me Robert-Jan's contact information.

"You found what you needed?" she asked.

"Yes and no."

She seemed to understand. She took the chocolates but

told me to keep the bike. It didn't belong to anyone, and I'd need it in Amsterdam, and I could take it with me on the train or pass it along to someone else.

"The pink White Bicycle," I said.

She smiled. "You know about the White Bicycle?"

I nodded.

"I wish it still existed."

I thought about my travels, about all the things that people had passed on to me: friendship, help, ideas, encouragement, macarons. "I think it still does," I told her.

Anamiek has written me instructions on biking from Utrecht to Amsterdam. It's only twenty-five miles, and there are bike paths the whole, flat way. Once I get to the eastern end of the city, I'll hook up with the tram line nine, and I can just follow that all the way to Centraal Station, which is where most of the budget youth hostels are.

Once out of Utrecht, the landscape turns industrial and then to farms. Cows lolling in green fields, big stone windmills—I even catch a farmer in clogs. But it doesn't take long for the bucolic to meld with office parks and then I'm on the outskirts of Amsterdam, going past a huge stadium that says Ajax and then the bike path dumps me onto the street and things get a little confusing. I hear the *bring-bring* of a tram, and it's the number nine, just as Anamiek promised. I follow it up the long stretches past the Oosterpark and what I assume is the zoo—a flock of pink flamingos in the middle of the city—but then things get a little confusing at an intersection by a big flea market and I lose the tram. Behind me, motos are beeping, and the traffic of bicycles seems twice that of cars, and I keep trying to find the tram, but the canals all seem to go in circles, each one looking like the last, with tall stone banks and every kind of boat—from houseboat to rowboat to glass-domed tour boat—on its brackish waters. I pass by improbably skinny gabled row houses and cozy little cafés, doors flung open to reveal walls a hundred years' worth of brown. I turn right and wind up at a flower market, the colorful blooms popping in the gray morning.

I pull out my map and turn it around. This whole city seems to turn in circles, and the names of the streets read like all the letters in the alphabet got into a car accident: Oudezijds Voorburgwal. Nieuwebrugsteeg. Completely lost, I pedal up next to a tall guy in a leather jacket who's strapping a blond toddler into a bike seat. When I see his face, I do another double take because he's another, albeit older, Willem clone.

I ask him for directions, and he has me follow him to Dam Square and from there points me around the dizzying traffic circle to the Warmoesstraat. I pedal up a street full of sex shops, brazen with their lurid window displays. At the end of the block is one of the city's cheaper youth hostels.

The lobby is boisterous with activity: people are playing pool and Ping-Pong, and there's a card game going, and everyone seems to have a beer in hand, even though it's barely lunchtime. I ask for a dormitory room, and wordlessly, the dark-eyed girl at the desk takes my passport info and money. Upstairs in my room, in spite of the NO DRUG USE IN THE DORMS sign, the air is thick with hash smoke, and a bleary-eyed guy is smoking something through a tube on a piece of tinfoil, which I'm pretty sure is neither hash nor legal. I lock my backpack in the locker and head back downstairs and out onto the street to a crowded Internet café.

I pay for a half hour and check out the budget airline sites. It's Thursday now. I fly home out of London on Monday. There's a flight to Lisbon for forty-six euros. One to Milan, and one to somewhere in Croatia! I Google Croatia and look at pictures of rocky beaches and old lighthouses. There are even cheap hotels in the lighthouses. I could stay in a light-house. I could do anything!

I know almost nothing about Croatia, so I decide to go there. I pull out my debit card to pay for the ticket, but I notice a new email has popped up in the other window I have open. I toggle over. It's from Wren. The subject line reads WHERE ARE YOU?

I quickly write back that I'm in Amsterdam. When I said good-bye to Wren and the Oz gang in Paris last week, she was planning on catching a train to Madrid, and Kelly and the crew were heading to Nice, and they were talking about maybe meeting up in Barcelona, so I'm a little surprised when, thirty seconds later, I get an email back from her that reads NO WAY. ME TOO!!!! The message has her cell number.

I'm grinning as I call her. "I knew you were here," she says. "I could feel it! Where are you?"

"At an Internet café on the Warmoesstraat. Where are you? I thought you were going to Spain!"

"I changed my plans. Winston, how far is Warmoess-traat?" she calls. "Winston's the cute guy who works here," she whispers to me. I hear a male voice in the background. Then Wren squeals. "We're, like, five minutes from each other. Meet me at Dam Square, in front of the white tower thing that looks like a penis."

I close the browser window, and ten minutes later, I'm hugging Wren like she's a long-lost relative.

"Boy, that Saint Anthony works fast," she says.

"I'll say!"

"So what happened?"

I give her the quick rundown about finding Ana Lucia, almost finding Willem, and deciding not to find him. "So now I'm going to Croatia."

She looks disappointed. "You are. When?"

"I was going to fly out tomorrow morning. I was just booking my ticket when you called."

"Oh, stay a few more days. We can explore together. We can rent bikes. Or rent one bike and have the other ride side-saddle like the Dutch girls do."

"I already *have* a bike," I say. "It's pink."

"Does it have a rack on the back where I can sit?"

Her grin is too infectious to resist. "It does."

"Oh. You have to stay. I'm at a hostel up near the Jordaan. My room is the size of a bathtub, but it's sweet and the bed's a double. Come share with me."

I look up. It is threatening rain again, and it's freezing for August, and the web said Croatia was mid-eighties and sunny. But Wren is here, and what are the chances of that? She believes in saints. I believe in accidents. I think we basically believe in the same thing.

We get my stuff out of my room at the hostel, where that one guy is now passed out, and move it to her hostel. It's much cozier than mine, especially since tall-dark-and-grinning Winston is there checking in on us. Upstairs, her bed is covered with guidebooks, not just from Europe but from all over the world.

"What's all this?"

"Winston loaned them to me. They're for my bucket list."

"Bucket list?"

"All the things I want to do before I die."

That curious cryptic thing Wren said when we first met in Paris comes back to me: *I know hospitals.* I've only known Wren a day and a half, but that's enough for the thought of losing her to be inconceivable. She must see something on my face, because she gently touches my arm. "Don't worry, I plan on living a long time."

"Why are you making a bucket list, then?"

"Because if you wait until you're really dying, it's too late."

I look at her. *I know hospitals.* The saints. "Who?" I ask softly.

"My sister, Francesca." She pulls out a piece of paper. It has a bunch of titles and locations, *La Belle Angèle* (Paris), *The Music Lesson* (London), *The Resurrection* (Madrid). It goes on like that.

"I don't get it." I hand back the paper.

"Francesca didn't have much of a chance to be good at a lot of things, but she was a totally dedicated artist. She'd be in the hospital, a chemo drip in one arm, a sketchpad in the other. She made hundreds of paintings and drawings, her legacy, she liked to say, because at least when she died, they'd live on—if only in the attic."

"You never know," I say, thinking of those paintings and sculptures in the art squat that might one day be in the Louvre.

"Well, that's exactly it. She found a lot of comfort in the fact that artists like Van Gogh and Vermeer were obscure in life but famous in death. And she wanted to see their paintings in person, so the last time she was in remission, we made a pilgrimage to Toronto and New York to see a bunch of them. After that, she made a bigger list."

I glance at the list again. "So which painting is here? A Van Gogh?"

"There was a Van Gogh on her list. *The Starry Night*, which we saw together in New York, and she has some Vermeers on here, though the one she loved best is in London. But that's *her* list, which has been back-burnered since Paris."

"I don't understand."

"I love Francesca, and I *will* see those paintings for her, one day. But I've spent a lot of my life in her shadow. It had to be that way. But now she's gone—and it's like I'm still in her shadow, you know?"

Strangely, I sort of do. I nod.

"There was something about seeing you in Paris. You're just this normal girl who's doing something kind of crazy. It inspired me. I changed my plans. And now I've started to wonder if meeting you isn't the whole reason I'm on this trip. That maybe Francesca, the saints, they wanted us to meet."

I get a chill from that. "You really think so?"

"I think I do. Don't worry, I won't tell my parents you're the reason I'm coming home a month later. They're a tad upset."

I laugh. I understand that too. "So what's on your list?"

"It's far less noble than Francesca's." She reaches into her travel journal and pulls out a creased piece of paper. *Kiss a boy on top of the Eiffel Tower. Roll in a field of tulips. Swim with dolphins. See the northern lights. Climb a volcano. Sing in a rock band. Cobble my own boots. Cook a feast for 25 friends. Make 25 friends.* "It's a work in progress. I keep adding to it, and already I've had some hiccups. I came here for tulip fields, but they only bloom in the springtime. So now I'll have to figure something else out. Oh, well. I think I can catch the northern lights in this place called Bodø in Norway."

"Did you manage to kiss a boy on top of the Eiffel Tower?"

Her lips prick up into a slightly wicked pixie elf grin. "I did. I went up the morning you left. There was a group of Italians. They can be very obliging, those Italians." She lowers her voice to a whisper. "I didn't even get a name."

I whisper back, "Sometimes you don't need to."

Thirty-seven

*W*e go to a late lunch at an Indonesian restaurant that serves one of those massive *rijsttafel* meals, and we stuff ourselves silly, and as we're wobbling along on the bike, I get an idea. It's not quite the flower fields at Keukenhof, but maybe it'll do. I get us lost for about twenty minutes until I find the flower market I passed this morning. The vendors are closing up their stalls and leaving behind a good number of throwaways. Wren and I steal a bunch of them and lay them out on the crooked sidewalk above the canal bank. She rolls around in them, happy as can be. I laugh as I snap some pictures with her camera and with my phone and text them to my mom.

The vendors look at her with mild amusement, as if this type of thing happens at least twice a week. Then a big bearded guy wearing suspenders over his butte of a belly comes over with some wilting lavender. "She can have these too."

"Here, Wren." I throw the fragrant purple blooms her way.

"Thanks," I say to the guy. Then I explain to him about Wren and her bucket list and the big fields of tulips being out of season so we had to settle for this.

He looks at Wren, who's attempting to extract the petals and leaves from her sweater. He reaches into his pocket and pulls out a card. "Tulips in August is not so easy. But if you and your friend don't mind to wake up early, I can maybe get you a small field of them."

— — —

The next morning, Wren and I set our alarm for four, and fifteen minutes later, go downstairs to the deserted street to find Wolfgang waiting with his mini truck. Every warning I've ever had from my parents about not getting into cars with strangers comes to me, but I realize, as improbable as it is, Wolfgang isn't a stranger. We all three squeeze into the front seat as we trundle toward a greenhouse in Aalsmeer. Wren is practically bouncing with excitement, which seems unnatural for four fifteen in the morning, and she hasn't even had any coffee yet, though Wolfgang has thoughtfully brought a thermos of it along with some hard-boiled eggs and bread.

We spend the drive listening to cheesy europop and Wolfgang's tales of spending thirty years in the merchant marines before moving to the Jordaan neighborhood in Amsterdam. "I'm German by birth, but I'll be an Amsterdammer by death," he says with a big toothy grin.

By five o'clock, we pull up to Bioflor, which hardly looks like the pictures of Keukenhof Gardens, with its carpets of color, but instead looks like some kind of industrial farm. I look at Wren and shrug. Wolfgang pulls in and stops alongside a football-field-sized greenhouse with a row of solar panels on top. A rosy-faced guy named Jos greets us. And then he unlocks the door, and Wren and I gasp.

There are rows and rows of flowers in every color. Acres of them. We walk down the tiny paths in between the beds, the air thick with humidity and manure until Wolfgang points out a section of tulips in fuchsia, sunburst, and one explosive citrusy combo that looks like a blood orange. I walk away, leaving Wren to her flowers.

She just stands there for a while. Then I hear her call out: "This is *incredible*. Can you *see* this?" Wolfgang looks at me but I don't answer because I don't think it's us she's talking to.

Wren runs around this greenhouse, and another one full of fragrant freesia, and I snap a bunch of pictures. And then Wolfgang has to get back. We belt Abba songs all the way, Wolfgang saying Abba is Esperanto for happiness, and the United Nations should play their songs at general assemblies.

It's only when we get to a warehouse outside Amsterdam that I notice that the back of Wolfgang's truck is still empty. "Didn't you buy flowers for your stall?"

He shakes his head. "Oh, I don't buy flowers directly from the farms. I buy at auction via wholesalers who deliver here." He points to where people are loading up their trucks with flowers.

"So you just went all the way out there for us?" I ask.

He gives me a little shrug, like, of course, why else? And at this point, I really have no right to be surprised by people's capacity for kindness and generosity, but still, I am. I'm floored every time.

"Can we take you out to dinner tonight?" I ask.

He shakes his head. "Not tonight. I'm going to see a play in Vondelpark." He looks at us. "You should come. It's in English."

"Why would a play in Holland be in English?" Wren asks.

"That's the difference between the Germans and the Dutch," Wolfgang replies. "The Germans translate Shakespeare. The Dutch leave him in English."

"*Shakespeare?*" I ask, feeling every hair on my body rise. "Which play?"

And before Wolfgang finishes telling me the title, I just start laughing. Because it's simply not possible. It's less possible than finding that one needle in a needle factory. Less possible than finding a lone star in the universe. It's less possible than finding that one person in all the billions who you might love.

Because tonight, playing in Vondelpark, is *As You Like It*. And I know with a certainty I cannot explain but that I would stake my life on, that he will be in it.

Thirty-eight

And so, after a year, I find him as I first found him: In a park, in the sultry dusk, speaking the words of William Shakespeare.

Except tonight, after this year, everything is different. This is no Guerrilla Will. This is a real production, with a stage, with seats, with lights, with a crowd. A large crowd. Such that by the time we get there, we are shunted off to a low wall on the edge of the small amphitheater.

And this year, he is no longer in a supporting role. This year, he is a star. He is Orlando, as I knew he would be. He is the first actor to take the stage, and from that moment on, he owns it. He is riveting. Not just to me. To everyone. A hush falls over the crowd as soon as he delivers the first soliloquy and continues for the rest of the performance. The sky darkens, and the moths and mosquitoes dance in the spotlights, and Amsterdam's Vondelpark is transformed into the Forest of Arden, a magical place where that which was lost can be found.

As I watch him, it's as though it is only us two. Just Willem and me. Everything else disappears: The sound of bicycle bells and tram chimes disappears. The mosquitoes buzzing around the fountain in the pond disappear. The group of rowdy guys sitting next to us disappears. The other actors disappear. The last year disappears. All my doubts disappear. The feeling of being on the right path fills every part of me. I have found him. Here. As Orlando. Everything has led me to this.

His Orlando is different from the way we played it in class or from the way the actor in Boston played it. His is sexy and vulnerable, the yearning for Rosalind so palpable it becomes physical, a pheromone that wafts off him and drifts through the swirl of floodlights, where it lands on my damp and welcoming skin. I feel my lust, my yearning and, yes, my love, coming off me in pulses, swimming toward the stage, where I imagine them being fed to him, like lines.

He can't know I'm here. But as crazy as it sounds, I feel like he does. I sense he feels me somewhere in the words he speaks, the same way I felt him when I first spoke them in Professor Glenny's class.

I remember so many of Rosalind's lines, of Orlando's too, that I can mouth them along with the actors. It feels like a private call-and-response chorus between me and Willem.

> *The little strength that I have, I would it were*
> *with you.*
> *Fare you well: pray heaven I be deceived in you!*
> *Then love me, Rosalind.*

And wilt thou have me?
Are you not good?
I hope so.
Now tell me how long you would have her after
    you have possessed her?
For ever and a day.

For ever and a day.

I hold Wren's hand in one of my hands and Wolfgang's with the other. We make a chain, us three. Standing there like that until the play is over. Until everyone gets their happy endings: Rosalind marries Orlando, and Celia marries Oliver, who reconciles with Orlando, and Phoebe marries Silvius, and the bad duke is redeemed, and the exiled duke is returned home.

After Rosalind gives her final soliloquy, it's over, and people are going crazy, just nuts, clapping and whistling, and I'm turning and throwing my arms around Wren and then Wolfgang, pressing my cheek against the broadcloth of his cotton shirt, inhaling the smoky tobacco scent mingled with flower nectar and dirt. And then someone is hugging Wren and me, the rowdy guys from next to us. "That's my best friend!" one of the guys shouts. He's got impish blue eyes, and he's a head shorter than the others, more Hobbit than Dutchman.

"Who?" Wren asks. She's now being passed around in hugs by the rowdy, and it appears, drunk, Dutch guys.

"Orlando!" the Hobbit answers.

"Oh," Wren says, her eyes so wide and pale they gleam like pearls. *"Oh,"* she says to me.

"You wouldn't be Robert-Jan, by any chance?" I ask.

The Hobbit looks surprised for a second. Then he just grins. "Broodje to my friends."

"Broodje," Wolfgang chuckles. He turns to me. "It's a kind of sandwich."

"Which Broodje loves to eat," one of his friends says, patting his belly.

Broodje/Robert-Jan pushes the hand away. "You should come to our party tonight. It's going to be the party to end all parties. He was fantastic, was he not?"

Wren and I both nod. Broodje/Robert-Jan goes on about how great Willem was and then his friend says something to him in Dutch, something, I think, about Willem.

"What did he say?" I whisper to Wolfgang.

"He said he hasn't seen him, Orlando, I think, so happy, since, I didn't hear it all, something about his father."

Wolfgang takes out a packet of tobacco from a leather pouch and begins to roll a cigarette. Without looking at me, he says in his rumbly voice, "I think the actors come out over there." He points to the little metal gate on the far side of the stage.

He lights his cigarette. His eyes flash. He points to the gate again.

My body feels like it's no longer solid matter. It is particle dust. It is pure electricity. It dances me across the theater, toward the side of the stage. There is a crowd of well-wishers awaiting the actors. People holding bouquets of flowers, bottles of champagne. The actress who played Celia comes out to whoops and hugs. Next comes Adam, then Rosalind, who gets a heap of bouquets. My heart starts to thunder. Could I have come this close only to miss him?

But then I hear him. He is, as always, laughing; this time at something the guy who played Jacques said. And then I see his hair, shorter than it was, his eyes, dark and light all at once, his face, a small scar on his cheek, which only makes him more strikingly handsome.

My breath catches in my throat. I'd thought I'd embellished him. But really, if anything, the opposite is true. I'd forgotten how truly beautiful he is. How intrinsically Willem.

Willem. His name forms in my throat.

"Willem!" His name rings out loud and clear.

But it's not my voice that said it.

I touch my fingers to my throat to be sure.

"Willem!"

I hear the voice again. And then I see the blur of movement. A young woman races out from the crowd. The flowers she is carrying drop to the ground as she hurls herself into his arms. And he takes her in. He lifts her off the ground, holds her tight. His arms clutch into her auburn hair, laughing at whatever it is she's whispering into his ear. They spin around, a tangle of happiness. Of love.

I stand there rooted, watching this very private public display. Finally, someone comes up to Willem and taps him on the shoulder, and the woman slides to the ground. She picks up the flowers—sunflowers, exactly what I would've chosen for him—and dusts them off. Willem slides an easy arm around her and kisses her hand. She snakes her arm around his waist. And I realize then that I wasn't wrong about the love wafting off him during the performance. I was just wrong about who it was for.

They walk off, so close I can feel the breeze as he passes by. We are so close, but he's looking at her, so he doesn't see me at all. They go off, hand in hand, toward a gazebo, away from the fray. I just stand there.

I feel a gentle tap on my shoulder. It's Wolfgang. He looks at me, tilts his head to the side. "Finished?" he asks.

I look back at Willem and the girl. Maybe this is the French girl. Or someone altogether new. They are sitting facing each other, knees touching, talking, holding hands. It's like the rest of the world doesn't exist. That's how it felt when I was with him last year. Maybe if an outsider saw us then, that's exactly how we would've looked. But now I'm the one who's the outsider. I look at them again. Even from here, I can tell she is someone special to him. Someone he loves.

I wait for the fist of devastation, the collapse of a year's worth of hopes, the roar of sadness. And I do feel it. The pain of losing him. Or the idea of him. But along with that pain is something else, something quiet at first, so I have to strain for it. But when I do, I hear the sound of a door quietly clicking shut. And then the most amazing thing happens: The night is calm, but I feel a rush of wind, as if a thousand other doors have just simultaneously flung open.

I give one last glance toward Willem. Then I turn to Wolfgang. "Finished," I say.

But I suspect the opposite is true. That really, I'm just beginning.

Thirty-nine

I wake up to bright blinking sunlight. I squint at the travel alarm. It's almost noon. In four hours, I'm leaving. Wren has decided to stay on a few more days. There's a bunch of weird museums she just found out about that she wants to see, one devoted to medieval torture, another to handbags, and Winston has told her that he knows someone who can teach her how to cobble shoes, which might keep her here another week. But I have three days left, and I've decided to go to Croatia.

I won't get there till tonight, and I'll have to leave first thing Monday morning to make my flight back home. So I'll have just one full day there. But I now know what can happen it just one day. Absolutely anything.

Wren thinks I'm making a mistake. She didn't see Willem with the redhead, and she keeps arguing that she could be anyone—his sister, for instance. I don't tell her that

Willem, like me, like Wren herself now, is an only child. All last night, she begged me to go to the party, to see how it played out. "I know where it is. Robert-Jan told me. It's on, oh, I can't remember the street name, but he said it means 'belt' in Dutch. Number one eighty-nine."

I'd held up my hand. "Stop! I don't want to go."

"But just imagine," she'd said. "What if you'd never met Willem before, and Broodje invited us to the party, and we went, and you two met there for the first time and fell in love? Maybe that's what happens."

It's a nice theory. And I can't help but wonder if that *would've* happened. Would we fall in love if we met today? Had I really fallen in love with him in the first place? Or was it just infatuation fueled by mystery?

But I'm also starting to wonder something else. If maybe the point of this crazy quest I'm on wasn't to help me find Willem. Maybe it was to help me find someone else entirely.

— — —

I'm getting dressed when Wren opens the door, clutching a paper bag. "Hi, sleepyhead. I made you some breakfast. Or rather Winston did. He said it's very Dutch."

I take the bag. "Thanks." I look Wren, who's grinning like crazy. "Winston, huh?"

Now she's blushing. "He just got off work and he's going to take me for a bike ride and introduce me to his cobbler friend as soon as you leave," she says, her grin now threatening to split her face. "And tomorrow he says I have to go to an Ajax football game with him." She pauses to consider. "It wasn't on my list, but you never know."

"No, you don't. Well, I should go soon. Let you get to your, um, cobbling."

"But your flight's not for ages yet."

"That's okay. I want to leave enough time, and I hear the airport is amazing."

I pack up the rest of my things and go downstairs with Wren. Winston points me toward the train station.

"Are you sure you don't want me to come with you to the station or the airport?" Wren asks.

I shake my head. I want to see Wren ride away on the pink bike as if I'll see her again tomorrow. She hugs me tight and then kisses me three times like the Dutch do. *"Tot ziens,"* she calls. "It means 'see you later' in Dutch, because we aren't saying good-bye." I swallow the lump in my throat. And then Winston gets on his big black bike and Wren gets on the little pink bike, and they pedal away.

I hoist my backpack up and make the short walk to the train station. There are trains every fifteen minutes or so to Schiphol, and I buy a ticket and a cup of tea and go sit under the clattering destination board to eat my breakfast. When I see what's inside, I have to laugh. Because Winston has made me a *hagelslag* sandwich. For all our talk, I never did get to try this particular delicacy.

I take a bite. The *hagelslag* crunches, then melts into the butter and still-warm bread. And what's left over tastes just like him.

All at once, I finally understand what it means for time to be fluid. Because suddenly the entire last year flows before me, condensing and expanding, so that I'm here in Amsterdam eating *hagelslag,* and at the same time, I'm in Paris, his hand on my hip, and at the same time, I'm on that first train to London, watching the countryside whiz by, and at the same time, I'm in the line for *Hamlet*. I see Willem. At the canal basin, catching my eye. On the train, his jeans still unstained, me still unstained. On the train to Paris, his thousand shades of laughter.

The destination board shuffles, and I look up at it, and as I do, imagine a different version of time. One in which *Willem* quits while he's ahead. One in which he never makes that remark about my breakfast. One in which he just says good-bye on that platform in London instead of inviting me to Paris. Or one in which he never stops to talk to me in Stratford-upon-Avon.

And that's when I understand that I *have* been stained. Whether I'm still in love with him, whether he was *ever* in love with me, and no matter who he's in love with now, Willem changed my life. He showed me how to get lost, and then I showed myself how to get found.

Maybe accident isn't the right word after all. Maybe miracle is.

Or maybe it's not a miracle. Maybe this is just life. When you open yourself up to it. When you put yourself in the path of it. When you say yes.

How can I come this far and not tell him—he, who would understand it best—that by giving me the that flyer, by inviting me to skip *Hamlet*, he helped me realize that it's not *to* be that matters, but *how* to be?

How can I come this far and not be brave?

"Excuse me," I say to a woman in a polka-dot dress and cowboy boots. "Is there a street in Amsterdam named after a belt?"

"Ceintuurbaan," she answers. "Tram line twenty-five. Right outside the station."

I race out of the train station and jump onto the tram, asking the driver where to get off for Ceintuurbaan number one eighty-nine. "Near Sarphatipark," he replies. "I'll show you."

Twenty minutes later, I get off at the park. Inside, there's a small playground with a large sandpit, and I go sit down under a tree to summon my bravery. A couple of children are putting the finishing touches on an elaborate sand castle, several feet high, with towers and turrets and moats.

I stand up and make my way to the building. I don't even know for sure that he lives here, except that the feeling of rightness, it has never been stronger. There are three bells. I ring the bottom one. An intercom squawks with a woman's voice.

"Hello," I call. Before I say anything else, the door clicks open.

I walk inside the dark, musty hallway. A door swings open, and my heart skips a beat, but it's not him. It's an older woman with a yappy dog at her heels.

"Willem?" I ask her. She points a thumb up and shuts her door.

I climb the steep stairs to the second floor. There are two other flats in the building, so this could be his, or the one upstairs. So I just stand there on the doorstep for a moment, listening for sounds inside. It is quiet, save for the faint strains of music. But my heart is beating fast and strong, like a radar pinging: *Yes, yes, yes.*

My hand shakes a little bit as I knock, and at first the sound is faint, as if I'm knocking on a hollowed-out log. But then I tighten my grip, and I knock again. I hear his footsteps. I remember the scar on his foot. Was it on the right foot or the left? The footsteps come closer. I feel my heart speed up, in double time to those footsteps.

And then the door swings open, and he's there.

Willem.

His tall body casts a shadow over me, just like it did that first day, that only other day, really, when we met. His eyes, those dark, dark eyes, hiding a spectrum of hidden things, they widen, and his mouth drops. I hear his gasp of breath, the shock of it all.

He just stands there, his body taking up the doorway, looking at me like I am a ghost, which I suppose I am. But if he knows anything at all about Shakespeare, it's that the ghosts always come haunting.

I look at him as the questions and answers collide all over his face. There is so much I want to tell him. Where do I even begin?

"Hi, Willem," I say. "My name is Allyson."

He says nothing in response. He just stays there for a minute, looking at me. And then he steps to the side, opens the door wider, wide enough for me to walk through.

And so I do.

COMING SOON!

Their story continues with Willem's journey in

just one year

On my wrist is a watch, small and delicate, bright and gold. It's not mine. And for the quickest moment, I see the watch on a girl's wrist. I travel up the hand to a slender arm, a strong shoulder, a swan's neck. When I get to the face, I expect it to be blank, like the faces in my dreams. But it's not.

Black hair. Pale skin. Dancing eyes.

I look at the watch again. The crystal is cracked but it's still ticking. It reads nine o'clock and again, I begin to suspect what it is that I've forgotten.

I try to sit up. The world turns to soup.

The doctor pushes me back onto the bed, a hand on my shoulder. "You are agitated because you are confused. This is all temporary, but we will need to take the CT scan to rule out a hematoma. While we wait, we can attend to your facial lacerations. First I will give you something to make the area numb."

The nurse swabs off my cheek with something orange. "Do not worry. This won't stain."

It doesn't stain; it just stings.

ACKNOWLEDGMENTS

This book begins with Shakespeare, and so my thank-yous begin with Tamara Glenny, who, when I told her I was writing something with some Shakespeare in it, promptly wrote me up notes on plays to look at, got us tickets to a number of those plays—including that fateful production of *As You Like It*—and answered dozens of ridiculously obscure questions with her usual enthusiasm and good humor.

The book then moves on to France, and I would like to thank Céline Faure and Philippe Robinet, for helping me discover Allyson and Willem's Paris, and for not blinking when I asked for such translations as: "shut your piehole." Laurence Checler graciously helped with so many more of the translations in the book. Marie-Elisa Gramain helped me find the perfect French band name. Also thank you to Taly Meas for the hospital tour, Willy Levitanus, Patricia Roth, and Julie Roth for orchestrating it all.

We move on to Holland then, and to Heleen Buth and Emke Spauwen who gave me such a fantastic tour of Utrecht and provided me with so many details that sparked so much of Allyson's and Willem's stories. My brother-in-law, Robert

Schamhart, helped me with many of the Dutch subtleties, and allowed me to steal a few key aspects of his identity, down to his nickname. *Hartelijk bedankt*!

Back stateside, my inimitable editor, Julie Strauss-Gabel, once again, helped me figure out the book I *meant* to write and remained a steady, optimistic force whenever I became discouraged that I'd ever actually write it. "I'm not worried about you," she frequently says, such reassuring words, when I'm in a tizzy. Thank you for not worrying—and for worrying. Thank you also to the other extraordinary member of Team Dutton: Liza Kaplan, as well as to Scottie Bowditch, Danielle Delaney, Deborah Kaplan, Rosanne Lauer, Elyse Marshall, Emily Romero, Don Weisberg; and the entire staff of Penguin Young Readers Group: the amazing sales and marketing team, the wonderful school and library department, the ever-brilliant online department, and all the fantastic field reps—who give so much heart to the authors they publish.

Sarah Burnes is my agent, my advocate, my reality check, my Mama Bear, and above all, my wise and generous friend. I feel thankful to have someone who understands all the sides of me—and by extension, my characters and books—in my corner. The powerhouse team of Logan Garrison, Rebecca Gardner, and Will Roberts have propelled my books to places I never dreamed of. You couldn't imagine a nicer, smarter group of bulldogs!

I would like to thank Isabel Kyriacou for, among many other things, helping me curse more proficiently in Spanish. I would like to thank my YA cohorts, particularly Libba Bray and Stephanie Perkins, who provided the writerly equivalent of therapy: lots of listening, combined with the occasional, laser-beam insightful question or comment. (I believe they accept most insurance.) Thank you also to Nina LaCour, E. Lockhart, Sandy London, Margaret Stohl, Robin Wasserman, and whoever else might've listened to me jabber about complicated plot threads. Thank you Onome Edodi-Disowe, Victoria Hill, and all the ladies of the BK/BNS crews, for taking hold of the reins so that I might let them go. Thank you to Veronica Brodsky, for helping me understand what this book is truly about. And to Rebecca Haworth for taking that first trip with me. We had our Melanie moments—and came out the other side. Thank you, Marjorie Ingall, for reading, hand-holding, and geeking out with me about Shakespeare.

Speaking of, I know he is long dead and there's no collecting royalty or praise from the grave, but I must thank Shakespeare anyway, for giving me the surprise of this book, and for providing me a play that keeps working on so many levels. Thank you Royal Shakespeare Company, for bringing *As You Like It* to New York City just as I was starting this book. Thank you Fiasco Theater Company for turning me onto *Cymbeline*—and for all your help with this book, and the next.

Thank you to my parents, for passing on their love of travel, for being proud when, the week after high-school graduation, I took off on a one-way ticket to Europe to attend "The University of Life," and for teaching me to be self-sufficient enough to travel on my own, and on my own dime, for the next several years. Thank you to my siblings, Tamar and Greg, for being such cheerleaders and supporters of their little sister and for, each in their own way, showing me how to say yes. Thank you to Karen and Detta, Rebecca, Hannah, Liam, Lucy, and all of my extended brood.

Thank you to all the people I've met in my travels over the years—some of whom I kept in touch with, some of whom I put into this book, and some of whom have changed the trajectory of my life. Without you, I would not be here now, writing these words.

Thank you to my readers, for packing their mental suit-cases and coming off on another trip with me. Without you, I would not be here now, writing these words.

Finally, thank you to Nick, Willa, and Denbele: You are the ones I travel with now. And how wild and wonderful the journey is.